*Johanna Drew Her Skirts about Her
with a Swish of Red and Gold Silk
and Marched Toward
the Bower Stairs . . .*

Rochambeau caught up with her on the stairs. "Let's continue our quarrel in private," he growled.

"I have nothing more to say to you!"

They passed through the bower and into the great bedchamber, where Rochambeau made haste to shut the door. Johanna whirled to face him. The gilt embroidered ends of her long red sleeves and the curling locks of her loose black hair streamed behind her with the speed of her turn, and Rochambeau found himself forgetting their quarrel in his delight at the vision of angry beauty she presented. The soft silk clung to her breasts when she moved, showing each tantalizing rounded curve.... She was as lovely as he'd ever seen her—and as unattainable. He sighed. How had his clever plan gone wrong? "Now, love, don't let's quarrel any longer," he said, crossing the room so that he could put his arms around her....

She didn't push his hands away. He felt the softness of her under the clinging silks, and his desires increased until he could scarcely bear the time it would take to peel away her soft surcoat and tunic . . .

Books by Catherine Lyndell

Alliance
Ariane
Captive Hearts
Masquerade
Tapestry of Pride
Vows of Desire

Published by POCKET BOOKS

Tapestry of Pride

Catherine Lyndell

PUBLISHED BY POCKET BOOKS NEW YORK

Another *Original* publication of POCKET BOOKS

POCKET BOOKS, a division of Simon & Schuster, Inc.
1230 Avenue of the Americas, New York, N.Y. 10020

ISBN: 0-671-62328-1

First Pocket Books printing September 1987

10 9 8 7 6 5 4 3 2 1

POCKET and colophon are trademarks
of Simon & Schuster, Inc.

Printed in the U.S.A.

Tapestry of Pride

Chapter One

Malvern, 1274

"ROCHAMBEAU IS BACK."

Sometimes a chance spark will blow onto some poor cottar's thatched roof, from his own fire or a neighbor's. If the season has been dry and the winds are in the right quarter, such a spark can glow into leaping flames that dance from rooftop to rooftop, reducing half a dozen daub-and-wattle huts to ashes before the neighbors can do more than cry out in alarm. So the news of the baron's return spread through the steep, muddy lanes of the village below his castle of Malvern, carried on bright gossiping tongues that flickered like the flames of scandal. The first spark, in this case, was brought by Gospatric the pig-boy, who'd run breathless through the woods to announce the sight of a cavalcade of armed men winding their way up the road from the lowlands.

"He said the leader was the Archangel Michael."

"His breast shining silver, and his head shining gold."

"Or possibly a devil, for didn't Gospatric say that his eyes were so cold a blue they paralyzed him for as long as it takes to say a Paternoster and three Aves?"

"A devil indeed! You'd be lucky if that were all!"

The knot of women who'd gathered in the muddy lower lane of the village to speculate over Gospatric's story dispersed like frightened chickens as Goodwife Simpkin stalked forward, swishing her cane and her skirts to shoo them out of the way.

"Aye, you'll soon be wishing 'twas a mere devil." She laughed at the startled peasant women. " 'Tis my lord of Rochambeau himself, from the description: gold hair, blue eyes, a devil's face—Nicolas de Rochambeau," she summed up with satisfaction.

"Back from the dead." Gospatric's mother, Elfleda, crossed herself.

"No," said Goodwife Simpkin dryly, "from France."

There was more excited babbling at this supposition. Everyone knew that while the lord of Rochambeau was making his leisurely way home from Prince Edward's abortive crusade, he had been captured and held for ransom by Joscelin d'Avranches in France. Most of them had heard some garbled story about his lady's response to the ransom demand. If this new arrival should be Rochambeau himself—miraculously escaped from d'Avranches and come to claim the estates his lady had been running so competently—what would this change mean for the village? It had been four long years since the lord had left for the Holy Land, and the young girls who giggled and ran through the village lanes with the news could barely remember him, save as a tall, magnificent figure who'd occasionally tossed the children a coin or a handful of sweetmeats. But their mothers had darker and more interesting stories to tell of the great baron.

"Ah, me," sighed Elfleda, smoothing her long flaxen braids with one hand. "If 'tis Rochambeau indeed, perhaps there'll be some life about the place at last. He was a devil with the women, in truth. Not a girl in the village but would have come to him if he did but snap his fingers—and some didn't wait for that. It's a wonder he didn't fill the village with yellow-haired children. They do say some witch gave him a magic spell to prevent the girls conceiving by him."

She looked down with a sigh at the muddy hair and scarcely less muddy features of her son, who was lingering, full of importance at the news he'd brought to the village. No, she concluded for perhaps the twentieth time, there was no hope of passing off Gospatric as my lord's son, although there had been certain pleasant passages between them after her first man had died and before she had married again. Gospatric had been born just three months after her man had died, and everybody knew my lord had never dallied with a married

2

woman. Besides, every line of the pig-boy's blunt-featured square body showed his peasant origin.

Two of the young girls whispered together and giggled shrilly before racing off to the high point of the village, the stone cross before the church where they might hope to catch a first glimpse of the legendary lord. Goodwife Simpkin's cane caught a third girl neatly by the ankle and whisked her into the mud before she could join her friends.

"Into the house with you, Hawise," she commanded, ignoring her daughter's whimpers of protest.

"I w-want to s-see the baron!" Hawise blubbered, trying in vain to escape from her mother's bony clutch.

"And I," her mother said between her teeth, "don't want him to see you, with your skirts hiked up in that shameless way. You'd think the entire village had to appreciate your pretty legs!" Goodwife Simpkin thrust her daughter unceremoniously into the mud-plastered hovel behind them and propped a stout branch against the door to make sure she remained there. "Not that I believe for one minute there'll be any of that sort of nonsense now," she said grimly over Hawise's howls of protest. "The baron always respected other folks' marriage vows, and now he's got a wife of his own to come back to."

"If he doesn't kill her," sneered Elfleda. She loosened her long plaits and spread the shining golden hair over her shoulders, where it gleamed in the sun, covering the food stains on the front of her smock. "What kind of a wife is that? Everybody knows how my lady Johanna refused to pay his ransom when the messengers came from France. Said it suited her very well to have him remain abroad—and I'm sure it did, the skinny bitch! Riding astride like a man, running the estates like a man. What does she want with a fine man like the baron to warm her bed? A pile of account books is all *she* needs to keep her warm at night, as anybody'd know who'd heard that song the baron made after their marriage. I heard—"

A sharp crack on the cheek silenced Elfleda. She spun around, startled, only to find her shining hair yanked back into a meaty fist that pulled her head backward until she almost lost her balance. "If it's foul, malicious, or sinful, I'm sure you heard it first—if you didn't make it up," growled

3

her husband the smith. "Come, wife. You've my midday pottage to heat up, and the baby's dirty. You do your work in the house, and I'll watch the baron ride by."

Not daring to protest, Elfleda stumbled off disconsolately at the side of her husband, while the other women slipped away to their own houses before their men should come home from the fields and offer similar punishments. Goodwife Simpkin, who enjoyed the free life of a widow with a thriving alehouse of her very own, watched Elfleda's disappearance with a slight smile. The lady Johanna was severe but just, a good mistress to folk of castle and village. Such malicious words as Elfleda spewed out deserved no less than a slap on the side of the head. All the same . . .

"I wonder what he *will* do to her?" Goodwife Simpkin mused, and it wasn't Elfleda she was thinking of.

The same question occupied the minds of the castle folk—that is, all those who didn't have their own fates to consider. The lord of Rochambeau, generous to a fault with loyal vassals, never forgave two things: deliberate stupidity and deliberate injury. Which would have been very well, the chamberlain of the hall thought, if Rochambeau weren't so damned clever that he tended to assume other men were deliberately acting stupid when they were actually doing their best. Those cracked mazers in the cellarer's care, for example, should have been replaced long ago. But the chamberlain had not wanted to confess his carelessness in letting them get cracked to begin with. Johanna had never questioned him, but what if my lord wanted to know why they hadn't been mended or replaced? Sweating profusely, he bawled for the cellarer and his assistant to set to work polishing the already gleaming stores of plate that would be brought out to celebrate Rochambeau's return.

In the stables, the grooms hired for the season from the village also sweated and cursed, as the marshal of the stables drove them to scour out the stalls and groom the horses as if they were preparing a lady's bedchamber. Racing for fresh buckets of water, the grooms collided with the squires who were searching for sand to scour their masters' armor. Both groups cursed the boy from the buttery who'd gotten underfoot while he watched the carters roll fresh tuns of wine into the storeroom under the kitchen. The butler in turn took out his excitement on an unfortunate new carpenter's assistant who had left his tools in the way of the carts.

And in the midst of their panic, every once in a while the stammering, chattering members of the household found time to stand up, massage aching backs, and glance up at the narrow slits of windows in the bower where the lady Johanna sat with her women. Chamberlain and cellarer, marshal of the stables and head groom, butler and pantler, and cook and larderer all wondered exactly what fireworks would be set off when the lord and his lady were reunited after their four long years of separation.

"Is it true he left on crusade the day after they were married?" the butler's boy asked his master. "After a regular dingdong fight with his lady?"

The butler aimed a perfunctory blow at his assistant's head. "Certainly not. It was a good five weeks later—and they did *not* quarrel. You can't believe everything you hear."

"Well, I wager we hear something now. I know a spot where you can see whatever goes on in the bower. Want me to show you? Ah, no, you're too fat to climb up there, master." The boy turned away, whistling insouciantly, and got a much more serious slap on the head for his pains.

"And don't whistle that song!" the butler roared. "If my lady hears you . . ."

But the boy had taken to his heels, scuttling up one of the four narrow spiral staircases that decorated the four corners of the new tower, moving too fast for a middle-aged man with a serious ale paunch to catch up with him. The butler went back to tasting his supply of locally brewed ales and imported wines, trying to decide which, if any, were smooth enough to serve to a much-traveled man like the baron of Rochambeau. To be sure, the lady Johanna had never complained about the quality of the wine—not since that unfortunate incident when the water had unaccountably leaked into the barrel—but everyone knew that women had no palate.

Climbing as nimbly as a little monkey, the butler's boy scurried up to the very top of the keep tower. He burst forth from the damp gray chill of the stone staircase into a world dazzling with the blue and gold of the warm September season. From the flat roof of the keep, he could see the fields belonging to the manor of Malvern stretching off toward the north and west. Long, undulating strips of golden-ripe wheat marked late-ripening fields where the harvest was not yet in; golden strips of stubble showed where the wheat had already been harvested from the sunny south-facing slopes.

To the southeast, the forest crowded right up to the edge of the village, a tangle of dark woods where the lord had hunted and the villagers grazed their pigs. A winding white road appeared at the edge of the forest, the way to the southern port cities. A sparkle of sun on metal caught the boy's sight now, confirming the rumor. He leaned over the battlements for a moment, striving to distinguish individual points of light: a shield, a lance, maybe a man's flat-topped helm? The first riders were already out of the wood and approaching the village, and Rochambeau's triangular pennon floated from the top of the leader's lance. So it was true—the baron was coming home! And in a few minutes he'd be meeting his lady for the first time in four years.

His heart beating fast with excitement, the boy crawled out along the lead guttering that bordered the flat roof. He swung from hand to hand, from lead gryphon's head to carved stone spout, until midway between one corner and the next his feet found the tough branches of the ivy that grew up the side of the tower. He clambered down along the vines until he reached the carved stone course that ran around the second level of the tower. Then he edged back toward the safety of the corner, where the projecting wall of the staircase and a gnarled root came together to make a niche just big enough for one small boy . . . and, by the grace of Providence, just beside one of the narrow slit windows of the bower.

"The Warhawk stoops!"

A girl's laughing voice quoted the old war cry of the Rochambeau family, and all eyes in the bower turned to the lady Johanna. Here, in contrast to the frenzied activity below stairs, all was calm and peaceful. The only sign that something unusual might be afoot was that the bower was somewhat more crowded than usual. Every woman who could make an excuse to be there had suddenly developed an interest in the never-ending work of spinning, weaving, sewing, and embroidery with which Johanna kept her small household too busy to get into mischief.

Girls wound silk into long skeins or twirled great carved spindles to spin their distaffs of wool into thread, while the great loom in one corner and the two small ribbon looms in another clacked as regularly as the ladies' tongues. In the center of the bower, seated straight-backed upon a high stool with a pillowed seat, Johanna of Rochambeau stabbed a needle through the tapestry frame before her as though her only concern was to achieve a perfectly even shading of colors from green to gold. If one did not know that the lady's practice was to retire to her bedchamber with the account rolls for an hour of private clerkly work after the midday meal, one might have taken the scene for a completely normal one of everyday work. If one did not know the lady's courage, one might have thought that she had changed her habit and surrounded herself with her ladies in waiting so as to prevent her returning lord from making a public scene.

The butler's boy had had the highest respect for the lady Johanna ever since the day she'd demonstrated her ability to string a bow, shoot a crouching hare, and skin her trophy faster than his big brother the poacher. He did not suppose that Johanna needed her ladies to protect her from Rochambeau. He thought it more likely that she'd chosen this public setting for their meeting so that no one should say later that she'd cowered in her bedchamber when the lord returned.

Whatever her reasons, the boy was grateful for the decision. The great bedchamber where Johanna had slept alone the last four years was safe from prying eyes. Here, he could both see and hear all that went on, providing him with some pleasurable thrills now and with an eyewitness report that could be sold in the kitchen for sweet cakes later.

Now Johanna turned her bright green eyes on the girl who'd teased her with the old war cry of Rochambeau. Slender and still and white, she made the butler's boy think of a cold flame. The massive loops of her black hair, shining brighter than all the cellarer's polished plate, framed a pale face whose perfect features were dominated by those sea-green witch's eyes. "If the hawk stoops," she said in a cool voice that nonetheless filled the narrow room, "vermin should hide. You may leave us, Clairemonde."

Blushing, the girl Clairemonde dropped her distaff and slipped out of the room.

"She's a cool one, our lady," whispered Dilys, one of the matrons who'd been entrusted with the delicate work of handling the silk-ribbon looms. "Married at sixteen, and not five weeks wed before her lord rode off to the crusades. Yet to see her now, you'd think the man coming up those stairs would be no more than a chance visitor, or a bailiff from one of the outlying manors come to report on his harvest." A dangling thread of crimson silk was snipped off, and the new shuttle full of white thread took up the pattern in time with the whispered words. A rose with a heart of gold grew slowly under the weaver's skilled hands.

"Well, she'll soon find out different, if I remember Rochambeau's temper aright. Blessed Virgin! We've not seen such a day at Malvern since the old baron's three mistresses clawed one another's faces over his bier, fifteen years ago."

The steady clack of the ribbon looms never ceased while the women exchanged comments, but Johanna's sea-green glance darted to that corner of the room, and the matrons fell abruptly silent. The lady of the manor turned her slanted oval eyes back to consideration of the tapestry before her, and the long trailing ends of her embroidered silk veil floated over her shoulders to follow the quick motions of her head.

In the hush that followed, when not one of the girls and women gathered in the bower dared to speak, the clatter of horses and armor in the courtyard below announced Rochambeau's arrival. Johanna would have done a stranger the courtesy of greeting him in the great hall; for her wedded lord, she remained obstinately at her seat, hands busy with the flashing needle that sprinkled green leaves against a gold background. She would not even turn to face the door. Only two spots of color, high on her cheekbones, betrayed her awareness of the coming confrontation.

The open door let in a clanking noise that grew louder and nearer with each repetition—the sound of a man in armor, coming up the wide flight of stone steps that led from hall to bower. The women stirred uneasily, like birds startled from their place on a tree, and two of them crossed themselves when a dusty hand threw back the tapestry that covered the door opening. Johanna turned then and leisurely surveyed the man standing in the doorway: his helm under his arm, the rest of his armor half unlaced, dusty and sweaty from long hours of riding. His shoulder-length yellow hair was darkened with sweat and clung close to his neck; his cold blue eyes were dark also, like bruises in his tanned face.

There was a hysterical titter from one of the girls. The rest of the women waited, agape, to hear what words the lord and lady of Rochambeau would exchange on this, their first meeting in four years. Johanna's cool glance swept over them and silenced them. "You have my leave to go now."

As Rochambeau stepped into the room, moving slowly and heavily like the footsteps of doom, the waiting-women scurried around him and down the steps. Before they'd reached the bottom of the steps they were talking again, high babbling voices chattering away all at once in a perfect frenzy of gossip and speculation. The heavy oaken door slammed shut behind them and cut off the noise abruptly.

"I wonder you have the patience to abide that flock of chattering chickens." Rochambeau let fall the tapestry that covered the oak door and regarded his wife with a neutral look, neither welcoming nor inimical.

Johanna shrugged and pretended to be occupied with choosing another skein of silk for her embroidery work. "Well you might wonder. As I recall, patience was never your strong point."

"Nor yours. Don't you want to know how I left Joscelin d'Avranches?"

At the name of the old enemy who'd held her lord for ransom, Johanna put down the skeins of silk she'd been playing with and let her shears fall to swing from the ribbon at her waist. Hands folded, she regarded Rochambeau's impassive countenance with a slight smile. "All right, if you want me to ask. How did you leave d'Avranches?"

"Wounded," said Rochambeau. "Thigh and shoulder. And bellowing at his men to go after me."

"You fought your way out?"

"Since my dear wife refused to send ransom," Rochambeau pointed out, "I had no other option. Disappointed to see me again, are you? You didn't really think d'Avranches was strong enough to hold a Rochambeau prisoner indefinitely?"

She shrugged, and Rochambeau's face hardened.

"Perhaps it will cheer you to learn that the escape was not without cost. When Joscelin captured me and my men, I chose to send for ransom rather than fight my way free and lose lives in what was bound to be an unequal battle. Too many of my men had been wounded in the initial fight. I knew I might be able to free myself, but I didn't want to risk their lives on such a point."

"No." Johanna's sneer was overdone. "A point of honor never did mean much to Rochambeau."

Taking two strides forward, Rochambeau gripped his wife by the shoulders and lifted her bodily from her stool. "It ill beseems you to prate to me of honor! He asked only a hundred and fifty marks ransom—less than one-fourth the revenues of the estate in a good year, and less than half what I received of him when I captured him in the melee at the Poitiers tourneys. All he wanted was to make the score even between us, and I'd gladly have paid him that to end the old feud. Your duty—your *honor*, wife, since you so like that word—would have lain in obeying your lord's commands when I sent for the money. Instead you shamed me before my tenants, left me with no choice but to fight my way out of d'Avranches's hold, forced me to turn an old grudge into new and deadly enmity."

"My," murmured Johanna with a mocking smile, "I never guessed I was so powerful." There would be bruises tomorrow where Rochambeau's fingers dug into her shoulders, but she would not give him the satisfaction of wincing under his grip.

"He'll not forgive me the men he lost when I fought my way free. To get our arms, I used a ruse of war, but he'll call it treachery. And I'll not forgive him—or you—the death of old Marc."

That news drew a gasp of pain from Johanna. "Marc dead?" The old man had been Rochambeau's squire and his father's before him. Always refusing to be knighted—preferring the freedom of a lowlier station to the responsibilities of knighthood—he'd trained two generations of Rochambeau tenants in the art of war.

Johanna had only known him for the few short weeks between her wedding and Rochambeau's departure for the crusade, but in that time she'd come to love and revere the gentle spirit hiding behind Marc's years of experience in warfare. He'd never given up trying to reconcile the lord of Rochambeau and his reluctant bride, and Johanna sometimes thought that with a few more weeks to work on both of them he might well have succeeded. But that, of course, was before Rochambeau's deadly insult to her which had ended any hope of their marriage being a success.

"Yes. One of d'Avranches's crossbowmen hit him between the shoulders when we were riding for freedom. Does it sweeten your sense of power to know that I can lay his death at the door of my own wife?"

Johanna twisted blindly out of his grip, throwing up one arm to hide the ravages of grief on her face. "No wife of yours by any choice of mine!" She spat at him, head averted. "Nor shall I ever be!" How dare he blame her for Marc's death! The old man should never have gone on crusade. He should have remained there, on castle guard duty, where he would be safe. It was Rochambeau's fault he'd risked himself so.

Before she had time to do more than dash the tears from her eyes, Rochambeau had grabbed her in a rough embrace, forcing her against his chest. His hands were hard and strong; he smelled of horses and the dust of the road. In four years no hands but the delicate white fingers of her waiting-women had touched Johanna; no scents but lavender and rose water had invaded this bower. She shivered and told herself it was revulsion she felt.

"You were willing enough once, as I recall." He was still wearing his fighting coat of boiled leather reinforced with steel plates; the hard edges of the plates hurt her and killed any possible flickering spark of desire. She raised her head and stared at him with defiant green eyes—slanted witch eyes, the village folk called them. Rochambeau was the only man who never quailed under that look.

"Willing? Perhaps—before I found you out for what you are."

"Found out what?" Rochambeau released her so abruptly that she staggered and would have fallen, had he not caught her around the waist and lowered her to her stool again. Johanna bit her lip in vexation. He'd not been back five minutes, and already this lean, hard-faced man was taking the initiative away from her. She'd not intended their interview to go like this.

"Found out what?" He was leaning over her, blue sparks flashing in his hooded hawk's eyes. In spite of herself, she flinched away from the taut anger revealed in every line of his body. "Perhaps it's time we came to a reckoning of accounts, madam. I always wondered what turned you against me so suddenly."

If he had to wonder—! Johanna bit her lip again, clamping down hard against the hysterical anger that swirled and bubbled within her like a witch's brew. This man had forced her to marry him by the vilest threats against her family, yet now he could look her in the eye with an unclouded brow and say he'd always wondered why she took against him.

"Need you ask?" she flung back at him. "If I seemed to favor you once, it was before you showed your true colors to me. How could I love a man who forced me to his bed?"

Rochambeau's hard blue gaze softened, and he laid one hand on her shoulder, gently stroking where his fingers had bruised before. Johanna winced at the light touch and felt almost sorry to see the hurt look on his face. But she'd wanted to hurt him. She still did. What was between them could hardly be forgiven by a few soft words and this lecher's practiced caresses.

"And yet there was a time," he murmured, "when no force would have been needed. Can't we start over, Johanna? Can you remember what it was like when I first came courting you? From the moment I set eyes on you, I knew you were the only woman for me—and I did not think you hated me, either!"

She hated him now, though. Hated the growing confidence with which his big hands moved over her body. Hated the deep-throated chuckle as he called to mind those early days of their courtship, those days when her whole body had quivered with eagerness under his hands, quivered with the desire for him to take her and make a woman of her.

The same treacherous desire was melting within her now, as his wandering hands grew bolder with their adept caresses. His fingers moved lower, dipping beneath the loose neckline of her overtunic. Johanna gritted her teeth in fury at her own weakness. He had wronged her in every way possible. Should she now forgive him and be tumbled on the bower floor like any of the light wenches he'd met in his travels?

"Can't we go back?" he murmured again, bending his head low to receive her answer. It wasn't fair, the way his breath curled around her neck and ears and the way the warmth of his lips heated her skin. "Will you let me court you again, Johanna?"

In desperation, she wrenched her head away from those treacherous lips, jumped up, and ran across the bower to the shelter of the great loom. The trailing edge of her mantle caught the stool as she fled and sent it crashing to the ground.

"So it's courtship you want, is it?" she cried from the double safety of the great loom and her own carefully nurtured anger. "Aye, my lord, perhaps you should *write me a song.*" And, pursing her lips, she whistled the opening notes of the melody that had haunted her for four long years, since after Rochambeau had left for the crusade.

She had the satisfaction of seeing him pale under his crusader's tan, his lips set as if to conceal the pain caused by a sudden blow. So he had not known that his mocking words had come back to her ears? Good! If the surprise of that discovery hurt him one-tenth as much as the song had hurt her, she would begin to be avenged.

"I never meant you should hear that song."

"It makes little odds to me what you *say* you intended. Although indeed I believe you, for it must greatly hamper your style in courting now, my lord, knowing that I know what you truly think of me and my charms! 'Colder than winter's frost,' " she quoted the mocking song, " 'harder than steel, I didn't know whether I was in bed with a woman or a coat of mail!' I wonder you should pretend such eagerness to bed me again, my lord. Don't you fear to cut yourself on my sharp edges?"

"Johanna . . ." He took one step toward her, and she dodged back behind the great loom. "That's not what I truly think of you. You know better than that, if you'll just take time to think it over."

"I have had time," she reminded him. "Four long years."

The beginnings of a smile creased his stern face. "So they've been long years—without me?"

"I didn't mean that." She retreated another step, until she was standing where the weaver would stand, her hand on the great breast beam of the loom and the screen of warp threads between them.

"And I didn't mean what that song said," said Rochambeau softly, "I was hurt when I composed it, Johanna, hurt and drunk. Or didn't it ever occur to you that you could cause me pain too?"

"No," Johanna answered honestly, "but it pleases me well."

Rochambeau threw one hand up in disgust. "So I made a mistake. I was too drunk to know anybody else had heard me singing in my tent. By the next day it had spread through the camp. It was too late to suppress it, and we were leaving anyway. How did you hear it? I suppose some poor bastard of a wandering jongleur picked up the catchy tune and carried it back to you? I can't help that unlucky coincidence, Johanna."

"Oh, no! I suppose you can't help any of the wrongs you've done to me and mine! Poor Rochambeau, too weak to master events, at the mercy of every chance wind!" Johanna threw back her head and laughed shrilly.

"Hellcat!" He moved toward her again, one hand upraised threateningly, and she dodged around to the far side of the great loom. She stumbled again as her thrice-damned fashionable trailing mantle wrapped itself around the leg braces of the loom. Throwing out one hand for balance, she grabbed something cold and pointed that pricked her palm. Rochambeau laughed, and Johanna threw the thing at him without looking to see what it was.

It was the iron-pointed shuttle, still loaded with white wool yarn, with which Dilys had been weaving at the loom when Rochambeau came into the bower. It went whizzing past where Rochambeau's head had been a scant second earlier. If he had not ducked, the iron point would have torn out his eye. The shuttle clattered against the wall, and Johanna seized three more from their places on the woven web, throwing them one after another with furious energy.

With a juggler's dexterity, Rochambeau caught the missiles and threw them back. Johanna retaliated as fast as she could grab up the shuttles. The air grew full of white and gray and

crimson-dyed yarns, weaving a spider's web of wool between
Johanna and the loom and Rochambeau. Strands of weft yarn
floated around her, clung to her throwing arm, and fell across
her face. She broke them with furious chopping gestures, but
more yarns followed. Too late, Johanna realized that Rochambeau was deliberately aiming his shuttles to entrap her
in the web of yarn. She tried to dodge his next throws, but
the web of weft threads slowed her movements. Almost before she had fully realized his plan, she was cocooned in soft
floating yarns whose dyed and undyed and bleached fibers,
red and gray and white, clung to her tunic, crawled under her
dress, and prickled up and down her arms.

And he was laughing.

"Well, wife." With long, easy strides, sure now of his
victory, he advanced upon her. Johanna stood perfectly still,
too proud to fight the entrapping mesh of yarns. "There are
more ways to tame a vicious wife than beating her. Now, are
you prepared to be friendly?"

One hand under her chin, he lifted her face to meet his.
She could feel her lips softening in expectation of his kiss.
And he was still smiling as he bent his head to receive her
submissive tribute. Oh, it was too much! Johanna bit down
hard on the lips that met hers. She tasted blood and heard an
outraged bellow from Rochambeau. He jumped back, clap-
ping one hand to his bleeding lip, and Johanna suppressed a
giggle.

"Before God, woman, you go too far! Is there no one of
your duties as a wife that you'll perform without being beaten
into submission?"

"You'll never beat me into submitting to you," Johanna
spat back. With quick, impatient gestures, she pushed the
clinging web of yarns down over her arms, down past the
jeweled girdle where wisps of yarn clung to her keys and
chatelaine, finally trampling the last woolen strands under her
feet. Her skirts were covered with woolen fluff; the laundress
would have to brush and beat them for days before the clothes
were fit to wear again.

"No. I've never struck a woman yet." Rochambeau stroked
his chin with one hand, watching her with the wary glance
of a man approaching a wildcat's lair. The bleeding had
stopped already. "You tempt me to set precedent, though.

Perhaps a short stay in my dungeons would cool your blood and remind you that a woman's rightful place is in submission to her husband."

"Would you admit to the world that you're such a weak fool that you cannot master your own wife without whips and chains?" Johanna was beginning to feel better. This was more the way she'd meant her first meeting with Rochambeau to go. No more of his cloying, false love talk! Let them meet as the enemies they were; let him see what dragon's teeth had come to harvest since he had left the land.

"It seems to me," Rochambeau said slowly, "you've already broadcast that to the world. With your refusal to raise the money for my ransom, for instance. Do you think any baron in the land would question my right to imprison you for that? My dear, your little gesture of defiance has not made you popular. The gentle knights of the Marches will be quaking in their boots next time they go to war, for fear that their own wives will demonstrate such poorly timed independence. They'd applaud me if I dragged you through the village pigsties by your hair, and say it was no more than your due."

Johanna had been expecting such threats as these. She sat down on the weaver's bench behind the loom, brushing flecks of white and crimson-dyed wool off her skirt, and folded her hands with every appearance of calm. "You can, of course, treat me as you wish, my lord." Her downcast eyes and demure tones sent Rochambeau's eyebrows dancing up into his forehead. "But if you ever wish to read the accounts for your own estates, you will wish to treat me gently—very gently indeed."

"Accounts?"

"For the estates." Johanna smoothed her skirt and smiled down at her hands. "You've been away so long, perhaps you've forgotten how much business a great estate like yours requires. You've upwards of twenty manors scattered the length and breadth of England, my lord, some enfeoffed and some in demesne. Rents must be collected and fines paid. Your villeins must do their week work or pay their way out of it; your tenants must pay for your rights of high, low, and middle justice; your gentlemen that hold fees of you must send knights to your service or pay—pay—pay again!"

"I'm familiar with the workings of a large estate," said

Rochambeau mildly. "What puzzles me is what this has to do with you, or why you should think my treatment of you should concern my seneschal of the estates."

Johanna lifted her eyes at last, ready to let him see the triumph that lit them from within.

"Because, my lord, I am your seneschal of the estates."

"No, you're not," Rochambeau contradicted immediately. "You're only my wife. I left Aubrey in charge of the estates, just as he's always been. He serves as my steward in payment for his own manor of Spelsham that he holds from me. God's blood, woman, d'you think I'd forget such basic matters as who runs my estates?"

Johanna's green eyes flashed with irritation that Rochambeau had spoiled her climax. "Things have changed around here since you left, my lord."

"I can see that." Rochambeau crossed to the window slit and leaned against it, brushing the long hair away from his forehead with one hand. In the courtyard below, the castle servitors were still scurrying around like ants whose nest has been dug up. "I'm back now, though, and I mean to have things back in order. Including," he warned with a threatening frown in Johanna's direction, "such matters as disobedient wives who think they can wear the breeches in the household."

Johanna took a deep breath to calm herself. "If putting things back in order means putting Aubrey in charge of the estates again, you'll be making a mistake. That bumbling idiot was managing to run half of the demesne manors at a loss until I took over the books."

"Ridiculous! Everybody knows women don't have the intelligence to manage accounts. Doubtless you misunderstood what he was doing. Aubrey is my half-brother, even if he is a bastard, and he must therefore be at least half as clever as I am—which puts him well ahead of any gossiping girl! I'll see him tonight, and we'll get all this straightened out."

"No," said Johanna quietly, "I don't think you will."

Rochambeau's head snapped up, and he stared at her unbelievingly. "Open defiance? To my face? By God, madam, it's time you learned who's master in this castle. I'll have those account rolls from you if I have to have my men hold you down while I search your rooms for them." A slow grin began to spread over his face as he took in Johanna's outraged expression. "On second thought, maybe *I'll* hold you down while the men do the searching. It might be more fun that way, don't you think? Now, I wonder," he mused, coming slowly toward her with arms outstretched, "I wonder if somewhere on your person there is concealed a little key—for instance, a key to the chest that holds the accounts?"

Johanna yanked the heavy ring of keys free from her girdle and flung it at him. "Here are all the keys to all the locks in the castle, and much good may it do you! Go ahead! Try them out, but leave me alone!"

"Ah, but I feel sure you wouldn't give me the key to the account books so easily." Rochambeau grinned and feinted to one side, darting immediately the other way to catch Johanna as she attempted to slip by him. "Most likely you're trying to distract me while you go and hide the key somewhere else. Now, where would a lady hide a little key that she valued so highly? Here perhaps? Or here?"

One broad hand slipped under her bodice and explored the firm, high breasts held up by her wide jeweled girdle. Johanna felt close to fainting as his callused palm moved in gentle circles over her skin. Damn the man! It wasn't fair that his casual touch could turn her knees to water and her will to curdled porridge. Just because she'd slept alone for four lonely years; just because her dreams were haunted by memories of the pleasures he'd taught her in five short weeks of marriage, need not mean that she would give in to him now as though nothing else mattered.

"Nothing above the girdle," mused her wedded lord, this stranger, Rochambeau. "Perhaps we'd better search below? Gently now, my sweet, don't struggle so. I don't want to hurt you."

Johanna shivered and shook her head in vain while Rochambeau's searching fingers slid up under her skirts. "Stop," she breathed. "Please. You're not looking for the key."

"No? But I have the strangest feeling." Rochambeau's head bent to touch the milky skin of her breasts, where he'd left her garments in tempting disarray. "That I might find . . ." Flames danced up and down her skin wherever he touched. It had been four years since any man had held her so intimately. Too long. Johanna moaned and clenched her teeth against the treacherous desires that were weakening her. "That I might find the key to something under here . . ."

With a last effort of her despairing will, Johanna wrenched herself free of Rochambeau's exploring hands. She yanked her skirts down and straightened her dress as best she might. "You won't find anything you want under my skirts," she told him. "I can assure you of that. As for this mythical key, it doesn't exist. The account rolls are in my bedchamber, and you're welcome to take and read them if you can."

"In our chamber! Ah, now you're seeing reason. But I think I won't leave them in there. The proximity of the bed might prove all too distracting." Rochambeau's smile lit up his stern features, flashing like sun across a cloudy day. The stupid man didn't even have the sense to feel uneasy at this apparent surrender. How could he imagine she would give in to him so easily? As he moved past her with his light, catlike tread, incongruously graceful in such a big man, Johanna tucked a few loose strands of her hair up under her headdress and tugged at the loosened neck of her tunic. She looked down to conceal her secret smile.

"Don't be downcast, wife." Rochambeau had come out of the bedchamber with rolls of parchment tucked under his arm. Johanna jumped at the sound of his voice so close to her ear. She had barely time to compose her features before his fingers raised her chin once more, forcing her to look at him. "You've lost this joust," he said with a grin, "but I'll give you the opportunity to join me in combat again. This evening. After I've looked over the rolls and straightened things out with Aubrey." His three-cornered cat's grin broadened and deepened. "I think we might both enjoy a continuation of this tourney."

He dropped a swift, surprisingly gentle kiss on her lips and then was gone, down the stairs with his unwieldy load of parchments.

"This evening?" Johanna muttered. So Rochambeau thought they were going to share a bed again, just as if nothing had happened? Thought she'd given up so easily? Well, he'd learn better when he took a closer look at the account rolls. She'd been looking forward to telling him just why it would do him no good to have the actual parchments in his possession, but perhaps it was better this way. Let him find out on his own. Then he would understand that he must deal with her, not ride over her as if she were a conquered territory!

"Another tourney, is it? Ha! I'll wager your lance droops when you look at those records."

The bower filled with rustling skirts and sweet scents again. All in a rush, Johanna's ladies came crowding around her with little shrieks of excitement and curiosity. They must all have been on the stairs with their ears to the door.

"Did he beat you?"

"Is he going to send us away?"

"Was he very angry?"

"Isn't he the handsomest man you ever saw? How can you stay angry with him?"

"Stop!" Johanna all but shrieked, hands over her ears. "God's blood! Your babble is worse than a flock of geese waiting for their corn. Get out of here, all of you. I want to think!"

"But the weaving—"

"My tapestry work—"

"The Michaelmas liveries to cut out—"

A shriek of pure anguish rose from the corner where the great loom stood. "My weaving! Oh, that pig of a man!"

Dilys had discovered the wreckage of her carefully strung web and her pile of loaded spindles.

"Later." Johanna shooed the women out with flapping gestures of her hands and skirt, just as if they'd been the flock of silly geese she'd compared them to. "Dilys, we can repair the weaving. The other work can wait. God's teeth, you girls must have something to do outside the bower! Weed the herb garden. Help the cook. Play with the laundress's new baby. Flirt with the soldiers. Just—stay—out—of my way for a while!"

Given this blanket permission to do anything they wanted, the waiting-women disappeared as quickly as they'd come. Only one girl lingered—a pale, slim girl whose flowing golden locks proclaimed her to be unmarried, just as her rich dress with its jeweled border showed her to be of a higher rank than her companions. "Lady Johanna, do you really want to be left all alone? If that horrible man should come back—"

She broke off, her cheeks flaming crimson at the images conjured up in her mind.

"He won't be back, Alais." Johanna smiled at the tall girl whom she'd taken for fostering and to keep her company in Rochambeau's absence. "But, yes, do stay for a while. I find you restful, unlike those clacking geese. I didn't mean to shout at you, child. It's just that I have the headache."

The excuse was true, though she'd not realized it until just then. She felt hot and cold by turns when she remembered Rochambeau's impudent exploration of her body, and her temples were throbbing wildly under the tight binding of her headdress.

"Let me comb out your hair." Alais gently urged Johanna to her stool and loosened the tight square of embroidered silk that held her hair back. Cool, gentle fingers stroked away the pain in Johanna's temples, and a comb smoothed the masses of curly black hair that fell from the loosened headdress.

"Lady Johanna," Alais asked timidly after she had been combing for some time, "would you mind telling me—what was all the uproar about?"

Johanna jerked her head incautiously and felt a tug on the curl Alais was holding. "Don't you know? I thought everybody in three parishes knew that I'd refused to pay Rochambeau's ransom out of France. For heaven's sake, girl, you were with me when the messengers came."

"Yes," said Alais with unexpected spunkiness, "but you never said why, and that old Dilys won't tell me anything. She says I'm too young to know. But I'm sure you must have had a good reason."

Johanna laughed and stood up, too restless to settle down under Alais's patient hands. "Good reason? Aye, so it seemed at the time. We've both had good reasons for everything we've done to each other, I suppose. I forgot that you'd be too young to know the old stories. How old are you now, Alais? Rising fourteen? No, you're not too young to know. Your father will be looking for a good husband for you soon, and you'd best not be so ignorant as I was when I wore the bride crown.

"Almost fourteen," Johanna repeated to herself. "And you came to me the winter after Rochambeau left, a little maid of nine . . . *Dieu!* That means I must be almost twenty-one now." Her hands flew to her cheeks, feeling for wrinkles, and she examined her face anxiously in the polished steel mirror that Alais held for her inspection. "Tell me the truth, child. Am I quite old and worn?"

"You are the most beautiful woman in the Marches," said Alais calmly. "And everybody knows it, you included, so stop fishing for compliments."

"Indeed?" Johanna's eyes grew misty as she looked in the mirror, seeing her own face no longer, but a host of shadowy images crowding out of the past. "Ah, but four years ago they said I was the most beautiful girl in England and Wales together. My father meant to take me to court to find a husband. But then Rochambeau came riding across our land on his great black horse . . ."

Now the shadows in the mirror cleared and came together, like a reflection in a pool taking shape again after the water has been disturbed by ripples. Gazing into that polished surface, Johanna saw the image of a tall and wondrously handsome knight who'd come riding into her life a little over four years ago, when she was just turned sixteen and known as the most beautiful girl in all England and Wales.

Chapter Two

Pomeray, 1270

IT WAS HIGH summer, and the fields around Johanna's father's manor of Pomeray were golden with the ripening wheat. Soon, perhaps at the end of the week, the reeve would go out to call all the villeins to work on those fields, for the lord's wheat must be harvested and safely under store before the peasants were free to work on their own plots. Already the household was preparing for that first day of reaping, when it was customary to give the villeins their fill of food at noon and ale throughout the day. Johanna's mother, Gwynne, was herself overseeing the making of massive quantities of dark bread in the manor ovens—more loaves than the small household used all the rest of the year, special bread baked from the coarse scrapings that made a dark, heavy loaf.

It was a hot, sticky day, and the dark strands of hair that escaped from Gwynne Lespervier's coif clung to her forehead, while her cheeks grew mottled red with the heat from sun and bakehouse. Johanna should have stayed by her mother, learning the tasks that she would one day supervise as mistress of her own household. Instead, she had slipped away from the stifling heat of the ovens by creating an excuse.

"Gillie and Francoise are in your way," she'd informed her harried mother. "I'll help you by taking them down by the river to play."

Gwynne looked at her three daughters—Johanna, already sixteen and not yet wed for all her beauty, and the two little ones whose twin birth eight years previous had sent her husband into despairing bellows. Where, he'd demanded, was he to find dowries for *three* daughters, out of this poor manor with only twenty plough teams all told? Could an income of seventeen pounds sixpence a year establish one girl creditably, let alone three? And why couldn't Gwynne give him a son for a change?

Lately two things had eased Hugh Lespervier's depression about his houseful of daughters. The first was that Johanna, as she shot up from childhood into ripening girlhood, gave promise of a beauty so rare that already she was famed throughout the Marches. The second was the birth of his long-awaited son, William, now a baby in his cradle up in the bower.

Hugh had taken to declaring, too loudly and in the presence of the girls, that all his problems were in a fair way to being solved. Gwynne had finally borne him an heir to take over Pomeray. As for his gaggle of daughters, Johanna was beautiful enough to make a fine match without dowry. She shouldn't be wasted on any local knight with estates no better than Hugh's own. No, one of these winters, when they'd had a good harvest, he would take her to London to show her off before men who would appreciate her beauty and could afford to pay for it. Then, as mistress of a great household, she could find matches for her little sisters.

Gwynne had often wished that Hugh wouldn't praise the girl's beauty so loudly and in such extravagant terms to her very face. And yet, what more harm could it do? Half the men within a day's ride of Pomeray, not to mention both the young squires who waited on Hugh and his men, were madly in love with Johanna. With Piers making songs about her eyebrows and Gautier teaching her how to shoot a specially cut-down longbow he'd had made for her, well, it was a wonder the girl wasn't even more spoiled, and that was the truth!

"Johanna, you should stay here and learn how to manage a large baking," she automatically reproved the girl. "Soon you'll have a household of your own to run. You're not a baby to go paddling in the river when there's work to do."

Johanna tossed her head. "Pooh! Father says that I'm going to marry a great lord who'll have stewards and bailiffs and chamberlains to oversee all the work, and I shall have nothing to do but go hunting and hawking all day long with my husband.''

Spoiled indeed! Gwynne sighed as she looked at her tall, slender daughter. The masses of black hair that spilled out from under a scarlet ribbon were glossy as a raven's wing, but they'd not been combed out since Sunday before Mass. She refused to wear a surcoat in this heat, and her old tunic was far too thin for decency. The swelling curves of breasts and hips thrust out against the old worn fabric, showing a burgeoning womanhood in her body that had yet to be mirrored in her spirit. Her eyes were bright and dancing with green lights of mischief, and her full red lips were brighter around the corners with—could that be paint? No, Gwynne concluded with relief as Johanna chewed and swallowed the last of whatever was in her mouth. Only berry stains. Why, she was only a child after all, for all her sixteen years and her father's plans of a great marriage! This winter, surely, would be the time to see those plans come to fruition. Gwynne's heart twisted within her at the thought of losing this firstborn daughter, this fey creature who had always been secretly dearer to her than all the others. Why not let her have this last summer to run and play? This time next year, according to Hugh's plans, she'd be a married woman with a babe of her own under her girdle.

''Oh, go on, then. I can see you'd be less than no use to me here, the mood you're in, and it's true the little girls need some fresh air.'' As she spoke, Gwynne's hand automatically went out to smoothe Francoise's mousy hair, to straighten Gillie's tunic.

Johanna heard only the sharpness in her mother's words and missed the underlying tenderness in her eyes. She blinked back the momentary hurt she felt and grabbed her sisters' hands with a whoop of joy. ''To the river! I'll race you both.''

It was cool under the tall overarching oaks that shadowed the river bank. The little girls tucked their tunics up into their girdles and paddled happily in the shadows, looking for pretty stones that had been rubbed smooth by the current. Johanna dived into the deep pool that swirled around the roots of the oldest oak and swam back and forth once, nonchalantly, just to show the children what she could do if she chose. Then she climbed out and lay on the grassy bank, letting her clothes drip dry around her body, chewing a stem of grass and dreaming of the future.

It was a somewhat shadowy, misty future that her mind's eye presented to her, for she had only visited London as a child and could not remember it. Hugh had taken her to Shrewsbury last year, though, for the fair, and Johanna had wandered entranced down three whole lanes filled with stalls of bright ribbons and cheap pottery and mysterious bags of spices from the East. London must be like that, she thought, only bigger and finer—perhaps as many as a hundred shops on five or six big streets, with gaily dressed knights and ladies in fine floating veils looking at the merchandise. When she went there, the knights would cluster around her as Piers and Gautier did now, vying for her favors with presents. Only they would buy her silk robes and strings of pearls, not ginger nuts and gilt comfits. And in some unexplained fashion, all this attention would lead to her getting a husband who was very rich and very indulgent and would let her do whatever she chose, all day long, instead of making her go to lessons and learn to embroider and sit inside like a lady.

"And he'll let me have my own hawks," Johanna promised herself, "gerfalcons, with silk hoods and jesses, and little golden bells to put on their legs . . ."

Her little sisters' shrill, excited cries awakened Johanna rudely from her dream. She sat up, rubbing her eyes, and stared blankly at the empty pool where the little girls had been wading. Where had they got to? It sounded as if they were on the other side of the low ridge that separated the river's course from the fields of ripening grain. Johanna scrambled to her feet and raced for the top of the ridge, her heart pounding. She heard a man's deep shout rising over the cries of her sisters, and a long high scream pierced her ears.

She came over the top of the ridge, barefoot and breathless, to find Gillie and Francoise dancing up and down in the dirt and pointing at a dark track where the wheat had been crushed. The rider was just visible now, in the middle of the field, and as Johanna shaded her eyes she could make out a hawk returning to his glove with some limp furry thing dangling from its beak. The scream she had heard had been nothing more than a dying rabbit.

Without pausing to think or to straighten her garments,

Johanna shouted at the rider and pelted down the trail of trodden-down wheat. How dare this idiot come riding across their land, trampling the grain and frightening her little sisters!

"You fool!" Johanna railed when she was still a dozen steps away. "Can't you see the grain's almost ready for harvest? What possessed you to come trampling our fields? You should be hanged for this! You *will* be, if I've aught to say . . ."

He reined in his horse at her shout and sat waiting for her, smiling as though he'd come to pay a social call. He was a stranger; he should make his apologies, she thought, to her father before he left the manor of Pomeray. He should know it was not some petty sergeant's land he'd insulted thus! But breath and words alike deserted her as she reached the horseman. She grasped his stirrup to keep him from running away. The horse was fully a hand taller than any in her father's stables, and glossy black all over—a color of ill omen, betokening an ill-tempered beast. But the man didn't seem to care. He, too, was tall, with hair that shone as golden as the wheat he had carelessly trodden down, eyes whose deep blue rivaled the summer sky.

"Well, here's a sweet addition to my day's sport!" he exclaimed as she reached him. "D'you want a ride, sweetheart?" Without waiting for an answer, he reached down and scooped her up with one arm, as effortlessly as if she'd been a wisp of the straw that he had broken just now.

"Gillie! Francoise! Run!" Johanna screamed before panic about her own fate overtook her. The hard grip crushed her ribs and bruised her side. Johanna struggled, kicked, and found herself sitting before the stranger, with the hard bright eyes of his falcon staring incuriously at her. Her sisters had disappeared, and she desperately hoped they would have enough sense to run back to the manor for help. But what could happen in the time it took them to get there? Nothing much, Johanna told herself. This impudent fellow wouldn't dare harm the daughter of the lord of the manor.

She wished she felt quite sure of that. "You'd better put me down," she told him, sitting straight-backed before him, disdaining to struggle. "*Now*. If you let me go at once," she added, "I'll not speak of this to anybody."

"I'm sure you'll have better sense than to do that," said

the stranger consideringly. "But I don't think I will put you down. Not yet. You're too pretty an armful to be wasted on some churl's hut. Tell me where you want to go, girl, and I'll take you there . . . eventually." He smiled down at her, and she felt herself swimming again, floating in the deep blue of his eyes as she'd floated on the river.

"Put me down," she said again. "You're hurting me."

"I don't think so." But he shifted his grip slightly so that she could lean back against his arm. Indeed, she had no other choice if she wanted to keep her balance; the saddle was a slippery edge on which she was most insecurely perched, and the ground seemed a dizzyingly long way down. She let her head fall back so that she could look the fellow in the face again, and that was a mistake. Lips as hard and warm as the strong arm that held her covered her mouth, taking away her breath and leaving her, if possible, dizzier than before. His arm tightened around her, and his mouth demanded more than she was prepared to give—more than she'd known she had to give. Oh, this was a world away from the chaste peck on the cheek which she'd permitted Gautier last Fair day! Senses awhirl, Johanna sank down into the magic of the kiss, forgetting everything but the intoxication of the moment.

"There, that's not so bad, is it, lass?"

The deep, amused laugh that accompanied the words brought Johanna to her senses.

"I think you will regret that. My father will have the flesh from your bones if he finds out how you've abused me."

"Oh, I haven't started abusing you yet," laughed the stranger.

"God's body and bones!" Johanna almost shrieked as he bent his head toward her again. "Can't you understand anything? My father is Sir Hugh Lespervier, dolt, and he owns this manor!"

"Sir Hugh!" In his surprise, the stranger's arm loosened and let Johanna slip to the ground. Her bare heels thudded against the soft earth; broken wheat straws prickled her insteps. She felt strangely and sharply aware of these minute sensations, and of a hundred other messages from her body—the heat of the sun striking through her long damp ringlets to warm the back of her neck, the shivering coolness of her skin under the damp tunic that clung to her like a villein's only robe.

If she had any sense, Johanna thought in her confusion, she'd run away. Apparently she didn't have any sense, for she stood her ground, staring up at the stranger and taking in the details of his features that had been blurred by fear before. A proud face, she thought, and a secret one. He'd keep his thoughts hooded like the cold eyes of his gerfalcon. But his eyes were not cold—nor his lips. Blushes seized her at the memory of her shameless response.

"Lespervier's daughter," he repeated. "And does he recognize you as his own?"

He took her for a serf's bastard. Anger made Johanna's cheeks burn brighter than the faded red of her tunic. "I am," she said, biting off the words one by one, "Sir Hugh's oldest daughter by his wife, Gwynne. Does that make the situation perfectly clear to you?"

"Perfectly." The strange knight should have been stark terrified to find he'd been manhandling the daughter of the lord. Johanna had just time to wonder at his surprising calm before he spoke again. "There's just one slight misunderstanding we have to clear up. Your father doesn't own this manor. He holds it from one Nicolas de Rochambeau." The blond man tapped his chest with a grin whose meaning was unmistakable.

"You're the baron?" Johanna couldn't believe it. She'd never seen this mysterious Rochambeau to whom her father owed fealty, but it stood to reason that a man so rich and powerful, with so many manors scattered over England that he never even bothered to visit Pomeray, would be . . . "I thought you'd be old." The words spilled from her lips with the careless haste her mother had so often decried. "And ugly!"

Nicolas de Rochambeau dismounted and looped the reins of his horse over one arm, taking care not to disturb the falcon. Johanna found that she was no longer afraid of him, even now that she knew he had enough power to dispossess her family and turn them all out like landless villeins if she had displeased him.

"I'm glad to learn that I find favor in your eyes, demoiselle," he said, moving toward her with a soft, catlike step that surprised her—so graceful for such a big man!

"I didn't say that." Johanna stepped backward and reminded herself again that she was *not* afraid. Besides, it was time somebody stood up to this Rochambeau. Everything in his manner showed that he was not accustomed to encountering any opposition.

"At least you don't think I am old and ugly," Rochambeau pointed out. "After the sharp words with which you belabored me before, I'm inclined to take heart at the smallest sign of gentleness."

It wasn't fair that he should be able to smile at her like that, so sweetly that she forgot how rude and overbearing he'd been. Head swimming, Johanna wondered what it would be like to receive such smiles every day. What woman could resist him? What woman would want to?

Well, she wasn't likely to find out. He would be angry that she'd called him names and kicked him. This softness was most likely only the prelude to the storm.

"I'm not going to apologize for anything I said." Johanna planted her bare heels firmly in the furrow where she stood and glared up at Rochambeau. "It's your own fault if you weren't greeted properly. You should have told us you were coming. You should have told me who you were to begin with. And I don't care if you are the baron, it's wicked, sinful waste to ride through the ripe wheat just before harvest!"

The sun behind his head turned his long golden hair into a halo of fire, blurred his features, and made her squint most unbecomingly. So she dropped her eyes again, preferring to seem meek rather than make herself ugly. His chuckle took her by surprise.

"I cry your pardon, gentle lady. I will not even point out that it is my right, as your father's seigneur, to ride where I will over the lands of my vassals. You are perfectly correct. Even a baron should know better than to waste the good wheat, the golden bounty of our Lord. Will you not pardon me?"

There was a rustling sound. Johanna glanced through her eyelashes and saw Rochambeau kneeling before her, head bowed in a mockery of penitence.

"Oh, get up, for pity's sake," she said, too cross at his

gentle mockery to remember how one ought to address one's father's seigneur. "You're only crushing more wheat with this foolery."

"If you don't consent to walk a while by the river with me, in token of pardon," Rochambeau countered, "I shall be thrown into such despair that I'll very likely fall down in a fit, rolling around and making a perfect mess out of your beloved wheat field. My horse, too."

"Your *horse?*"

"He has the greatest sympathy with my feelings." Blue eyes peeped up at Johanna's face. She tried to restrain the smile that threatened the corners of her lips. "If I roll over in a fit, he will probably imitate my actions. And, being bigger than I am, he will crush proportionately more wheat. And this time, my lady Johanna, the fault will be all upon your lovely head. Dare you accept the danger of so nearly mortal a sin?"

The laughter would sputter out, no matter how Johanna tried to restrain it. "All right, all right! I pardon you. I apologize. Whatever. Now, will you get that horse out of the wheat?" While Rochambeau had been making his mock apology, his horse had been peacefully grazing on the grain.

"Your slightest wish is my command." Rochambeau rose in one fluid motion, with that incongruous and disturbing grace, and snapped his fingers at the horse. "Come, Marchgai. The lady graciously permits us to accompany her."

Marchgai. The name meant "the proud walker." Johanna thought it might equally apply to the man beside her.

Afterwards she never could remember what they'd talked about in that enchanted stroll under the cool shady trees, or how long they'd been there. It was an hour out of time, when Nicolas de Rochambeau teased her one moment with outrageous flirtation, then treated her like a little girl and gravely inquired if she was frightened of his hawk.

"Frightened! No, indeed!" cried Johanna swiftly. "He is the most beautiful creature I have ever seen." Her admiration was real enough, but she didn't know whether it was for the lord of Rochambeau or for the lordly creature sitting brighteyed on his wrist with its fierce talons digging into the arm guard of leather embroidered with fine gold and silver wires.

What he holds, he will never let go, she thought, and again

she wasn't sure whether she thought of the hawk or of his master, whose crest was a stooping falcon.

This thought led naturally to another. "You're not wearing your arms," she reproved him. "I would have recognized the crest of Rochambeau."

"I don't normally dress in full armor for a day's hawking in the country," said Rochambeau. Then, as he saw her blush, he added, "But perhaps I should have done, had I guessed at the dangers lurking in these peaceful fields! Behold me stricken to the heart!"

"I thought we'd agreed to forgive each other for what we said." Johanna pouted. She tossed her head and turned a little sideways, enjoying the way Rochambeau's eyes followed her. She was used to the adoration of Piers and Gautier, but it was something else to attract a man like this—a knight, a powerful baron, who could have his pick of any court lady. Just for a little while, she would pretend that his sighs and flirtatious jests were real, that this great man would be so stricken by her beauty that he'd want to make her his lady.

"It was not your words that wounded me," said Rochambeau gravely, "but the darts sent by your bright eyes that have pierced me to the heart." His broad hand, the back sprinkled with sun-bleached golden hairs, covered Johanna's fingers where they rested on his arm. She felt a not unpleasant thrill within her at that touch, and at the deep meaningful look he bent on her.

"There is a medicine for that hurt, my lord," she said, eyes modestly downcast to conceal the fluttering in her heart.

"If I might crave one kiss to heal my wounds . . ."

"Prayer and fasting were a better medicine!" Johanna laughed, and she spun away from Rochambeau before he could claim the kiss her gestures had half promised him. He reached for her, laughing likewise, and she knew a moment's breathless fear and anticipation. What was it she had thought? What he takes, he'll not give up; what he grips, he'll not let go. In a moment he would catch and hold her, would kiss her again, and this time they wouldn't be on the back of his tall horse, but all alone under the trees, with the soft green grass underneath . . .

"Hold! A Lespervier! A Lespervier!"

The thundering of hooves broke in on their enchanted

dream. Johanna spun around and shrieked in dismay at the sight of her father, armed and mounted, bearing down on them with his long shining sword raised. Behind him came two other figures, men-at-arms in hard boiled leather, with their long lances of fire-hardened ash pointed directly at Rochambeau's breast.

Johanna shrieked again and threw herself in front of Rochambeau, only to be tossed aside as lightly as a leaf. She fell on her knees halfway down the bank, her shoulders bruised from the casual grip with which Rochambeau had hurled her out of danger. She scrambled upright again to find the moment of danger already past. Sir Hugh had reined his horse to a halt just inches from Rochambeau; the long muddy marks in the turf showed where the stallion's hooves had slid in a panic-stricken halt. Already her father had dismounted and gone down on one knee before his feudal lord, while behind him the two men-at-arms shuffled uneasily.

"My lord baron, forgive me! I thought—my foolish daughters said Johanna had been carried off by a robber knight. I had no idea it was you, my lord!"

"The misapprehension appears to have been widespread," said Rochambeau in a dry tone that Johanna had not heard before. "Your daughter called me a thieving tramp with nothing better to do than spoil other folks' hard work." With a sweep of his hand, he pointed behind them, where the dark track of his passage still showed against the golden fields of wheat.

"I'll beat her," Hugh promised. Rising to his feet, he grabbed Johanna's wrist and dragged her to his side. "How dare you speak to our liege lord that way!" His face was crumpled as if he wanted to cry. How could he act so cringing before Rochambeau, just when Johanna wanted so desperately to impress the man with her poise and her family's standing? Johanna opened her mouth to rail at her father, but stopped abruptly as she saw herself reflected in his pale gray eyes. What a pitiful sight she must present—hair streaming down her back, her single tunic torn and wet from the river. Rochambeau must have been inwardly laughing at her all the time they strolled by the river and played at courtly love. She glared at him, turning his way all the anger she could not bestow on her father.

"No, don't beat her," said Rochambeau in a lazy, considering voice that only made her hate him worse. "I don't hold with beating lovely women. I do believe we can find some better use for her, Sir Hugh, if we put our heads together."

A bright, calculating glitter came into Hugh Lespervier's eyes, and he stroked his short reddish beard with one hand. "Indeed, my lord baron? Ah . . ."

With that sigh of contentment, the world turned upside down for Johanna. Her father sent her back to the manor house on the saddle pommel of one of his men-at-arms, with a message to Gwynne to prepare a feast for the baron. Gwynne heard the words and sighed sharply at the thought of this new task added to a day that had been too long already. She looked at her daughter's large dark eyes and bruised lips and sighed again with belated understanding.

From then until long after supper, Johanna had not a minute's peace. She was plunged into a tub of cold water to wash off the mud of the river, then into hot water scented with rose petals. Her mother's tiring-woman scrubbed her hair with the sweet market-bought soap that Gwynne saved for special occasions, made her sit still while every last snarl was combed out, and then began a ruthless attack on her short splitting fingernails. After supper, Gwynne came running up to the bower to report that Sir Hugh and Rochambeau were sitting mighty cozy over their tankards of mulled wine.

"And your father brought out the good Gascony red wine, too!" she reported in awed tones.

"I'm sure the baron deserves no less than the best our house has to offer." Johanna knew her mother would be hurt at her cool, uninspired response, but she herself was hurting in a dozen different ways—her scalp aching, her nails tingling from Elys's probes with the ivory nail cleaner, her skin stiff and itchy from the paste of tansy and tincture of pearls that Elys had slathered on her face in a desperate attempt to cure a summer's sunburn in one evening.

Fortunately, Gwynne was too excited to heed her daughter's tone of voice. She went on enumerating the delicacies she'd found to enliven their customary plain supper of soup and bread, quoting Rochambeau's praise of the crayfish ragout and his admiration of the tapestry of Jonah and the whale as though she really thought a great baron could be impressed by their country hospitality.

"Mark my words, my girl, something great will come of all this!" she said over and over, until Johanna could have screamed for sheer weariness. What was the good of meeting a man like Rochambeau if all it meant was that you were dragged away to the bower while he sat and discussed dull business with your father? It was more fun flirting with Piers and Gautier, after all.

"I'm hungry," she complained. "Nobody brought any supper to the bower."

Gwynne frowned, smiled, and patted her daughter on the shoulder. "Listen to the girl! Thinking of supper at a time like this. There's no time to eat. We have to make you beautiful. You silly girl, don't you understand what it means to have attracted the attention of a man like Rochambeau?"

"Yes," said Johanna sharply. "Apparently it means that I'm to be included with the crayfish ragout and the marzipan cakes, served up at the rere-supper to tickle the baron's appetite!" She didn't want to be paraded like a special dessert, stuffed into an unfamiliar gown with her hair trussed up in imitation of the court ladies they had none of them ever seen. Hadn't Rochambeau liked her well enough by the river, in her old tunic and with her hair about her shoulders? She wished passionately that they could have kept that enchanted time just a little longer. Oh, she understood well enough what her father and the baron were at downstairs; she wasn't as stupid as her mother seemed to think. She was of too high a rank for Rochambeau to consider taking her as his mistress, so it could only be a marriage that they were discussing. They were taking away her magic afternoon and turning the attraction she and Rochambeau had felt into a dull matter of settlements and rent rolls and property.

But apparently this had to be gone through, before one could be alone with a man without fear of interruption, without one's father galloping up and waving his sword and babbling about honor. She'd never heard of a marriage that wasn't preceded by such tiresome talk. So Johanna gritted her teeth and resolved to be polite about it. As long as she and Rochambeau understood what nonsense it all was, she could get through it. Presently her father would be through talking business, and then Rochambeau would take her out into the little walled garden behind the orchard, and they would be together again. Johanna tried to ignore the pull of the drying paste on her face and hands, tried to ignore the giggling of the waiting-women who came to empty the tub. Instead, she dreamed of a quiet place scented with flowers and herbs, and Rochambeau coming to hold her in every sense.

Toward midnight, when the candles in the bower were burning low and sputtering and stinking of the tallow that had been used to dip them, Gwynne sighed and unpinned the elaborate arrangement of pearls and brass pins with which she'd put up Johanna's hair. "You'd best put off your good dress," she told her daughter, "and go to bed. I don't know when the menfolk will be done talking." She kissed Johanna lightly on the cheek. "You want to be pretty for him in the morning, you know!"

"In the morning," Johanna promised herself, and quickly changed the time of her dream from evening to pearly dawn, with dew on the roses and the birds singing in the garden.

In the morning Rochambeau was gone before Johanna came down to Mass, and Sir Hugh announced with beaming satisfaction that everything was settled. "Bit of luck for us, having him drop by like this. Said he was making a tour of inspection of his demesne manors, got as far as Rhuthun and decided to take a day off for some hawking, drop in and talk to me and some other tenants. He's granting me the good bottom lands on the other side of the river. They used to belong to Rhuthun, but they're so far from the rest of the manor lands that his seneschal never sends anybody over to work the land anyway. Dead loss to him, profit to us! *And* he's remitting the knight service we owe for ten years. Ten years!" He rubbed his hands together. "Not having to pay him every year for three armed knights we don't have and can't afford to support—that'll help me get this place back on its feet! Let's see, we can reroof the stables now with the shingles from the kitchen and do the kitchen roof in lead as you've been after me to do, Gwynne, and then maybe next year I'll put in some of these newfangled beans instead of leaving half the fields fallow, and with two more plough oxen we could break some new land—"

"And what did you offer him in trade for all these favors?"

Johanna asked sharply. As her father rambled on and on about his plans for improvement to the manor, she began to know a sinking fear that the discussions last night had not involved her at all. Perhaps she and Gwynne had been merely spinning romantic dreams. After all, Rochambeau hadn't even troubled to see her again before he rode away. Probably he'd forgotten all about her by now.

"Don't interrupt your father," Gwynne reproved Johanna. Her voice was gentle, but the whiteness of her clasped hands told Johanna that her mother, too, was feeling the strain of waiting. But, as Hugh Lespervier's wife, it was her duty to wait and listen patiently and accept his decisions when he felt ready to tell her about them in his own good time. Johanna vowed that when she married she wouldn't let her husband beat her down like that, as though she had no right to a voice in the family affairs. Probably it was just as well she wasn't marrying Rochambeau. He seemed to be cut of the same inconsiderate, selfish cloth as her father. And yet . . . something in her heart yearned uncontrollably after the tall, bright-haired figure on the black horse. She pictured him riding away from Pomeray, never to return, and there was a strange ache deep in her chest.

" . . . And with the extra money from selling the beans, I'll hire a stonemason to repair the old water mill, and we'll make all the tenants use that instead of going to the monastery, so I'll take in the profit from the grinding as well as the grain they pay in rent. I might even be able to start on the mill this fall. After all, he's generously offered to pay the entire expenses of the wedding feast himself."

"Wedding feast?" Johanna's heart thudded irregularly between her ribs, and she found it hard to breathe.

"Why, yes. What did you think he's giving us all these favors for—the love of my pretty gray eyes?" Hugh chuckled and tousled his daughter's hair. "You're to be married next spring, on Lady Day," he informed Johanna.

"In trade for a few hectares of mud and ten years' remission of knight service." And her prospective husband hadn't even bothered to inform her of the arrangement, much less ask her how she felt about it. All that love talk by the riverside had been just a game to him; in the real world, she was nothing more than a commodity to be bought and sold.

37

"A few hectares! Nothing of the sort. Nearly twenty virgates, enough to support a couple of dozen villein families, and the best rich bottom land in the country. It's a damned good deal, and I'll thank you not to put on that sour face about it. Enough to curdle milk, it is, let alone scare Rochambeau out of the wedding. You'll like being married well enough when you get used to it, and he's a fair man. Don't give him any trouble, and I'll wager he'll be generous enough to you. And once you're settled in, you can find husbands for Gillie and Francoise among your lord's rich friends. Nothing could be better! Eh? What could be better?"

Chapter Three

THE MEWS WERE cool and shadowy, a welcome contrast to the glaring heat of the summer sun. Her father's three hawks stirred uneasily on their perches as Johanna entered. They were restless from long hours cramped in the mews. During the harvest no one had time for such amusements as hawking, and Gwynne flatly forbade her family to carry the hawks around indoors or to take them to Mass in the tiny chapel as great lords and ladies did.

"I don't care what your cousin's wife's aunt says the court ladies do," she told Johanna. "It's a dirty habit, and there'll be no flea-bitten birds fouling the nice clean rushes in my hall!"

"They're not flea-bitten," Johanna had protested when she was younger and thought she could win points by arguing. "They're beautiful birds, and they're cleaner than our serfs!"

"Very likely," said her mother dryly. "Certainly they're better lodged."

But on this point she'd remained adamant, and the three aging hawks remained lonely on their perches in the mews, hoping for someone to take them out after game. That morning, in the disappointment of finding Rochambeau gone already, Johanna had slipped away from her prescribed morning tasks in bower and stillroom to snatch a few minutes talking to her favorite hawk, Gaimont. She had felt dull and rebellious as Gwynne outlined the new tasks she must master be-

39

Tapestry of Pride

fore she could be considered ready to take over a great baron's
household. A winter of hard work, learning to perfection each
dull domestic chore so that she could be fit to oversee it, was
a poor trade for the visit to London her father had promised
her.

"Why can't I go to stay with Aunt Jehane? Father promised
this winter would be the time!"

Gwynne sighed sharply. "You don't need to go now, since
we've found you a husband nearer home. And we can't afford
the expense."

"He's paying for the wedding feast, isn't he?"

"And who's to pay for your bride clothes, and all the linen
you'll need to take with you to be decently outfitted? Your
father forgets these little details."

Johanna's spirits had lifted momentarily at the mention of
new clothes, only to be dashed by the information that her
mother intended to make the trousseau into a learning experience. "Of course we'll have to buy a lot of the cloth; there's
not time for you to weave it all, even if you had the skill.
And there'll have to be some silks; that will cost a pretty
penny," Gwynne sighed. "But you can weave some, at least,
of the linens and woolens right here. It's time you learned
how to work the great loom without leaving your cloth flapping loose at the selvages. And there'll be no need to waste
money on embroidered hems and edgings. The good nuns in
the convent where I was educated taught me to embroider
finely on linen, and you'll have the whole winter to practice
and make your underlinen ready."

Before her mother could think of any more projects for her
to take on that winter, Johanna had seized the advantage of a
momentary disturbance in the kitchens to slip away. Now she
kicked the loose straw that covered the floor of the mews,
watched the golden strands floating slowly down around a
shaft of sunlight, and cursed under her breath. Gaimont stirred
again on his perch, ruffling his feathers out and jerking his
head, and Johanna made up her mind. She'd not stay there,
to be called back to the bower as soon as her mother tracked
her down. She would saddle a horse and ride out with Gaimont, giving him some much-needed exercise and perhaps
coming back with some nice plump rabbits for the pot.

Cautiously, she sidled from mews to stable, staying under

the covered passage that connected the two buildings so that she couldn't be spied from the windows of the keep. What luck! The stable was all but deserted; only one boy squatted in the far corner, pretending to clean a harness with lackluster, desultory strokes.

He raised his head as Johanna came in, fixing her with dark, melancholy eyes.

"Piers! I thought you were a stable boy," Johanna exclaimed. What was one of her father's squires doing there at such a menial task?

"I might as well be," said Piers glumly.

She questioned him further and found that the marshal who kept the squires and men-at-arms busy had sent him away from the morning's arms practice. "He said I was so clumsy I must have been up all night, either with a girl or drinking; and I might as well make myself useful in the stables until I got my coordination back together."

"Were you? With a girl, I mean?" If so, it would be an interesting sidelight into Piers's character. Johanna had never thought he had the gumption to take one of the villein girls into the straw, though there were plenty who switched their skirts and tossed their heads at the sight of his darkly handsome young face.

"In a manner of speaking." Piers bowed his head, black hair falling across his forehead, and rubbed with unnecessary vigor at the piece of harness in his lap. "Thinking about one, anyway."

"Who? Do I know her?"

"Johanna! How can you ask?" Piers's dark eyes were raised to her face, brimming over with liquid melancholy. "You know how I feel about you. There's never been anyone but you in my heart. Oh, I know you're far above me. Your father is a knight with a manor of his own, and I'm only a landless squire, a third son whose father can't even afford to buy him a set of arms. It'll be years before I can earn my knighthood. Now that all the rebel barons have been put down, we'll probably have peace forever. I'll never get to prove myself in battle, so I'll probably stay a squire all my life. But a man can dream."

"And you . . . dreamed of me?" Johanna had never taken Piers's sighings over her too seriously, not with her father continuously telling her what a great match she would make someday. She'd even thought him rather boring. But today, when she was smarting from the businesslike way in which Rochambeau had bought her for a couple of muddy fields, Piers's innocent adoration touched a responsive chord within her.

"You know I did. And now it's more hopeless than ever! That's why I said I might as well be a stable boy. You'll be a great baron's lady. Even if I won my knighthood on the field of battle, even if I did some great service to the king and got a manor like Pomeray, I'd still be as far below you as one of the grooms. But I have one thing *he'll* never have," Piers declared with pride.

"What's that?"

"My love for you. I wouldn't have bought you the way he did, Johanna. I would have courted you as my very fair lady and cherished you tenderly forever. And in my heart you'll always be my lady. He can't take that dream away from me."

Johanna closed her eyes for a moment to savor the sweetness of Piers's words.

"Are you insulted?"

"No, Piers." The right words came to her lips unbidden, fed into her mind by a hundred romances that she'd heard sung or told in the bower all her life. "What lady can be offended by true devotion? I, too, shall cherish the memory of our few short hours together all my life." For the moment it was true. She saw herself cold and unloved in Rochambeau's baronial hall, a possession bought for its beauty like his embroidered hawking glove.

"You mean—if it had not been for this marriage—Johanna, of your mercy tell me!" He was kneeling, incongruously still clutching the harness in both hands, and Johanna noted the detail with annoyance. It detracted from her picture of a romantic encounter, to have her suitor kneeling among horse droppings and holding a broken bridle. "Might I one day have dared to dream of—of what I dare not even say now?"

Johanna dropped her eyes. "Even a baron's lady may dream," she murmured. "That, at least, is one thing they cannot take away from us."

Piers's upturned face blazed with such joy that she felt a moment of fear. Springing to his feet, he moved toward her with arms outstretched. "If I could beg one kiss to remember?"

Johanna closed her eyes and proffered her cheek. His lips were cool and moist, and he dared do no more than brush the surface of her face. It wasn't at all like Rochambeau's hard, demanding kiss. But then, she reminded herself, Piers respected her.

She controlled the impulse to wipe her face, but when he would have repeated the kiss, she stepped back. "No, Piers. Remember that I am promised to another. We must not let our emotions run away with us."

"If I could have some token then?" suggested Piers. "A scarf, a ribbon—something to cherish, to remind me of you?"

Before Johanna could answer, a loud, cheerful whistling broke in upon the silence of the stables. They sprang apart without a word. When Gautier entered, Piers was again working on the harness, while Johanna patted the mane of the nearest horse with great absorption.

Gautier staggered into the stables without noticing Johanna and dropped his chin-high load of swords and bucklers and rubbed his back. "Whew! I swear those things get heavier every day. I bet old Horse-Piss sits up at night hollowing out the wooden handles and pouring in lead. 'Good for your training, my boy,' " he mimicked, waggling his fair head in imitation of the marshal. " 'Keep your wrist up, and quit complaining. What'll you do if you meet one of Dafydd's Welsh raiders, tell him you're tired and you want to knock off for an hour's rest?' As if anybody ever raided Pomeray! You were clever to get sent off, Piers. I think I'll be clumsy tomorrow."

Johanna giggled, and Gautier whirled in surprise. "What the—oh, it's you," he said in almost comically altered tones. "How may I serve you, Johanna?"

"I was looking for an escort to take me out with Gaimont," Johanna said. After all, that had been what brought her into the stables originally.

Gautier pulled a long face. "Wish I could be the lucky man, but I'm due to work in the armory in half an hour. Tell you what, though, I'll escort you as far as the garden."

"And what game will you find there?" Piers gibed.

Gautier grinned. "Oh, we'll find some amusement." Taking Johanna's silence for consent, he offered her his arm with a courtly bow.

On the way out of the stables, she contrived to loosen the faded ribbon that tied her hair back. It went fluttering to the straw in the doorway, a flash of blue on gold that reminded her of Rochambeau. But when she glanced back a moment later, the blue ribbon was gone. Perhaps that would make Piers happy.

In the walled garden beyond the orchard, Johanna quickly discovered that it would take more than a ribbon and a kiss on the cheek to make Gautier happy. He too was upset at the news of her coming marriage, but his way of showing it was to press her immediately for more favors than she'd ever considered granting him. "We've only this winter," he pointed out when she protested. "Next year you'll be the baron's brood mare."

Johanna shuddered at the thought and did not put Gautier off quite so firmly as she might have done. Was she never to know any of the joys of being courted? She closed her eyes, let Gautier taste her cool, closed lips, and pretended that his strong young arms were the arms of a husband-to-be.

"You're my lady," he told her after that sealing kiss. "To hell with the baron! We've a whole winter to find some way out. You're not properly betrothed yet, are you?"

Johanna shook her head. Rochambeau hadn't even stayed for that exchange of vows; seemingly he thought the business decisions he'd discussed with her father were all that mattered.

"Well, then. We'll find some way to get out of this marriage. Now that I know you love me too, I can do anything!" In sheer exuberance, Gautier leaped high into the air, clicking his heels and snapping his fingers like an acrobat.

Johanna didn't recall having said that she loved Gautier, but she supposed the kiss she'd permitted him might be interpreted that way. The memory of his hot lips inexpertly pressed on hers did nothing for her, but she was taken with his cheerful assertion that she didn't have to marry the baron after all. Instead of moping in a corner like Piers, Gautier evidently meant to do something to claim her as his own— although just what he meant to do was rather vague. However, she didn't get out of the garden without granting him another kiss and a curling lock of her hair as a token of her favor.

"Chin up, sweetheart," he advised her. "We'll think of something. I won't let you go to the baron without a fight."

Johanna couldn't picture a fight between Rochambeau and Gautier ending any way but in Gautier's utter discomfiture, but it warmed her heart that he was willing to struggle for her.

"Let it be our secret," she whispered to him before they left the garden. "Don't tell anybody. I should be so ashamed!"

Gautier promised not to breathe a word.

"Especially not to Piers!"

"Of course not. What do you take me for?" Gautier scowled down at her. "I'm not some puling Italianate song master who has to make a song about it every time he kisses a pretty girl. And speaking of kissing . . ."

"I think I hear my mother calling." Johanna fled the garden, only half reassured by Gautier's promises. What a coil there would be if Piers and Gautier compared notes! But as long as they didn't . . . well, it was pleasant to be courted and fought over, to know that at least some people in the world thought she was worth more than a business deal struck over the supper table and settled without so much asking her opinion.

Over the next few days, Johanna tried with varying degrees of success to keep both Piers and Gautier from simmering over into open rivalry for her affections. Not that she was entirely averse to the idea, but something told her that if her father guessed at the games she was playing, she'd be deprived of both admirers at a stroke. And it was pleasant to hear Piers whispering the words of a new aubade he'd made in her honor, or to have Gautier maneuvering to catch her alone and report on his latest plan for freeing her from the marriage to Rochambeau. The only thing was, both squires were quite busy with arms practice, caring for their lords' horses and armor, and manifold other duties—and the times when they were off duty were much the same. Johanna could never enjoy a quiet tête-à-tête with Piers without fearing interruption from Gautier, and vice versa. To her annoyance, she found herself spending more and more time in the bower, spinning and weaving as her mother wished. It was the only place where she didn't have to juggle the stories she'd told both men!

One cloudy morning, Johanna found that both the squires were helping with the harvest. Separately they'd both grumbled to her about being set to such menial work, but all the able-bodied men were pressed into service that week to finish the harvest before the threatening rains came down and spoiled the wheat. And her mother was down in the fields too, overseeing the serving maids who brought ale to the thirsty workers and making sure that none of them disappeared into the long meadow grasses where they might simultaneously lose their virtue and crush the hay.

Johanna couldn't pass up the opportunity to get outside without worrying about being caught in one flirtation or another. Without even bothering to make up an excuse, she deserted the quiet shady world of the bower to visit her favorite place on the manor, the herb garden that had been slowly drying up under neglect and summer sun.

Gwynne had no taste for gardening and spared little attention for this part of the manor, though she liked to spend long hours in the stillroom or kitchen concocting new sauces with the sweet and pungent herbs that Johanna brought her. Now Johanna was ashamed to see that her beloved plants were wilting from thirst and neglect. She draped her good surcoat across the low stone wall that bordered this section of the garden, unbuttoned the long tight sleeves of her tunic, and set to work with her own hands.

With all the men and boys at work on the harvest and the women servants trying to fill their places around the manor, there was no point in looking for someone to haul water for her. Johanna did it herself, splashing bucket after bucket over the roots of the thirsty plants until the rows ran with sludgy mud and she herself was sweating. She tilted the last bucket up to her mouth, balancing the weight of water precariously in an attempt to gulp a cooling draught out of the wooden bucket. Totally absorbed in her task, she did not notice the stealthy noises behind her until a pair of strong hands gripped her around the waist.

Johanna screamed, choked, and dropped the bucket. Water splashed down her front and soaked her tunic. Wet and spluttering with rage, she kicked backwards at her assailant. "Look what you made me do, you great oaf!"

"Is that any way to greet your betrothed?" inquired a familiar voice.

The hands on her waist loosened, and Johanna turned to face Rochambeau. "You! I might have known."

"I thought you would know," said her not-yet-formally betrothed. "Surely there can't be anyone else who's in the habit of stealing kisses from you in the garden?"

As a matter of fact, Johanna had thought it was Gautier.

"You haven't kissed me," she pointed out. "All you did was make me spill a bucket of water. Even our serfs can be that clumsy."

"Oh, I wouldn't call you clumsy," said Rochambeau, infuriatingly pretending to misunderstand her insult. "And if you're complaining about my tardiness in kissing you . . ."

"No!" The heat of his hands, the lithe strength in the body so close to her own, filled Johanna with a primitive fear. She backed away, and he made no attempt to hold her. "I . . . wouldn't want you to get your pretty clothes wet."

Today he was sleek and smooth in tunic and chausses of silky black stuff. The neckline of his tunic was embroidered an inch deep in gold and set with blue stones. The colors matched the sapphires and gold chasing on his swordbelt, the blue of his eyes, and the summer's gold of his hair. Johanna felt keenly the contrast with her own state—hot, sweaty, and once again wearing nothing but a water-soaked tunic.

"I don't mind," said Rochambeau. "And you must learn not to be afraid of me."

"I'm not afraid of anything." And to prove it, she stood quite still when he reached for her again, planning to be cool and disdainful of his hot and heavy kisses. She felt the last week's dual flirtation with Piers and Gautier had taught her a little something about these games between men and women. Their kisses hardly excited her at all, and she had all but convinced herself that she would have felt as calm about Rochambeau, had he not been the first man ever to use her so.

In the hard, warm grasp of his arms, Johanna discovered just how wrong she'd been. His mouth on hers was fire and honey and all the spices of the Orient, a heat more potent than that of the sun that had burned off the morning clouds overhead. She grasped his arms, feeling the hard swelling of muscles that spoke of years at the tiltyard and at swordplay. She felt her body molding to his as simply and naturally as the wet tunic clung to her own form.

Dazzled by a glory and sweetness beyond her comprehension, she forgot all her anger and her resolves against this impossibly arrogant man. Had he bought her? Good! Then she was his. She ran her palms down the muscular length of his back and let her head fall back over his arm so that he could kiss her throat right down to the vee of white flesh exposed in the neck slit of her tunic. His lips strayed over the soft curves displayed when her tunic fell open, and she felt herself turning to water, to sunshine, to music . . . to everything free and joyful and shimmering with life.

Then his hands were hard about her waist again, forcing her away from him, forcing her to stand up. "Gently, sweet lady!" There was a ragged edge of laughter, and maybe something else, troubling his voice. "Your father would think ill of me if I shamed you before the wedding day."

Shame. It had been glory to her. Johanna's head felt thick and stupid, and her lips stung from his kisses.

"Don't be angry," he said in sweet, coaxing tones. "I'd no idea you were so . . . responsive." Again that unvoiced laughter, hardly more than a turbulent breath, but enough to make Johanna sure he was laughing at her.

So responsive, he had said, and laughed. What did he really mean? So cheap? So easy? Now he had one hand raised before him, as if fearing that she'd throw herself on him and beg for him to love her, like some sluttish serf girl.

The bucket with which Johanna had been watering the garden lay where she'd dropped it, propped at an angle against a thick bush of lavender, with a little water puddled in the bottom. Without consciously thinking of what she was going to do, Johanna grabbed the rope handle and swung the bucket around her head. The water splashed out over Rochambeau's face. He jumped back with hands up, and she shoved the bucket into his midsection just as his booted feet came down on a muddy furrow. His fall crushed a row of herbs and landed him smack in the middle of the wettest spot in the garden.

"What a pity," said Johanna. "You've spoiled your lovely suit, after all."

Head high, she stalked out of the herb garden without deigning to look behind her.

News of Rochambeau's arrival had reached the manor before her. Gwynne was all in a flutter between searching for Johanna and trying to make arrangements for a much more sumptuous dinner than was customarily served during harvest time. "Oh, why couldn't the man send word he was coming?" she wailed, and in the next breath, "Look at you, child! A great girl of sixteen, with no more sense than to play in the mud like your little sisters! What a mercy Rochambeau didn't see you like this!"

Fortunately, she was too agitated to ask Johanna exactly where she had been or whether she'd seen her future husband yet. Johanna bowed her head with unaccustomed meekness and suffered the attentions of Gwynne and her tiring-woman without complaining—behavior which made Gwynne wonder, in the midst of her other distractions, whether her daughter was ill or suffering from sunstroke.

It was something very like sunstroke. No matter how she tried to control her errant thoughts, Johanna was drawn back to the memory of Rochambeau. Not as she'd last seen him, sprawling in the mud, but as he'd first appeared to her in the garden, his gold head blazing in the sun, his lips setting fire to hers. Damn the man! So arrogant, so sure of himself!

Johanna glanced in the polished steel mirror held up for her inspection, and a smile curved her red lips. She was beautiful. Somehow the casual way Rochambeau used her, in such contrast to Piers's and Gautier's worship, always made her doubt the fact. The mirror reassured her, as did the sight of the two squires hovering behind Hugh at the table in the great hall. Their parted lips and stunned gazes told her she was as lovely as ever. Rochambeau should see, she vowed, that some people both appreciated her and knew how to treat a lady!

She had ample time to encourage the boys, as Rochambeau did not appear in the hall until halfway through dinner. "He sent his squire to say he'd be a bit delayed," Sir Hugh told the ladies. "Said we should go on without him. Sensible man.

No point in letting good food get cold." And without further delay he plunged both hands into a plate of roasted ortolans, crunching the small birds whole and chewing and swallowing with noisy appreciation.

Gwynne's lips thinned to a narrow, disapproving line, but she said nothing. What would have been unconscionable rudeness for a man of their own rank was acceptable for the baron to whom they did homage for their lands. As for Sir Hugh's eating habits, she had long since abandoned hope of reforming her husband. It would be enough if the girls did not grow up absolute savages. Johanna's marriage, with the hope of fostering Gillie and Francoise in noble households, offered Gwynne the best hope.

Johanna was more pleased than annoyed by Rochambeau's lateness. She guessed correctly that he had lingered to make hasty repairs to his person, and she hoped that he would appear somewhat bedraggled and a shade less proud when he finally arrived. She put the interval to good use, beckoning Piers to fill her cup and Gautier to carve her meat, while bestowing sweet glances on both squires until they were glaring daggers at each other behind her back.

Rochambeau's appearance in the doorway was like a clap of thunder in the midst of a peaceful summer day. It took all Johanna's willpower to keep from staring as he stalked down the length of the table to his place at her side. She smiled sweetly at Piers and thanked Gautier for his service. She pretended surprise when Rochambeau seated himself beside her and felt real surprise as she took in his immaculate appearance. The suit of black and gold had been changed for a magnificent tunic, cut short for riding, of dark green cloth with a border worked in emerald silk.

Damn the man! she thought again while murmuring the appropriate responses to his greeting. He must be vain as a peacock. Did he always ride with a complete change of clothing in his saddlebags?

"Your lady mother doubtless thinks I owe her an apology for my lateness."

"Perhaps you do." Johanna dipped her spoon into a dish of herbs and fish and toyed with the contents. Somehow, with Rochambeau's eyes upon her, she was finding it difficult to recover her usual hearty appetite.

Rochambeau picked up the tall carved mazer that stood between them and saluted Johanna before raising it to his lips. At the first taste, he coughed and set the cup down again quickly, swearing under his breath.

"Is the vintage not to your taste? What a pity! We cannot all dine daily on fine imported wines, my lord," Johanna said with a sweet smile. She had no taste for wine herself and had directed Piers to fill the mazer with some thin sour stuff—results of her father's failed experiment in grape-growing—rather than with the good wine he had brought out in honor of the baron's visit.

Rochambeau eyed her sweet smile with gathering suspicion. "I believe somebody around here owes some apologies," he said, "and I intend to see that you make them!"

"And if I don't?" Johanna inquired.

Rochambeau lifted the mazer toward her. "Take your choice. Apologize or drink to my health with this delicious vintage which I suspect you ordered especially for me."

Johanna was spared a decision by the uproar that broke out near the head of the table.

"Fool! Dolt! Idiot!" her father shouted, pounding the board with his fist at each word. "Have you no more sense than to look where you're serving? You poured hot bread sauce into my lap while making moon eyes at my daughter!"

Piers stammered apologies while dabbing at Sir Hugh's lap with the linen napkin he carried over one arm.

"What business have you to be gazing at the lady, boy?" demanded Gautier. With one foot he hooked Piers around the ankle as he was getting up, jerking him off balance so that he measured his length in the rushes. The remains of the bread sauce went flying and struck Sir Hugh in the face.

"And you're as bad!" Sir Hugh's backhanded blow knocked Gautier sprawling just in time to save him from a worse fate. Piers sprang to his feet, drawing his belt knife, and slashed forward just where Gautier's face would have been if Sir Hugh hadn't knocked him down.

"What business have you to be interfering between me and my lady?" Piers panted. His arm slashed down in a wicked sweeping curve that came within inches of castrating Gautier.

"Yours! *My* lady Johanna!" Red-faced with fury, Gautier threw himself at Piers's knees and brought him down in the rushes for the second time. They rolled over and over, wrestling like half-trained puppies, but the flash of steel in Piers's hand and the straining muscles of Gautier's arm showed they were both in deadly earnest. Gwynne screamed, Sir Hugh kicked both squires impartially, and two men-at-arms ambled up from the far end of the long table to separate the boys.

"Now," Sir Hugh demanded when the combatants stood breathless and snarling at each other, each restrained by a brawny man-at-arms. "What's all this about?"

"The lady Johanna and I have an understanding." Piers pulled the scrap of blue ribbon out of his tunic.

"You lie! You stole that! She's *my* lady, and to prove it she gave *me* her favor!" Gautier produced his own trophy, the long black curl which he had bound with silk and carried next to his breast ever since Johanna gave it to him.

Johanna edged back from the table. Somehow she didn't feel that she would enjoy being in the hall for the next few minutes. Before she could quite get up, a steely hand clamped down on her shoulder. With her eyes she begged Rochambeau for mercy, but he shook his head and held her in place.

Sir Hugh began roaring in the same vein as before about fools, dolts, idiots, et cetera, while at the same time he tried to wipe lumps of bread sauce off his balding head and mop puddles of sauce out of the creases of his flowing tunic. When he started to discuss Johanna's behavior in terms more suited for a strumpet off the streets of London, Rochambeau stood up and cut across the flow of invective with a single quiet sentence.

"Your pardon, Sir Hugh, but I believe I also am concerned in this matter."

Johanna's father turned bulging eyes at the baron. "You don't want her now? Listen, my boy, you don't want to take these things so seriously. She's still pure, whatever childish games she may have been up to with these two hell-born brats. I'll stake my life on it."

"And I my honor," said Rochambeau.

Sir Hugh misunderstood him. "No, no, your honor's not in question. If you like, you can have a surgeon examine her. We'll get a signed testimony that she's still virgin. We can—"

"I would not dream of humiliating your daughter in such

a fashion.'' Rochambeau's hand ground into Johanna's shoulder. His face was pale, and his blue eyes were dark as summer storm clouds. For the first time, looking at his tightly controlled fury, Johanna felt real terror. She'd meant to show him that he wasn't as important and wonderful as he thought himself. She'd never meant matters to come to such a pass as this. Now he was going to throw her back to her father in disgrace. He'd never marry her now. But wasn't that what she wanted? To make him go away? No, not like this. She felt queerly desolate and empty inside.

"However," Rochambeau went on, "since you seem utterly incapable of controlling the girl, I feel it might be a mistake to postpone the wedding until March as we'd planned. We'll have the betrothal now, and I'll marry her next week. I promise you," he said with a grim smile, "there'll be no such scenes as this when she's my wife."

"I'll wager there won't," said Sir Hugh with a grin. "Beat the foolishness out of her, eh, my boy!" He chuckled and rubbed his hands together, smiling foolishly until a sudden unwelcome thought struck him. "Er . . . the fields you promised? And the remission of scutage?"

"Nothing need change. My cousin Aubrey, who acts as my seneschal of the estates, has already been instructed to draw up the necessary papers. I shall bring them with me next week when I marry her."

Johanna's momentary relief that Rochambeau didn't mean to reject her had turned to hard, cold anger by the end of this interchange. Nothing had changed, except that now, not only was she to be deprived of her winter in London, but she wasn't even to have the bride clothes and the wedding feast that were every girl's right. Instead, she was to be hustled off to some cold, damp castle where her husband would beat her into submission to his slightest whim. And who would defend her? He would have bought the right to her, as men buy an ox or a cow or a strip of grazing land.

That cold flame of anger carried her, still and proud and pale, through the hasty betrothal ceremony that followed. She wanted to scream out her denial, to slap Rochambeau's hand away from hers, but she knew better than to defy her father openly in his present mood. If she refused to go through with the betrothal, he would lock her up on bread and water until she agreed. If she pretended to go along with this charade, she would have a modicum of freedom in the few remaining days before the wedding. And if she used those few days well, the betrothal would be only an empty charade in truth, and Rochambeau could whistle for his promised bride.

Chapter Four

THE LAST RAYS of the setting sun illumined a deeply rutted
track which ran through a roughly cleared area of waist-high
underbrush, and was bordered by the dark walls of the forest.
Down this track limped a single figure in a coarse hooded
robe who, from time to time, glanced anxiously at a sky
whose sunset glow was almost gone. The flowing black hood
and gown, girdled with a single strand of rope, suggested
that the wayfarer was a member of some religious order; the
blisters rubbed raw by rope sandals suggested that she was
not accustomed to this mode of travel.

The land on either side of the road had been cleared for
two hundred feet, as ordained by the king's statutes; but the
clearing had evidently not been performed regularly, for the
wild grasses grew high enough to sway in the evening breeze,
and clumps of small trees and bushes sprouted up at random.
A ripple of movement ran from one such clump of trees
through the tall grasses as the wayfarer passed. She started
nervously, staring about in all directions, and only then remembered to cross herself.

"Benedicite, 'twas only a hare," Johanna murmured. She
looked nervously at the dark stretch ahead of her, where the
forest had been allowed to grow right up to the edge of the
road. Even at noon it would have been a dark, forbidding
place, redolent of secret lairs and men with secret lives. Now,
in the deepening shadows of twilight, every motion of the

leaves and grasses was transmuted in Johanna's imagination into a lurking bandit.

She had only traveled this way once before in her life, when the whole family had gone to London to stay with her aunt Jehane for a winter. Johanna had been a little maid of six then, but she remembered clearly how her father had commanded his men-at-arms to ride in close about the wagon carrying the womenfolk and how they had made their best speed through this dark section of uncleared forest.

The ringing of a bell spurred on her lagging footsteps. That would be the great bell of the convent of St. Sulpicia, where they'd stopped for the night on that long-ago journey. Now Johanna hoped to find refuge there in her disguise as a humble pilgrim from a distant religious house. And the ringing betokened that the holy sisters were about to shut their gates for the night. After that no latecomer would be offered entrance. Johanna crossed herself again and limped into the shadows of the forest, muttering imprecations on the careless seigneur who let his lands be so overgrown in defiance of the statutes and to the danger of those forced to travel across his territory. Her father had said something about the man who owned this forest, but she couldn't remember what it was.

"Probably Rochambeau," she muttered. "Why should *he* care what happens to hapless wayfarers? He's rich; he can travel everywhere with twenty knights to guard him. He probably doesn't want to spoil his hunting by cutting back the bounds of the forest. It's just the sort of careless, arrogant way he'd behave."

Cursing Rochambeau distracted Johanna from her fears and helped her to remember why this flight from her father's house had been a good idea, something that had been harder and harder to remember as the weary road stretched on and her blistered foot pained her. At least Rochambeau, when he returned to claim his bride, would discover that she was not so easily bought and sold as he thought!

Johanna had pretended meek acquiescence to her father's wishes until the sleepy hours after dinner on the day following her betrothal. Rochambeau had left that morning, saying there were things to make ready at his nearby manor if he were to receive a bride there within the week. Johanna watched him go with a smile, and her parents thought she was smiling at the thought of being married to such a rich, handsome young baron. Seemingly it never occurred to either of them that nobody had consulted her about her feelings.

Once Rochambeau was safely gone and her father was dozing in his high seat after dinner, Johanna had asked her mother for permission to retire to the sleeping chamber she shared with Gillie and Francoise. She wanted to go through her clothes and see what she could do about making them fit for the wedding, she said. Gwynne was predictably charmed by this evidence of domesticity in her wayward daughter and made no objection. While her mother was in a good mood, Johanna added a further request: might she be excused from supper that night? She wished to remain in her chamber, to pray and meditate on the duties of a wife which were so soon to fall upon her.

Less than an hour later, Johanna was disguised as a pilgrim nun in a coarse black robe, a hastily sewn hood and a rope girdle. Johanna then slipped away from Pomeray and turned her face toward London. She had no idea how far away London might be or how long it would take her to get there, but she felt sure that she could get far enough to evade pursuit in the day and night that would pass before she was missed. With new rope sandals on her feet, a staff in her hand, a knife concealed under her girdle, and a loaf of coarse brown bread from the harvest baking knotted in her sleeve, Johanna felt equal to any challenge. She struck out gaily down the hard-baked dirt track, only reminding herself at the last minute not to whistle the dance tune that was running through her head.

Now, feet blistered and sunset falling before she'd reached shelter, Johanna felt somewhat less confident. The tall trees and dense undergrowth of the forest crowded in menacingly on either side of the road, and the last beams of sunlight made the shadows seem to move in curious ways. She pursed her lips and tried to whistle, but the merry tune died away as if choked by the thick darkness around her.

Never mind, Johanna told herself. Soon enough it would be Rochambeau who was whistling—whistling for a vanished bride! She tried to raise her spirits by envisioning how it would be when she stayed in Aunt Jehane's house, finally in a setting where her beauty could be appreciated as her father had always promised. By the time Rochambeau tracked her down, she would have been in London long enough to acquire a whole train of suitors—real knights, not boys like Piers and Gautier. She would have some fun, and Rochambeau would have to apologize for his high-handed ways and court her properly before he won her.

Somehow, she never doubted that he would come after her.

A rustling in the underbrush to her left startled her. She jumped, composed herself hastily, and moved casually to the other side of the road. No doubt it was just some small beast settling in for the night. She'd feel a proper fool if she ran and screamed at every little noise, wouldn't she?

The rustling was repeated to her right, and this time Johanna heard an unmistakable low chuckle. Her veins chilled as if icy winter sleet were falling down her back. Forgetting the blisters that had forced her to slow her pace, she strode out at a good speed, grasping her stick firmly and looking neither to left nor to right. Her mind whirled with alternatives while she marched on, pretending not to notice the stealthy movements of the men keeping pace with her on either side of the road. How many were there? Two on her left, one on her right. She might be able to hit one with her stick, but the other two would have her down before she could strike again. If she took off her sandals and hitched up her robe, she might be able to outrun them, but what if they pounced on her when she was bending to untie the sandals? And how far was it to the convent?

"Blessed Virgin, Mother of God, *ora pro nobis.*" Johanna's lips moved silently beneath the shelter of her hood. "Holy Saint Agnes, *ora pro nobis.*" She fumbled at her girdle for the rosary she'd tucked there at the last minute as the finishing touch to her disguise. The large beads of carved wood, set in silver and separated by tiny silver beads, had been an extravagant Christmas present from her parents last year. Johanna was grateful for their size and flashiness now. Holding the rosary ostentatiously in front of her, she prayed aloud and clicked the beads through her fingers as she walked. Surely no man, even a skulking outlaw in the forest, would sink so low as to attack a holy nun on her way back to her convent?

Ahead of her, the road curved slightly. Johanna prayed that

she would see the convent bell tower rising above the trees. Instead, she heard the thump of hooves and the jingle of bridle bells, and a mounted man came onto the road from a narrow path that wound back in among the bushes. Johanna caught her breath, first in fear, then relief. This was no bandit, but a gentleman. The red glow of the setting sun behind her danced off his polished mail and embroidered silk and cast long jagged shadows across a deeply scarred face, turning his smile of greeting into a demon's grimace. But he was a knight, gentle born, and sworn to protect all women. Johanna forced herself to smile and step up to his side.

"Good day, sir. Might I beg of your courtesy to give me a ride as far as my convent?"

"What, you and all your friends?" The knight sounded amused, and he was looking past Johanna at something behind her on the road. She glanced back and saw that her pursuers had come out of the bushes. There were not three but four of them, evil-looking men in dark clothes with surcoats of stiff boiled leather. One held a knife; the others, bare-handed, moved in a half-circle about her with arms spread wide, as though taunting her into a children's game. The knight's horse stood across the road, blocking the narrow track before her.

"No friends of mine," Johanna said, lifting her arms imploringly toward the strange knight. "Nor of yours, sir! Will you not aid me?" She could not believe that he would just sit there, hands loosely holding the reins of his horse, while these men attacked them both.

"They seem to want to be friendly," he observed.

Rough hands closed on Johanna's arms from behind, yanking her backward. Her stick went flying, and she was hauled against a broad, hard chest. "Pretty little nun," grunted the man who held her. "Want some fun, little sister?"

"She must," said one of his friends. "Nuns ain't supposed to be out of their convents after dark, and alone. You sneak out for a little fun and games?" He pushed back the dark hood that half covered her face and examined her closely, exhaling a long, stinking sigh of contentment. "Ah, you're too pretty to be locked up in a convent, little holy woman. We'll show you a better time than that." He ran his hands over her coarse robe, feeling her breasts and thighs like a horse coper examining merchandise.

"Sir! Won't you help?" Johanna cried in anguish to the strange knight, who still sat his horse as if he had no interest in the scene one way or another.

"Why? They seem to be doing quite well on their own. Redbeard! Give me that bauble." He pointed at the rosary of silver and dark polished wood, glittering in the road where Johanna had dropped it.

"A pretty toy," the knight mused, running his fingers over the beads. "A rich bauble indeed. Why would a holy nun, so vowed to poverty that her habit is of the coarsest woolen, carry a rosary fine enough for a court lady? And what is she doing out of her convent at night?"

Dismounting lightly, he pushed the man who'd been fondling Johanna out of his way. He seized the neck of her black woolen robe and tore it into two halves, neck to waist, with only a slight flexing of his powerful wrists. Underneath, Johanna was wearing her best tunic, the one of scarlet cloth with a narrow band of gold and silk embroidery.

"Well, well," the knight mused softly. "Well, well, *well*. You've caught us a nice little prize this time, lads. Not so good as a rich merchant, but well worth the time and effort. No, you can't play with it now. We'll take it back to Trichard and see what sort of tune it sings there. Not such a holy one, I'll be bound!"

Trichard. Now, sick with fear, Johanna remembered what it was her father had said about this stretch of forest. It was owned by a robber knight whose castle, Trichard, was concealed behind the trees. He lived by preying on unwary passersby, preferring the weak and helpless travelers who couldn't fight back. Rich merchants could pass unmolested if they had the sense to hire guards; the Lespervier family with their escort of armed men were safe enough. But pilgrims were murdered for the silver settings of their palmers' shells, and peasants had their feet burned for the coins that might be concealed in the recesses of their rags.

"My father will pay well to have me back. You had better not harm me." Johanna gave his name and that of his manor.

"Lespervier?" The knight shook his head. "Ah, Pomeray's a poor manor, and I hear all your daddy's spare cash goes—other places.'' He chuckled, and Johanna stared at him blankly, not understanding what he could mean. "No, pretty, I think we'll keep you for a while. He'll pay later.''

"I am betrothed to Baron Rochambeau!'' In desperation, Johanna played her last card. "He can pay whatever you want.''

"My, my,'' the master of Trichard mocked her, "how your social status keeps rising. From simple nun to knight's daughter to baron's lady. Who knows? Perhaps by the time we get you back to Trichard, you'll have become a close friend of the king's. Truss her up and put her over my horse, Fumble-fingers.''

The man who held Johanna's arms behind her back reached one hand to pull at her rope girdle, fumbling around her waist to untie the knot in front. She twisted and broke loose, swinging the weighted sleeve of her habit around in a full circle. The loaf of coarse brown bread she'd tied there struck him in the face with a sickening crunching sound. Fumble-fingers yelped and started back, both hands clapped over the fountain of blood that sprayed from his nose, and Johanna threw herself at the underbrush. Someone was close behind her, hot fingers closing over the rope sandals. She screamed as the rough grip jerked the ropes over her blisters, screamed again in helpless fury as she was slowly dragged backward into the road. No answer came, only the pounding of a horse's hooves and the jingle of mail—another of the nameless knight's confederates coming to share in the spoils.

"A Warhawk! A Warhawk!''

The full-throated roar that split the air was incredibly, impossibly familiar. The galloping horse went past Johanna and her captor at full speed, and she heard a dual scream as if a man and a horse had perished at once. There was a dull sound like an ax cutting green wood, and the hands on her legs fell away limply. Johanna crouched in the dust at the edge of the road, gathering the torn rags of her habit about her and staring up at Nicolas de Rochambeau.

An ash lance had pierced right through the master of Trichard as he tried to mount his horse. The tip of the lance had plunged on into the horse's belly, and it was still struggling. The man who'd flung himself on Johanna was lying face down in the road, surrounded by a red puddle. One of his hands was no longer attached to his body. The other three men had disappeared.

Rochambeau looked down at Johanna, one eyebrow slightly raised, smiling in a way that frightened her more than the threats of the robber knight. "Did you wish to escape me so much that you planned to take religious vows?"

"I b-begin to think even that wouldn't work." Johanna rose to her feet, resolutely averting her eyes from the dead men in the road.

"It wouldn't," Rochambeau said briefly. "But I should much regret the necessity of taking you from the convent. Isn't it fortunate that I found you earlier?"

"Fortunate indeed." Johanna swallowed carefully. She was in severe danger of disgracing herself in front of Rochambeau. If she looked down at the bloodstained road, it would certainly happen. "My lord, I have much to thank you for."

"You have *nothing* to thank me for." Rochambeau cut off her attempted speech of gratitude with a quick downward chopping motion of his hand. "What I have, I keep. That includes you. You were a fool to think otherwise. Are you going to be sick?"

"I don't think so." She drew a deep breath, then another, and willed the words to be true.

"Of course you're not." A rare spark of approval flashed deep within Rochambeau's sapphire eyes. "I knew when I saw you that you were fit to be lady of Rochambeau. You don't faint either, do you? Good girl. We'll be off as soon as I've finished this little business."

He dismounted, sword in hand, and Johanna shrank back involuntarily. Now he would beat her for running away. She couldn't blame him; her father would have half killed her, and he'd come after her in her father's place. She was startled when he walked past her, toward the bloody mess his lance had made of the robber knight and his horse.

"A pity about the horse," he said. "It was a good beast. Don't look!"

The sharp words extorted unthinking obedience. Johanna turned her head away. A moment later the horse stopped struggling and there was a strong smell of fresh blood in the air. Rochambeau mounted again and reached down one hand to help her up behind him. "Hold on to my waist. And see what you can do about pulling up those stupid skirts so you can ride astride. You're going to be damned sore by the time we get to my manor, but it's no more than you deserve."

Clinging to his waist, dizzy and sick with the events of the evening, Johanna could not argue with his verdict. He had already set off down the road, returning the way she had come, when she began to understand what he had said.

"*Your* manor?"

Rochambeau half turned his head to regard her with amusement. "Do you really want to go home? I wouldn't advise it. Your father's even angrier with you than I am."

"My father's not so frightening," said Johanna truthfully. "I can usually get around him."

Rochambeau's broad back quivered; it took a moment for her to realize he was trying to suppress a laugh. "Oh, you'll usually be able to get around me too. I can see it coming."

"How?"

He clicked his tongue and the horse stopped. Looping the reins over the pommel, he took her chin between two fingers and pressed a brief kiss on her lips. "I'll teach you how. Later," he added. "After we're married."

Johanna felt her spirits rising. Apparently he wasn't going to beat her.

By the time they reached Rochambeau's manor of Rhuthun, several hours after sunset, Johanna was tired and stiff and sore, just as Rochambeau had predicted. The light of torches carried by the squires who ran out to greet them showed a simple stone-built manor house, fortified with stout walls and high crenellated parapets, but nothing to compare with the keep at Pomeray. And there were chickens in the courtyard, pecking and scratching around the horse's hooves.

Rochambeau looked down at her face with a glimmer of amusement. "Disappointed? I must confess, it's not my best manor. After the wedding I'll take you to Malvern, where I grew up. It's not the biggest of my estates, but it's a pretty little castle, and I built on a new hall and tower some years ago. You'll like Malvern."

Johanna wanted to dispute his casual assumption that there was to be a wedding, but she was too tired to fight any longer. She'd never ridden for so long at a stretch, and after the first couple of hours there had been no such thing as a comfortable position. Sitting pillion behind him, both legs decorously dangling over one side of the horse, twisted her spine unmercifully. When she changed her position to ride astride as he'd suggested, she had to hike her long narrow tunic skirts up to her hips, and her bare legs were rubbed sore.

When she dismounted, her legs were so numb that they folded under her and she crumpled toward the ground. Rochambeau caught her and lifted her in his arms, holding her against his broad chest as easily as her little sisters cradled their dolls. He paused a moment in the circle of light cast by two guttering torches to give brisk instructions to the squires. One was to rub his horse down well and feed him; the other was to find someone named Aubrey and set off in an hour for Pomeray.

Pomeray! Johanna stiffened in his arms. "You're going to send me back." Which was, of course, what she wanted; but she didn't relish the thought of the beating her father would give her for this escapade. Oh, she'd talk him around in the end, but there would be some uncomfortable hours first. It would be much better if Rochambeau let her stay there at Rhuthun for the night; perhaps she could escape and make for London again. If she could stay awake . . . A yawn caught her unaware, and her head dropped down against his shoulder. He was an overbearing brute, but that warm solid shoulder made a very comfortable pillow.

"Send you back? No such luck," Rochambeau growled. "I'm going to marry you. Tomorrow," he added in an undertone, carrying her toward the keep while the squires went about their errands. "As soon as your father can get here. I'm tired of your games."

"If you didn't marry me," Johanna pointed out, "you wouldn't have to put up with my tiresome games." A second jaw-cracking yawn caught her at the end of the sentence and all but smothered the last word. Her head fell back against Rochambeau's shoulder as he climbed the steps leading up from the hall to the private chambers on the floor above.

"Lady, I won't put up with them in any case." Rochambeau laid her down on a massive tester bed whose smooth red covers were richly trimmed with marten fur. He turned away slightly to loosen his girdle, and she thought she understood.

"You can't . . . force me . . . to sleep with you." Ridiculous. He could do anything he wanted, and the humiliating part was that he could probably make her like it. But could he make her stay awake long enough to participate? Johanna's giggle turned into a yawn, her eyes squeezed shut of their own accord, and her head sank into the heavenly softness of a pillow stuffed with goose down.

"Don't worry, I only seduce girls who are wide enough awake to enjoy the experience. Tonight I have serious doubts that you'd qualify. I can wait till tomorrow, when we're married. But you'll have to sleep in here tonight, all the same. What else can I do?" With his back modestly turned so as not to offend his bride-to-be more than necessary, Rochambeau stripped off his stained clothes and dropped them in an untidy heap on the floor. His body-squire could pick them up in the morning; no point in embarrassing Johanna by having Marc in there now. It wouldn't kill him to wait on himself for once.

Crossing to the basin of cold water that stood in a wall niche, Rochambeau plunged his head into the water, shook his wet hair vigorously, snorted, and splashed more water over his chest and shoulders. "You see," he explained while toweling his head dry again, "I don't quite believe this act of total exhaustion you're putting on. I have a feeling that the minute I close my eyes, you're going to be up and trying to climb out the window. And I really don't have the energy to chase you halfway to London again tonight, not to speak of killing off a few scum. So what am I going to do? You're going to be my lady. It wouldn't be fitting to your degree to chain you to the wall. This damned one-plough manor doesn't even have a room with a proper barred door for keeping debtors. And I certainly can't set anybody else to watch you. It's not right, and besides I'd never live it down. So I'll have to watch you myself, and the easiest way to do that is to keep you right beside me in the bed where I'll sense your every movement. And believe me, dear lady, I will know! I'm a very light sleeper, and . . ."

A gentle snore interrupted his monologue. Turning to look at the bed, Rochambeau caught his breath at the sight of Johanna's delicate white features outlined by the tumbled mass of her dark hair. The glossy black curls spread out like a cloak over the red-dyed coverlet, framing her face in black satin and forming a shining, scented waterfall that a man could drown in. His hands trembled with the desire to bury themselves in her dark hair and press his body against her softness, to wake her with hot, demanding kisses and wrest from her the acknowledgment of the passion that they both felt. Although he'd just dashed cold water over his body, he felt the heat of his skin burning off the last remaining droplets.

"More likely the heat of your overactive imagination, you fool," Rochambeau admonished himself in an undertone. "She's only a child, and she's had a rougher day than you have. Do you want to scare her half to death? Tomorrow night will be soon enough, after she's got used to the idea of being married."

The sound of his voice penetrated Johanna's dreams. She murmured something and stirred slightly in her sleep, throwing one arm up above her head. The movement stretched the thin fabric of her tunic so that the cloth molded itself to the rounded shapes of her high, firm breasts. Her red lips were slightly open, moist and glistening in the light of the candles that flickered from high on the wall.

Rochambeau tied an extra knot in the drawstring of his linen drawers, as a guard against temptation. He blew out the candles and lay down on the far side of the bed, arms crossed behind his head, staring up at the darkness and trying not to think about the tempting young body beside him. A light sleeper, had he said? He snorted in amusement. It would be a miracle if he got any sleep at all that night.

Chapter Five

JOHANNA WOKE IN the half-light before dawn. Somewhere
in the distance a bell was ringing for lauds; there must be a
religious house nearby. Closer at hand, the raucous cries of
a rooster in the courtyard and the scuffle of servants already
going about their duties told her that the new day was about
to begin.

She felt a moment of bemusement. The morning sounds
were familiar yet subtly wrong. Why didn't she hear her little
sisters giggling in the next bed? Why did she have such a
heavenly comfortable feeling, as if she were floating on clouds
instead of sleeping on the straw pallet that was all her father
allowed his daughters? And what was this weight across her
chest that pinned her down?

Her eyelids slowly fluttered open. The first thing she saw
was a man's face pressed against her shoulder, firm tanned
features smoothed out in sleep, harsh lips softened by a pleasant dream.

Rochambeau!

The soft clouds surrounding her were only a billowing
feather mattress. She was sleeping in the exact center of the
bed, all but trapped by the weight of her own body sinking
into the cloud of down-stuffed coverlet, and Rochambeau's
arm above her completed the trap. He was insecurely sprawled
between her body and the edge of the bed, one leg flung over

her thighs, his arm resting just under her breasts. And he was still sound asleep.

Johanna pushed unavailingly against the heavy arm he had flung across her body. He stirred, mumbled something, and curved his arm about her, gathering her firmly into a warm and sleepy embrace. His unshaven chin, sprinkled with golden bristles, brushed against her neck. Johanna shivered at the light intimate touch. Had they been sleeping like this all night? Or, worse, had he—?

She searched her memories but could recall nothing except the arrival in the torchlit courtyard and her own embarrassing collapse when her numbed legs refused to hold her up. Then Rochambeau had scooped her into his arms and . . . and . . .

"And *nothing*," Johanna told herself firmly. Not that she would have put it past that brute to take advantage of her helplessness, but somehow she felt sure the experience would have been quite memorable. Hateful, perhaps, but memorable. Not the sort of thing a girl could doze through, no matter how exhausted she was.

And definitely the sort of thing a girl *could* expect if she woke up in the bed of this oversexed yellow-haired beast. She had to get away before he woke up! Oh, why hadn't she kept herself awake last night? He was sleeping so soundly, it would have been child's play to creep away in the middle of the night. Now, with the manor servants already stirring, it would be all but impossible to make her escape.

Time enough to think of that later. For now, if she didn't get out of Rochambeau's bed, there wouldn't be any question of getting any farther away. Already he thought he owned her; possessing her body would be, in his mind, the final seal. Johanna pushed again at Rochambeau's encircling arm, and only woke him enough to make the fingers of one hand open.

His hand moved over her chest with a vague searching motion and closed over her breast. Johanna felt a fiery heat there, as though his palm had scorched right through the fabric, and a throbbing ache that could only be assuaged by a firmer touch. As if receptive to her feelings even in his sleep, Rochambeau began fondling her, opening and closing his fingers and gently rubbing across the firm curving underside of her breast.

The heat was spreading, gathering between her thighs, robbing Johanna of strength and will. She had to get away! But her treacherous body only curled closer into the curve of Rochambeau's, as if ignorant of her commands. With a last, despairing effort of will, she rolled over, placed both hands against his chest, and shoved with all her might. He rolled over the edge of the bed, caught himself on his hands, and sprang upright with the agility of a tumbler.

"What did you do that for?" he asked reproachfully. His blue eyes were wide open, and he showed no sign of the confusion one might expect in a man so rudely awakened from deep slumber.

"You rat! You were awake all the time!" Johanna scrambled to the other side of the bed and stood with hands clenched, glaring at him.

"So were you," Rochambeau pointed out reasonably, "and I didn't notice you objecting that much."

"Well, I—I do object. You can't use me like one of your light women!"

"I've no intention of doing so. I'm going to use you as my wife. And all the signs indicate you'll like it very much. Why don't you relax a little bit and let me demonstrate what you've got to look forward to?"

"I already know more than I want of what I'd have to look forward to in your bed." And looking at his naked chest, sprinkled with curling golden hairs that arrowed down to the tightly knotted drawstring of his linen underdrawers, was giving her more of those strange unsettling feelings. It was too much. He was too powerful for her. If once she gave in to him, she'd be nothing but his toy in truth, just as he thought she was now. Johanna could see it coming, inevitable and sweet and destructive as the rush of waters in the Severn Bore. She could drown in the feelings he aroused, lose herself forever, become utterly dependent on his sensual enchantment—the slave of a man who thought less than nothing of her, who treated her like a serf girl placed on this earth for his amusement. Johanna folded her arms and turned her back, pretending indifference. "And it's not going to happen. I wouldn't marry you if you were the king!"

"King Henry's not available. Besides, he's too old for you. You'll have to settle for me."

"Maybe you're too old for me too," Johanna fenced wildly.

Rochambeau's deep chuckle told her that the shaft had failed to strike home. "And maybe I'm not. Why don't you wait for our wedding night to pass judgment? I'm not thirty yet, and I've never had any complaints from my bed partners."

"There won't be any wedding night! There won't be any wedding! I'm not marrying you!" Her refusals battered in vain against Rochambeau's imperturbable certainty. Johanna felt like a child, kicking and screaming and refusing to be washed and dressed. But there was one weapon still at her command. The marriage vows would have to be made in public, at the church porch. He couldn't force her to say the words, and no priest would declare the marriage valid without her consent.

Rochambeau sighed and sat down on the edge of the bed to lace his shoes. "Johanna, has it occurred to you that you've never told me exactly why you object so much to this marriage? At one time," he said almost plaintively, "I thought you liked me." He smiled at her, lifted her hand, and turned it over to kiss her palm; despite herself, Johanna felt a shiver of desire at the touch of his lips. "I still think you do," he added.

Johanna sighed in her turn. "You wouldn't understand." She wasn't sure she understood herself. It was some compound of panic at the feelings Rochambeau aroused in her and anger at the light way he treated her. It was the deep knowledge that once she gave in to him she would never belong to herself again. Did she want to marry him, to lie naked with him in this great soft bed, to feel his skin burning warm against hers, to mold her softness to his body?

Yes. She wanted all that so much she could hardly breathe when she thought of it. But it had to be on her terms, not his. If she let him pluck her out of Pomeray like a ripe apple off a tree, whisk her off to be wedded and bedded without bothering to ask how she felt about it, what would become of her after she gave in to his impetuous wooing? He'd be up from the marriage bed to buckle on armor and spurs and set off for some more interesting prey, while she'd be left at home to pine away for the crumbs of his attention. Only if he had to court her, woo her, and win her against competition would he value the prize he'd won.

"I might understand better than you think. Want to try explaining it to me?"

Johanna shook her head until the crisp black curls on her shoulders flew out around her face in a crackling halo. What good were words to a man like Rochambeau? Deeds were all he was capable of understanding. Somehow she had to find a way of putting off this marriage until he understood that she had no intention of becoming a meek, obedient chattel like her mother.

She heard him rise from the bed, heard his footsteps coming around toward her. "In that case," he said in a voice soft with menace, "you'd better . . ."

"I won't do anything you tell me to!" Johanna whirled and spat at him, her hands opening like claws to score his face if he came a step closer.

"You'd better comb your hair and wash your face. I sent for your parents last night. They'll be here before dinner. After Mass, we can spend the morning walking around the manor lands. And I promise you this much, Johanna." His face was grave and tender, the blue eyes alight with a gentle promise that won her heart more surely than all his cocksure courtship had done. "If you can find words to tell me why you object to this marriage, and if I can understand your objections, I'll not force you to it. If you're just indulging in a tantrum, I can deal with that, but I've no wish for a truly unwilling bride."

"You want me to do *what?*"

Hugh Lespervier, standing in the somewhat dilapidated hall of his overlord's manor of Rhuthun, raised one hand as if sorely tempted to knock his defiant daughter spinning into the ashes of the central fire. Johanna planted both fists on her hips and glared up at him. Everything had been so simple until her father started roaring like a baited bear. What had she done to deserve this explosion of temper? Rochambeau had said quite clearly that he didn't want an unwilling bride, hadn't he? Very well. She was unwilling. She wanted to go to London for the winter. She wanted a year of freedom. Then, she'd told her father, perhaps she would consider wedding the baron.

Now her father was turning purple and going into his usual

rant about disobedient spoiled brats, while Gwynne held on to his arm and prevented him from knocking his daughter down. Most humiliating of all to Johanna was her awareness of Rochambeau's seneschal, Aubrey, listening from the other side of the hall. At least Rochambeau himself had tactfully departed "on estate business," leaving Johanna and her parents to discuss the marriage among themselves. It would have been the last straw to have had him witness her father's incoherent bellowings. Aubrey was bad enough. Sent to Pomeray last night to reassure her parents of Johanna's safety and to bid them to an immediate wedding, he'd brought them back with him that morning and had hung around ever since as if the family affairs were his business too.

In a sense, she supposed this was true. Aubrey was like a younger, smoother, softer version of Rochambeau; it had come as a shock to her to find that he was actually two years older. Somewhat less of a shock was Rochambeau's quiet explanation that Aubrey was actually his bastard half-brother, fruit of his father's liaison with a merchant's daughter just before his marriage. That much Johanna could have guessed by looking at the two men together when Aubrey came back that morning with her parents. Rochambeau was like a scarred, cracked mirror image of Aubrey, his skin roughened by wind and weather, his blue eyes hard and piercing where Aubrey's were gentle, his face and body scarred . . .

With great effort, Johanna wrested her mind from the image of Rochambeau's naked torso as she'd seen it that morning, the long white lines of old scars running diagonally across his chest and the striations of another wound striping one shoulder. Her fingertips had tingled with the desire to trace out those lines with which his enemies had marked his flesh, to feel if the scars were as hard and the surrounding muscular body as warm and taut as her eyes told her. Perhaps she would do that. Next year. After Rochambeau had learned he couldn't have her for a whistle, to run at his heels like a tamed hound.

"You listen when I'm talking to you, girl!" This time Gwynne's hands were not strong enough to restrain her husband. A ringing box on the ear knocked Johanna into one of the trestles that supported the long dining table. "Yesterday's escapade disgraced you beyond any hope of marriage with a decent man," Sir Hugh went on while Johanna dragged herself up again. "You ought to thank God fasting if the baron is still willing to have you. And by God, if you refuse this marriage, there'll be no London jaunt for you, my girl! I'll throw you into St. Sulpicia's and divide your dowry between Gillie and Francoise."

"You're not giving me any dowry," Johanna snapped back. "Remember? You sold me for some muddy fields and a remission of your knight's fees. Rochambeau wants to buy me—like a cow."

"At least cows give milk! That's more use than you've ever been!" Sir Hugh turned on his wife. "I'll be damned if I know how you managed to raise such a spoiled, worthless brat. Didn't you put anything into her head but pride in her own beauty?"

His face was rapidly attaining an alarming hue of royal purple. Gwynne thrust herself between Johanna and Sir Hugh, pleading incoherently with her husband to calm down. Her words had no visible effect; Aubrey was more fortunate.

"Pray do not excite yourself, Sir Hugh," he said, stepping up to join the little group. "I'm sure we're both aware of many excellent reasons why this marriage must proceed as planned."

To Johanna's astonishment, her father subsided faster than her last disastrous attempt at a risen pudding. Aubrey put one arm around Johanna's shoulders and the other around Gwynne's. Johanna felt her own anger cooling at his brotherly comforting.

"And there's no need to discuss these . . . private matters . . . in open hall. Indeed, I assure you the baron would prefer not to raise the matter again, nor will it be necessary if you just hand over Johanna as promised."

Johanna stiffened at the phrasing. Surely her father would see now how humiliating this treatment was, not just for her but for all of them. But he had shrunk in on himself at Aubrey's first words, and now he only nodded dully.

"Perhaps you'd care to take your daughter upstairs to the private chamber," Aubrey suggested to Gwynne, gently urging them both toward the stairs at the far end of the hall. "You can help her ready herself for the wedding in privacy, and perhaps you can explain the matter to her?" He smiled down at Gwynne, and she gave him a tearful, tremulous smile in return.

"Whew!" Johanna sank down on the high, soft bed in Rochambeau's chamber with a sense of relief that made absolutely no sense, considering how recently she had looked on that same chamber as a prison. "What was that all about? Oh, I suppose you're going to tell me it's none of my business—even though," she added bitterly, "it seems to me this marriage is more my business than anybody else's, for all no one has bothered to consult me about it. Never mind. I don't care what Father says about disgrace and a nunnery. I'm not marrying Rochambeau, and that's final!" Once Sir Hugh's roaring had calmed down, Johanna felt confident of being able to coax him into a good mood as she'd always done before.

"Not this year, anyway," she added thoughtfully as the memory of Nicolas de Rochambeau's broad shoulders and gold-furred chest revived those strange stirrings deep within her. God's body and bones, but that was a man! If only somehow, by trick or force or simply keeping him waiting, she could get the strength to meet him on equal terms, there was no man she'd rather have. But not this way, not to be handed over like a piece of property. He would absorb her, burn her up in a blaze of sensuality, and then put her back in a carved chest until the next time he was ready to play with her.

"And just what makes you think you'll have another chance? You silly girl, do you think it's every day that one of the first men of the realm marries the daughter of his least important vassal? Men like that don't come asking for favors, Johanna. They take what they want, and you can count yourself lucky that you're what he wants this season. If you don't take him now, by next year he'll have found another pretty face he likes better or an heiress whose lands march with his."

"And if I do marry him now and his fancy changes anyway?"

"You'll be a wedded wife, with dower rights and the keys of the estate. And you'll be the one to give him heirs." Gwynne spoke as if these things were the most that any woman could hope for in marriage.

"Is that all you had from my father?" Johanna asked.

Gwynne flushed and looked down, twisting the embroidered border on her veil. "Not at first," she said, almost inaudibly. "But no woman expects that to last. You're lucky, as I was. Your husband will begin by loving you. Many women of our rank don't even have that much."

"Lucky! No, thank you, Mother. I want more out of life than to have my husband hopping into my bed on a regular basis for the first two years, then turning to other amusements when the babies come."

Gwynne winced, and Johanna wished the cruel words unsaid. She hadn't needed to make it so clear what she thought of her parents' marriage. And worse, she feared that her careless speech had reminded her mother of the string of little graves in the churchyard, the graves that explained the long gap between Johanna and the twins and between the twins and the newborn heir of Pomeray. "Mother, I'm sorry. I didn't mean to make you think about . . ." For once at a loss for words, Johanna enveloped her slightly built mother in a tempestuous hug.

"It's all right," Gwynne reassured her. She wiped her eyes with the end of her veil. "I never forget them anyway. You'll understand when you have children. Oh, dear, to think that this time next year I may be a grandmother!"

"Not if I have anything to say about it." Johanna felt guilty for hurting her mother, but not nearly guilty enough to agree to the marriage. She folded her arms and stared at the wall.

"You don't." Gwynne's voice held a crisp note that was foreign to Johanna's experience. Shocked, she turned her head to see that Gwynne was standing over her, white hands twisting together until the fingers reddened under pressure. "I didn't want to tell you this. But there is no question, Johanna, of your refusing this marriage. When Aubrey came to bid us to Rhuthun, he brought an additional message from Rochambeau. The baron knows something about your father."

"What?"

"Did you never wonder why Pomeray doesn't suffer from Welsh raids, like the rest of the manors so near to the border?"

Johanna shook her head. "We're a poor manor. And your people are from Wales originally. Perhaps it's not worth Dafydd ap Hywel's while to raid us, or perhaps he doesn't attack his own kin?''

"My family's no kin to that freebooter," said Gwynne, "and he doesn't scruple to attack poor hamlets. Your father made an agreement with Dafydd—oh, years ago, before Gillie and Francoise were born. He pays him five marks yearly, and Dafydd's men leave us alone."

"Five marks!" It was a substantial portion of the manor's yearly income. "It can't be worth all that, surely."

"You don't remember what a raid is like."

No wonder her father always complained of being purse-pinched! Johanna's blood boiled. She would rather have fought it out with Dafydd yearly than meekly give him the third part of the manor's rents just to be left in peace.

"All right. We're even poorer than I thought. But why does that mean I have to marry Rochambeau?"

"Because in the wrong hands, told the wrong way, your father's dealings with Dafydd could be twisted to look like treason. Do you realize that for ten years he's been having secret meetings with Dafydd quarterly to pay the accounts? And for most of those ten years we've been at war with Wales. And, as you pointed out, I'm Welsh by origin, with relatives on both sides of the border. Suspicious circumstances, all of them. It wouldn't be hard to make out that your father was passing along more than money—information, perhaps, or arms. And no one would question a man like Rochambeau if he accused one of his own vassals. The best we could hope for would be to be turned out of the manor. At worst, it could be your father's life."

Gwynne frowned. "I only hope Aubrey doesn't make Hugh so angry that he cancels the marriage and snatches you back home in spite of everything. That young man has no tact. Rochambeau must have charged him with explaining the matter so that there'd be no direct contact between Hugh and himself, but somehow everything Aubrey says makes it seem as if Hugh has no choice but to give in, and you know how your father hates that. You'd better go downstairs and agree to the marriage right away, before Hugh loses his temper and storms out of here with us."

The words pounded down on Johanna like the roar of a summer hailstorm, bending the crops to the ground and creating devastation where moments before there had been a field of ripe grain. She crouched on the bed, putting her hands over her ears, but she couldn't shut out the knowledge that Gwynne's speech brought. All this morning, while Rochambeau strolled around the manor with her and made pretty speeches, he'd known that he would have her by the end of the day. The net was already limed, and the stupid bird was already inside; only let her flutter her wings, and she'd know herself a prisoner.

No wonder he could promise so easily that he'd not force her agreement; no wonder he was so sure that she'd say the vows with him. She had no choice, and he'd known it all along, even while he was glibly promising her that she could be free if she wished it.

And this was the man she'd feared to marry because he would be so easy to love and because she doubted her ability to win his love in return. This man who knew neither truth nor decency. She would be forever ashamed that he'd won half her heart already; she was lucky, she supposed, that her burgeoning love had been killed so quickly.

It seemed to her that years passed while she bent under the storm of her mother's words. When at last she raised her head again, she felt infinitely older than the passionate girl who'd been so afraid of the feelings Rochambeau had evoked in her. "All right, Mother," she said. "I understand. I will marry the baron." The words seemed to come from a place far outside her; she had retreated into a cold, remote core of herself. Nothing that Rochambeau could do would touch her now; he could buy her body, but she would never be fool enough to let herself love him. And so she was safe, and there was no reason to fight against the marriage.

"Well, you needn't look as if you were going to a pagan sacrifice!" Gwynne snapped, her relief spilling over almost instantly into ill humor. "Plenty of girls would be delighted to have such a chance in life. Stand up now, and let me try the new tunic on you. Elys and I were up most of the night stitching it."

Johanna submitted to her mother's ministrations passively, turning her head and raising her arms as required when Elys was called in to stitch the new-fashioned tight sleeves closed, letting the women attack her tangled hair with brisk yanks of their combs that brought tears to her eyes. Gwynne's own eyes threatened to brim over when they had finished preparing Johanna for her wedding.

"My little girl," she whispered, permitting herself one of her rare caresses. Usually she was careful not to let Johanna see how much she loved her; the girl was spoiled enough by her father. Now, belatedly, she wondered if Johanna could not have done with more gentle loving and less of her father's buffeting alternation between pride and anger. She was too proud, too prickly, too independent to submit meekly to the demands of marriage. A wife must always bow her will to her husband's, must learn to offer gentle meek words to his anger. That was ordained by Scripture, and, besides, it was the only practical way to get on with a man. Johanna was likely to have a hard time learning that lesson.

Johanna felt some faint surprise at the sight of her mother's tears. She started to tell her not to cry; they should carry themselves more proudly before this great baron who thought he could buy or bribe his way to everything he wanted. But some unexplained impulse curbed her tongue. Perhaps it was fitting that someone should cry at this mockery of a marriage, and Johanna was past being able to weep for herself.

Chapter Six

I T WAS AS unlike Johanna's childish dreams as any wedding could be. Rhuthun, even closer to the Welsh border than Pomeray, was a poor remote manor that had not been visited by the baron in years. There was no chapel and no resident priest. They said their vows in the porch of the village church, before a nearly illiterate priest who stumbled over the Latin of the Mass so badly that Johanna bit her tongue with wanting to correct him. Even without knowing Latin herself, she was so familiar with the lovely pattern of the words that every slip hurt her ears. She concentrated fiercely on the responses, trying to keep from thinking about the meaning of this Mass that changed her life forever.

There was no store of wine and spices suitable for a great baron's wedding feast, nor would the serf who cooked for the manor have known what to do with them. They dined off coarser fare than was served in her father's hall and drank ale brewed by the reeve's wife. There had been no time to summon neighbors to the feast, even had this remote corner of the Marches held seigneurs to equal Rochambeau's standing. Johanna's parents and sisters sat above the salt with the reeve and his wife, simple villagers who were uncomfortable with such a signal honor.

And the day was cloudy, threatening rain that would spoil the harvest. The reeve and Hugh Lespervier could think of little else. Presently, abandoning a halfhearted attempt to make such jokes as were customary at a wedding, they fell into a worried discussion of the crops at Rhuthun and at Pomeray. Rochambeau joined in the discussion, all but ignoring Johanna, and Gwynne had her hands full with soothing the tired and fretful little girls. If it hadn't been for Aubrey, Johanna would have sat in splendid isolation at the head of the long table, with nothing to do but pick at her supper and worry about the night to come.

She would be forever grateful to Aubrey for the lighthearted, charming conversation with which he beguiled her during that long dinner hour, demanding nothing of her but an occasional smile or murmured meaningless response. He had all Rochambeau's charm, this graceful older brother whose bastard birth condemned him always to be the servant of the younger; and in his case the charm was not contradicted by the warrior's hardness that always showed under Rochambeau's courtly mask. It was clear that he'd set himself the task of pleasing Johanna and distracting her from the unhappy circumstances of the rushed wedding, and even while the intent was obvious, she had to acknowledge that he succeeded very well. By the end of the meal she was even able to laugh at his jokes and to smile at him without strain. But the smiles still faded when she glanced to her left, at the man who would take her away to his great chamber that night.

And that night there would be no reprieve for her. He would demand the surrender that his kisses had already half forced from her. There would be no drawing back on the brink of those new, dangerous waters; like it or not, ready or not, she would be subjected to the full force of his sensuality. Johanna remembered the heat of his lips and hands on her, the sweet, dangerous desire that had overcome her in his arms. What would it be like when he no longer felt obliged to draw back after a certain point, to respect her innocence? Her heart beat faster at the thought, but she could not say whether fear or desire dominated the insistent pounding in her pulses.

Too soon, the supper was over, and Johanna's parents announced their intention of returning to Pomeray at once. Panic seized Johanna by the throat. She cast a pleading glance at her mother, and for once Gwynne rose to the occasion.

"I'll see her properly bedded first," she declared, ignoring Sir Hugh's grumblings about the clouds and the threatened rain and the chance of being caught by darkness before they were halfway home. "Since there are no waiting-women here to serve, it's only proper that I should see to the task."

It was the closest she'd come to a criticism of the arrangements at Rhuthun. Johanna was pleased to see Rochambeau slightly embarrassed. While he was repeating his explanations about the poverty of this manor and promising that Johanna should have all the servants and luxuries she could desire when they moved on to Malvern, she slipped away to the great chamber behind the hall. A few moments later, Gwynne and Elys joined her there.

It seemed to Johanna that summer's heat had never penetrated to this stone-floored room. There had been no fires lit in here to counteract the damp that penetrated the old walls of the manor; the narrow windows showed only the gathering storm clouds outside. Her skin prickled with goosebumps, and her nipples contracted with the chill while her mother and Elys snipped at the stitches holding her new sleeves in place, folded the fine new tunic and laid it aside, removed the gilt ribbons from her hair, and combed it out in a full crackling cloud that clung to her naked back and shoulders. Elys made the customary jokes about how glad the baron would be to see his lovely young bride. Gwynne embraced her daughter and shed a few last tears. Nothing penetrated the cold that seemed to have struck inward to Johanna's very bones.

Presently Sir Hugh shouted for his womenfolk to join him in the hall. It was time to start for Pomeray, and what did they want, to stand there and watch while the baron bedded the girl?

Gwynne led Johanna to the great chilly bed, tucked the down-stuffed comforter around her, and kissed her pale cheek. "You're not afraid, are you?" she whispered. "After all, it's not as if . . . I mean, last night . . ." She flushed. "I didn't know what it was all about on my wedding night. Perhaps you're lucky to have had it over with before the night."

She was gone before Johanna grasped her meaning, and then a bright flush of indignation warmed her shivering body. Gwynne thought that she and Rochambeau had been lovers already. Of course! They'd shared this very chamber last night; no doubt everybody on the manor thought so too. They must admire the baron's generosity in buying and wedding a girl he'd already bedded. It was all of a piece. Even while pretending he had no intention of forcing her into marriage, he'd done everything possible to see that she had no other option. Ruining her reputation, threatening her father's livelihood and very life. Was there anything he wouldn't stoop to?

"He may have bought my body," Johanna vowed silently, "but that's all he'll have, by God!" She was Rochambeau's wife now; he had certain rights over her. Very well. She would comply with his demands. But that was all. He could not seduce her into passionate response, should not believe that he could keep tricking her into doing whatever he wanted. Soon enough, no doubt, he would tire of a coldly compliant wife and would go back to his old mistresses, of whom she didn't doubt there were plenty. Good. She wanted as little as possible to do with this man.

In the first few minutes of waiting alone in the chamber, expecting Rochambeau to stride in any minute with his conqueror's smile and his insolent hands to run over her body, indignation kept Johanna warm and alert. As the time passed, and he didn't come and didn't come, she began to feel that pride was a very chilly bedfellow.

Presently there was a discreet tap on the door. Johanna wrapped the top coverlet around herself and tiptoed across the room, trailing red woolen cloth and marten fur behind her. A serving girl informed her that the master had said he would be somewhat delayed, some matter of estate work that could not be put off. In the meantime, he'd sent up a pitcher of warm spiced wine with his apologies.

Apologies! Johanna fumed. It seemed the man wasn't even going to wait for her cold reception of him before losing interest in her. How could she refuse him what he didn't even trouble to ask for? But the wine was warm, steaming invitingly, and the spices gave it a tempting flavor. She wondered where he'd found this hidden treasure. It seemed Rhuthun wasn't quite as miserable a manor as it appeared at first.

While she was wondering, Johanna found that a first cup of the hot spiced wine slipped down quite easily. But it left her thirsty and longing for a little more to drink. Well, there would be no harm in helping herself. She was the baron's lady now, not a little girl who had to wait for her elders, and he had sent the wine for her. It would be his own fault if there wasn't enough left for him. That would teach the man to ignore her in favor of estate business!

A third cup of wine shared the fate of the first two, and Johanna found that the room was becoming comfortably warm after all. But the floor was moving. She dropped the empty pitcher, made her unsteady way to the bed, and curled up under the coverlets to rest until that bastard Rochambeau should appear. If he did. She was beginning to suspect that Rochambeau didn't mean to visit his newly wedded lady that night—and that, she told herself, was perfectly all right with her!

The wine muddled her brain and sent her into a series of strange, half-waking dreams that gradually merged with sleep. Memories of Rochambeau rose out of nowhere: the golden knight in her father's wheat fields, the hard hands that had held her so tenderly, the lips whose pressure awakened her body to new wellsprings of delight. Once again her breasts flowered under his touch; in the dream, he was tenderly caressing her bare skin, fingers cupping her breast, one thumb brushing back and forth across the nipple until she could hardly bear the intense pleasure he caused her.

The crackling of flames and the weight of something on her body slowly penetrated Johanna's consciousness. She moaned and tossed her head from side to side until the warm pressure of lips on her throat stilled the movement. She didn't want to wake up from this pleasant dream!

Reality intruded slowly. First she was aware that there was a real fire in the hearth, throwing a leaping golden light over one wall. She must be awake then. But the dream didn't stop. The kisses that were so pleasurable on her throat moved down, tracing a path of trembling delight over her flesh until the insistent tugging of a mouth replaced the hand that had covered her breast. Rochambeau's naked body, all golden in the firelight, lay beside and half over her, and now his hands too had moved downward to awaken her to new and more urgent pleasures.

She felt a melting heat between her thighs even before he touched her there. His lips and hands were still gliding over her body with agonizing slowness, and she knew instinctively that she needed him to release the taut knots of desire that were building within her. She arched upward under his hand, sighing with pleasure, and a new shaft of pure delight shot through the center of her being.

She moaned her pleasure aloud, clasping him to her, even while her tardy mind cried, *But this is Rochambeau . . . the man you hate!*

It was far too late for that warning. The wine had heated her blood, the surprise of finding him beside her had penetrated her defenses, and the passions he had awakened were crying out for release. She was helpless to resist his embrace, drawn without volition into the demands of her body and his, and it was just as she had always known it would be: dark, consuming, wonderful, frightening. Once, when he entered her, there was a brief stab of pain that almost broke the sensual bonds he was weaving about her; but she didn't have time to free herself from his spell before he had subdued her again, using his expertise to charm her senses into a magical world where nothing existed but the next peak of delight. Together they climbed into those enchanted gardens where lovers lie, lost to the world around them and knowing nothing but fulfillment in each other.

Johanna cried out aloud in the culmination of their passion, and while she was still trembling with the waves of delight that rolled through her body Rochambeau found his own fulfillment. Yet that was not the end but only the beginning of a long night in which the leaping fire burned down, the carefully arranged coverlets of fur and scarlet and down were kicked into a tangled mess at the foot of the bed, and the old manor of Rhuthun itself shook with the passion unleashed between them.

The golden flames had become a pile of white ash when at last they were both sated. In the dying reddish glow of the last embers, Rochambeau admired the pale perfection of Johanna's white body, sweetly curved against the tangled sheets. The coverlet at the foot of the bed, the dying red light of the fire, and the bloodstains on the sheets were notes of scarlet and crimson against the whiteness of her skin and the cream color of the linen sheets. Had he hurt her very much? She was young; he'd meant to be more gentle this first time. But all her responses had cried out against gentleness; she was made for the wildest demands of passion, a sensual body only waiting to be released from the twin spells of ignorance and innocence.

"I could look at you forever," he murmured, stroking her cheek with one finger. Even now, when desire should have been long since sated, he felt a stirring in his loins at the touch of her satiny smooth skin. She was even sweeter in other places, pure silk and fire and honey, and if he let himself think of that neither of them would get any sleep that night. Passionate though she was, it didn't do to use a woman so roughly on her first night; she would be sore in the morning, if she didn't feel it now.

"Did I hurt you? Tell me you forgive me." The sooty sweep of her long dark lashes over the perfect curve of her cheek entranced him; a coil of her wild dark hair caught around his finger, holding him with springy strength. Her face was in shadow; one might almost have thought that she slept, but that only moments earlier she'd been responding with wanton eagerness to the demands of his passion.

"I know it's not what you wanted, this hasty wedding," Rochambeau told his bride. "But do you see why now? I couldn't have kept my hands off you much longer, Johanna. We were made for each other. Your body knew it, if your mind resisted. And now that you are mine, I promise I'll make it up to you. As soon as you like, we'll leave this dreary manor in the back of beyond and set out for Malvern. You'll like Malvern. And there you'll have your silk gowns, your great wedding feast, dancers and jongleurs to entertain our guests, hunting and hawking as you will."

"Gerfalcons," sighed a breath from Johanna's lips, "with silver bells . . ." She sighed and flung one arm out carelessly, and he realized that she was all but asleep already.

"Yes, gerfalcons if you want them," Rochambeau agreed, smiling inwardly. He'd judged aright in his list of proffered treats. She was a child still, albeit a child in a disturbingly sensuous woman's body! He'd win her with love at night and toys in the daytime, he'd keep her always a little off balance as he'd done tonight, until she forgot that she'd ever resented the speed of his wooing. Until she was his, body and soul, as her body had been his tonight.

He flattered himself that it had been a wise move, making her wait until she fell asleep. Hard on him, pacing up and down outside the manor house with an ache at the root of his manhood, while Aubrey laughed at him and asked if he was afraid of his new bride. But he'd sensed her chilly resentment during the wedding feast, had seen the flash of panic in her eyes when Gwynne took her away to be bedded. Never mind that she had no reason to hate and fear him; he'd teach her that later. Meanwhile, he had no mind to come to a cold, frightened girl who would have to fight him for the sake of her own pride. Much better to warm her blood with the spiced wine, warm her imagination with waiting, and then to take her by surprise when, half asleep, she would be ready to surrender to the dictates of her own body.

Now that she knew what pleasures marriage could bring, he felt that he'd have very little trouble with her. Why had she been so resentful of him, anyway? Just because she hadn't had the courtship and presents and feasting that she thought her due? After her warm reception of him in her bed tonight, he certainly couldn't believe that she found him personally repugnant. And he'd told her that very morning that he would not force an unwilling bride; if she had refused the marriage, he would not have pressed his claim. He'd even left her alone with her parents to talk the matter over in privacy.

And she'd come to him after that and said she would be his wife. Her own choice. So why this glowering resentment that he'd felt from her, first during the nuptial Mass, then during dinner?

It was a mystery to Rochambeau. But then, he'd learned early in life that many things about women were mysteries, and few of their little secrets were important. What mattered was the way their eager bodies responded in his arms, the way they softened and smiled if he but took the trouble to chat with them and pretended to treat them as equals. A man like Hugh Lespervier, forever roaring like a bull at his poor womenfolk, was a fool who made unnecessary trouble for himself. Rochambeau never had woman trouble, and he didn't anticipate any real problems with Johanna. His practiced lovemaking would win over the little witch's body, and the presents he meant to shower on her would conquer her childish resentment.

The next morning, he began to find out just how wrong that easy assumption had been. Waking to reach out a sleepy hand for the warmth of his little bride, he felt only cold rumpled sheets beneath his hand where he'd hoped to cup a firm young breast. He sighed, rolled over, and opened his eyes to find Johanna already up and dressed in a plain brown tunic that did nothing for her ink-and-porcelain coloring. The rebellious black curls were tucked under a white linen coif, and her hands were folded before her. She sat on a three-legged stool that he did not remember as part of the furnishings of this chamber.

"You're up betimes, little bird," he said, smiling lazily at her. "Come back to bed a while. There's not so much business on this manor that the baron and his lady must work like serfs to keep track of it. I'll call a servant to bring us up something fit to eat—in a little while." Already the stirring in his loins was reminding him that there were more rewarding things than eating with which to begin a morning's work.

In a chilly voice Johanna informed him that she had already dressed, attended Mass in the village church, and broken her fast.

"And then you came back to wait for your lazy husband to stir," applauded Rochambeau. "Why didn't you wake me, sweetheart? You're not still shy of me now that we're married, surely? Come here, and I'll teach you to forget shyness." He reached out one hand, beckoning, inviting, but Johanna did not respond to his invitation.

"I came back," she told him, "because we have some matters to discuss in private, my lord."

It began to sink into Rochambeau's sleep-fuddled brain that his bride's cool manner might stem from something more than maiden shyness. He sat up, alarmed, and the rumpled covers fell away to reveal his naked torso, gleaming with golden fuzz and scarred with the white lines of old wounds.

Johanna caught her breath and looked away. He was the finest-looking man she'd ever seen. He put to shame the peasants she'd covertly watched from time to time as they labored in her father's fields, stripped to a pair of baggy breeches. And she remembered all too clearly the fiery intoxication of being pressed against that body, the heat of his skin entering and warming her, the practiced caresses of his hands making her forget everything but the passion of the moment. It wasn't fair that he should be so seductive in looks and manner and so foul in spirit!

"I have complied with your demands," she said, staring at the worn tapestry on the far wall of the chamber. "I want to know if that is enough."

Without looking, she could tell that Rochambeau was grinning. "It's a start. Come here, and we'll improve on it. Seems to me I had a little more than compliance from you last night."

"You tricked me!" Johanna clenched her hands and slid the fists into the loose ends of her sleeves so that Rochambeau shouldn't see how upset she was. But she could do nothing about the blushes that mounted to her cheeks. "I didn't mean . . . that is, I submitted to your embraces because it was my duty," she lied, cheeks aflame. "I want you to understand, my lord, that I will uphold my end of the bargain, no matter how distasteful I find it to do so. All I want is reassurance that you'll do the same."

"Bargain?"

Oh, the man was a consummate actor! From the tone of innocent surprise, one might think he'd never sent Aubrey to threaten her father with ruin or possible death if she did not submit to him. And Johanna felt too ashamed of the way her family had given in to him to spell the matter out. There would have been more honor in it if her father had defied Rochambeau to do his worst, trusting in his innocence and the king's justice to bring them safely through the ordeal. Now that she'd been sold to Rochambeau in return for his silence, who would ever believe that there was no real reason for the sale? By giving in, her father had named himself traitor in truth, should the news ever come out. By discussing the matter with a clever bastard like Rochambeau, she would only give him new tools to use against her family.

"I see no need to discuss the matter," Johanna said between her teeth. "I merely wish to know if you'll keep your promises."

"Gerfalcons? With silver bells?" That was the only promise Rochambeau could remember making, apart from the usual wedding vows. Why was the girl making such a pother over the matter? Did she really fear he might be so mean as to deny his wife a few small luxuries? He gave a rueful glance around the barren chamber that was the best Rhuthun had to offer its lord, with its faded tapestries and antique bedstead, and granted that she might have some reason for apprehension.

"Oh, you are impossible!" Johanna jumped to her feet. "If you were a man of honor, you would not play these games with me."

"I have that name," said Rochambeau. His own temper was beginning to rise. At sixteen, the girl should have been better schooled than to greet her new husband with demands for toys, let alone gratuitous insults. Anybody would think she'd been forced into a hateful marriage—and from his memories of last night, one thing he felt tolerably sure of was that she didn't hate him. At least, she didn't hate making love with him, and the rest should follow without difficulty.

"Good. Then there's nothing more to be said." Johanna attempted a sweeping exit from the chamber but was hampered by the trailing hem of her tunic getting entangled in the three-legged stool she'd brought in. The pause while she freed herself gave Rochambeau time to jump out of bed and grasp her by her shoulders. Her blushes flamed even higher, and she averted her eyes from his nakedness. Well, too bad. It was time she gave up her shamefaced maidenly airs—and, he thought, it would be a pleasure teaching her. He'd make a willing scholar out of her yet.

"One more thing," he told her, holding her tightly against his naked body. He could feel the softness of thighs and breasts through her tunic, and the involuntary trembling of her body told him that she could feel him too and that the contact was having the same effect on her. Oh, she wanted him as much as he desired her, let her play what games she would!

"Pray state your demands and allow me to go, my lord." Her voice trembled, her eyes were modestly downcast, and her lips were roses spewing forth poisoned darts. Rochambeau burned to kiss the nonsense out of them.

"You mentioned a matter of duty," he said with a grin, releasing her as she'd requested. She backed away from him, and her downcast eyes were inevitably directed on that portion of his anatomy which was causing them both so much trouble. Her lids flew open, and she looked up into his face, as he'd wanted.

"I just wanted you to know, madam wife, that you'll have to do your duty regularly. Quite frequently, in fact." He was still confident that he could force her to love him, if only she were reminded at frequent intervals of the wondrous accord between their bodies. And what better time than the present? Morning was the traditional time for lessons. "Starting—"

Johanna clasped her hands in front of her and assumed a martyred expression.

"—after we reach Malvern." Rochambeau quickly changed the end of his sentence. No point in forcing the girl into bed when she was all set to resist him. If he had to take her by surprise a few more times, well, he was well versed in the siegecraft of love. He'd never expected to have to apply the art to his own wife, but already he could see some amusement and some sweet rewards in the game.

And it was almost worth denying the renewed ache in his loins to see the look of surprise on her face.

Malvern was indeed very different from the shabby, isolated manor of Rhuthun. Although Rochambeau had told Johanna that it was by no means the largest of his manors, merely his childhood home and his favorite estate, it was to be many months before she could imagine a baron's hall whose lord lived in greater comfort and dined in greater state than at Malvern.

Unlike the semifortified house at Rhuthun, Malvern was a real castle with keep and hall and bailey, a pile of golden stone rising magically above the huddled village outside its walls, enclosing garden and pleasance and orchard for her delight.

"Small," Rochambeau said, but his words of apology were contradicted by the pride in his eyes when he showed her the new bower and private chamber that he'd had built at the end of the great hall, with fine stone-vaulted storerooms beneath them to keep food and wine and spices cool through the year. "In my father's day the only private quarters were in the old keep tower, which I've made part of the inner wall now. It was damp. You'll like this better; see how convenient it is to the hall? We can retire to the bower after meals and enjoy some private time without my men-at-arms and your maid-servants fluttering around us. And there are rooms above for the women to sleep, or for our children when God sends them.''

He smiled down at her with an intimate confidence that made Johanna's cheeks grow warm. Children! There'd be few enough of those if Rochambeau went on as he'd begun. Why, he'd not so much as touched her since that first disastrous night at Rhuthun—not, she hastily told herself, that she had any objection to this state of affairs. If she lay long awake at night, it was from apprehension at this new life into which she'd been thrust, not from missing the caresses of this hateful man. But even so, she found it hard to meet the deep glow of those blue eyes. She turned away and said the first thing that came into her head.

''The chapel is not very convenient, is it?''

Rochambeau's new building formed a truncated L shape, with the hall and private chambers making up the long part of the L, the chapel the short end. But there was no way into the chapel from hall or bower; one entered by a flight of steps from the courtyard outside.

Rochambeau grinned. ''It's more convenient for the servitors than for us,'' he acknowledged. ''That's all right—their souls stand in more need of it.''

''I sincerely doubt that!''

''Oh, do you have a sin on your conscience?'' Rochambeau's tone was all solicitousness, but there was a spark of mischief dancing in his eyes. ''Coldness to your newly wedded lord, perhaps? Come into the bower, Johanna, and confess to me.''

''In broad daylight!'' Genuinely shocked, Johanna scurried down the flight of steps that led from the bower into the great hall. ''We—we haven't finished the tour.''

Rochambeau accepted defeat with good grace and spent the rest of the afternoon ceremoniously escorting Johanna around the castle and grounds, introducing his new lady to all his people. That first night at Malvern was almost a repetition of their wedding night. Johanna went up to the private chamber alone after their evening meal, while Rochambeau vanished on some masculine errand. She was almost asleep in the great tapestry-hung bed, thinking he'd forgotten his promise—no, his threat!—to come to her at Malvern, when he woke her with well-aimed kisses and seductive caresses that quickly moved beyond her powers of resistance. She stretched like a cat, cried out shamelessly in his arms, blazed with the fires he lit—and came down to earth to resent, all the more, his conqueror's smile.

"I trust I perform my duty adequately, my lord?"

"Not bad . . . for a beginner."

Johanna seethed.

"You need more tutoring, though. Allow me?"

Taking her in his arms again, he began to teach her the slow refinement of the senses that allowed them to stretch over hours the delightful dance that had taken only minutes before. Now nipping her earlobe with strong white teeth, now kissing her indecently wherever her sense-drugged limbs fell back, he kept her shivering with delight and frustration for an eternity, then demanded that she serve him the same way—and she complied. Far into the night, he wove his magic spell around her, until at last sleep and exhaustion overtook her, and she knew nothing but the warmth of his love enfolding her.

In the morning she woke to find him dressed and watching her as she lay, sprawled indecently naked with arms and legs outflung, covering two-thirds of the bed. All the coverlets were dragged down to the floor, and the sun was pouring in through the barred windows. Johanna felt angry at him for catching her at such a disadvantage. She'd meant to be first awake, to greet him with a display of freezing dignity. Somehow that dignity had been most thoroughly misplaced last night; she couldn't quite figure out how. Snatching up a crumpled linen sheet, she covered herself and sat up in one motion, ready to repel any assumption of love or intimacy on his part.

She was somewhat taken aback to find that no such repulsion was needed. He'd courteously looked away while she covered herself. Now she saw that he had brought in a small writing desk and was scratching out some words on a piece of parchment, head bent over his task as though this scribework was more important than greeting his wife in the morning.

"Ah, you're up? Good. I have to go soon—estate business.

92

I'd like you to start taking care of the household. Aubrey's my seneschal; he can tell you what's involved.'' He showed her the parchment. "This is an order for . . ."

"I can read."

"You can?" Rochambeau's eyebrows shot up. "Convent?"

"And cipher." No need to add that the convent had kicked her out after one short season. She'd already learned all they had to teach except Latin, and the priest had said it was unfitting to teach girls Latin. But the order scrawled in Rochambeau's distinctive hand shocked her. He wanted Aubrey to give her more silver than she'd ever seen at one time. Was such a vast sum of money really necessary, even for a baron's household?

"Well, good." The parchment fluttered down onto the bed like a dried leaf in the wind while Johanna reached for it with numb fingers. "You'll soon find your way around. I recommend that you start by inspecting the stores. I suspect the cook's been passing haunches of meat on to the village butcher, but it's been too much trouble to check on him."

"What do you want me to do about it?" Johanna asked. And how was she supposed to find out if it were true?

"If it's true, hang him. I've the right of the high justice, and for sour meat pottage like he served last noon he should be hanged anyway. Else find somebody who can cook food the way I like it—one of the assistants may do—and promote him. I'll be back for dinner to see how you're doing."

And with no more farewell than that, he was gone, leaving Johanna with the distinct feeling that she'd just been locked into a small room with a pile of straw that she was supposed to spin into gold. Presently she dressed herself, squared her shoulders, and went in search of the peculating cook.

It took more than that first morning for Johanna to find her feet as lady of Malvern, but Rochambeau showed no impatience with her initial efforts. He merely suggested more and more things that she might want to do. She quickly learned that if she didn't follow his suggestions, he would see to matters himself, and not always in the ways that best pleased her. He had hired the blond slut Elfieda as a waiting-woman, while Johanna was summoning the courage to interview and hire village women ten years older than herself. After that, she tried to anticipate Rochambeau's suggestions and maintain control over the side of manor life that was supposed to be hers. But it wasn't easy.

The brief tour on the first afternoon had done little good. For the first weeks Johanna was continually losing her way in the maze of wooden passages that connected the stone-built keep with the cluster of outbuildings in the bailey. On her way to the mews she would accidentally stumble into living quarters where half-dressed men-at-arms polished their armor and told smutty tales on rainy days. Trying to find the kitchens, she discovered herself in the smithy instead. She would then be distracted from her errand to the cook, watching Coluin the smith beat out a glowing miniature horseshoe which he presented to her as a luck charm.

Slowly she began to know her way about Malvern and at the same time to learn some of those things Gwynne had meant to teach her about the management of a great lord's estate. It was far more complicated than she'd imagined from her experience at Pomeray, but also more interesting. If the lady of Malvern had no need to burn her fingers and heat her face with bread baking, she did need to see that flour of the right quality was available to the baker, from fine-milled white flour for the lord's bread to coarse scrapings for the alms-basket loaves. When the pantler came to request her order for spices, Johanna, who'd never thought twice about a recipe, frowned over her mother's closely written recipe book, trying to figure out how many times in the next quarter she would want gingered chicken—keeping in mind that she needed enough for the crowd Rochambeau customarily seated above the saltcellar, where the best food was served. Then there was cloth to be bought for the servants' liveries, she had to engage waiting-women for herself, and the butler wanted to know what to do about the wine that had been sent from Gascony.

"I can't figure it all out!" she wailed in frustration at least a dozen times a day. Rochambeau was trusting her with more silver than she'd ever seen in her life, enough to buy all the pretty luxuries she'd dreamed of before her marriage. He didn't even ask her to keep account of it. But she also knew that he expected this silver to cover the household accounts without her troubling him for more before the next quarter-day, and the responsibility scared her.

"You needn't try," suggested Aubrey one cloudy day when he found her covered with ink splotches and close to tears at the problems posed for her to solve. "I'm sure it's not what Nicolas intended—and if he did, he shouldn't have," he added with an abstracted frown. "Look at you! Pale and tired and . . ." He broke off as a sudden thought struck him. "You're not breeding, are you?"

Johanna shook her head. The blunt question didn't even embarrass her, coming from Aubrey, whom she was fast coming to look upon as the elder brother she'd never had. He didn't make impossible demands on her like Rochambeau; he didn't frighten her with his sensual wooing or trick her into responses she would later regret. He was just always there—lounging in the doorway as she struggled with accounts, stealing a honey cake from the kitchen while she went over the cook's tasks, laughing at her seriousness and making her laugh too.

No, she wasn't pregnant yet, and she supposed that was another reason for Rochambeau's daytime neglect. Perhaps already he was beginning to regret his hasty wooing. At night he was as attentive as any bride could wish, and far more so than Johanna wished, regularly bringing her to the peak of trembling passion in his arms even while she resented the skill that ravished her senses. In the daytime he went about his own business, hearing tenants' complaints in the morning, hunting or hawking the rest of the day, and generally acting as if he didn't have a wife at all. In between times, he casually tossed her a bunch of keys or a heavy purse and recommended that she look into this, that, or the other thing about the running of the manor.

"Well, then." Aubrey casually smoothed back the curls that had escaped from the edges of Johanna's coif. "If there's no reason for you to stay housebound, why don't you come riding with me? Perhaps we'll catch up with Nicolas and the rest of the hunters. Or—no, that might not be a good idea."

"Why not?" asked Johanna languidly. Not that she'd felt the slightest interest in joining her husband's hunting party, of course, but Aubrey's quick quashing of the notion made the damp summer day seem more boring than it already was.

"Nicolas," said Aubrey slowly, "is . . . not kind to those who disobey his wishes. As you, I think, have already had too sad cause to learn. There are tales in the village of men he took prisoner in the wars . . ." Again he broke off and shook his head, apologizing for having started such a topic. "Not tales for a lady's ears. But come riding anyway. Who knows? Perhaps we'll find some game of our own to pursue."

His infectious smile and sparkling blue eyes were like a shaft of sunlight brightening the gray day. Johanna was not sure why she resisted the offer, but she sighed and shook her head. "I've got to figure this out first." She pointed at the blotched sheet on which she was trying to add up the quantities of spices to be ordered from London merchants and the amount of money that would have to be sent with the pantler's assistant.

"No need." Aubrey deftly twitched the parchment out of her fingers. "That's my job, not yours. I'm seneschal of the estates, remember? Don't look so worried, my dear. The honor of Rochambeau, from Wareham in Dorset to Rhuthun in the Marches, was running smoothly before you were more than a gleam in your father's eye. For the last ten years I've had all this responsibility and more to bear, while little brother Nicolas jaunted about with Prince Edward and played at war. Now come, change your clothes. You can't ride properly in that long tunic!"

Laughing, Johanna let Aubrey tempt her away from her self-imposed task, though she was later horrified when she discovered how much money he'd casually tossed to the pantler's assistant for the spice account. Still, the ways of a rich barony had to be different from the penny-pinching life she'd known at Pomeray, and, as Aubrey said, he'd been taking care of much greater estate matters for years and years. Why should she worry, if Rochambeau didn't care?

And, for that matter, why should she care what Nicolas de Rochambeau thought of her and her skills as lady of the manor? He'd made it all too clear that he had no use for her except as a bedtime toy, something he'd bought in a fit of passion and was already growing bored with. Oh, to be sure, he sat cross-legged before the hearth at night and sang her meltingly sweet love songs of his own composition. But the words seemed like mockery when she remembered that his true style of courtship was composed of lies and threats. When he coaxed her into bed, he was tender and loving, passionate and skilled at arousing her responses, but he gave her no choice in the matter. Since the first day he'd set eyes on her, she'd never had a choice; what he took, he kept. Johanna held with equal tenacity to her own stubborn resentment and felt herself justified when the mornings took him off on his own errands. She never saw him in the daytime. What clearer proof did she need that she was only a toy to him?

And soon, like any spoiled child, he'd tire of playing with this toy and demand another, Johanna thought. She involuntarily shivered with fear at the thought of ending those nightly encounters where he and she burned with an equal fire, composed of hatred and desire, mastery and revolt. She firmly told herself that nothing would please her better than to have Rochambeau desert her bed for good. Sometimes she even made herself believe it—in the daytime.

"You should spend more time with your lady during the day," old Marc, Rochambeau's body-squire since his sixteenth year, reproved him. "Why don't you invite her to go hawking with you after you finish your work in the manor court?"

"She hasn't much use for me in the daytime," Rochambeau said as he stripped off his heavy hawking gauntlets and tossed them to Marc. Marc caught them one-handed without being distracted from his argument.

"You could change that."

Rochambeau's smile was brighter, more dangerous, than that of his half-brother. "I mean to. But I've wasted enough energy trying to coax her out of her sullens. She doesn't want to take an intelligent interest in the manor. She's made it clear enough to me that she doesn't want my company outside of bed. The only time we get along decently is . . ."

"Stop. Don't tell me anything indecent. Anyway, I know where Rochambeaus always get along best with the ladies," Marc grumbled, fixing his beloved master with bright bird-like eyes.

"Well, then, old man. If you know it all, then you know she'll come around in time. As soon as she grows up and accepts the fact that she's a married woman now, not a girl teasing her suitors. And until that time, I'll be damned if I'll coax and bribe her. She can have her damned gerfalcons as a reward when she's willing to act reasonably friendly.''

"You could at least tell her you're planning to give a great feast at the end of harvest," Marc pointed out. "Married in that drafty hut of Rhuthun, then whisked off here and loaded with the household accounts, the poor girl probably thinks you wed her for a brood mare and a housekeeper.''

"No.'' The tone of the denial was something that even Marc, who'd given Rochambeau his first lessons with a wooden sword and shield, dared not question. "She'll hear about the feast, and the silks I've stored away for her bride clothes, when she's ready to act like a bride. And believe me''—again that flashing, dangerous smile—"it won't take me many more nights before she's as sweet in the daytime as she is in my bed.''

"Wouldn't hurt to give her a few days too.''

Rochambeau regarded his squire with cold distaste. "You begin to harp a one-note tune, old man. I find it distinctly boring. Give me my gauntlets again. I'm going to take my hawk out and look for some more game. If you think the girl needs courting and coaxing to behave like a wife, why don't you try it and see how far you get?''

"All right. I believe I will. You certainly don't need my help to go out and kill a few more defenseless rabbits.'' Old Marc stumped out the door of the mews without a backward look.

Chapter Seven

THE CLOUDS THAT hung over the Welsh Marches, threatening Pomeray's harvest, also threatened the southerly manor of Malvern. Fortunately, the summer had been hot and the grain had ripened early. Rochambeau ordered that harvest also begin early, and he made it clear that he expected his tenants to work as though it were the traditional date for full harvest. By the grace of God, the threatened rains held off until the harvest of Malvern was safely gathered and sheltered. Even the villeins, though they had to give their usual boon-days to the lord's harvest, managed to get their own strips of grain reaped and under cover before the autumn rains broke. This expeditious harvesting was due partly to the generosity of the lord of Rochambeau, who hired itinerant day laborers to help with both his own harvest and that of his villeins. It was also due partly to the harshness of that same lord. Two lazy sots who'd been accustomed to lounge in the village alehouse while their young sons were sent to do a man's work on the lord's land found themselves dragged out of the alehouse by the ears and set to work under the hayward's eye and under threat of his long white-tipped cane.

"My lord, everybody knows Alfwin and his brother are too old and sick to work," protested Alfwin's wife.

Rochambeau gave the panting woman a mirthless grin and just touched the handle of his long-lashed dog whip. "With proper motivation, they may recover their strength."

99

A few lashes curling about the luckless pair's ankles on the first day of harvest reinforced the lesson, as did the widely disseminated news that my lord had given the hayward permission to flog any man who gave less than his best. The incident was reported with some indignation by Aubrey.

"Beating the peasants! It's harking back to the worst times of old Nicolas, his grandfather, when the villeins could be required to haul stones for the mill on their backs."

"They still can," Johanna pointed out. "It's in the custom book that his father had the clerks compile." The clerkly commentary on the customal was in Latin, but the original statements were in the English spoken by the villeins.

Aubrey gave her a surprised sidewise glance. "So you can read as well as cipher?"

"Not all women are totally brainless," Johanna told him. "Even if you and Rochambeau would like to think so."

This drew aggrieved protestations from Aubrey. His brother, he admitted, thought of women as nothing but toys with which to while away an idle hour. But he, he swore and vowed, was different. He had only been surprised to hear that Johanna had enjoyed an education so far beyond the lot of most females—though he ought not to have been so surprised, because her intelligence, like her beauty, shone out as a rare jewel in a diadem . . . and so on and so on. Johanna wondered why the compliments she'd always dreamed of seemed faintly boring in real life. Perhaps it was because she sensed that Aubrey, for all his protestations, was not entirely pleased at these signs of her ability to do more than sit and embroider in the bower. Underneath, for all his charm of manner, he was probably of the same cut as his brother.

Eventually, as though sensing her inattention, Aubrey drifted off into a vague round of complaints against Rochambeau's interference with the running of the manor. For years he'd paid no attention to the business affairs of the estate; he was always off with young Prince Edward, engaged in putting down the numerous small wars that had followed the barons' rebellion ten years earlier. Meanwhile Aubrey had been left on his own as seneschal of the estates. Now Rochambeau came on a whim to look over his lands, and what must he do but thoroughly upset the established order of things? One day he showed his brutality by having Alfwin flogged, the next he squandered the silver of the estate by hiring day laborers to do work that the villeins should, by rights, have done. And doubtless on another day he'd lose interest in the entire project and leave the mess in Aubrey's hands to straighten out, just as he seemed to have lost interest . . .

Aubrey stopped there, almost biting his tongue, and Johanna noted with interest that the tips of his ears grew red when he flushed. She had nothing to say; she didn't even feel any particular anger against Aubrey. Why should she? It was true. Except for their stormy nights together, Rochambeau seemed to have lost interest in his new bride. But it was not a matter that she cared to discuss with anyone, even Aubrey.

"He may be interfering with the running of the estates," she agreed now, trying to steer the conversation back into safer channels, "but it would do nobody any good if the villeins' harvest were ruined by rain. We couldn't let them starve, and the expense of feeding them might well be greater than the cost of hiring extra labor for these few weeks."

Aubrey gave her a long considering look. "You're a clever woman, Johanna. Reading, ciphering, balancing the cost of hired labor against the cost of buying extra grain through the winter. No wonder Nicolas . . ." He stopped with a funny, agonized look, as though he'd just bitten his tongue.

"No wonder Nicolas doesn't care to spend time with me?" Johanna interpolated swiftly. "But Aubrey, he did tell me to take over the household accounts." And she'd been struggling with the effort to understand not just the household but the entire running of the estate, to make Rochambeau see that she was more than a child bride he'd taken for passing amusement. How ironic if that very effort were what was driving them farther apart!

"The household, that's one thing. But it's not fitting for a girl like you to go riding about the fields and inquiring into the serfs' work. Only the other day Nicolas commented to me that such matters might do for a girl from a small farm like Pomeray, but not for a baron's lady."

Pride and anger stiffened Johanna's back. She reminded herself that she didn't want or need Rochambeau's approval; she didn't even like the man! "I see. Thank you for the advice, Aubrey. Should I ever wish to please Rochambeau, I'll know how to go about it, won't I?"

"Now you're angry with me," Aubrey said as he gave her a rueful grin and spread his hands. "I was only trying to help."

"I know that, Aubrey." She couldn't stay angry with Aubrey, the one soul who'd been consistently kind and sympathetic toward her. It wasn't his fault that everything he said about his brother proved Rochambeau to be just the kind of man she could never care for: cold, hard, cruel, withering her beneath his lordly disapproval. Aubrey's very attempts to excuse the man only pointed out how hopeless this marriage was. The next time he came to her bed, Johanna resolved, she would plead illness, and she would stay ill until he got the message.

The next few days gave Johanna no chance to demonstrate her resolve. All hands about the manor were working frantically to bring in the last of the crops before the threatening rain clouds dumped their torrents on the valley. Although Rochambeau didn't strip to the waist and work alongside his villeins as her father had done, he seemed to be everywhere at once these days—overseeing, exhorting, and directing men and materials to where they were most needed. Once she came upon him with a group of slow-moving carters threatening them with his whip if they didn't stop overloading carts to the brink of disaster. Another time, while volunteering to help the women bring bread and ale to the fields, she saw him put his shoulder to a mired cart. When the heavy wheel pulled clear of the mud with a sucking sound, one of those same carters clapped Rochambeau on the back and the rest applauded his achievement.

Was he a good lord or bad, considerate or brutal? Johanna couldn't decide. The streak of hardness in his nature appalled her; the ease with which he achieved results appealed to her. Aubrey thought him needlessly cruel. Old Marc, his body-squire, thought he could do no wrong. Johanna spent a great deal of time sitting with Marc, as much to keep the aging squire from tiring himself with harvest work as for her own amusement. In consequence, she heard many stories about Nicolas de Rochambeau: his prowess in the tiltyards and at the tourneys, his swift moves and sudden strikes in time of war, his knightly virtues too many to name. On the night following the harvest feast for the tenants, Johanna was still

deciding what to think of this man she'd married. The sound
of music coming from their chamber surprised her as she
prepared to retire for the night. During the last frantic days
of the harvest, Rochambeau had hardly even slept at the
manor, and she had no idea where he'd lain on the night of
the feast. But that was unmistakably the sound of his lute.
Heart beating a little faster with excitement, she dismissed
her waiting-women and went alone into the chamber.

Not, she told herself, that she wanted him to spend the
night with her. Not that she'd missed his practiced assaults
on her senses. She just wanted to talk to him. After all, they
were married, and they might as well act like lord and lady
rather than a couple of strangers cooperating in the task of
running Rochambeau's great estates. Soon it would be time
to move on to one of the northern manors where harvest was
just about to begin. She wanted to know where they stood
with each other before she set about getting to know the next
group of tenants and dependents.

All this did not quite explain why the music rippling from
the lute sent a corresponding ripple through her body, like a
buried drumbeat echoing in her blood, like the memory of
birdsong in her heart.

Rochambeau was seated cross-legged on the bed, his
shoulder-length blond hair glistening in the candlelight and
his head bent over the lute. His hands moved deftly over the
instrument, releasing a gay ripple of sound that made Johanna
think of springtime, of dancing, of new green leaves and
flowers budding.

"That's pretty," she said involuntarily.

"Me," inquired her lord and master, "or the music?"

"If I said I was praising the music, would you be disappointed?" For the first time, Johanna felt able to enter into
Rochambeau's lighthearted banter, perhaps because for once
he wasn't trying to force a response from her before she was
ready to give it.

"By no means. I made the music, whereas I can take no
such credit for myself."

"I thought you took credit for everything!"

"Since you don't praise me," Rochambeau countered, "I
needs must praise myself. Tell me again you like the song,
then. It's the first kind word I've had from you."

"Let me hear the words."

"I haven't composed them yet." A bright blue mischievous gleam lit his eyes. "I was thinking of an aubade in praise of the happy night I spent in my lady's arms. Care to inspire me?"

"Why do you always have to turn everything into sex!"

Rochambeau shrugged. "When a man's around you, Johanna, everything seems to turn that way naturally." Discarding the lute, he reached one hand to hers, tugging at her to make her come and sit beside him on the bed. "And sometimes I think you don't object."

Digging her heels into the stone-flagged floor, Johanna freed herself.

"And sometimes you turn cold on me again," he concluded with a sigh. "What's the matter, Johanna? I know I'm older than you, and I've not had much time to spend with you lately, but surely we could deal together better than this? I'm tired of making every night a mix between a seduction and a rape." He brushed the clinging strands of gold hair away from his brow and looked up at her with wide, innocent blue eyes. "Damned if I know how we got into such a tangle, anyway. You liked me well enough at first. What went wrong?"

Johanna had honestly meant to try and achieve some sort of accord with her husband, but this wide-eyed innocent act galled her immeasurably. "We? You're the one who got into a tangle when you forced me into this marriage."

"I did not force you! Damn it, I told you you didn't have to marry me if you didn't want to!" With an angry gesture, Rochambeau swept the lute from the bed. It shattered on the stone floor, and he stood up and kicked the pieces aside.

Standing, he was much taller and broader than she remembered when she was away from him. The sheer physical force that emanated from his outraged frame was almost too much for Johanna to stand against, unless she matched it with anger of her own.

"It seems you forgot to inform my father of that little detail," she spat at him, hands curved like claws.

Rochambeau sighed and passed one hand over his forehead again. Suddenly he seemed more tired than angry. "If he bullied you, I'm sorry, but I wish you would choose to hate him rather than me." Holding out one hand to her, he smiled. "Come, sweetheart. I didn't understand at first how much you disliked being rushed into marrying me. Perhaps I made a mistake in how I went about things. But I think I can make this marriage more to your liking."

Johanna's ebullient spirits bounced back upward again. Did this mean that Rochambeau was finally recognizing that she couldn't be bought or bullied? If he was willing to put some effort into improving their relationship, if he cared enough to treat her like a person rather than a toy . . .

He smiled down at her, deep blue eyes lit by the candle-flames, and she felt weak at the knees at the thought of what it might mean to be loved in every sense of the word by a man like Nicolas de Rochambeau. If he didn't treat her so casually, if he really cared for her, anything might be possible. Her red lips trembled slightly as she returned his smile. The least she could do was show him that she, too, had been trying to change.

"I've learned a little since I've been here," she told him. "The spice account . . ."

"Devil take the spice account! That was just something to keep you amused while I was busy elsewhere. If I'd wanted a housekeeper, I could have hired one," Rochambeau declared, completely forgetting his earlier complaints to Marc that Johanna was too childish to take an interest in anything but herself. What did that matter? She'd grow up soon enough; all he wanted was to see her smile at him again, with the tremulous lips and glowing eyes of a woman on the verge of love. Marc was right—they'd been in a state of tension long enough. He was ready to give her anything she wanted, just so she'd be happy with him.

But her smile was fading, and the green eyes darkened as her lashes dropped over them. Damn! He'd frightened her again with his vehemence. Well, that could be repaired. When he showed her the pretty things he'd been saving for her, she'd be happy again.

"Come with me." Seizing her by the arm, he towed her into the wide chamber of the bower, the large room between their private chamber and the stairway down to the hall. It had been used as a storeroom until Johanna's arrival; now her women were setting up looms and using the storage chests as tables for the marking and cutting out of liveries. But at this hour the bower was empty; the women who lived outside the castle were back at their village homes, and the others were abed on the upper floor. Johanna looked around in bewilderment as Rochambeau raised a branch of candles high to illuminate the dusty crevices of the room. He turned the light this way and that as if searching for something. What was he up to now? A moment ago she thought they'd been on the verge of some new understanding. Now he thrust the candles into her hand and was down on his knees before an assemblage of locked chests in one corner.

"Keys," he muttered impatiently. "Keys, keys . . . oh, the cellarer must have them. He was always at me to move this stuff into the strongroom anyway, but I knew I was right to keep them handy. Ah!" The tip of his belt knife pried open the lock on the topmost chest. He threw the lid open and beckoned Johanna closer, taking the candles from her hand and holding them close so that their light cast a flickering, golden, magical glow on the contents of the chest.

"Samite. Purple silk from Outremer. Brocades." A sweep of his arm spilled folds of rich fabric over the side of the chest, glittering with gold and silver threads, glowing with their own jewel-bright colors. "I sent for this green silk the day after I met you. I told the merchant I must have silk the color of willow leaves reflected in running water, silk that rippled like water and changed color with the changing light, silk as green as an emerald and as bright as a star, to match the eyes of my lady for her bridal gown."

"But . . ." Speechless, Johanna remembered the hastily cobbled tunic in which she'd spoken her wedding vows.

"It didn't arrive till after the wedding as things turned out. Well, that's all behind us now." Rochambeau glided hastily over this unfortunate reminder of the hasty marriage and delved into the chest for more treasures. "Look. Ivory combs for your hair, white as your skin, to set against the black satin of your curls. A hand mirror of real glass." The mirror was framed in ivory to match the combs, with an intricately carved border of dragons and hawks around its outer edge. The small dinner knife he pulled out next had a handle of dark polished wood, inlaid with fine gold and silver wires forming the image of the Rochambeau crest, a stooping hawk. Johanna's fingers itched to touch it. "I put everything into these chests. Even these, though the cellarer all but cried when I took them from the strongroom."

Reaching into the very bottom of the chest, he drew out a glittering triple chain of gold set with glowing red stones. The fine, supple, heavy chains ran through his fingers like a golden waterfall, and the rubies flashed like living coals, like the eye of a phoenix rising from the flames.

"The Rochambeau family jewels." He held out the mass of entangled chains spread out on both hands. "They're yours now. There hasn't been a woman here to wear them since my mother died. And everything else here is for you, too. Fine silks, ivory and gold and bronze work, everything you want, Johanna, if you'll only love me."

Johanna felt sick with disappointment. After all, he still thought she was a child to be bribed with toys. He thought an insult to herself and her family could be wiped out with these trinkets. Love? That wasn't what he wanted, though it was what she ached to give. All he wanted was for her to come willingly to his bed at night and pretend compliance to his wishes in the daytime. And as long as she cooperated, as long as she was his pretty doll, he'd deck her with silks and jewels and surround her with luxury.

"Don't you like them?" The shining confidence on his face wavered a little. "Perhaps they're too heavy for you for now, but you'll grow into them. In the meantime I'll send to London for some lighter jewels. A silver chain with an emerald, some gold rings perhaps." His confidence grew visibly as he enumerated the presents his wealth could buy her. "And that's not all. You were angry because we married so quickly, because you never had a proper wedding feast, weren't you? Well, I've taken care of that too! I've invited all our neighbors to join us for an after-harvest feast, to meet my new bride. You'll be honored and admired as you deserve, Johanna. I never meant to treat you lightly—it's just that things happened so fast."

His eyes glowed with that deep blue fire as he gazed up at her. "No one else could see you and not admire you, Johanna," he murmured. "And never fear, I mean to show you off as you deserve. All our neighbors will be green with envy at our good fortune, and you'll be queen of the feast.''

Two months earlier, the fine clothes and jewels and feasts he was promising would have been the sum of Johanna's dreams. But that was before her life was turned upside down by a golden-haired, hawk-faced knight who snatched her up out of her father's wheat fields. Nicolas de Rochambeau had ended her girlhood in a blaze of desire and anger, and now he didn't know what to do with the woman he had created.

He lifted the heavy mass of golden chains and rubies toward her, and Johanna slapped his hand away without thinking. Half blinded by tears of disappointment, she saw the golden fire of the jewels slither to the floor in a glittering mass.

"Do you think I'm a baby, to be distracted with baubles?" she cried out. "You force me into your bed, you ignore me out of bed, for weeks you've never a word to spare for me, and then when you happen to remember my presence you try to buy my love. You don't know the first thing about love, Nicolas de Rochambeau, and you never will!"

"I know this much," Rochambeau grated out as he rose to his feet, "I'm tired of begging for what ought to be mine by right! Must I lay siege to your heart like our crusaders outside the walls of Jerusalem, praying for entrance to the holy city?"

"An apt analogy! How long has Jerusalem been back in the hands of the infidels now? How many crusaders have failed to win it? Maybe the holy city will fall to a man with sufficient strength and determination, and maybe I'll love a man someday, but you can be sure of one thing, Nicolas de Rochambeau, in neither case will that man be you.''

Rochambeau set the branch of candles down very carefully on the bower floor, with a slow delicacy of movement that frightened Johanna worse than his open blaze of anger. "You seem mightily sure of yourself, madam. Have you forgotten so soon how you lay in my arms those long nights before the harvest? I didn't hear such spitfire pride then. No, you seemed glad enough to have me in your bed."

He caught her by the shoulder and held her while his free

hand ran along her arm, under the long loose sleeve of her tunic, sending unwelcome shivers of desire along her bare skin. Did he thing he could have her this easily? The truth was, he was not far from it. Let him get close to her, and she would be in terrible danger of succumbing once again to his practiced kisses and his relentless lovemaking. He wouldn't stop until he had won, once again, the cries of fulfillment which signified his triumph over her flesh—and then, like all men, he would think the argument over.

"Seemed?" Johanna's unsteady laugh was high and piercing as a curlew's scream. "Aye, *seemed,* my lord! For once you choose your words well. As well as I've played my part in your bed. Did you think I wanted you to touch me? I loathe you as I would any man who forced me so. But my mother instructed me well in how to please a husband, and what she didn't know I practiced with Piers and Gautier."

"You came pure to me!" He was white to the lips.

Johanna laughed again. "There are many sweet games between man and maid, my lord, that leave no mark upon the flesh for a husband to discover." She groped in her memory of half-understood bawdy jokes in her father's hall. "Did you think Piers's lips were only good for singing? You've never sung so sweet a tune as he played upon me. If I pretended ecstasy in your brutish embrace, it was because I knew well what the reality felt like."

He released her so suddenly that she might have fallen. "I'll sleep in the hall tonight. If I stay longer, I might strike you."

"Go ahead!" Johanna taunted him. "It's not so bad, my lord, compared to what you've already done. I prefer your blows to your kisses. I prefer—"

The oaken door that shut off the bower from the head of the hall stairs slammed, cutting off her shrill defiance in midstream. He was gone, and the draft of his passing blew out all but one of the candles that still flickered valiantly from the stone floor where he'd laid them. Johanna sank to her knees on the floor, surrounded by flowing jewel-toned folds of fabrics costly behind her imagining, kneeling in a puddle of gold and rubies. Presently she laid her head on her folded arms and spoiled the purple silk from Damascus with saltwater stains.

* * *

The messenger came in the small hours of the night, thundering on the locked gates of the outer palisade, demanding immediate entrance to my lord Rochambeau in the name of Prince Edward of England. Rochambeau met him at the second gate tower, and they held a hasty meeting there, lit by sputtering torches in the hands of two sleepy squires. Neither the messenger nor the meeting disturbed Johanna's heavy slumbers, all alone in the great chamber on the second floor of the keep.

"Aye, if you must go, you must," Marc agreed when he heard the tenor of the message. "But surely it will keep till morning? The messenger requires rest, and you will wish to take a proper farewell to your lady."

"The messenger can stay overnight and give her my messages in the morning. You'll go tell twenty of my men to ride with me. The rest can stay here to defend the castle. Aubrey will look after affairs until I get back."

"And I'll stay to look after the lady Johanna," Marc pressed.

"You," Rochambeau snapped, "ride with me, as always. The lady Johanna is, believe me, quite well equipped to look after herself."

"And the wedding feast?"

"Will be better celebrated without me." Rochambeau's mirthless death's-head grin made three of his men fall back, crossing themselves. For a moment, in the wavering and uncertain light of the torches, he looked like the old lord of Rochambeau come back to life. They remembered stories from the old baron's time, tales of men flogged till their backbones showed white through the bloody, mangled flesh. The temper of the Rochambeaus was legendary; it was said in Malvern village that you'd do better to raise a demon than to anger a Rochambeau. And for all his smiling ways and generous hand, this lord who'd spent most of his life at the wars had the blood of the old baron in his veins. No one who'd seen his summary ways of dealing with disobedient serfs and disorderly soldiers could doubt that. They privately vowed not to mention the lady of Rochambeau again in my lord's presence.

In the morning Johanna woke to learn that Nicolas de Rochambeau had departed in the small hours of the night, between matins and lauds. The messenger said only that Prince Edward had taken vows to go on the crusade being planned by the French king. The prince wished to speak with Rochambeau before he left; he had commanded my lord to meet him at Dover, where his men were assembling to sail. If there was more than that to my lord's hasty departure, he did not know it. No, my lord had not said when he would be back, although rumor had it that he was very recently married. Doubtless he would not stay away overlong!

This last suggestion was drawled out with a lazy look up and down Johanna's slender figure, a look of admiration so bold that Johanna flushed and forbore to ask any further questions. Doubtless, she reassured herself, Rochambeau would return well before the feast he had planned. Not that she would say one Ave for the return of such a husband, but it would be difficult, to say the least, to entertain unknown neighbors at a wedding feast from which the bridegroom had casually absented himself.

On the day before the feast, when Johanna was up to her elbows in orders to the spicer and the pantler and the larderer's assistant, a second message arrived. This one was brought by a wandering jongleur who freely admitted that he had taken a roundabout route to Malvern, stopping off at every castle or manor or hall that promised a night's food and lodging. Why not? The lord of Rochambeau had not indicated that the matter was especially urgent.

"Oh, hadn't he?" said Johanna between her teeth. She tore open the folded scrap of parchment the jongleur had been carrying in his breast. The heavy wax seal with its emblem of a hawk in flight fell to the floor. When she'd read the message, she ground the wax seal under her foot, slowly and deliberately, and wished it was Rochambeau's face she was grinding into the stones.

"He won't be back," she told Aubrey, who was inconspicuously waiting to hear what word his half-brother and master had sent. "He's decided to join Prince Edward on the crusade. They sailed for Tunis last week."

Aubrey's lounging pose transformed into bolt-upright surprise. "But that's . . . he could be away for months!"

"If he could not find time to attend the wedding feast to

which he himself bid all our neighbors," said Johanna, "then the longer he is away the better, as far as I'm concerned." Head high, she sailed out of the hall, feeling in sore need of a moment of privacy in which to compose herself before she faced the demands of the next few days. Beyond that she could not, dared not, think.

Chapter Eight

THE WISHED-FOR MOMENT of privacy was interrupted even before Johanna reached the safety of her chamber. She was on the stairs leading from hall to bower when the noise of the first arrivals reached her. Sir Ilbod de Marti, his lady, their four daughters, and their grooms and servitors had traveled a long way from their manor at the northern edge of the Marches, and they arrived expecting to spend that night and the next in the hospitality of Rochambeau. As the wagon containing the four unmarried daughters creaked into the outer bailey, Sir Ilbod rode ahead and trumpeted forth his intentions in a hoarse, gravelly voice that carried through the hall and up the stairs where Johanna stood as if frozen. On the morrow they would be ready to well-wish the blushing bride, Sir Ilbod announced, and on the day after they would return to their manor. For the present, he required only lodging for his family and servitors and horses; they would not trouble Rochambeau and his new lady with a visit that evening. Doubtless the young lady was fully occupied in preparing for the feast.

Johanna correctly interpreted this disclaimer as meaning that Sir Ilbod was annoyed not to have been greeted in the courtyard by the lord of Rochambeau and his bride. Cheeks burning, she lifted her skirts and hurried out to say all that was proper in welcoming the de Marti family, while politely evading Sir Ilbod's hints that he expected to see Rochambeau at her side. By the time they were settled in their lodgings, one of those long-nosed, ferret-faced daughters would have found out the truth of the matter. If Sir Ilbod and his lady had any tact at all, they'd forbear inquiring after Rochambeau again.

By dint of paying extravagant attention to Sir Ilbod's youngest and prettiest daughter, a flaxen-haired little girl who reminded Johanna of her own sisters, she was able to avoid answering his wife's prying questions. Following the chamberlain's discreet hint, she settled the family in the upper story of an old keep tower, a large, barren room that had been strewn with fresh rushes and filled with straw pallets in anticipation of the visitors for the feast. Blessings on the hall chamberlain! Johanna had not even thought about the problem of extending hospitality to her guests before and after the feast; she had been thinking solely of how she would get through the banquet itself. Now, by the time she had hurried downstairs again, more guests had arrived. And some of these were not as easily put off as Sir Ilbod had been.

"Called away on the prince's business?" repeated Esclairmonde de Lacy, a plump dowager whose dimpled old face held two eyes as bright and sharp as black glass beads. "Of course, child, we must all obey such a summons, but it seems strange, with no war in the land, that Prince Edward would detain a newly wedded bridegroom so long at his side."

Johanna flushed. "I do not recall mentioning exactly when my lord of Rochambeau departed, my lady."

"No, but I heard it from the bastard Aubrey—I mean your seneschal," the old lady said frankly.

In which case, she had had no need to inquire of Johanna at all and had simply wished to see what revelations she could tease out of her. Johanna curtsied and excused herself on the plea of needing to greet the other guests who arrived close on the lady Esclairmonde's heels.

"It seems strange he should not hurry back to you, child," sniffed Judith, the wife of Leofric of Thonglands. "You are far too young to be entrusted with the management of such a great estate."

"My lord's seneschal, Aubrey, is familiar with the working of the estates," Johanna answered. Turning away to greet another guest, she pretended not to hear Judith's sneer about bastards raised to overhigh places. Johanna privately resolved to see that Aubrey was seated at the high table tomorrow, while Judith and Leofric were squeezed down in humiliating proximity to the silver saltcellar that divided noble from humble.

The men in general accepted her excuses for Rochambeau's absence without question, though Johanna found their repeated comments on the difficulty of leaving such a lovely young pride rather hard to bear. Nicolas de Rochambeau did not seem to have found the parting difficult at all.

The women were more difficult to put off. As the afternoon wore on, Johanna developed a pounding headache and a hearty dislike of her own sex, with their penchant for penetrating questions and embarrassing asides. When, at nightfall, all the overnight guests were settled, and she had seen to the serving of a rere-supper of hot soup and ale, Johanna took her own soup to the bower and settled down among her waiting-women. At least they wouldn't be asking prying questions to find out what had happened between her and Rochambeau. Why should they? They already knew as much as she did.

Just as Johanna was beginning to recover from the stresses of the day, Sir Ilbod de Marti's long-nosed wife, Adelina, swept into the bower without knocking and demanded to inspect Johanna's bowl of soup. Too shocked at the intrusion to fight, Johanna meekly held out her soup to the lady and hated herself for doing so. "Too highly spiced," said Adelina with a single sniff at the bowl.

"I am sorry the food is not to your liking."

Adelina gave a high-pitched titter that reverberated along Johanna's strained nerves like the scrape of a fingernail over polished place armor. "Goodness, I've no complaint for myself, child! But a breeding woman should stay away from spiced foods, which engender dangerous heats in the belly."

"I'm not breeding," snapped Johanna, and she realized too late that she had been baited into volunteering the very information the lady Adelina angled for.

"Indeed? What a pity. There's nothing like a family to keep a man at home where he belongs," said the lady. "Perhaps you will be luckier when Rochambeau returns, although it does seem, from all I hear, that his seed gets few children, even where it's had plenty of opportunity.'' Her sharp, ferrety gaze circled the bower and fixed on one woman, a fair-haired widow named Elfleda whom Johanna already disliked without exactly knowing why. She resolved to ask Aubrey a little more about this Elfleda's antecedents in the morning.

"My mother taught me, my lady, that these matters were best discussed between husband and wife,'' Johanna said politely, rising and retrieving her soup bowl from Adelina's hands. "Now I must beg you to excuse me.''

It was rude, she knew, to retire into the sleeping chamber and shut the door, but it would have been much ruder to follow her first impulse and dump the bowl of soup over Adelina's pointy head. Johanna perched rather disconsolately on a three-legged stool and tried to choke down the cooling soup for which she no longer had much appetite, pretending not to hear Adelina's sharp-voiced questions to the waiting-women.

The banquet on the next day was almost easy by contrast with the previous afternoon. At least she had the night in which to prepare herself. And during the day, the duties of a chatelaine in seeing that the proper hospitality was offered to each of her guests protected Johanna from having to spend a tête-à-tête with any one of them. From Mass in the chapel at sunrise until the feast was prepared at midday, she saw to it that there were constant calls on her attention. By the time the visitors were washing their hands and sitting down at the linen-spread table, she was genuinely too tired to care what embarrassment Rochambeau brought upon her next.

Or so she thought, until the jongleur struck up his newly learned song.

It had seemed only proper to invite him to stay for the feast, in partial recompense for his labor in bringing the message from Rochambeau. Johanna had charged Aubrey with issuing that invitation and with giving the man some coins and one of Rochambeau's old mantles in further payment. She knew it was irrational, but she did not want to see or speak with the jongleur again.

"You're generous,'' Aubrey said. His blue eyes lit with an admiration that should have warmed Johanna, but all she could think was that his look was a pale echo of the one she'd wanted from Rochambeau himself. "Some nobles would have a man flayed who brought such a message, or at least let their hounds upon him to chase him from the bounds of the estate."

"He didn't know what was in the letter," said Johanna wearily. Her head was aching, and already a new batch of guests was below, clamoring for attention. "It's not his fault. And he'll come in handy to entertain our visitors tomorrow. I'm surprised a place of this size doesn't have a resident minstrel."

"Nicolas always preferred to entertain his guests himself."

Johanna nodded. Of course, she should have guessed as much. It was like the man's peacock pride. Not only must he be the best at everything he chose to do, but he had to demonstrate as much to all less gifted mortals. Swordsman, musician, lover, horseman. She had grown heartily sick of hearing and seeing Rochambeau's numerous talents demonstrated!

Now, as the feast drew to a close and the jongleur struck up the old song of King Horn, she was grateful for the impulse that had made her bid him to stay for the feast. No matter that the very sight of the man who'd brought Rochambeau's contemptuously short letter caused a stab of pain to go through her heart. His singing would entertain her guests, if it pleased her not, and would perchance keep them from speculating in her hearing about the true reasons for Rochambeau's disappearance. She knew that such speculation must be going on, and at this point in the feast many of the visitors were too drunk to remember to curb their tongues before Rochambeau's lady. The jongleur would be a welcome diversion.

Unfortunately, the song of King Horn was not quite so welcome.

"Musty old stuff!" decreed one of the squires who sat close to the salt, bringing his wooden mazer down on the table with a crash that splattered drops of strong ale over his companions. "Give us a new tune, minstrel, or hold your peace!"

The jongleur rolled his eyes apologetically and tried three or four other songs, all common currency with minstrels since Johanna's childhood. Clearly his repertoire was not great, nor was his skill. Johanna began to understand why he looked so shabby and half starved. Such an inept entertainer would hardly receive generous hospitality except at the most remote manors, where peasants and lord alike would be too poor to reward him with more than a bowl of soup and a loaf of black bread.

Her heart went out to the frightened little man, now ducking his tousled head as the rowdy squires pelted him with their hard crusts. In a moment someone would think it great sport to set the dogs on him, and then there'd be a brawl such as would do no credit to her hall or hospitality. Already the lady Adelina was sniffing that such manners were what one might expect when the lady of one of the great manors of the kingdom was no more than an untrained, ill-bred girl.

In the last twenty-four hours, Johanna had become adept at not hearing Adelina de Marti's ill-natured asides. She ignored this comment now and rose to command the attention of the squires. At first she could not make herself heard over their drunken shouts. She glanced imploringly at Aubrey, and he leaped down the length of the table to bang a few heads together. Slowly the boys fell silent, and the shabby little jongleur crept out from under the serving table where he had taken refuge.

"My lady, I do have a new song, one I learned but two weeks since from Prince Edward's crusaders at Dover," he volunteered. "But perhaps it is not suitable for a mixed audience?"

Something new was needed, and quickly, before this wedding feast degenerated into an outright brawl. "Go ahead," Johanna told him. "If I judge it unsuitable, I'll tell you to stop." Very likely it would be one of the bawdy trifles that men bawled out to one another at the end of a drinking bout, but no matter; such a song would probably suit the mood of the assembled company better than one of the old epics.

"Aye, sing out!" commanded old lady Esclairmonde in her high, cracked voice. " 'Tis a wedding feast you sing for, minstrel. A little gaiety would not come amiss!" She fell into a fit of laughing and coughing under cover of which Adelina de Marti could be heard to mutter that a girl of sixteen was scarce fit to judge what was or was not decent to hear at a feast.

The jongleur bowed and pushed his thinning strands of black hair across his sweating forehead, attempting to recover his poise. "Well, then, lords and ladies gay, this too is in some sort a wedding song, though the bridal it celebrates is scarcely the sort that would be the lot of the glowing young bride I see!"

A cold shiver of premonition swept through Johanna. Before the jongleur put his hand to the strings of his old-fashioned cittern, she knew that she should not have told him to proceed with his song. The dancing burst of notes that sprang forth under his shaking hands only confirmed what her evil angel had whispered in her ear before he began to play.

The song was the one Rochambeau had been composing before their last quarrel.

And God only knew what words he'd put to it.

A rippling murmur ran through the hall before the jongleur even began to play. "Rochambeau's own song," Johanna heard from one side, and from the other, "So he finally found words befitting his music!"

"But in a crusader camp?" Esclairmonde's voice had the high, thoughtless pitch of old age and deafness. Two of her nephews, seated on either side of her to serve the old lady, tried in vain to hush her. "Did Rochambeau go with the army, then? The bride spoke not of crusades, but only of the young prince's summons . . ."

"Hush, Aunt Esclairmonde," murmured one of the boys. "Don't you want to hear what words Rochambeau put to his own song?"

The jongleur, absorbed in coaxing from the strings of his cittern the melody that flowed almost too swiftly for his stumbling fingers, was oblivious to the stir in the hall. His head had been bent over the cittern, greasy strands of dark hair dropping forward again to expose his bald spot, while he chased after the dancing run of notes that seemed always to be a little ahead of him. Now, sure of the catchy melody, he lifted his head and raised his voice in song.

The song was, as one might expect of something learned in an army camp, short, pointed, witty, and extremely indelicate. It was also very well wrought; words and music fitted together into one unforgettable whole. Anyone who heard the tune would go away whistling it, and anyone who whistled the music would have to remember the words without even trying. But such artistic nuances escaped Johanna on this first hearing, pinioned and exposed as she was by the meaning of the words. In a series of short, pungent, unforgettable phrases, Nicolas de Rochambeau made his reasons for going on crusade abundantly clear. The sands of the Holy Land were warm, he said, while the bed of his bride had proved as cold as the winter sleet that froze the birds' tails to the trees. His own tail was well nigh frozen by the welcome she'd given him, but by God's grace and with the help of a warm-blooded Saracen maid, he hoped to undo the damage.

Johanna herself felt as if alternating bands of fiery iron and pure ice were closing about her body, heat and cold chasing each other through her shaken frame until she could neither move nor speak. Through the red mist of shame and anger that veiled her sight and hearing, she was dimly aware that people were looking at her and murmuring, wondering why she did not stop the song as she'd promised to do if it proved too indelicate. A gesture of her hand would stop the jongleur. But that gesture was beyond her, as was any movement. Perhaps the second verse would reverse the first, would say that it had all been a joke and that Rochambeau was hastening to her side even now. Surely that was what was coming next. No man, however angry, would put such an insult on his own wife in their own hall. It would be a killing matter between them.

The second verse began with a satiric description of the warm welcome the author of the song expected to receive in the Holy Land. The Saracens would be glad to see him, he declared, for they had long been deprived of good fighting. They would welcome him with sharp lances and flights of arrows and well-sharpened swords. Yet such a greeting would be as soft as a maiden's speech to a man whose own lance had been blunted by the greeting he had from his sweet bride. Alas, let the hearers have pity on a poor broken knight whose strength was all unequal to the combats he faced at home, who had to flee to the Holy Land for a little peace in his old age!

Before the verse was over, an irrepressible snicker broke from one of the squires whose foolery had started this incident. Higher up, between the saltcellar and the high dais, Sir Ilbod de Marti spluttered, then guffawed. By the end of the second verse, most of the wedding guests were giggling helplessly into their sleeves, sneaking apologetic glances at Johanna. She could think of nothing to do but stare straight ahead, her smile frozen to her face, and pretend she did not recognize the insult. There was always, she told herself, the slender chance that if she didn't act upset the guests would think the song must not have been aimed at her.

A violent movement broke the spell that held Johanna pinned to her high carved chair. Aubrey had sprung from her side. Picking up one of the laughing squires bodily, he threw him into the jongleur. The cittern cracked with a screech of protest from tortured strings and mangled wood. The little jongleur went down into the ashes of the hearth, and the squire landed on his stomach, still clutching a bowl of meat and broth that splashed all over them both. While the wedding guests broke into unrestrained laughter, two of Rochambeau's hunting dogs that had been snoring by the hearth trotted over and licked the meat broth off the jongleur's greasy head.

"Enough!" Aubrey declared. He stood over the prostrate pair, dusting his hands off with satisfaction. "Be gone, jongleur, and see you come not within these lands again with your lying, canting songs." Striding back up to the high carved chair where Johanna sat, he bowed and offered her his hand. "My lady, I fear you are tired with the strains of the day. Pray allow me to escort you to your chamber. I will see to the comfort of our visitors."

His sympathy was the last straw. Johanna felt her icy composure about to give way to the tears that would shame her forever before all these curious, peering, gossiping strangers, these strangers among whom she had to live out the rest of her life. Clenching one hand into her palm, she laid her other hand on Aubrey's arm and managed one sweeping curtsy to her guests before retreating up the stairs at the end of the hall.

She could not but be grateful for Aubrey's support. Yet she could have wished that he had not shown it in such a dramatic manner. If there were any guests who'd been fooled by her apparent calm into wondering if the song could really be about her, they would wonder no longer. Aubrey's explosion of temper and her own retreat made that quite certain. Before she had reached the head of the stairs, she was regretting her departure from the feast, yet to go back down again at that moment was quite beyond her.

"If you will be all right," Aubrey suggested, "I should go back and say farewell to our guests. I doubt any of them will wish to stay longer."

"I doubt it, too," Johanna agreed.

"And I'll have that scurvy jongleur beaten through the village."

"No, no, don't do that. He didn't know what he was doing!" Johanna all but stamped her foot in vexation at the mulish, blind look she saw on Aubrey's face. "Don't you see, he would never have sung that if he knew it came from Rochambeau. He must have picked it up from some other knight in the camp, never knowing the source. It's not his fault." And here, at least, was one piece of damage she could partially repair. "Wait a moment."

Johanna dropped to her knees in the inner chamber and went through the chest where Rochambeau's best clothes were stored. Serve him right if he'd departed in too much haste to pack, she thought with a glimmer of satisfaction through her misery. She drew out his very finest cloak, a mantle of soft leather trimmed with sooty black fur and ornamented with a collar of glistening sapphires, and held the garment out to Aubrey. "Take this to the jongleur with my compliments. Tell him that after hearing his music, I feel that our original gifts were not sufficient and that my lord would wish him to have this mantle in token of gratitude for the fine entertainment he has offered us. And tell him—oh; say I am sorry that my sudden indisposition made it impossible for me to hear the rest of his repertoire."

"But—but—" Aubrey stammered, holding the black-dyed leather at arm's length. "I don't understand. He should be soundly punished!"

"Then don't understand!" Johanna snapped. "Just do it! And make sure all our dear departing guests hear you! Oh, and if you can hint that I'm indisposed because I'm breeding, that would help too. At least it'll give them something else to talk about!" And they'd all be gone before that particular lie could be exposed.

Aubrey's eyes glazed over with the effort of comprehension.

They seemed pale and dull beside the glitter of the sapphires in the leather cloak he held. "Are you?"

"Just do it," Johanna repeated. "And in God's name, hurry!"

She all but pushed Aubrey out the door, praying that he would get the message right and that he would be in time to undo at least some of the damage caused by the nasty scene in the hall. Oh, she'd been weak to leave like that! But the stunning magnitude of the insult put upon her by Rochambeau had temporarily paralyzed her brain.

It was a killing matter between them now, sure enough. If her father was too craven to defend her, as Johanna guessed he might be, then she would do it herself. Poison or a dagger? Either was too swift. What she really wanted to do was hang Rochambeau over a bed of slow-burning coals, as King John was said to have done to his Jewish moneylenders when he applied for another loan. But it would be difficult to arrange . . .

With a mirthless laugh, Johanna sank down on the wide, soft, empty bed that she and Rochambeau had shared for their few passionate nights together. Any revenge at all would be difficult to manage in the immediate future. By now, the crusaders had already left for the Holy Land—Rochambeau among them. She might have to wait a while before building that slow fire.

In the end, it was to be more than four years before she had an opportunity to humiliate Rochambeau in public as he'd humiliated her. But when the chance came, it was everything she could have asked for, and more.

Johanna had more to do in those four years than brood over her departed husband and the sting of his abandonment of her. She began to take a serious interest in the running of his estates, at first just to give herself something else to think about. As she discovered that her aptitude for reading and ciphering could be translated into a skill at figuring out how many bushels of wheat they should get from an outlying manor or how many suckling pigs a vassal should deliver in payment for his knight service, she began to take some pleasure in following the estate business. It was intellectually absorbing, more fun than the feminine tasks of weaving and baking which her mother had tried to teach her, and best of all, it was a way to show her new neighbors that, barren and deserted wife though she might be, she was yet a power to be reckoned with in the land. When Sir Ilbod de Marti consulted her about ways of getting the best yield from his stony upland acres, or Lady Esclairmonde's two nephews sent her a newly caught peregrine falcon in gratitude for her help with their tangled accounts, Johanna began to feel some of the humiliation of that wedding feast being wiped out.

Finally, as she understood the business of running a great estate better and better, she took the seneschal's tasks entirely into her own hands, for the best of all reasons: Aubrey was clearly incompetent. Charming he might be, devoted to her and Rochambeau he might swear he was, but under his direction manors that had been profitable in the old lord's time were now mysteriously losing money and supplying very little in rents and services. Unable to read Latin herself, Johanna could not decipher Aubrey's accounts to tell just where the problem was, so she borrowed one of the chaplain's assistants to help her with the task. He wrestled with the matter for the best part of two days, grunted and groaned and sprayed himself and the rolls with brownish ink, and finally announced that the Lord had not seen fit to grant him the gift of figures.

"Nor Aubrey either, I suspect," said Johanna, dismissing the man in the midst of his apologies. She had requested him to translate a few passages from the rolls for her, and what he produced bore out her suspicions. The accounts were a garbled collection of mislabeled numbers and mysterious scrawls, not kept in the same format for two seasons running. Clearly Aubrey had wrestled mightily with the problems of managing an honor comprising nearly twenty separate estates with their different rents and customs; equally clearly, he had failed to keep up with the complexity of the task. And he was surprised that she had the brains to read and cipher! Johanna thought with some amusement. No, worse than surprised, unhappy. Well, it was ever so; the men with least wit were most resentful of those who had it. Aubrey's thick head was doubtless better suited to the simplicities of jousts and swordplay than to the complex interrelations which Johanna found in the estate accounts. A pity that his bastard birth debarred him from the honor of knighthood, while his pride in being an acknowledged son of the old lord would have kept him from being happy as a simple squire or man-at-arms. Doubtless Rochambeau had thought to find the ideal solution in giving him the socially ambiguous position of seneschal of the estates; it was a pity it hadn't worked out better.

As tactfully as she could, she took the management of the estates into her own hands, at first using Peter the clerk a little when she needed something translated from the Latin, later keeping her own accounts in plain English. Here she found Aubrey a decided nuisance. Laughingly rueful over the muddle he himself had made of the accounts, he still insisted on hanging over her shoulder while they traveled with the household from one manor to the next, making well-meant suggestions and disrupting her thoughts. When Johanna found him making his own notations in the midst of her carefully kept rolls, and getting the numbers in a hopeless muddle once again, she devised a cipher of her own to use in place of plain English. Thereafter the account rolls looked like a collection of sorcerer's incantations in some unpronounceable foreign tongue, and she had to take extra time every day to work the cipher. But she could read them, Aubrey couldn't interfere, and she had avoided an open confrontation with him over the matter.

Johanna had no wish to insult Aubrey by pointing out his utter incapacity to be any help to her in this matter. He had always been kind to her, though she wished he would not make so many flirtatious suggestions implying his envy of Rochambeau. Of course, she knew he didn't mean her to take him seriously, and she had become adept at laughing off his sallies. But sometimes his game of courting gave her a little pang, when his resemblance to Rochambeau caught her unaware or when dreams of her absent lord troubled her sleep.

They were not totally without news of Rochambeau in those quiet years. In the spring after the crusaders' departure, word was brought that Prince Edward and his small force of a thousand men had landed at Tunis only to find that King Louis, the moving force behind the crusade, had died and his son was taking the main crusading army home again without ever meeting the infidel.

"He'll have to come home now," the waiting-woman Elfleda predicted, with a languishing look toward the east and a hand caressing her flaxen tresses.

"Will he?" Johanna snipped off the end of a dangling thread and set another stitch into the tapestry she had begun. She had as little liking for needlework as ever, but as her household grew she needed the produce of the home looms and the sewing of her own women to supplement the cloths bought from merchants for the yearly liveries. And she had found that where the mistress did not supervise, the work was ill done. So, as Gwynne had predicted, she must sit with the gossiping women and prick her fingers with a needle.

Somehow she was not surprised to learn that Price Edward had declared his intention of going on to conquer the Holy Land even if he had no companions but his groom Fowin; and she was even less surprised to learn that the one thousand crusaders who went with him had vowed to follow him, trying to do with a thousand men what a hundred thousand had failed to do in earlier years.

"If they're all of Rochambeau's temperament, each one thinks himself the equal of a hundred ordinary men," she commented, and went doggedly on with her tapestry.

"In his case," murmured Elfleda, "it's true." Her pale eyes rolled heavenward, and she sighed as though remembering secret delights.

Johanna drove the needle into her thumb and made a mental note, while she sucked away the spot of blood that appeared, to see if she couldn't dower the widow Elfleda to a good second marriage. Coluin the blacksmith had taken to hanging about the courtyard when she appeared; perhaps he'd like to take the woman and, with her, enough money to start his own smithy in the village. Outside the castle. Away from Johanna's bower.

In the next year, they heard that Edward and Baibars had made a truce and that the prince had already sailed for Sicily with his followers. He was there when the sad news reached him: King Henry was dead, and Edward was ruler of England.

"Now they must all come home," said Aubrey.

"Will they?"

Over the next two years the crusaders did indeed come straggling home, a few at a time. Johanna let it be known that any of the manors belonging to the honor of Rochambeau would be happy to offer hospitality to returning crusaders.

"It's a vow I have made," she told the priest of each village owing service to the honor. "For my husband's sake."

Many a tired knight or purse-pinched squire was happy to take advantage of the offer, and in this way Johanna heard news of Prince Edward and his companions, often before that same news reached London. From all accounts, the young prince—for king he was not, not till he was crowned—was in no hurry to return to England. While his ministers ruled in his name, he tarried in Rome, jousted in France, and made a side trip to punish a rebellious vassal in Gascony. Then, at last, the bells rang in London and at Dover. In August of 1274, four years after his departure, Prince Edward returned to take up his crown.

Rochambeau did not return with him. And this time Johanna's news came not from a footsore returning warrior but from a messenger sent directly by her absent lord, the first such messenger she had received in four years.

That morning she was presiding over the manor court at Ainscourt. The household was preparing to move on to Malvern, which had become Johanna's favorite of Rochambeau's many residences. Most of her women had already left, riding on the slow four-wheeled carts that carried the heavy baggage of bedding and portable furniture from one manor to the next whenever the household moved on. In a few days Johanna and Aubrey, with the few officials who traveled with them—chamberlain and wardrober and marshal of the stables—would set off on horseback. They would probably reach Malvern at the same time as the slow-moving carts. Meanwhile, there were a few cases yet to be heard in the great hall. The villeins crowded into the long room, now stripped of its tapestries and other furnishings. Their voices echoed off the rafters, and the smell of their infrequently washed woolen garments rose higher and higher in the warm room.

When the messenger demanded entrance, Johanna was nodding off over a long and complicated argument between Aylwin Godwin's son and Hugh de Leofric about whose beasts had first grazing right on the strip of common between their holdings. The matter would not be decided by her but by the jurors who had been chosen from the tenants of the village. But custom of the manor, that iron chain that bound lord and freeman and villein and serf in an unbreakable sequence of rules, decreed that the lord of the manor or his seneschal should personally hear each and every such argument.

The entrance of a man in Rochambeau's personal livery, dusty and tired from a punishingly long ride, was a welcome diversion. Johanna's eyes brightened when the interruption occurred, sparkling with anticipation when she recognized the messenger. "Fulke d'Evroul?" He'd been little more than a chubby page when he'd left in Rochambeau's train; now he was a man with battle scars to prove his experience. But there was no mistaking the sharp nose and chin of a d'Evroul, nor the mop of curly red hair that burst out from under his helm. He held himself straight and proud and announced himself as Rochambeau's second squire, under old Marc. Johanna was glad to hear that Marc had survived the vicissitudes of the crusade, but she wished Fulke would get to the point.

"You bring news of my lord?" For the moment she forgot all her old and carefully nursed grudges. All she could think of was that Rochambeau might even now be on the road to her. Would he stride in and take her in his arms as though they'd never quarreled? Or would they fence with each other like cats in strange territory? She didn't know what to expect, but the rapidly beating pulses at her neck and wrists were sign enough of what her love-starved body anticipated.

"I do, my lady." Johanna meant to beckon Fulke into a private room where she could give him some refreshment while she heard his news, but before she could do so he had blurted it out before the assembled peasantry. "My lord was captured during the fighting in Gascony. He commands you to send his ransom, in the sun of one hundred and fifty marks, to Joscelin d'Avranches in Gascony."

Fulke paused uncertainly. A moment ago, as he pushed his way into the hall, he had been greeted by a living, breathing, warm, excited woman with tendrils of black hair curling around her flushed cheeks and setting off the emerald sparkle of her slanted green eyes. Now that same woman seemed to have turned into a statue, cold and hard as an ivory carving.

The only sign of life was in the rapid rise and fall of her breast and the dangerous light in her eyes.

"Is there no more message than that?" Her voice was quiet and low, an excellent quality in a decent woman; Fulke couldn't have said why it sent shivers down his spine. But then, this lady Johanna was hardly a decent woman. Look at her now, sitting in my lord's high seat in the manor court, dispensing justice and collecting fines as though she, not Rochambeau, were lord of the manor! From the lofty height of his nineteen years, Fulke disapproved of such uppity ways in women and vowed privately that his own wife, when the time came, would be properly meek and biddable. The resolution did nothing to make the lady Johanna look less intimidating as she waited, imperious as a queen, for his answer.

He swallowed and added the last word of the message he'd memorized before Joscelin's men escorted him to the boundaries of the Avranches estate. "Immediately."

Johanna sat quite still while she absorbed the insulting content of the message. So! After abandoning her for four long years, Rochambeau thought he need do no more than send his commands for her to perform immediately. These were words for a servant, not for a wife. Her long-nourished grudges against the man rose up like a choking cloud in her throat, filling her with bitter words that she must either spit out or be poisoned by.

"Only one hundred and fifty marks for a great baron! It seems Joscelin d'Avranches does not set a very high value on my dear lord. Nonetheless," Johanna went on, raising her voice slightly so that it carried over the uneasy murmur of the huddled peasants in the hall, "it is a higher value than I am pleased to give him. Pray return to my lord Rochambeau, Fulke, and tell him that I am well content to live alone and to take all the responsibility of managing his estates, as I have done these four years. He has been in no hurry about returning to take up his duties here; he should not expect me to be so hasty about arranging his ransom."

"B-but—if I return empty-handed—when will you send the ransom, my lady?" Fulke stammered.

"Approximately two weeks after hell freezes over!"

As the peasants' murmur grew into an outright babel of

surprised comment, as Aubrey reached out to catch Johanna's sleeve, she stood up and swept out of the great hall with no concern for messenger, manor court, or anything else except the satisfaction of finally, after all these years, having had a chance to show Rochambeau exactly what he was worth to her.

Chapter Nine

Malvern, 1274

As JOHANNA NEARED the end of the long, unhappy tangled tale that lay between her and Nicolas de Rochambeau, the misty figures before her eyes swirled into nothingness, and she became aware once again of her surroundings: the stone walls of the bower at Malvern, the skeins of wool flung helter-skelter about the room, the brightly colored piles of cloth to be cut out for the Michaelmas liveries. Alais was sitting at her feet. As Johanna's voice died away, the girl stirred slightly.

"Heavens, child, what am I thinking of, to sit and gossip so long! You must be dying of the cramp! Take a stool, for heaven's sake! Or, no, why don't we sit in the inner chamber, where that pig of a man hasn't made such a mess? I never meant that we should sit in this disaster of a bower all afternoon!"

The low slant of the light that gilded the eastern walls showed that the sun was about to sink down below the Welsh hills to the west. Johanna was appalled to find how easily the afternoon had slipped away, how strongly the memories of Rochambeau came back to her once she let herself go. She shouldn't have taken that dangerous plunge back into the past. Rochambeau was here now, very present and very dangerous to her hard-won independence and peace of mind. She should have been making preparations against whatever trick he thought of next, though just what preparations, she couldn't say.

How did you guard against such a man, when you never knew from what angle he'd come at you next? There was only one thing sure about Nicolas de Rochambeau, Johanna thought with a wry smile, only one path you could be certain he'd not take, and that was the simple, straightforward one of treating her like another human being with needs, desires, and will. He'd bully, trick, cajole, or wager, but never would he simply talk with her and find out what she wanted. She gave a sharp sigh and sank down again on the bench of the great loom, hands twisting idly in her lap. Once again, as always when Rochambeau was around, she seemed to be waiting on his pleasure.

"Well." Alais drew a shaky breath and straightened out her cramped legs. "I certainly understand why you wouldn't want to ransom him. But maybe it would have been better— I mean, since he's back anyway—and now he's so angry?" Her voice quavered uncertainly on the last word.

"Oh, I did send the ransom," Johanna said calmly. "I just didn't want to give him the satisfaction of thinking I'd jump to his bidding like a servant—or a wife who's been beaten into submission."

Had she ever seriously contemplated leaving Rochambeau in his enemy's hands? If so, it was only for a few minutes. Before Aubrey had cleared the manor court of people, Johanna had known she couldn't abandon him like that. In the first place, she didn't believe any castle walls could hold Rochambeau if he didn't want to be held. He would be back, ransom or no, and she didn't even want to think about the temper he'd be in if she really withheld his ransom. No, she'd had the revenge she wanted by showing in open manor court just how little she cared for him. The story would be told for years. The peasants would snicker wherever he rode on his own estates: the great lord couldn't be so great a lover if his wife didn't even want him back!

And in the second place? Johanna shook her head, trying to shut out the wanton images that had sprung to her mind as soon as she saw Fulke, when she thought for one dazzled moment that Rochambeau himself was about to ride into the manor courtyard. No, it couldn't be that she missed him and wanted him back; it was just that she missed having a man in her bed. She should have taken a lover years ago—that would really have shown Rochambeau what she thought of him—only for some reason she couldn't stomach the thought.

No, she didn't want him back, she told herself. She was just looking forward to the opportunity to show him, in person, how little she needed him.

"The money came from the sale of hunting rights in Ainscourt woods to the abbot of Saintsbury," she told Alais. "I thought that was fair. Let Rochambeau's pleasures pay for Rochambeau's mistakes! I didn't want to take it from the ordinary income of the estates; it's taken me long enough to repair the damage Aubrey's carelessness did."

Before his marriage, Rochambeau was often absent and demanded only money from the estates, enabling Aubrey to fall into slipshod practices. Johanna hadn't been able to trace the precise flow of money through his tangled accounts, but he had explained to her that Rochambeau drained most of the ready cash from the estates, leaving him insufficient income to see to necessary repairs and upkeep. Johanna couldn't hold Aubrey entirely blameless in this matter; as seneschal of the estates, he should have seen to it that such matters as new roofs and sluice dams were paid for first, before he filled Rochambeau's hands with silver. And having criticized him thus, if only in her own mind, she could hardly repeat the mistake the first time Rochambeau demanded money from her.

It had taken a few days to arrange for the sale of the hunting rights. When the business was concluded, Johanna had pressed the gold into Aubrey's hand and had requested him to find a reliable man to take it to Gascony, one of the men from his own employ, if possible; she didn't want it to be seen publicly that she had anything at all to do with the ransoming of Nicolas de Rochambeau. Let the world think that Rochambeau could have rotted in prison for all his wife cared; only the three of them would know the truth.

"But then, if you did ransom him after all," said Alais, "I don't understand. Why is he so angry?"

"He didn't wait to be ransomed," Johanna said dryly. "Fulke, with my message, must have reached Gascony before Aubrey's man could get there with the money. Rochambeau broke out of Avranches without my help, some of his men got killed in the process, and he is not very pleased with me."

"But surely if you explained?"

"Explain!" Johanna's temper flared up. "I, Johanna Lespervier de Pomeray, am to humble myself to *explain* to this man who bought me like a piece of property? Perhaps you'd like me to go down on my knees to him and sue for pardon while I'm at it!"

"That will not be necessary, madam wife," said a deep, unmistakably masculine voice behind her. "I require only that you scrub my back."

Both women whirled around to discover Rochambeau standing in the doorway of the bower. "I've been riding around the manor," he announced—unnecessarily, in view of the mud splashes that decorated his legs and the strong smell of horse that arose from his person. "I've given orders for hot water and a tub to be brought to our chamber, wife. You can give me a bath, and then we'll have a nice little supper in private and enjoy our reunion."

"A bath!"

Rochambeau paused in the act of stripping off his muddy gauntlets. "You've heard of the custom, surely? Even in England I believe it is not totally unknown, though I must grant the Saracens are much more cleanly in their persons than we English. And the Saracen girls!" He gave a blissful sigh as though words failed him. "Did you know they sprinkle essences of perfumed oils in their bathwater? And they burn braziers of incense on the floor and stand over the braziers so that the smoke scents their—"

"We've no desire to hear about these heathenish customs." Johanna cut him off sharply before he could embarrass Alais further. "If you wish to bathe, I suggest you call a squire to attend you. I certainly have no intention of playing the meek little wife to your bidding!"

Rochambeau shrugged and pulled off his embroidered surcoat, dropping the gaudy, muddy garment in a crumpled ball on the floor. Two of the hall usher's assistants staggered in bearing the large wooden tub.

"Put that in my chamber," Rochambeau directed them. He unfastened the brooch that held his short riding tunic together at the neck and yanked that garment over his head, exposing a chest tanned by the sun and wind of the Holy Land and scarred by new marks since Johanna had last seen his body. As his fingers went to the drawstring of his short linen underdrawers, Alais shrieked and covered her eyes. Johanna noticed that her fingers were not completely closed; she'd left space enough to peep through.

"My lord, I must beg you to refrain from shocking my waiting-woman!"

"Send the chit away," Rochambeau advised, grinning. "I mean to be private with you, dear wife. We have a lot to catch up on between us, do we not?"

"Private!" A train of servitors was crossing and recrossing the bower, carrying buckets of steaming water which they dumped into the wooden tub in the inner chamber. Quite a lot of the water was spilling on the floor, as the servitors were looking at the lord and lady of Rochambeau instead of watching where they were going.

"You have developed a strange habit of parroting my words," Rochambeau remarked. "Is there anything so strange in a long-separated husband's desire to be reunited with his wife?" He tugged again at the linen drawstring, and Alais shrieked and fled.

"In this case, yes! Did you really think I'd share your bed again?" Johanna couldn't take her eyes off the bronzed, muscled, white-scarred expanse of Rochambeau's chest. They had only been together for a few short weeks. Why was it that she could remember in such torturing detail exactly how that golden fuzz of crisp hair had felt pressed against her own naked breasts? Her nipples tingled with memory or anticipation and she felt a treacherous, gathering warmth between her thighs as Rochambeau came toward her.

"I don't recall mentioning bed," he said, taking her arm in an iron grip. "Only bath. Although it's true one thing sometimes leads to another, and most pleasantly, as the Saracen slave girls sent by my lord Baibars to Prince Edward were fond of demonstrating. You might take a lesson from them, my dear wife. I'll be happy to teach you what they showed me about that art of pleasing a man."

"I want no such lessons from you!" Johanna spat at him. "Nor do I need them."

"What, have you been educating yourself since I left? I'll have to judge of that for myself."

The bench of the great loom was hard behind her knees. Rochambeau's hand held her arm. She moved her head backward as he bent toward her, unable to escape the tantalizing contact of his hard thighs against her legs. His bare chest pushed her backward even farther, and his lips covered hers. Breath and sense deserted her at that first touch, so much more powerful than all the memories and dreams that had tantalized her night after night since his departure.

Her mouth opened slightly beneath his, and when the tip of his tongue demanded entrance she felt as though a fiery power coursed through her whole body, weakening her until she no longer had any hope of withstanding him. Rochambeau's free hand slipped behind her head, supporting her as he bent her back over the loom bench until only his hold was keeping her upright. One of his legs thrust between hers, forcing an intimate quiver of desire that was too strong for her to bear in silence. When she moaned and returned the pressure of his kisses, he stepped back suddenly and jerked her upright again.

"Oh, I think you want my lessons, my dear lady," he said, grinning. "I think you'll enjoy the schooling more than you admit. But do, pray, contain your ardors until we are alone together."

The train of water carriers had slowed their pace to a mere shuffle, gaping and doubtless storing up every word to be retold downstairs. Johanna stared past Rochambeau into the goggling eyes of a boy of fourteen whom she dimly remembered having seen downstairs, assisting the butler. Dear God, was every underservant in the castle of Malvern using this bath as a pretext to shuffle through her rooms? The thought made her angry enough to withstand Rochambeau.

"Alone together!" She pushed at his bare chest. "That will never be, my lord, unless you force me. I had rather take the veil and be the bride of Christ than share your bed again."

"Unfortunately for Christ," said Rochambeau, his hand closing over her upper arm so hard that she winced with pain, "I have a prior claim. Your marriage vows, my lady, do not leave you the option of denying me your bed. Or any other service that I may desire you to perform! Now, you may begin by kneeling behind the tub and scrubbing my back. Later on," he said with a distinct leer, "I'll doubtless think of more interesting things for you to do for me."

"Think as you like, my lord!" Johanna clawed unavailingly at his face; he caught her wrists and held them together, laughing in a way that only infuriated her further. "I vow that thinking is the only pleasure you will get of me. Did you think I'd nothing better to do these four years than wait for you to graciously return to the marriage bed? I've no more need of you, my lord Rochambeau, than you have of me!"

"Ah, but I have a most definite need of you," he said, forcing the lower part of his body against hers so that she could feel the risen hardness of him.

There was a muffled snicker from the butler's boy. With the last of her strength, Johanna pushed Rochambeau away. She was surprised at how easily he released her, now that she was fighting him in earnest.

"Then you'd best find one of those Saracen slave girls to satisfy your needs. Or perhaps one of the pretty boys would be more to your liking," she taunted him. "I've no need to hear any more about the perversions you learned in the Holy Land, my lord. If you force me to your bed, it will be no more than a rape. Such a triumph for the man who fancies himself a great lover because he can seduce innocent young girls or peasants with no escape from him! It's time you learned that a real woman has no use for you and your perverted tricks!"

"There will be no rape, madam!" Rochambeau shouted back. Grabbing his tunic from the floor, he pulled it back on and fumbled with the brooch at the neck. The sapphire-encrusted silver front of the brooch slid back to reveal a tiny box of glass and silver, holding a sliver of bone. "By this saint's relic that I brought back from the Holy Land, I vow that I will not come to your bed again until you yourself invite me there!"

He'd been loud enough that not only the boys carrying water but half the castle staff in the hall heard him. Now he lowered his voice and bent his head toward her, adding words that were meant only for the two of them. "And I'll add a prediction to my vow, my lady. I won't have long to wait!" He wheeled and was gone before she could think of a fitting insult with which to reply. The water carriers trailed out disconsolately after him, leaving Johanna alone to stare at the puddles of mud and water on the floor. In the inner chamber, the hot water with its sprinkling of rose petals steamed invitingly, mute witness to the pleasant time she and Rochambeau could have shared if only he had asked like a gentleman, instead of storming in and demanding his rights like a bully.

Johanna closed the bower door before Alais could come back. She didn't feel like dealing with the child just then. Frowning slightly, she wandered into the bedchamber and stood for a long time looking down at the bathtub with its swirling pattern of rose petals and dried herbs to scent the water.

As her anger cooled, she found herself thinking that there'd been something rather strange about the quarrel they'd just had. Something that didn't ring quite right in her memory. Something different from Rochambeau's usual style.

"The only thing different," she muttered to herself, "was that Rochambeau doesn't usually lose so easily."

Nor did he usually come on so crudely. Had he lost his charm in the Holy Land? There was a time when, if he'd wanted to share bath and bed with Johanna, he would have cajoled her into the inner chamber so gently that she'd have been naked in the tub with him before she knew what was happening to her. Time and time again he'd demonstrated his ability to wring that response from her body, even in the early days of their marriage when she'd been an inexperienced girl with fresh cause to hate him. Now, after he'd already taught her the delights of sensuality, after she'd slept for four years in a cold bed . . .

Johanna sighed and admitted to herself that now Rochambeau would have found it easier than ever to seduce her if he'd gone about it in the old gentle, charming way. In fact, she half regretted that he'd failed to do so. The sight of his half-naked body, the grinding kiss he'd forced on her, had been just enough to remind her of the piercing sweetness their bodies had shared, even when their minds had been least in accord. Was she never to know that sweetness again? There'd been lonely nights enough, in these last four years, when she'd raged against her fate—deserted by her husband, not free to marry again, and for some reason too squeamish to take a casual lover as did so many ladies in like circumstances.

Rochambeau, of course, hadn't been sleeping alone for the last four years. His teasing comments about the Saracen girls had made that abundantly clear. So perhaps he didn't feel the same aching need that now filled every crevice of Johanna's body. But in that case, why storm in and make his impossible demands in front of half the servitors of the castle, shaming her and goading her until she was almost forced to reply in kind? One would almost think he'd wanted this quarrel.

"And Rochambeau," whispered Johanna to herself, "always gets what he wants." If they'd quarreled publicly, then that was the end he'd been aiming for. Not to get her into bed with him—to get her to insult him and rant at him like a peasant. But why would he want to make a public show of their marital differences?

The answer to that was almost chillingly clear. He had just goaded her into denying him his marital rights, loudly and publicly. The church was very clear on that point. Refusal on the part of either husband or wife to pay what was euphemistically called the marriage debt was a sin; if the parties involved were rich and powerful enough to get the pope's favor, it could even be considered grounds for annulment.

Rochambeau was certainly rich and powerful and well connected, and while he and Prince Edward were in Rome he must have made friends with a number of highly placed churchmen. Doubtless one of them had suggested to him this way of ridding himself of a hot-tempered wife of whom he'd already tired.

"Well, good!" Johanna clenched her fists. "That suits me perfectly well! There's nothing I'd like better than to be free of that brute. Then I could seek a husband more to my liking."

She bent over the brimming tub of bathwater, looking anxiously at her reflection. Was she still beautiful? The face that looked back at her—with cheeks and lips still burning from Rochambeau's kisses, black curls framing her head, green eyes alight from within—was surely beautiful enough to get her any husband she might desire. The froth of pink rose petals on the surface of the water gathered like a garland over her head, floated across her reflected neck, and set off its porcelain whiteness.

But, for no reason at all, the silly girl in the reflection seemed to be crying.

Chapter Ten

Nicolas de Rochambeau was whistling under his breath by the time he reached the bottom step of the stairs leading from bower to hall. The slam of the bower door behind him seemed not to disturb his equanimity, nor did the fascination with which some thirty pairs of eyes followed his jaunty progress across the hall. At the outer door, he stopped to speak to the chamberlain.

"If all these people have nothing better to do than gape in the hall," he said, "my manor is sorely overstaffed."

Before he'd finished speaking there was a general exodus. Rochambeau grinned and raised his hand to his half-brother, who was waiting in the shadows by the unlit hearth. "Aubrey! Come and help me inspect the mews."

As they left the cool shade of the hall, a buzz of conversation and speculation rose behind them. Rochambeau paid no attention to the sound, though Aubrey glanced over his shoulder several times. Alternately humming snatches of an old tune and making pleasant conversation about trivialities, Rochambeau led his half-brother toward the mews as though he had nothing on his mind but the chance to visit his long-neglected hawks.

Once inside the mews, Aubrey anticipated that the storm would break. From the shouts and screams that had been heard upstairs, it was fair to guess that both the lord and the lady of Rochambeau had quite thoroughly lost their tempers.

It would be strange indeed if Rochambeau were really so calm as he now appeared! But his younger brother said not a word about the fight. He wandered about the sun-speckled interior of the mews, observing the condition of the hawks, tightening a pair of jesses here, slightly raising a hood there. Mostly he just moved slowly about the building, hands behind his back, humming to himself and giving an occasional nod of approval to the hawkmaster.

"Clean," he approved. "And I see you give them good fresh food. Mutton, fresh fowls—what's this?"

"Eels, my lord. The lady Johanna commanded they be brought from the river once a week to vary the birds' diet."

Rochambeau nodded and glanced at the floor of the mews. "Plenty of grit and gravel, I see, and the castings are a good color. And clean water in the tubs for them to bathe themselves. I see I am well served, better than a man might expect who's been gone for four years!" He had expected to have to reform the order in the mews and stables, even if Johanna had learned to run the household efficiently; but so far he had found nothing to criticize.

The hawkmaster bowed, hands shaking with relief, and mumbled that the lady Johanna had been accustomed to oversee the keeping of the mews herself, visiting daily when she was in residence at Malvern.

A quick frown marred the smooth contentment of Rochambeau's face. "Hardly a task for a lady!" He could not have said why he felt displeased at this news, but he was beginning to feel that Johanna had circumvented him at every turn. The stables, too, were in perfect order. Couldn't she fail at one little thing so that he could feel his presence was needed here at Malvern?

"Now, Nicolas," said his brother pacifically, "many ladies enjoy hawking—though I must admit, few show such devotion as your wife!" He attempted to smother a laugh. "Good Father Osmund threatened her with excommunication once for carrying her new peregrine falcon to Mass as though it were a favorite child!"

"And very proper, too," said Rochambeau at once. "A hawk shouldn't be separated from its owner during the training period. I should think you'd know that, Aubrey. Although . . . where did she get a peregrine? It's not a lady's bird."

Aubrey shrugged slightly. "I believe one of Esclairmonde de Lacy's nephews gave it to her. Both lads have been . . . frequent visitors . . . in your absence."

If Rochambeau noticed the slightly strained tone that indicated Aubrey was holding something back, he gave no sign of it. "Oh, well, if she can handle a peregrine, I suppose there's no objection. But I fail to see the necessity for my wife to concern herself personally with the sweeping of the mews and the provision of fresh game for the birds."

"Oh, the lady concerns herself personally with a great deal more than you'd expect!" said Aubrey with a slightly bitter laugh. On seeing the slight frown that crossed his younger brother's face, he hastened to reassure him. "I meant no slight, Nicolas. You wanted her to grow up and act as the lady of the manor, did you not? She's done that. Perhaps to a greater extent than you ever anticipated. I must confess, when you left for the crusade, I hardly expected to see a girl in her teens sitting in your high seat at the manor court and taking management of the estate accounts out of my hands!" Another laugh, as if to indicate that he did not mean his words to be taken too seriously.

Rochambeau's frown became two deeply chiseled lines between his brows. "Nor did I. I was under the impression that I had left you in charge of the estate management, Aubrey. How did this change come about?"

Aubrey shrugged and spread his hands. "Perhaps the young lady was bored with our quiet life here on the manor. We have few amusements besides hunting and hawking and occasional visitors, and she was young when you left. It's only natural if she cast a longing eye on the gaiety of court life. There was no one here to make sonnets in praise of her eyebrows!"

He paused and cleared his throat, peering at Rochambeau's shadowed face. "I must admit that I am partly at fault, Nicolas. Fearing lest she run off to London once again, I sought to interest her in matters of the estate."

"You would say that my wife is a giddy girl with no more sense than to desert her home for the pleasure of an adulterous flirtation with some London gallant."

"Oh, no. I'm sure it was not so bad as that. But she was young, Nicolas, and as for desertion . . . well, there were those here who were quick to whisper in her ear that you were to blame, having in some sort deserted her first. I did but seek to distract her from such malicious whisperings as might tempt her away from her duty." Aubrey gave an embarrassed laugh. "I took her around the manors with me on the yearly tour of inspection, thinking the change of pace might amuse her. I fear it amused her all too well!"

"What do you mean by that?" Rochambeau's scowl grew thunderously foreboding. "Do you imply she had secret meetings? A lover on one of the other manors?"

Aubrey spread his hands again. "I'm sure there was nothing of that sort," he said, but his voiced tailed off uncertainly at the end of the sentence. "It would have been most unseemly, and in any case I was with her nearly all the time. At least, on that first round of inspection. Later, of course . . ." He bit his lip. "No, no, Nicolas, you mustn't accuse her of such things. There's not a soul on Malvern but would swear she's been a good and virtuous wife to you all these years. I meant only that the young lady is pleased to vaunt herself on her skill at ciphering. She can read and write, too—not Latin, of course—but she's mightily proud of such little learning as she's managed to pick up. She more or less insisted on taking the account rolls into her own hands."

Rochambeau's blue eyes glinted as hard as the blue sapphires set into the brooch at his neck. "Are you saying that you let a child of—what was she then, seventeen?—bully you into resigning your charge as seneschal of the estates?"

Aubrey shrugged slightly. "She was your lawful wife, my lord. Many women manage their husband's estates when the man is away. She had the right, if she insisted on it. And I thought it would please you little to come back and find us embroiled in a suit at law over the management of your estates."

"In that, at least, you were correct," said Rochambeau.

"I thought it better," Aubrey rushed on, "to stay here and offer her whatever help she was not too proud to take from me. I hoped to keep her from doing too much damage in her inexperience. She did need an older and wiser counselor, Nicolas, little though she liked to admit it."

"And have you managed," inquired Rochambeau with just

the faintest shade of irony, "to preserve the estates from ruin at the hands of my child bride?"

Aubrey flushed painfully. "I've done what I could. In these last years she's kept the accounts very much under her own hand. But I talk with the reeves of the manors, and where there's been unrest or discontent I do what I can to keep matters under control."

"But, of course, you can tell me nothing of how the financial matters of the estates stand."

Aubrey shook his head. "She keeps the accounts in a cipher now."

"The devil you say!"

"No, your wife. There is a difference, you know."

Rochambeau ignored the feeble jest. "And you couldn't figure it out? Come now, Aubrey. I find it hard to believe that a woman would be able to devise a code you couldn't see through. Doubtless it's a simple matter of substituting one letter for another, like the secret messages that boys send one another under their tutor's eye."

"I took it as a sign," said Aubrey simply, "that she considered my well-meant offers of help to be meddling in what she construed to be solely her own business. As I explained before, Nicolas, I did think it best to avoid an open break. The lady is very strong-willed."

"So I have observed," said Rochambeau dryly. "Well, no matter. I took the rolls away from her just now, and I'll go over them at my leisure. She can hardly argue that it's not *my* business. As for the financial standing of the estates, at least I'm already prepared for the unpleasant news that I'll doubtless find confirmed in the accounts. I can only assume that matters are very bad indeed, since she evidently found it impossible to raise the hundred and fifty marks for my ransom."

"Oh, that wasn't because—" Aubrey bit his lip and swallowed the end of his sentence with a visible effort.

"Do go on," Rochambeau urged him. "You meant to say, I presume, that the lady Johanna would have had no difficulty in finding this sum of money, had she wished to obey my commands in the matter of the ransom?"

"She *should* have had no difficulty," said Aubrey in a strangled voice. Like one grasping at straws, he went on,

"But you said yourself, one can't tell what condition the finances of the estate are in now. It's not inconceivable that an inexperienced young girl could have frittered away most of the ready cash on unnecessary expenses, leaving her embarrassed when you demanded a sum equal to a quarter of the year's income—or what should have been a quarter of the income when the estates were well managed. Yes, I'm sure—I'm almost sure that's why she . . ." His voice trailed off under Rochambeau's keen-eyed stare.

"Why she refused, in open manor court, even to make any attempt to raise the money for my ransom?" Rochambeau inquired with gentle irony. "Why she announced before a mixed assemblage of knights, officials, servants, and villeins that she would be very well pleased if I should languish in captivity forever?"

Aubrey's tunic of soft green woolen seemed to have grown two sizes too small for his well-built frame. He tugged at the gold-embroidered neck lacings without uttering a word.

"Tell me, Aubrey." Rochambeau's quiet voice held a menace behind the soft words. "You were at that manor court, I believe. Are the reports I heard true? Did she really flout me so, before all my people?"

Aubrey gulped, yanked at his neck lacings, and looked desperately around the shadowy mews, eyes darting from one corner to another like a captured mouse seeking shelter from the hawks.

"M-my lord. Nicolas," he managed with a sickly smile. "What profits it us to think of matters long past? Surely it is time that you and your lady should make a new beginning. And there's no need for you to trouble yourself with the rolls. Let me have them, and tell her it's your will I should be seneschal of the estates again in future. I'll soon have your lands back on their old footing, and there will be no need for you to be annoyed with looking at the mistakes she's made."

Rochambeau regarded his bastard brother with a very slight smile on his lips. "But Aubrey, if you couldn't break Johanna's cipher in all this time, what makes you think you can do it now?" He strolled to the door of the mews, where the last golden rays of the setting sun streamed in to create a dusty halo around his head. "No, brother. Let's to supper. I'm sharp set, having traveled all day and for many days before.

We'll make that new beginning over a good meal, and to-night—or perhaps the next day," he amended with a smile, "I'll see to this childish cipher of hers."

Aubrey nodded, but he looked somewhat doubtful. "She's been used to having everything in her own hands," he warned. "She may not take it well if you try to change things too fast."

"I'm not concerned with what the lady has been used to," said Rochambeau. "Now that I'm home, I do not intend to allow matters to go on as they have in my absence."

The grim statement had the tone of a warning. "I just hope you don't expect me to tell the lady that!" Aubrey laughed.

"I don't expect you to tell her anything." Rochambeau glanced at his half-brother; the effect of his blue gaze was that of a falcon marking its prey. "Or to warn her of anything. I'll deal with this matter in my own way, in my own time."

"And if *that* wasn't a warning," murmured Aubrey beneath his breath as the lord of the manor went off to his supper, "I don't know one when I hear it. All right, Nicolas. You deal with the lady—and I wish you joy of her!"

The normally simple meal of supper had been augmented on Johanna's orders by a number of more elaborate and highly spiced dishes usually reserved for feast days. Rochambeau's hints about a cozy little meal in their private chamber had not been lost on her. She still hadn't figured out exactly what his plans were, but one thing was sure: whatever he wanted her to do, she would do the exact opposite. If he meant to tease her into another quarrel for some reason, she would be careful to keep their conversation general and public, bringing Aubrey and Alais in to defuse any tension. And if, on the other hand, he meant to seduce her in the privacy of their chamber, he could just think again.

That, Johanna told herself, was a very unlikely contingency in any case. Hadn't she already decided that his whole object was to set up grounds for an annulment by making it publicly clear that she denied him her bed? He'd hardly compromise such a plan by seducing her before the quarrel was properly over. And yet . . . and yet . . .

She pressed cold hands to her burning cheeks, willing away the images of desire and seduction that filled her mind. Oh, she could imagine just how it would be! He'd get her alone, ply her with good strong Gascony wine, tell a few stories, sing a couple of songs, then move in with an arm casually draped around her shoulders. The back of his hand would just brush the underside of her breast, as though by accident. A fire in the hearth, the suggestion that it was really too warm for all these clothes, then the capable, experienced hands sliding under her tunic, inflaming her love-starved flesh with subtle caresses while his lips, hard and knowing and sure, taught her again the sweetness of a man's kisses . . .

Johanna felt the flush of desire that traveled over her white skin, burning her surcoat of purple baudekin and her gold-embroidered girdle and her silky tunic until she thought the heat of her body must radiate outward like the light of a fire. Yes, once she let him get her alone, once she dropped her guard and allowed herself to forget for a moment how he had insulted her, it probably would be that easy. And in the morning, he'd be laughing and triumphant, and the whole castle would know it had taken Rochambeau exactly one evening to make his lady forget her vows to keep him out of her bed.

"Don't be ridiculous," Johanna told herself. "It's not going to happen. He's already made it perfectly clear that he doesn't want you in that way anymore."

But her grounds for that belief rested only on the certainty that if he had wanted her in his bed that afternoon, he could have had her there with very little trouble. This left her with very little faith in her ability to withstand him if he changed his mind about what he wanted. What a sorry choice—to be cast off as an unsatisfactory bedmate or to be taken casually as his pleasure toy, relegated again to the position of a child bride who need not be taken seriously. And worst of all was the weakness that tempted her to invite him into the private chamber, the voice that whispered it was better to be loved by Rochambeau—at whatever cost—than to sleep cold at night forever more.

"Merciful Virgin!" she prayed in most unprayerful tones. "Have I learned so little in these four years? Am I still a silly girl to be seduced by the first man to kiss me like a real man?"

But in that area of experience, Johanna ruefully admitted to herself, she had advanced very little. While Rochambeau was off plundering Saracen tents and amusing himself with their slave girls, what had she learned about men? Nothing! Instead of taking a lover and discovering for herself that there were other men in the world who could give pleasure, she'd been ruining her eyesight and staining her fingers with his inky estate accounts. Managing his property for him! And now he was back, and she was expected to be grateful if he didn't punish her for failing to ransom him—if he so graciously allowed her to be his bed toy again. Meanwhile he snatched the account rolls away from her and probably had given them to Aubrey.

The thought of the accounts stiffened Johanna's spine. Evidently Rochambeau hadn't yet had time to look at the rolls he'd so rudely snatched from her. When he did look, it would be a different story. Maybe he'd come to her a little more politely when he discovered that he had to have her help if he ever wanted to find out what had been going on with his vast estates in the last few years.

All she had to do was hold him off until then. And the first step was to see that he didn't get any ideas about a private supper in their chamber. Johanna locked the door of the inner chamber and set two of her waiting-women—strong, stupid middle-aged widows—to clean up the bower. "And don't let anybody in without my consent," she instructed them.

"Even my lord Rochambeau?"

"*Especially* my lord," said Johanna. She clasped the key of the inner chamber onto the ring of keys that hung from her girdle and sallied downstairs to consult with the cook about supper. Rochambeau should have no cause to complain of the fare that night, no excuse to propose that they retire for a daintier dish than was set before the rest of the inhabitants of Malvern.

By the time her lord and his half-brother had cleaned themselves up and joined the rest of the folk gathered in the great hall for supper, an array of appetizing smells drifted through the courtyard from the kitchen shed. Aubrey sniffed appreciatively while he and Rochambeau held out their hands for the boy at the hall entrance to pour a thin stream of scented water from a silver ewer.

"Rabbits in onion gravy," he announced. "A nice fat roast bird of some sort—a capon, d'you think, or a goose? And a silver mark to St. Geoffrey's shrine if I don't smell cinnamon patties! She's welcoming you home, Nicolas. Usually it's soup and bread in the evenings.''

"Delightful.'' Rochambeau strode down the length of the hall to the high dais, set crosswise to the two long tables, where Johanna was already seated. This evening she had chosen to be resplendent in purple baudekin, the hem and sleeves of her tunic stiff with a foot-deep band of gold embroidery, her hair concealed under a severe hood of matching fabric. When she moved one arm, the wide bell of the sleeve fell away to reveal cloth-of-gold inner sleeves cut tight to her arms. The stiffly formal dress was more suited to a matron of mature years than to a girl who could not, by Rochambeau's swift reckoning, have reached her twenty-first birthday yet. He suppressed a smile. She was still a child trying to gain dignity from her finery. She would be easy to deal with.

Rochambeau's greeting to his lady was, to the great disappointment of those assembled in the hall, too quiet and formal to be heard more than a few steps away. An unnatural hush fell over the room full of castle officials, servants, pages, kitchen boys, and dogs, but only those closest to the high table were able to catch a few disappointingly polite words.

"They're gonna be civilized in public,'' grumbled the cook's second assistant to his master, who stood anxiously waiting at the screened passage to see how his special dishes were being received by the lord and lady.

"And a good thing,'' the cook reproved his assistant. "If the lady throws that dish of young rabbits in onion gravy at the master's head—after all the trouble I had to prepare it just to her taste—well, see if I ever let her turn my kitchens upside down an hour before supper, that's all!'' He folded his arms and scowled at the gentlefolk seated on the high dais, proudly aware of his mastery in his own small kingdom.

The meal began pleasantly enough, if on a somewhat strained note, as Rochambeau shared a dish with his lady and Aubrey seated himself beside Alais. The girl shrank back like a scared child whenever Nicolas de Rochambeau moved; he resolved to remedy that situation before beginning on his plans to tame his wife.

"I don't believe I've been introduced to your charming friend, wife.'' He nodded pleasantly at Alais and suppressed a frown of irritation as she clutched with whitened fingers at the edge of the table.

"Alais is the daughter of your friend Sir Ilbod de Marti," Johanna explained. "I took her in fosterage when his lady, Adelina, offered to take my little sisters, Gillie and Francoise." It had been less an offer than a bullying statement of intention, but Johanna had to admit it had turned out well. Alais was a sweet, biddable girl and a pleasure to have in the manor, if somewhat wishy-washy, while Johanna had been hard put to control her own little sisters when her father dumped them on her.

"I should have thought it would be your mother's task to arrange the fosterage of her daughters." But of course, Rochambeau thought, he should have known that damned impecunious family of Johanna's would move in as soon as his back was turned. He was lucky he hadn't encountered the lot of them camping in his courtyard.

"My mother died the winter after you left," said Johanna in a flat tone that did not encourage further discussion. Even now she found it difficult to remember that unexpected bereavement, coming just when she was most despairing at her position as Rochambeau's deserted wife. If Gwynne had lived, she might well have run back to hide at her mother's skirts. Instead, her father had appeared with the two little girls in tow and the news of her mother's death in childbirth. With a disapproving glance at Johanna's own slender waistline and a hint that he'd already found consolation with Gwynne's waiting-woman Elys, he was off again without delay.

"If you get Elys with child," Johanna had told him bluntly, "you'd better marry her."

Sir Hugh flushed red. "Why? I'll acknowledge the little bastard. That's enough. I've already got an heir."

"It's not enough," Johanna said, thinking of Aubrey. He never complained to her about his ambiguous position, but she had already seen how it ate at his soul—the knowledge that he, the elder brother, the gentle and polite man, was debarred by his birth from inheritance, knighthood, and the church. There was no place for him in this world but service to Nicolas, and it wasn't fair. Little as Johanna cared for Elys or for her father's indecent speed in consoling himself, she didn't want to see her little brother grow up with the guilty responsibility for a swarm of bastard half-brothers and half-sisters, too well born to be ignored yet never eligible for their proper place in the world.

She sighed now and tore her mind away from those painful recollections. A page was standing behind her, offering a dish of chicken meat pounded into a smooth paste with almonds and cinnamon. "It was a long time ago, my lord. Pray do not trouble yourself to offer condolences. Will you try some of this blancmanger?"

Rochambeau shook his head. "Too bland for me, though I understand it may be to a lady's taste." He allowed the page to place a helping of blancmanger on the plate he and Johanna shared, but he barely tasted the food himself.

He greeted the other special dishes Johanna had ordered with similar casual lack of interest. The cook's pride—his fricassee of young rabbits with onions, shallots, forest mushrooms, and a dozen subtle spices—drew only the comment, "I prefer this dish with saffron." Of the roasted goose, Rochambeau suggested, "Next time you might try rubbing the skin with galingale and stuffing it with ground coriander."

"Galingale," said Johanna stiffly, "is an unsubtle seasoning to my taste. Too sharp. I prefer ginger."

Rochambeau chewed another mouthful of tender breast meat, slowly, as though the effort pained him. He washed it down with wine. "Indeed? But I see you're not wasteful of any spices. Why don't you give the cook the key to the spice chest and encourage him to improvise a little?" His blandly patronizing smile suggested only the natural desire of a husband to instruct his young wife. "I don't mean to disparage your domestic talents, my dear girl, but a man accustomed to the East likes to eat food with a little flavor. Surely this manor can afford a few spices for the lord's dishes?"

Lips tight with fury, Johanna signaled the cook's second assistant to bring forth the wheaten cakes filled with ginger and cinnamon and honey, their tops glazed with egg yolks, which she herself had prepared for an end to the meal. At least Rochambeau would have no cause to complain about lack of flavor in this spice-sweet dish. It was one of the few things Gwynne had ever taught her to cook.

Aubrey greeted the appearance of these special pastries with delight and began feeding one to Alais at once, in little bites, with sips of wine to go with it. Johanna could not keep herself from watching anxiously as Rochambeau took one of the sticky cakes from the proffered platter.

One bite, then he set the pastry down again. "Haven't you forgotten something?"

Johanna tasted the cakes herself. They seemed perfectly all right to her.

"I thought there was supposed to be ginger in this. I can't taste anything but a little coarse honey." Rochambeau shook his head sadly. "My very dear lady, I applaud your gallant efforts to manage the estates in my absence, but might suggest that your efforts would be better applied in a more traditional direction? This entire meal shows only too clearly that our supplies of basic spices are running dangerously low. As lady of the manor, I expect you to see that we are adequately supplied with foodstuffs and clothing before you turn your attention to rentals and ploughlands."

"We have," said Johanna through stiff lips, "entirely adequate supplies of anything we may need, my lord. If the food *and other services* around here are too bland for your taste, might I suggest that you go back to your Saracen girls? I'm sure they are excellent cooks in addition to their other talents!"

Rising from the table without ceremony, she stalked off in the general direction of the storage cellars next to the kitchen shed. She would personally take inventory of the spice chest and show Rochambeau that he had no reasonable excuse for complaint. If he wanted to burn everybody's mouths out and disrupt the cook's temper by demanding excessive quantities of spices in every dish, he was quite at liberty to do so!

Aubrey, looking upset, made as if to follow Johanna, but Rochambeau's hand on his arm forced him back down to his seat. "No hurry," Rochambeau told him. "let the lady simmer down of her own accord."

"I'm afraid that doesn't happen," said Aubrey with a rueful glance at the barely touched plate before his brother, "or not very quickly, at any rate. You didn't handle that well, Nicolas. If you want sweet cooking, you'd best not sour Johanna's temper."

Rochambeau regarded Aubrey with the same infuriatingly bland smile he had turned on Johanna. "Indeed? Remind me to ask your advice next time. Now, I think things are going very well indeed." Stretching luxuriously, he crammed the wing of a roast fowl into his mouth, followed it with three slices of bread, and washed the whole down with a cup of wine. Then he rose and announced his intention of going to the chapel, where he meant to offer up a prayer of thanks for his safe and happy return home.

Chapter Eleven

JOHANNA'S FRUITLESS SEARCH of the storerooms occupied her until the extinguishing of lights around the outbuilding warned her that it was nearly bedtime. Somehow, in the few hours since she had ordered the elaborate supper, the kitchen stores had been shuffled around into such a disorderly mess that it took her some time to locate the small brass-bound chest where she kept the spices. And when she did locate it, she found the contents reduced to a few dusty, half-empty bags of spices too old to hold much flavor.

Johanna stood over the chest, tapping one long pointed shoe and frowning into the sputtering light of the torch held by the cook's assistant. It was perfectly maddening. She could practically recite from memory the expenditures she had made in the last quarter for ginger and cinnamon, pepper and sugar and dried figs, and the fabulously expensive saffron that imparted such a delicate flavor to the finest dishes. But the spice chest was practically empty, and Rochambeau, God rot him, had taken away the castle's account rolls, so that she couldn't check her memory of recent purchases. Was her mind going? Was the cook stealing spices to sell for his own profit?

Johanna dismissed both possibilities out of hand. She had absolute faith in her own memory for figures, and nearly as much faith in the honesty of the cook whom she herself had promoted from pantler's assistant. With the rest of the high-ranking staff, he had been following her from manor to manor

155

for years. Besides, the key to the spice chest hung always at her girdle, save when she unlocked it and doled out a measured quantity of the precious goods for a specific meal.

As she had done only that afternoon—and then the spice chest had been quite full of its precious aromatic parcels! Johanna's eyes narrowed to icy green slits as she considered a third possibility. Had Rochambeau somehow arranged the entire scene, including the mysterious disappearance of nearly a pound of ginger, half a pound of cinnamon bark, and various other expensive delicacies, just to make her look incompetent? The presence of the spice-chest key on her ring of keys should have disproved this hypothesis, but Johanna had an irrational feeling that Nicolas de Rochambeau was perfectly able to get through iron padlocks when he wanted to. Perhaps he had added lock picking to his skills in the East, or, more likely, he had a spare set of keys for his own use that she'd never known about.

But what a mean, sneaking, low-down trick, to send somebody into the storeroom and steal his own supplies, just to show her up! He must want this annulment very badly indeed, if he was so bent on proving her an unsatisfactory wife in every possible way. She'd been a silly girl to set guards on the bower and bedchamber. The last thing Rochambeau would want would be to seduce her now, when he was setting up all this evidence so that he could get rid of her.

At that thought, Johanna felt a needlelike stab of pain through her chest, just above the wide, tight golden girdle that bound her waist. This dress must be too tight. Or perhaps she'd eaten too much at dinner. Or perhaps she was ill. Certainly it couldn't be that she was upset about Rochambeau's machinations! For heaven's sake, didn't she want an annulment just as much as he did, the lecherous, sneaking, conniving swine?

In the morning, she resolved, she would confront Rochambeau and tell him that he didn't need to create quarrels and play games in order to be rid of her. She was just as eager to end their mockery of a marriage as he was, and if the pope wasn't satisfied by the evidence that she'd refused to sleep with him, she would join forces with him to search their family trees. A little ingenuity could almost always turn up some long-forgotten relative whose existence related two people within the seventh degree, and that was really the best way to get a marriage annulled—no fuss, no scandal, and, no nonsense in the spice chest!

Slowly, feeling all the exhaustion of the day dragging down her usual springing step, she traversed the maze of wooden passages leading back to the keep and mounted the stairs to the bower. The two waiting-women she'd left on guard were gossiping quietly to themselves, while Alais nodded on a chest against the far wall.

"Go to bed, child," Johanna told the slim, sleepy girl. "I don't need help to undress tonight." Tired though she was, she was also too tense to endure Alais's gentle chatter while her clothes were unfastened and her curly black hair combed out. Nor had she any desire to discuss the scene at dinnertime. Rochambeau was just an annoying fact of life, like flies in summer or maggots in unsalted meat, and Alais would have to learn to put up with him as calmly as Johanna herself did.

Until the annulment . . .

Again that flickering stab of pain lanced through Johanna's chest above her girdle. This dress was definitely too tight!

"No, you go too," she told the two waiting-women. "With all these men of Rochambeau's in the castle, I need you to sleep upstairs where you can watch over the other women." The women and girls who worked in the bower during the day were housed in an upper story of the new keep by night. There was just one stair leading to that story, and some staid woman in her middle years always slept by that stair, to make sure there were no nocturnal comings and goings.

The girdle of her splendid outfit fastened in front, with gold buttons encased in stiff loops of gilt thread. Johanna had never worn it before and found it hard to free the buttons. Head bent over her task, she paced abstractedly into the bedchamber and kicked the door shut behind her. A branch of candles had been lit some time ago; though they were half burnt down by now, the wicks were freshly trimmed so that the candles did not sputter or smoke at all. Alais must have stayed awake to trim the wicks at intervals. Johanna smiled at this evidence of how well she was served. Never mind what Rochambeau might say—she had done well in the position in which he had abandoned her.

Something in the long shadows cast by the candle flames seemed not quite right. Had the women been rearranging the furniture in her absence? Surely that long chest used to lie against the wall, not catty-cornered out at the angle where she saw it now. And she always left the curtains around the bed drawn back during the day, so that the bedclothes might have a chance to air out. Someone would have to be spoken to in the morning. But for now—"God's bones, but I'm tired!" Johanna breathed with a sigh of relief as the stiff gilt loops holding the buttons of her girdle finally gave way. She dropped the girdle across the misplaced chest, where it twisted like a golden snake with glittering scales, and shrugged off the surcoat of purple baudekin with its indecently wide neck opening. Now for the tunic, with its prickly tight sleeves of golden cloth! Johanna tugged at them, swore under her breath, and began to regret her hasty dismissal of her women.

"Perhaps I can help with that."

Johanna gave a convulsive start that left her with the unpleasant feeling that her heart had moved up into the base of her throat. The embroidered bed curtains swung open, and a golden head appeared in the aperture.

"You!"

"You were expecting someone else in your private bedchamber?" inquired the lord of Rochambeau. He swung his long bare legs over the side of the bed and reached out an inviting hand. "Come, let me help you with those sleeves. Why women will wear those ridiculous things I'll never know."

"I suppose the Saracen girls run around bare naked!" Johanna snapped, retreating a step. "What are you doing here? How did you talk my women into letting you in? Get out of there! Alais! Dilys! Oh, my God, you're naked yourself! Have you no sense of shame? Get back behind the covers before they see you!"

But she'd seen him, tall and golden in the candlelight, the hard lines of his masculine body fully exposed to her view as he stood before her, and closing her eyes did no good. She knew exactly what he looked like already; why should the sight of him now arouse such feelings in her? Johanna took another blind step backward and felt the hard edge of the chest behind her knees.

"Your women won't hear you," Rochambeau pointed out. "I gave them plenty of time to get up to their beds."

"I'd like to know how you suborned them to let you in here." Johanna sat down on the chest and stared at her hands, afraid to look up.

"I didn't. There's an entrance to these rooms from the upper gallery of the chapel. When I had these private rooms built onto the end of the hall, I thought it would be a foolish lord who made himself a chamber with no back exit. But I saw no necessity for the rest of the castle folk to know about it. The master builder who contrived the device for me was well paid to keep his mouth shut." Stepping to the wall behind Johanna, Rochambeau laid his hand on a square-cut stone and demonstrated how the door pivoted smoothly in and out, concealed behind layers of thin facing stone that looked as solid as the great rocks that made up the rest of the wall. A rush of dank cold air whistled in from the chapel gallery and blew out three of the five candles.

"I wish I'd known about that all these years," Johanna said. "It would have been a lot more convenient than going around through the hall and the outside stairs to get to the chapel."

"I didn't design it for your convenience." Rochambeau swung the door shut and stood looking down at Johanna. Again she was intensely, painfully aware of the proximity of his naked body. She wished he would go back to the bed, or anywhere, just so she didn't have to keep averting her mind and her eyes from the sight that brought back so many memories. "Nor did you arrange the furniture in here for mine. I had the devil's own time pushing that chest away! At first I thought you'd discovered that door years ago and blocked it up without saying anything. It would be like you."

"For once," Johanna said shakily, "you overrate me. I never thought to check Malvern for secret passages. However . . ." She had started to say that in the morning she would have a mason block the door at once, but why warn Rochambeau of her plans in advance? Besides, in the morning it would be too late.

"Don't bother." The flickering light of the last two candles gave his smile a feral quality, most disconcerting. "No mason on my estate will lift a finger to do any work without my express orders."

"Then you'd better prepare to give a lot of express orders, my lord," Johanna retorted, thinking that at least she could pile a lot of nice heavy furniture in front of the door, enough to try even Rochambeau's legendary strength. "There are two mills needing repair, the drainage system for the low fens is only half done, the church tower is about to fall down, and . . ." She derived some pleasure from enumerating the building work that had to be done on the estate, showing Rochambeau that she really was quite competent.

"My God," said her lord and husband in awed tones, "you have been letting the place fall down about our ears, haven't you? I can see it's high time I came back!"

While Johanna was still sputtering in outrage, he seated himself on the chest beside her and clasped her around the waist with one firm arm. "But we'll discuss all that tomorrow. For now, how do these silly things come off? They're sewn on? Ridiculous system! Why don't you buy a decent set of buttons? No, I'm not going to fiddle about for hours with a pair of scissors. Are you kidding? I'm not having any sharp instrument that close to your hands, and me naked and helpless before you."

"Helpless!" Johanna muttered. As he spoke, Rochambeau's strong hands closed about the two edges of one sleeve and tore it open from wrist to shoulder, with no more effort than if he'd been tearing off a piece of soft bread from a new-baked loaf. The other sleeve went as quickly, the tunic went over her head with one brisk tug, and then his hands rested on her shoulders, their warmth striking inward through the soft fabric of her chemise.

"Don't tear this too," Johanna said quickly. "I like it."

"But not the gold sleeves?"

She shrugged, pretending indifference. "They were too tight. And scratchy," she added with feeling, remembering how stiff and itchy the gold threads in the material were.

"All right, wife." Rochambeau released her, but his hands were open at his sides, and his body was between her and the door. "If you'd rather take your own shift off, I'd rather watch."

"And if I don't cooperate?" Johanna felt a little better standing up. Not much. But at least now she could move away from him. The only difficulty was in making herself do so, when for some reason she wanted to reach forward and caress the taut skin of his chest. Did it feel different now, that skin that was tanned to glowing bronze by the sun of the Holy Land, marked with new white scars from fights she knew nothing of? She could remember the crispness of his body hair under the palm of her hand and the supple strength of the muscles sliding beneath the skin, and her breath troubled her in this room that suddenly seemed so narrow and so close.

"You always do cooperate. Eventually. As I recall." Rochambeau grinned and moved a little closer, hands outstretched on either side. "Although I'll grant it's been a long time. Wouldn't you like to refresh my memory?"

Johanna backed away from him until she felt the rough solidity of an old woolen tapestry against her back and, against that, the stones of another wall. He was so sure of himself and of his eventual victory. Bitterness was the only thing that could protect her against the spell of the senses; she clung to her bitterness as though to a holy relic. And that reminded her—

"What about your vow? I thought you weren't going to come in here or touch me until I invited you."

"I lied." Rochambeau grinned as though the matter were of no moment.

"On a holy relic!" Johanna felt an instant of cold shock. He would burn in hell for such a sin. Her eyes slid to the bed where the sapphire-crusted brooch that held the reliquary lay with the rest of his discarded clothes, half expecting a punitive shaft of light to strike him down before her. Rochambeau followed the direction of her gaze.

"Oh, that?" He shrugged as though the matter were of no moment. "That's no relic. It's the bit of a pig's knuckle that I found in my plate one evening. Doubtless the silver case was a reliquary at one time, but it was empty when it came into my hands. I thought a splinter of bone inside might come in handy sometime, and so it did. You certainly fell for it."

"You," said Johanna severely, "are a liar, a blasphemer,

and a lecher. And you're going to be carried away by the devil if you don't reform.''

''I never heard that it was a sin to lie over a pig's knuckle,'' Rochambeau countered. He was coming closer, and she had no more room to retreat and nowhere to look but at the taut, solid mass of his body. The smooth locks falling to his shoulders and the crisp gold wires of his body hair glistened more brightly in the candlelight than the golden belt she had discarded. He was strength and certainty incarnate. How could she resist him?

''This won't help your annulment,'' she warned.

For once an expression of genuine surprise crossed his face. ''Who said anything about an annulment?''

''But you—I thought—'' Frantically Johanna tried to grab onto the remnants of what had once been a system of rational thoughts. ''You engineered that quarrel earlier today. When you made that vow not to come to my bed until I invited you. I thought you were making sure that everybody knew I was refusing to sleep with you.''

''I had another reason. Perhaps you'll figure it out later.''

''And at supper tonight. All those complaints about the food—and I found the spice chest empty, and I *know* we had plenty of supplies earlier today. You did that, didn't you? To show that I'm incompetent?''

''To keep you busy,'' Rochambeau corrected. ''I wanted you rooting around in the storeroom until late in the evening, so you wouldn't start to wonder where I was. I told the rest of the people here that I didn't want to be disturbed at my devotions in the chapel, but I was afraid you wouldn't pay any more attention to that order than you do to any of my other wishes. And it wouldn't have been good if you'd marched in and found an empty chapel where everybody thought they'd left me praying.''

''Oh.'' Temporarily disarmed, Johanna dropped the hands she had raised defensively before her. ''You seem to have gone to an awful lot of trouble just to sneak into my bedchamber unobserved.''

''It used to be our bedchamber,'' Rochambeau murmured. ''Don't you remember?''

She remembered all too well, and the sensual memories that his presence evoked were clogging her brain and making her stumble over the simplest words. "That was—before you left."

"Did you mind my leaving so much?" He came after her again, but not in the brutal, grabbing rush she'd feared. Delicately as a cat stalking a bird, he moved forward till his open hands could slide down her arms. Despite her resolves, Johanna shivered under his touch.

"I'm back now, sweet, dear lady, my very dear and very lovely wife," Rochambeau murmured. One hand cupped under her chin, gently raising her head until she met his eyes. They glittered in the candlelight with a rich blue light that put the sapphires in the discarded brooch to shame. "And you are more beautiful than ever. Did you really think I could forget your beauty? Stop wanting you? Find any satisfaction in the embraces of some foreign slave girl?" The questions were punctuated by gentle kisses along her temples, where a mad pulse throbbed in response to his touch, on her burning cheek, on the corner of her mouth. Her lips pursed in anticipation of the next kiss, but he seemed maddeningly content to pause there.

"You forgot for four years." The husky uncertainty in her voice disgusted Johanna. She tried to turn her head away and found that the gentle hand holding her face concealed muscles as hard and unyielding as the very stones of the castle.

"Never," said Rochambeau simply. "If I stayed away, it was because I doubted my reception."

"You had good reason!"

"Indeed. I treated you abominably. Even before I knew that damned song had found its way here, I feared you might not forgive the way I hurried you into marriage and then left in a temper."

The simple admission took the strength out of her fury.

"It's a Christian virtue to forgive." One arm held her close to his body, his big hand outspread on the curve of her buttocks. She might have been naked in his arms already, for all the protection her fine soft chemise offered. With the other hand he held her face to receive his kisses. His mouth sought out the corners of hers, pressed her lips open, and tasted the sweetness within; she felt herself sinking into that sensual embrace, held up only by the strength of Rochambeau's arms and his indomitable will.

"This is a fine time—to be talking—of Christian virtues!" she gasped when at last he freed her lips.

"Why, my dear love, is there anything unchristian about seeking to pay my marriage debt?" Innocent surprise in his voice was belied by the knowing movement of his hands over her body, awakening the fires of passion that had been denied for so many years. His lips nuzzled at her throat, her breast, leaving a damp circle of fine silky clothes over the risen nipple. Johanna shivered, and he clasped her warmly in his arms.

"Now, love, there's no need to be cold. Come to bed? I've been keeping it warm for you!" He was drawing her that way, and she followed him, unresisting, unthinking. But it was not the chill in the air that made her shiver. Her skin was on fire with darting little flames that ran up and down all her tender, secret places. She was hot as though she burned in a fever, and only the touch of Rochambeau's hands could soothe her now. The things on the bed, sapphire brooch and velvet surcoat and fur-trimmed coverlet, fell to the floor in a tangle. Last of all, drawn off by Rochambeau's skillful hands, her shift floated down to the floor like a maiden's bridal veil of filmy white. And then she was naked in his arms, and there was nothing left to fight about. He wooed her with kisses and sweet words, made her senses drunk with soft, insinuating touches that grew hard and demanding when she least expected it.

"Nicolas," she moaned against his shoulder, wanting more than the subtle skill with which he inflamed her body, more than kisses and hands gliding over her yearning flesh until she was all aquiver with expectancy. "Nicolas!" she cried out again when at long last he took her, joining them into the one being whose two halves had been separated for so long. Then there was no more Nicolas, no more Johanna, but only the mutual desire that drove them both onward to new heights of ecstasy. She had nothing to refuse him, nothing to bargain with; all that she was belonged to him, and she possessed him equally. Until that first consuming desire had been slaked, there was no room for anything but the joy of holding Nicolas de Rochambeau in her arms and being held by him, knowing herself complete where she had been aching with empty loneliness all those years.

Only when all their long-denied desires had been satisfied,

for the moment if not forever, could she find herself again amid the tumbled bed linens and rich embroidered hangings, distinguishing her own white slender limbs from Rochambeau's long muscular legs. And then it hardly seemed worth the effort. With her head resting on his shoulder, she floated in a delicious, drowsy half-sleep feeling his heart beating in time with her own, his ragged breathing gradually slowing as her own pulses recovered from that fierce ecstasy.

"Johanna."

"Mmm?"

"Nothing. Only Johanna." The pleasure she'd given him was, as always, so intensely sweet as to make all his other experiences seem like the play of children scarcely out of their cradles. But that merely physical pleasure was nothing compared to the aching, piercing shafts of feeling that sank deep within him now, as he cradled her head on his shoulder and watched the sooty sweep of dark lashes across her cheek. She sighed like a sleepy babe and stretched luxuriously in his arms; the dim glow of the last dying candle cast a rosy light over the slender white curves of her body. Only looking at her aroused all the passionate desires that should, just now, have been thoroughly satisfied; if he looked longer, he'd stretch her out on the bed and have her again, all tumbled and sleepy as she was. Very gently, Rochambeau drew up the coverlet of scarlet with fur-trimmed edges and covered them both against the night chill.

Who was she, this intoxicating, infuriating child wife of his? No, he corrected himself, not a child any longer. He'd left behind a girl, sweet and yielding in his arms but tart as a green apple outside of bed. He'd come back to find a woman, a witch, whose green-eyed glance and long curling black hair could entangle him hopelessly in the net of her magic. A woman with all the spirit and fire of the girl he'd loved and left, but something more besides. It had taken courage to stand up to him that morning in the full tide of his anger.

Any woman with a grain of sense would have been humbly begging his pardon for her refusal to ransom him, would have counted herself lucky if he didn't throw her into his own dungeons in retribution. But not his Johanna! Rochambeau chuckled, remembering the scene upon his arrival, and smoothed the black curls away from her forehead with one big, scarred hand. She was so delicately made, he could crush her like an eggshell if he weren't careful. But did any of his strength and righteous anger make the slightest impression on her? Ha! Instead, she'd stood right up to him, never admitting her own fault, instead attacking with her grudges from four years ago. Rochambeau could respect that. It was usually a mistake to admit oneself in the wrong.

Still, when all was said and done, she was a woman, with all a woman's weaknesses. He'd never had any doubt that once he got her alone, they'd find their own sweet accord in the oldest and most natural way. Much as she liked to deny it, she was made for him. Her body had always known it; he had only to convince the rest of her! He'd been a rash young fool to go charging off like that in the heat of his anger four years ago, carrying his wounded pride first to Edward's camp and then to the Holy Land. When he cooled down, Rochambeau had known Johanna's tales of her lovemaking with Piers had only been made up to infuriate him. She had been not only innocent but ignorant on their wedding night. And whatever she said afterward, her response to his lovemaking had not been any acting taught her by her mother!

But by then, by the time he had calmed down, he'd already agreed to accompany Edward on crusade; it would have been a mortal sin to break his crusading vow and turn back. And, too, he'd already composed that bitter, unhappy, satirical song about his marriage, though he'd never meant for it to come to Johanna's ears. Still, the way things turned out, perhaps it was just as well he'd stayed away for four years. Considering how she'd received him that morning, all indignation over an unintentional slight four years old, there was no telling what she'd have done if he'd come home immediately after she heard the song! A dagger between his ribs would have been the best he could hope for.

And now? Frowning slightly, Rochambeau considered the half-closed eyes and dreamy smile on the white face upturned to his. She was all his at night, but who was to say she wouldn't turn into a spitfire again by morning? And if she ever discovered how deeply she'd insinuated herself into his heart, there'd be no controlling her. If she knew, for instance, that he'd not been able to work up the slightest interest in those dancing girls sent by Baibars to Prince Edward, that he'd lived as chastely as she in the years of their separation, that since he'd first seen her no other woman could stir his senses.

Rochambeau smiled and shook his head slightly. It did no good to let a woman think she could master you, even when it happened to be the truth. His only chance of a happy outcome to this turbulent marriage was to keep Johanna thinking that he had the upper hand. And for the rest—for the chance that she'd be a virago by morning—well, the best way to guard against that was to keep that dreamy smile on her face until dawn. And with four years' abstinence to make up for, with the stirring in his loins that the mere thought of her engendered, he felt quite capable of doing that.

"Wake up, my love," he whispered, sliding his hands under the weight of the fur-trimmed coverlet to enjoy the sweet, yielding warmth of her sleepy body. "The night's young yet, and so are we."

Chapter Twelve

JOHANNA WOKE SLOWLY, luxuriating in a feeling of warmth, comfort, and bodily pleasure such as she had not known for years. The sweetness of the night left a glow of pleasure in her limbs, and the warm bulk of Rochambeau's body next to hers created a snug nest in which she felt cherished, protected, safe, loved, all those things that had, up to now, been so conspicuously missing from the life of the lady of Rochambeau. What would it be like, having a man to turn to with knotty problems of estate management and bellicose neighbors? To share this big, empty bed with a man? To put aside the cares of the estate and the responsibilities of the lady of the manor with her tight coif and laced girdle, and to become in his arms a creature of the night and of pleasure?

It sounded too good to be true.

It was almost good enough to make it worth forgetting all the unhappy old grudges and insults that lay between them. Wriggling luxuriously into the softness of the down-filled mattress, Johanna peeped through her long lashes at Nicolas de Rochambeau and contemplated offering him a truce. If he would stop sniping at her in public, she would be willing to do the same for him. They might even live together in amity, strange though such a state would be for either of them.

As though sensing her movements in his dreams, Rochambeau rolled over and pulled her to him with one iron-hard arm, crushing her against his chest and side. His grasp landed on places that he had used urgently in his passion the night before, and Johanna squeaked and pushed his arm away from her tender ribs. "Let go, you brute! Do you want to mash me to a pulp?"

Rochambeau opened one blue eye and regarded her cautiously. The yellow hair falling untidily across his forehead made him look like a small boy caught with one finger in the honey pot. "I just want you. Any way possible. Night, morning, afternoon, in bed, out of bed." He grinned and held her more gently, but without allowing her to wriggle away from him. "The same way you want me."

Johanna tried to deny the thrill of pleasure she felt as her breasts rubbed against his naked side. "Don't be so sure. I'm one mass of bruises from your rough treatment last night."

"Are you?" He looked genuinely concerned. "Show me." With one swift gesture, he stripped the covers off them both and lowered his face to scan her white body. His lips brushed along her throat and the curve of her shoulder and teased her nipples into aching tautness. He moved lower to cover the white skin he had only caressed with his hands the night before. "Mmm, I think I can see definite contusions here . . . and abrasions . . . Lucky for you, I learned some secrets of healing from the Arab physicians. A warm compress is indicated. With moisture and some pressure. Like this . . ." Lips and tongue worked together, most sensuously, to follow his prescription. Johanna sighed with an involuntary surrender to pleasure and only startled back to wakefulness at the sound of rustling and giggling outside.

"My women! They're waiting in the bower." She sat up and grabbed at the trailing coverlet.

"Let them wait. We've got more pleasant things to do." With casual strength, he bent her back against the bed. Johanna began to feel annoyed.

"Do you ever *ask* first?"

"Only when necessary."

"And for your wife, of course, it's not necessary."

"After last night," Rochambeau teased her, "I hardly thought you'd be shy."

"That's not the point."

"Then what is it?"

Johanna wasn't sure herself. She only felt that somehow

her generous intention to offer a truce had slipped away from her. Rochambeau seemed to be taking that, and everything else, for granted.

"It's too early in the morning to be arguing." He pressed his advantage. "And you're so much lovelier when you smile. Come now, pretty wife, smile for your lord!" He tickled her under the chin, as if she were a baby who had to be coaxed into good humor, and Johanna's annoyance flared into definite anger.

"I'm not in the mood to play games!" She jumped from the bed, suppressing a gasp of shock when her feet hit the cold stones. What had happened to the pile of furred covers that had lain there last night?

"Aren't you? What a pity! And you play such enticing ones, too. How can you say that, after the game of the bear and the huntress?"

Johanna remembered what they'd done with the fur-trimmed coverlets, and a wave of color rose to her cheeks that did nothing to warm her bare feet.

"And the swinging tapestry? And the thing you thought of to do with your girdle? And—"

"Oh, stop!" Johanna buried her burning face in her hands. It was true, last night she'd been totally abandoned, lost to all sense of modesty and decorum. And perhaps she'd had some passing thought of showing Rochambeau that his Saracen dancing girls weren't the only ones who could be inventive in the bedchamber. But in the morning light, with her women giggling just the other side of the door, how could he humiliate her by recalling such moments? Anybody would think there was no more to their relationship than that.

"I have work to do," she reminded him. "Did you think the honor of Rochambeau runs itself? It's time I was downstairs. With all the preparations for winter to get underway, the days are hardly long enough for all I have to manage. And we must leave Malvern soon, to move on to the northern manors. I have to see that all's in good order here first."

"Not anymore." Rochambeau leaned back, arms folded behind his head, and favored her with a lazy, contented smile. "I'm home now, Johanna; you don't have to play at managing the estates any longer. I mean to take matters into my own hands. And you can go back to being my wife and serving me in pleasanter ways than with a pile of musty old account books—starting now.''

Johanna gasped in shock and outrage. "Just like that? Before you even see what I've done, you judge it worthless?"

"Not necessarily worthless," Rochambeau corrected her. "Just unsuitable. I thought last night would show you there are better ways for you to spend your time."

"I don't see that the two are incompatible." But Johanna could feel that her words made no impression. Oh, she'd been a fool to think she had anything to offer him outside the bedchamber! What did he need with a truce? He was doubtless quite content to make love at night and war during the day. It saved him the trouble of dealing with her in the daytime, while at night he had her exactly where he wanted her. It was all starting again, just like before he went away, and she'd been a triply damned fool to ever think there could be anything different between them! Why had she ever let him seduce her again? It wouldn't have happened, she told herself, if she'd known he was waiting for her. If she couldn't be his trusted and respected wife by day, she wouldn't be his toy at night.

"Last night," Johanna said stiffly, "you took me by surprise. It won't happen again."

Rochambeau lounged at his ease on the bed, wearing nothing but an infuriatingly confident smile. "Would you care to make a small wager on that?"

"It would be unfair." Johanna pulled some clothes at random out of her chest and dressed herself hastily. To armor herself against Rochambeau's contemptuous amusement, she made herself remember every humiliating detail of the way he'd taken her for his bride in the first place. Lying, practically kidnapping her, pretending he'd force her to nothing, while at the same time he was blackmailing her father. "You don't seem to understand, my lord, that I could never love a man who'd cheat to get me."

Rochambeau stared, then laughed. "Aren't you making too much out of a little thing, my dear? You didn't show much resistance once the matter was settled, as I recall." Sure, he'd tricked her last night, making her think he wouldn't come to her and then sneaking in by the back way. But such ruses were fair among lovers—and whatever else they might be to each other, last night had proved that they were surely that!

And would be again. He feasted his eyes on her tumbled curls, on the surprisingly generous curves of her breasts under the thin tunic she'd yanked over her head. Such a delicate girl, with slender waist and long ivory legs, but such a wealth of delights under her tunic! A pity she was working herself up into a fury over nothing. He'd dearly like to tumble her on the bed right this minute, pushing her skirts up and taking her as quickly and joyously as one enjoyed a peasant girl in the fields. And she'd like it too. But now that she was working up to a tantrum, she'd feel obliged to scream first, and that would be detrimental to the impression he meant to leave with her waiting-women.

"Perhaps you'd like to make another wager," he suggested. "I could make the stakes more appealing to you."

Johanna's sooty lashes lifted briefly to disclose a startling flash of green, like the light that flashes across a calm sea in the instant when the sun goes down. "I doubt that, my lord."

"No? Try this. Aubrey tells me you've been keeping the estate accounts in cipher. You think I'll have to come to you to get them translated, don't you?" She remained stubbornly mute, turning away from him on the pretense of fastening up her long black curls under the linen coil. "Don't you?"

"Are you asking for my help already?"

"By no means. I don't expect to need it."

Johanna's lips curved slightly. "I think, my lord, you will find yourself mistaken there. I am very sure that no man in this castle can read the cipher which I have devised. Plenty of them have tried it," she added in an undertone, thinking of the clerks and priests and wandering scholars whom Aubrey had teased by posing her enciphered accounts as a riddle.

"You're very sure of yourself."

Johanna gave him a cool, level glance that would almost have made him doubt his plan, if it weren't ridiculous to suppose that a woman could outsmart him—especially a girl like Johanna! "In any field where we fight on equal terms, my lord, I have no doubt of my victory."

"Ah. Woman's wit against man's intelligence? That's more fair than using my superior strength against you?"

"Isn't it?"

"Is that what you think I've been using?" Rochambeau challenged. "Did I have to hold you down on the bed and rape you last night?"

Johanna flushed and dropped her eyes. "You use your strength . . . and your experience with women. And," she added hotly, "you cheat!"

"Well. There's no way that I can cheat on this wager, is there? A simple test of wits, mine against yours. I should think that would appeal to you."

"You've yet to propose the terms," she reminded him.

"Ah, yes, the terms. How about this? If I can decipher the accounts, you'll come to my bed willingly henceforth and be a dutiful wife to me in all things."

"And when—if—you can't?"

Rochambeau noted the slight hesitation and smiled inwardly. So, the lady wasn't quite so sure of herself as she pretended! All the better. It was time she learned to face the reality of man's superiority, his natural leadership.

"If I can't decipher them," he offered, "I'll not trouble you again in these ways that you claim to find so distasteful. I'll leave you the authority to deal with the accounts and whatever estate matters interest you. We shall work together as lord and lady of the manor, but I'll not force you or seduce you or tempt you or cheat in any way. Your bed shall be as inviolate as a sanctuary of Holy Church."

Johanna regarded him with suspicion. "Why should I believe you'll keep such a promise? You've lied before."

"Because this time," he told her, "I will swear on something that really does matter to me."

"What is that?"

Now for the dangerous throw, the one that would win or lose all. Rising from the bed, Rochambeau went down on one knee before his wife and bowed his golden head. As he did so, he noted that the stones in the chamber were damnably cold and hard. "I swear it," he said, "on the hope which I shall never abandon, of one day gaining your love."

Johanna gasped as if he had struck her; when he raised his head, he saw a sparkle like tears in her eyes. "Oh, you are abominable!" she cried, and turned to flee the chamber.

He caught her by the wrist before she reached the door.

"Not so fast, my lady. Say then—do you accept the terms of the wager or not?"

"Oh, I accept! I accept! I would take any wager that offered me a chance of freedom from you!" Breaking free, Johanna lifted her skirts and hurried out to the sanctuary of the bower where some of her women were already at work. She knew she presented very little of the calm, composed appearance suitable to the lady of the manor, but she had to get away from Rochambeau before his teasing tricked her into revealing what he must never know: how easily she could fall hopelessly in love with him. If he even suspected her weakness, he'd soon be her master in truth as well as in law.

She tried in vain to blink away the tears that made her eyes sparkle, to straighten black curls that were crackling with indignation, and to control the fires that burned in her cheeks. The suppressed giggles and smiles of her waiting women told her that they had thoroughly misinterpreted her disheveled appearance.

"A good morning, mistress!" said one of the older women with a sly smile.

"And a good night for *some* of us," put in Dilys. Seated before the high loom, she was busily engaged in undoing the damage to her weaving that had been caused by Johanna and Rochambeau's fight on the previous day. Her eyes were fixed on the tangle of warp threads that her clever fingers were untangling, and Johanna felt that she dared not criticize the woman for her pointed comment. Dilys would only look up with wide, innocent eyes and say, "Oh, did my lady have reason to take it personally?" And then Johanna would feel more foolish than ever.

The woman who'd first spoken looked past Johanna with a silly smile on her face. Johanna didn't need to turn around to know that Rochambeau would be lounging in the doorway, making it abundantly clear to all concerned that he'd spent the night with her. She just hoped he'd bothered to get dressed first.

"And a good morning to all." His suave voice came from behind her. Strolling forward, he kissed Johanna on the cheek before she could object, then proceeded to salute the three nearest waiting-women in the same fashion. In the flurry of shrieks and giggles caused by this audacity, he thanked them all for their concern and interest in his and his lady's happiness. "I'm sure you are as glad as I am to know that we are happily reconciled."

He was out of the room before Johanna could object to this statement, and she was entangled in the soft embraces and smiling comments of a gaggle of silly women who should have known better.

"We are *not* reconciled! And stop that congratulating! I don't want to be reconciled with him!"

She felt like a silly child breaking toys in a tantrum. But it had to be said, didn't it? The women drew back with expressions of shock.

"But the vow—"

"But when we saw he'd stayed the night with you, we naturally assumed—"

"You must have invited him! He'd surely not break a vow on a holy relic!" And Dilys triumphantly held up the silver and sapphire brooch with its concealed reliquary.

"Holy relic, my behind!" Johanna snatched the offending brooch from Dilys' hand and hurled it at the far wall of the bower. "It's nothing but a pig's knuckle!"

Two girls knocked heads in the effort to rescue the holy relic, and there were murmurs that my lady was in an awful temper, for sure, to blaspheme like that.

"Are you all right, my lady?" That was Alais, hurrying to pat Johanna's curls straight and smooth her coif. She looked at Johanna with imploring, innocent eyes framed in her fall of long, straight, fair hair, the very picture of frightened virginal innocence. Johanna felt an unfamiliar stab of irritation at the girl's big-eyed stare. Anyone would think she'd just been raped by an entire crusading army, instead of spending a night with her lawful husband!

"Perfectly all right, Alais," she said, putting an arm around the girl's shoulders. "You have nothing to worry about, and there was no need for all you ladies to come to work in the bower so early. You know I never require anybody to begin work before they've had a chance to hear Mass and break their fast."

The mention of Mass gave her an excuse to sweep out of the bower with what was left of her dignity. Oh, the cunning of that man! It was just like the game he'd played with her at the time of their marriage. Then, he'd promised with one hand that he wouldn't force her to wed him, while with the other hand he was cunningly arranging matters so that she must agree to the marriage or see her family ruined. Now he promised to leave her alone if she won a wager, while making everybody in the castle think that she'd welcomed him to her bed. Johanna fumed about the duplicity of the man all the way down the bower stairs, through the hall, out through the inner bailey, and up the external stair that led to the chapel.

The sight of Rochambeau, comfortably lounging against a back wall of the chapel while the castle priest hurried through Mass, did nothing to restore her equanimity. Johanna took her usual place on a low stool at the left side of the chapel and bent her head in a pretense of prayerful attention, while her mind was busy with most unreligious thoughts.

There was one difference between her situation now and then. At the time of their marriage, Johanna had been forced into compliance by her fears for other people. Now there was little harm Rochambeau could do her family. If he cried treason against her father on the basis of evidence five years old, Kind Edward would legitimately ask why he had not spoken before, why he had married into the family and sponsored the fostering of the two younger girls. Rochambeau could not now accuse her family without implicating himself.

Now the battle was between the two of them. And there, though she might have lost the preliminary skirmishes, Johanna felt more confident. Let him beat her, torture her, throw her into the dungeons! Never would she bend her will to his!

By the end of the short Mass, her head was high again, red lips curving in a smile that boded Nicolas de Rochambeau no good, green eyes glittering like sun-dazzled emeralds. Rochambeau observed his lady's martyred smile with deep foreboding. Damn! This was not working out at all as he'd planned it. He'd hoped that his honest profession of desire for her love would have touched her heart; instead, God only knew why, it had infuriated her. He'd hoped that when she thought it over she would realize that she stood to lose as much as he did by his offer to stay away from her bedchamber; instead, she looked so happy that he began to think she really didn't want him.

"Maybe she's under an enchantment," he mused, watching her instead of the priest in the closing moments of the Mass. Sun sparkled through the high windows on the outer wall of the chapel and bathed her in a pool of pale clear light, accentuating the brightness of her slanted eyes and the porcelain whiteness of her skin. It was an unearthly beauty she had that morning, a witch's beauty, a contradiction in terms, like Johanna herself, with her eyes so cold and untouched, her lips bruised to ripe fullness from his kisses. Weren't there tales of a knight who'd won to marriage with a woman under an enchantment? She'd told him that she could be beautiful at night for him alone and cursed during the day for his friends and family; or she could be beautiful and charming in the daytime for him to be proud of her and a monster at night.

Rochambeau couldn't remember how the story had ended. Somehow the knight had made a very clever choice which dissolved the enchantment and gave him a loving, beautiful bride by day and by night. But how had he done it?

At the end of Mass, Johanna tried to brush past him without acknowledging his presence. He put out one hand and caught her by the sleeve. "Wait a minute. I want to talk to you."

She regarded him with cool disdain. "I thought you promised not to bother me."

"God's bones!" Rochambeau snapped. "I'm not going to rape you on the chapel floor. I just want . . ."

The cold look in her green eyes sparkled with amusement, like sunlight on sea water. "Yes?"

"I have the account rolls."

"Yes, I know."

"But in order to decipher them, I want some other information. The rest of your records."

"Records?"

"Merchants' bills. The cartularies of the manors. The customals." Rochambeau's confidence grew as he enumerated the items he might legitimately ask for. All he'd had in mind, at first, was not to let her brush by him with that disdainful air. But as always, his fertile brain had not failed him when it was time to manufacture an excuse for spending more time with her. Poor girl, how could she hope to outwit someone so clever as he was? The outcome of their wager was practically decided already.

"Ha! Already you're asking for favors. I don't recall anything said in the wager about handing over every scrap of parchment on the manor."

"You're afraid that I'll figure out your secret cipher if you give me enough information, aren't you?"

"Certainly not!"

"Then why not let me have the materials I'm asking for?"

Johanna capitulated with a sudden dazzling smile that unsettled him thoroughly. "Certainly, my lord." She dropped a deep curtsy and inclined her head in obedience. "If you'll be pleased to follow me, I shall show you the materials you require." In an undertone too low for the gaping clerks and servitors who stood outside the chapel, she hissed, "And they'll do you about as much good as that scrap of pig's knuckle you call a relic!"

Rochambeau smiled and followed his lady from the chapel. It seemed to him the pig's knuckle had already served him well enough. Already he'd taken Johanna by surprise, reminded her of the joys of their marriage bed, and seen to it that the entire population of Malvern believed her to have invited him back to that bed. One night's work well done! Now he had only to devote an hour or two to breaking this cipher, and her sense of honesty would force her to give him the obedience she'd so far withheld.

And was that what he wanted from her? Obedience? Would that be the magic that broke the enchantment? Frowning slightly, Rochambeau put the question out of his mind. He'd never failed at a siege yet, be it of a castle or of a fair lady, and he would not fail at this one. Victory was almost within his grasp.

Chapter Thirteen

THREE DAYS LATER, Rochambeau was not quite so sure of his victory. Somehow, every time he thought he was getting somewhere with Johanna's damnable cipher, his carefully built theories came apart, and he was left with a pile of meaningless letters. The trouble was, of course, that he didn't have time to concentrate. The damned girl had probably spent months putting the thing together, and he was trying to solve it in the nonexistent spare time left him between whipping the garrison into fighting shape, settling manor court disputes, and preparing for a round of visits to examine his other manors.

"I could do that for you," Aubrey suggested when he saw that Rochambeau was planning, on top of all his other duties, to start a round of inspection visits.

Rochambeau cocked one bright blue eye at him. "And just what would you inspect," he inquired, "since you admit you can't read her accounts? Without knowing what's in the rolls, you have no idea what revenues we should be getting, who's been excused or amerced, what the local conditions have been . . ."

"I take it you've deciphered the rolls?" Aubrey looked sick. Rochambeau felt uncharitable for not confessing his total lack of progress; it was cruel to make Aubrey feel even stupider than he really was. But his pride wouldn't allow him to admit he'd been bested by a woman. Not yet.

"I'm making progress," he evaded, "but there are still some minor points to be worked out. It's a very time-consuming project."

"I bet it is." From Aubrey's sly smile, Rochambeau knew he hadn't fooled his brother. Under his breath, he cursed all women and their low animal cunning; aloud, he gratefully responded to the hall chamberlain's request that he come to straighten out a dispute about the use of the common grazing land. For once, he was just as glad to be interrupted.

He was a little taken aback when, on striding into the hall, he found Johanna already seated on the dais, listening intently as a knot of clodhopping peasants shook their fists and shouted at each other. She didn't seem to be doing anything to stop them, and Rochambeau didn't know whether to be glad that she wasn't usurping his functions or annoyed that she was just sitting there uselessly.

"All right, what's the trouble?" As he took his seat, he picked out one of the peasants whom he remembered by name, a burly farmer named Eduin whose three-virgate holding made him one of the richer villeins. "Eduin, suppose you tell me."

As Eduin launched into a thick-tongued recital of his wrongs, interrupted from time to time by the other villeins, Rochambeau remembered with regret that Eduin's large holding did not indicate a corresponding superiority in brain power. Self-important and self-satisfied, he liked to take his own sweet time about getting to the point of a story. And Rochambeau had set himself up for this one. Bored, he let his attention wander while Eduin thickly reiterated his right to graze his beasts on ten acres of open fields as soon as the fields were harvested.

Johanna, sitting still and calm beside him, was a far worthier subject of contemplation than Eduin and his involved claim. Today she was simply dressed in a deep green overtunic whose sleeves and hem were slashed to reveal an underdress of home-dyed blue. There was nothing ostentatious about her dress, but the two colors blended to reflect the green light in her eyes, and the soft wool draped over her high, firm bosom in a way that set him thinking irresistibly of the white perfection of her unclothed body.

Rochambeau heaved a heavy sigh and crossed his legs,

startling Eduin so much that he broke off his peroration and started his complaint over again. Rochambeau hardly heard the drone of the farmer's speech; his mind was hopelessly entangled in the snare that was Johanna. How could a woman be so beautiful and so cursed? Ever since he'd proposed that unlucky wager, she had taken him entirely at his word, treating him in hall or chamber with a cool courtesy that carried with it no sign of deeper interest. If he hadn't already proved otherwise, he would have begun to think she really didn't want him! And that, considering how much he desired her, would be intolerable. Yet he was reluctant to break his word and come to her before he'd solved the stupid cipher. Not only would such an action provoke her to more hellcat screechings and fighting, but worse, she would laugh in his face for being unable to solve the riddle a simple woman had set him.

Tonight, Rochambeau decided, sighing and leaning forward in his chair to disguise the swelling under his tunic. Tonight they'd see an end to these games. He would give up his afternoon's sport outdoors, even though it was perfect hawking weather. He would lock himself into a private chamber, leave strict orders not to be disturbed, and solve that damned cipher before the sun went down. Then he'd begin collecting his winnings! He smiled at the thought, and Eduin stumbled again, lost the thread of his speech, and started all over at the beginning. This time, Rochambeau recognized what the man was doing.

"All right, Eduin, that's enough," he interrupted before he had to hear the same speech for the third time. "You have the same right to graze the land as anybody else; no one is questioning that. What seems to be the problem?" He nodded at the group of poor villeins who stood opposed to Eduin, wishing to hell he could recall any of their names.

They all spoke at once, naturally, and the only thing Rochambeau could make out of their babble was that one of them claimed Eduin had turned his beasts on to the field early, before the women had finished their gleaning.

"If your lazy slut of a wife had been out there gleaning after the harvest, Alsi, instead of tilting mugs in the alehouse with you, she'd ha' done gleaning a week afore I turned my beasts out!" Eduin riposted.

Rochambeau stepped between the two men before a blow could follow this insult. "Well, it seems there's just one way to settle this matter," he said pleasantly. "I'll look at the field myself and judge whether it was ready for grazing." He extended one hand to Johanna in wordless invitation, not really expecting her to take him up on it, and blessed his luck when she joined him. Instead of a dull, interminable session in the manor court, he was going to get a nice ride in the fresh air with his wife. Maybe after they'd finished these churls' business, they could go on to explore someplace interesting, like a little secluded copse by the river bank. She might be more forthcoming once they were out of the manor, where everyone's eyes were upon her.

The field in question was quite close to the village, hardly worth saddling horses and riding out to view it, but Rochambeau insisted, and Johanna didn't object. "You can meet us there," he told the villeins who straggled after them. "That way, I'll have time to inspect the land and let you know my decision."

"A clever move," Johanna applauded as soon as they were out of earshot of the villeins. Rochambeau looked at her in faint surprise. The fresh air and exercise were already putting roses in her cheeks, and the light fall breeze whipped tendrils of loose curls about her face. She looked much too lovely to risk being nice to him. What was going on?

"I'm glad you approve," he said cautiously. The obvious explanation occurred to him. "Were you getting as bored as I was, then? That smoky hall is no place to waste a nice autumn day, and as for listening to Eduin's prosy lecture—" He broke off and laughed in some confusion, remembering that he'd been the one who had invited Eduin to bore them.

"I meant riding ahead," Johanna explained. "It gives me a chance to explain to you what's really going on in this case."

"Explain!" Did the damned girl think she was still running the manor single-handed? "Johanna, I think I can manage to settle a trivial dispute between a couple of villeins without your guiding hand, thank you very much."

"Oh, I'm sorry. I didn't mean to interfere." Johanna dropped her eyes, and he was momentarily gratified to see that she'd taken his rebuke to heart. Her next words reminded him that he should never be grateful when Johanna acted the obedient wife. Suspicion was the only reasonable reaction to such circumstances.

"Then you already know about Gytha's affair and the business of the three spotted cows. Good. I was afraid you might seem foolish by making the wrong judgment, but as long as you're in possession of all the facts, I can see I overstepped my place by reminding you of them." Johanna spurred her horse so that it trotted on ahead of her husband's mount. The village street was narrow and lined on both sides by refuse. Rochambeau couldn't catch up with her until they were past the church and both horses were picking their way down the steep path that led to the open fields. By that time, he'd conquered his momentary irritation. The girl had neatly trapped him; the only thing to do was to take his defeat in good grace.

"All right," he said as soon as their mounts drew level again. "I don't have any idea who Gytha is or what she's got to do with the case. Let me guess. Eduin's favorite spotted cow?"

Johanna's lips twitched. "No. Alsi's wife. The one Eduin is calling a slut. He should know. Two springs ago she spent most of her time waving her petticoats at him, leading him on until he'd have done anything to get a moment alone with her. Finally, she agreed to meet him in the old tithing barn by the river, but when he got there she slipped out and locked him in the barn. And the result was that Alsi's herd now has three young spotted cows whose markings just happen to match those of Eduin's bull, the one he rents out to the other villeins when they want to breed a cow."

"Wait a minute. I'm getting lost again. How did we get from Gytha in the tithing barn to Alsi's spotted cows?"

"It was Eduin, not Gytha, in the barn," Johanna explained, "and he says that while he was locked in there, Gytha and Alsi drove all their cows into his pasture and put them to the bull. Alsi says the cows are spotted because their mothers looked too long at Eduin's pimply face while he was hanging around at Gytha's petticoats. The rest of the villagers say Eduin charges too much for the rent of the bull anyway. And Eduin's been swearing vengeance ever since."

Rochambeau nodded slowly. "And how do you know all this?"

Johanna's green eyes flashed with quickly concealed amusement. "I listen a lot."

"Instead of marching into the hall and demanding a coherent story, at which point everybody starts spouting their carefully prepared lies. I may have a little something to learn from you after all, lady wife," Rochambeau conceded with a grin.

Johanna seemed inches taller, and this time the smile she offered him had no concealed malice in it. The flashing brightness of her face reminded him of a fine sword unsheathed and glittering in the sun. "Need we go look at this damned field?" he asked, more plaintively than he meant. If they turned to the left instead of the right, they'd disappear into the greenwood before the villeins caught up with them, and perhaps he could explore other ways to make Johanna look at him like that.

"It's right here." Johanna pointed at an expanse of golden stubble among which ten placid cows stood munching. There was a stalk of grain still dangling out of the mouth of the nearest cow.

"I see," said Rochambeau. "Eduin got his rent back, it seems, if that was supposed to be Gytha's gleanings. I'd say both sides are square now, and they don't need to trouble me any further." He glanced sidewise at Johanna, hoping she would approve this easy verdict.

"Except," Johanna pointed out, "that five other families have the right to glean off this field before it's opened for grazing. Those were the other villeins with Alsi. They didn't do anything to Eduin . . . and he does charge too much for the services of his bull."

Rochambeau groaned at this new complication. "I almost wish we could have a tidy little war again. A bad baron rebelling or something. War," he said plaintively, "is so much simpler than peace."

"My lady! My lord! Thank God you've come!" A heavyset man in a torn smock ran across the field, waving his arms and barely dodging the placid cows that stood in his way.

Rochambeau's hand went automatically to his side before he remembered that he'd ridden out unarmed. "What's the matter, man? Bandits? A fight?" His eyes sparkled, and he glanced around for a likely branch or a scythe to use as an improvised weapon. "Johanna, get behind me. Just show me where the trouble is, man!"

The villein came to a halt before Rochambeau's tall horse. "Beg pardon, my lord, but you'd not be much help," he mumbled. "It's *her* we need now." He pointed at Johanna, who had already swung off her horse without help.

"What's the matter, Ivo? Your Maud? I thought so. The childbed fever?" Johanna rapped out the questions before Rochambeau had quite recovered from the shock of learning that his kind of help wasn't going to be needed in this emergency.

Ivo shook his head. "No, my lady. But her milk dried up three days gone. It's that old witch 'as done it, her as lives in the wood. We was going to drag her before Maud and cut the cross in her forehead to break the spell, but she got warning and hid, see? Now Maud's desperate afeared the babe will die for want of proper nursing, and I can't calm her no way. I can't lose Maud and the babe both, my lady! You know charms. I thought maybe you could break the spell!"

"That I can, Ivo," Johanna reassured the frightened man. "And don't fear. You shall lose neither child nor wife, not as long as *I* have anything to say about it!" Once again, her slight frame seemed inches taller, and Rochambeau admired the commanding light that flashed in her eyes. "But I'll need to go back to the manor for, er, my magic potions."

"No, my lady. Please. Maud needs you now. It's all as will calm her. Unless . . . ." The man looked hopefully up at Rochambeau. "Maybe you'd send for your dogs and hunt the witch down, my lord?"

"My lord will do all that is needful," said Johanna calmly. Stepping to Rochambeau's side, she whispered, "Never mind the old woman. Some poor crazed creature who was stoned out of one of Sir Ilbod de Marti's villages. She's got a hut in the woods, and my people haven't been able to persuade her to come into the village where I could look after her. She's afraid of people, and you can see why. But what I do need is —" She broke off, frowning. "Oh, you won't want to bother with such women's business."

"Just tell me what you need," said Rochambeau, "And I'll see you have it. But I don't like leaving you alone with this rough fellow."

The shining look of gratitude in Johanna's eyes was all he'd ever dreamed of. "Oh, don't worry about Ivo and Maud. But if you could bring me a few things from the stillroom and the herb garden? I truly think it will be easier to calm the poor woman if I go directly to her."

Rochambeau raised his brows at the list of herbs she named. "Can you remember all that?" Johanna asked. "If you can, Alais will help you find them."

"Certainly I can. It's only four things. But why—"

"Then go on, *go!*" Johanna slapped his horse on the rump, and Rochambeau found himself cantering back up through the village before it even occurred to him to take offense at being ordered about by a woman. On his way back to the manor, he rode through the group of villeins coming down to the field. They scattered, and he shouted, "All right—I've made my decision—tell you later!" They would be on tenter-hooks, waiting to find out what he had decided and who would be amerced for the quarrel, but that was the lot of a villein. Right now, Johanna was also waiting, and her needs came far before those of a bunch of peasants.

Getting the herbs Johanna had requested took longer than he had anticipated. The borage had to be picked from her garden, and the thorn apple leaves were kept under lock and key in a separate chest in the stillroom. A sensible precaution, but it seemed that only Johanna had the key to the chest, and Alais dithered for some time before Rochambeau lost patience and pried the lock open with his knife. All he could think about was Johanna, alone with some superstitious villagers and a half-crazed woman. What if harm came to her while he was dallying around in the herb garden like an old woman?

Ivo's house, a mean daub-and-wattle hut in the lower end of the villages, was readily identifiable by Johanna's sleek chestnut gelding tethered outside the door. Rochambeau jumped off his horse, throwing the reins to one of the urchins who stood in the lane, and strode into the hut. Two paces carried him from the clean, fresh autumn air into darkness, smoke, the stench of old blood and sour milk, the wailing of women, and the high-pitched, fretful cry of a child. The single room was crowded with villeins, mostly women. Johanna was bending over a pallet at one side of the smoky room, where Ivo held down a thrashing, wailing woman. When she turned to him, her eyes glowed like a cat's in the firelight.

"Oh, thank goodness!" she exclaimed in heartfelt relief. "You were quicker than I thought possible."

She stood to take the little bags of herbs from him, and their hands brushed with an electric touch that set Rochambeau's heart hammering. Here in this dirty peasant hut, with her coif pulled half off her head and her dress stained, she was as desirable as he'd ever seen her. "I wish I could always be so quick to serve your needs," he said, and for once Johanna didn't come back with one of her cutting, sarcastic rejoinders. He even thought she blushed slightly before turning away.

With great care she crumbled a tiny amount of the thorn apple leaves into a cup of hot barley water. "I wish I had time to prepare a proper distillation," she said with a worried frown. "But we must get Maud calmed down before I can do anything else. They're talking of burning the wood to get that poor old woman."

Rochambeau watched in some concern as she held the cup to the sick woman's lips and coaxed her to take tiny sips. Although it did not discolor unicorn's horn or toadstone, he had heard that the thorn apple was a deadly poison if taken in sufficient doses. Some people called it nightshade; witches gathered it, and peasants were careful to clear it from the fields where their beasts grazed. Did Johanna know what she was doing?

Evidently she did. After a few moments, Maud's hysterical screaming quieted, and Johanna was able to move on to the next stage of the cure. Taking some dried vervain leaves and caraway seeds from her bags, she handed them to Ivo with instructions to crumble the vervain at the threshold of the house and bury the caraway seeds in Maud's pallet.

"A *clean* pallet," she instructed, her nose wrinkling with distaste. "Has this straw been changed since her childbed? I thought not. It stinks of blood and sweat."

"Beg pardon, my lady, but 'tis unlucky to change a laboring woman's straw until she has been churched," Ivo protested.

Johanna stamped her foot, and her eyes flashed with a green sparkle that made several of the villeins start back, crossing themselves and mumbling prayers. "It will be more unlucky for you if you don't do as I say!" Calming down slightly, she reasoned with the man. "Vervain will keep a witch or her familiar from crossing the threshold, and caraway will protect Maud and the babe from any new spells against her milk. But first we must get rid of the old pallet, which may very well be harboring demons."

Ivo crossed himself and lifted Maud, while some of the other villeins dragged out the old pallet. While they were arranging a clean sleeping place for the woman, Johanna brewed another draught for her. This one was an infusion of vervain, caraway, and fennel leaves. "See that she drinks this four times a day," she instructed Ivo. "I'll leave the herbs with you so that you can brew more when it's needed. Steep a pinch of each one in barley water—a lot of barley water." She measured the quantity with her hands. "By the end of the day, her milk will be flowing again, and if you leave the witch alone she won't cast any more spells."

"It's coming in now!" squealed Maud with delight, fondling her heavy breasts. "I can feel it. Quick, bring me the babe!" Leaning up on one elbow, she gulped the hot infusion while pulling her shift open to give suck to her newborn child. Rochambeau beat a hasty retreat and occupied himself with the horses until Johanna came out of the hut a few minutes later.

"Will vervain and caraway really counteract the spell?" he asked as they were riding back up to the castle.

Johanna flashed an impish grin. "I don't know, but they'll certainly help her milk flow. The stupid woman hasn't been drinking enough liquids, and then she got hysterical and decided she was under a curse. I had to calm her down first. The thorn apple's good for that, but it's dangerous too, so I didn't want to use very much. Clean straw to lie on and plenty to drink will be half her cure, and the other herbs will help if she really has a problem with her milk after she relaxes, which I doubt."

"So do I," said Rochambeau with feeling, remembering the moment's glimpse of pendulous blue-veined breasts when Maud had opened her shift.

Johanna giggled, and they rode on in companionable silence until they reached the outer bailey. Here Rochambeau saw, waiting for him, the villeins whom he'd ignored earlier. He groaned and turned to Johanna. "They want a decision."

"Tell them to wait."

"Er, I told them I'd already made one."

"What was it?"

"Damned if I know!" Rochambeau groaned again at the thought of plunging into that tangled litigious skein of old wrongs, rumors, and complaints. He hadn't thought about the problem of the grazing fields since this other emergency came up, and he was difinitely not prepared to deal with it now. It looked like it was turning into one of those things that could drag on all afternoon, and he had more urgent business at hand. On the other hand, if Johanna could be persuaded to take it over, he'd be free of both the villeins and her for some time, free to pursue his own project.

"Johanna, you seem to know all the personalities and problems involved. Do you think you could hear the rest of the case for me and hand down a decision in my name?"

"What if you don't like it?"

"Whatever you say," Rochambeau promised recklessly, "I'll abide by. After all, you've been in charge for four years, and things don't seem to have quite gone to ruin yet. I suppose you can handle this major case on your own. Just don't hang anybody, all right?"

Her face lit up as if she'd just been handed a string of pearls and an invitation to stay at court, and she dismounted before Rochambeau could lift her from her horse. He watched her slim, eager figure as she hastened toward the waiting villeins and shook his head in bemusement. Truly, there was no telling what would please a woman! Well, when he'd finished his afternoon's project, he would please her in some tried and true ways. And once they were reconciled, perhaps he would take her to court, buy her some new dresses, teach her the latest dance steps.

His step light, whistling under his breath, Rochambeau headed off to the old keep tower where he'd stored the account rolls and other miscellaneous parchments until he should have time to concentrate properly on this cipher of Johanna's. It shouldn't take him more than an hour or two of private work to break the cipher, and then they could begin living together as man and wife again.

He settled down happily in a cubbyhole of the old keep tower that, by fortunate coincidence, had been used by the clerk of the accounts in his father's time. The room was still furnished with a slanted writing stand and some ancient quills, and the stand was angled so as to take advantage of the north light that came in through the single window. Still whistling, Rochambeau sharpened one of the quills with his knife and mixed up a little brownish ink. Of one thing he felt certain: no woman, however skilled with herbs, however knowledgeable about the gossip of the manor, could possibly have the intellectual ability to invent a cipher. Such abstract thought was entirely beyond them. Someone must once have told Johanna about the codes and ciphers that schoolboys and monks used to enliven the tedium of their copying tasks, and she'd been clever enough to adapt the concept to her own use.

All he needed was time to concentrate, to decide which of a half-dozen different systems she might have used, and to test his theory on a number of different selections from the rolls. He certainly didn't mean to go through the labor of deciphering the last three years' worth of accounts. Once he'd shown her that he could break her system, she could damned well write out the accounts all over again in plain English to make up for putting him through this in the first place. What the hell, he'd even lend her a clerk to help with the copying. If she was generous about paying up on the wager tonight, he was prepared to be generous in his own way.

The only question was, what system had she used and how was it applied? Rochambeau had already tested the cipher against the various codes he and Aubrey had played with when, as boys, they were subjected to two years of monastery training. Writing words and sentences backwards, garbling Latin roots with English endings and vice versa, transposing letters, substituting code words for vital parts of the sentence—none of these methods, applied to Johanna's rolls, yielded anything but gibberish.

Of course, she wouldn't have used something Aubrey had told her about, or even he would have been able to break the cipher. Besides, these boys' tricks were probably too complicated for a woman's limited brain to follow. Rochambeau recalled something he'd heard in Rome about the way Caesar used to send secret messages. It was much simpler than the codes he and Aubrey had worked out. A simple letter substitution, as he recalled. For each letter of the alphabet, one substituted the third letter down, so that A became D, B became E, and so forth. Perhaps Johanna had heard the same story. Such a trivial substitution would be well within even a woman's capabilities if she made herself a little chart to work with. And poor old Aubrey had probably never even tried anything that simple.

Whistling happily, Rochambeau selected a page of the accounts at random and tried his new theory. The original line read, "FNVJ ZM URPJ TPSAMRK EX PIRX."

The substition he had chosen gave him "CRSG WJ ROMG OMPXJOH BU MFOU."

Hardly an improvement. Oh, well, even Johanna could probably figure out that using the exact same cipher as Caesar's would be too obvious. She must have used the fourth or even the fifth letter down . . .

In fact, it was the seventeenth, and Rochambeau had covered one of his blank parchments with scribbles before he correctly translated the first three words as "OWES IV DAYS."

"Hurrah!" He capped the ink bottle and tossed it up in the air. Perhaps that wasn't the most exciting line in the accounts, but it was enough to make him happy. Was it enough to convince Johanna that he'd broken the cipher? What the hell, he might as well least finish the sentence and do a couple more into the bargain. Now that he knew the system, it wouldn't take him long to translate enough to make it crystal clear to Johanna that her secret was a secret no longer. Chuckling, Rochambeau replaced the ink bottle on the stand, filled his pen, and bent over the parchment. Let's see, the next three words would be . . .

"TPSAMRK EX PIRX." Which translated to "CYBJVAT NG YRAG."

"God's body and bones!" Rochambeau swore in disgust. Gibberish again! Had he made a mistake in counting? No, T was the seventeenth letter after C, and so forth. He was still using the same system that had worked so well for deciphering the first three words, and there was absolutely no reason why it should fail him now.

Unless the seeming sense of the first three words had been

an accident. That must be it. An unlucky coincidence. The true cipher wasn't the seventeenth letter down, but perhaps the eighteenth, or even the nineteenth . . .

He worked all the way down to the end of the alphabet, checking his work at every step. Nothing worked on the rest of the line. Well, maybe that line had been garbled in some way. Try another . . .

As he scribbled and tried various half-formed systems on randomly chosen lines, he got no closer than that first tantalizing glimpse of success. Every once in a while a word or two would seem to leap out of the babel of the enciphered accounts, but as soon as he tried to grasp a theory it was exploded by the garbage on either side of the apparent translation. Finally, the light fading, he laid down his quill and massaged his aching shoulders. He'd been standing at that damned writing stand all afternoon, like a damned clerk in a monastery, and what had he to show for it? Not a damned thing!

"You swear a lot," said an amused voice behind him. "Having some difficulty?"

Johanna stood in the doorway, her delicate features lit by the candle she shielded in one hand. The glow of light dazzled Rochambeau, and he realized that the daylight had been slowly fading while he puzzled over the cipher.

"A few minor details," he lied, pushing his scrawled parchments under a clean page before Johanna could see and laugh at his attempts. "I should have it wrapped up in a couple of days."

"My, my," Johanna marveled. "Who'd have thought it would take the clever lord of Rochambeau so long to figure out a mere woman's cipher?"

"It wouldn't take any time at all," Rochambeau snarled, most unfairly, "if I weren't interrupted every time I started to work!"

"I'm sorry," said Johanna, demurely dropping her gaze so that, instead of being transfixed by the flash of green eyes, he was hypnotized by the spread of sooty lashes against a white cheek. "I just thought you might like to know what decision you made in Eduin and Alsi's case. And you haven't eaten all day."

Both statements stung Rochambeau to the quick. Did she

have to rub it in that he had been so wrapped up in the cipher he'd forgotten to eat, forgotten his duties as lord of the manor, forgotten everything except his desire for her? She was probably secretly gloating over his frustration, enjoying the sense of her power over him.

"Go away," he snarled. "You distract me."

"Do I?" She stepped closer, and the faint fragrance of dried flowers and herbs from her clothes, mingled with the warmer, sweeter scent of her skin, rose to Rochambeau's head in a dizzying wave.

"Don't gloat too much, madam wife." He would be damned if he'd let her see how much he desired her—not until he'd broken this cipher, proved his superiority, and won his right to her bed. "I'll solve your little puzzle any minute now."

"I'm surprised you haven't solved it already. Surely a mere woman can't have the intelligence to keep you in suspense for long?"

"Some women," Rochambeau admitted, "including you, my dear wife, do seem to have a sort of low animal cunning that can occasionally substitute for true masculine intelligence."

"In other words," said Johanna loftily, "you're stumped."

"And you're disappointed that I may not be claiming my winnings tonight?"

"No, I'm delighted!" She whisked out of his reach and disappeared down the winding stair outside. Only a tantalizing fragrance remained in the room to remind him of her, a scent compounded of warm bread and honey and other delicious, sweet, desirable things.

After a few minutes, Rochambeau identified the source of the fragrance. Just outside the door, someone had set down a wooden platter covered with a linen napkin. Under the napkin were a small loaf of fresh-baked bread, a dish of honey and pounded almonds, and half a roasted chicken.

Perhaps she had not meant to tease him with that remark about his having forgotten supper.

Perhaps she'd really come up in a friendly spirit. And he'd been so sore about his failure to solve the cipher that he'd completely failed to exploit the opportunity. Rochambeau gnawed on a chicken leg, cursed his own stupidity, dipped pieces of bread into the honey sauce, tried a few more tricks on the enciphered rolls without much hope of success, and gradually grumbled and nibbled himself into a good mood. Johanna had been nicer to him that day than ever before. Perhaps she didn't really want him to stay out of her bed forever. Of course she didn't. No woman really wanted to sleep alone all her life, no matter how she protested to the contrary.

All he had to do was give her a face-saving way out, some excuse to take him back. And that didn't necessarily have to be tied to his breaking of this damnable cipher. A meditative grin spread slowly over Rochambeau's face as he polished off the last bit of meat on the chicken bones. Why was he wasting his time with parchment and ink? Children's games were no way to win a woman. What he needed was a game that would make Johanna value what she'd thrown away when she kicked the lord of Rochambeau out of her bed. And that was a sport in which he excelled.

Chapter Fourteen

THE MORROW FOUND the lord of Rochambeau packing his saddle bags for a quick, unheralded journey. He had had some thought of leaving during morning Mass without making any explanation to Johanna, but her habit of early rising foiled that plan. If he was in the courtyard before dawn, so was she, demanding to know where he thought he was going.

"I can hardly conceive that my movements would be of any great interest to you," Rochambeau said. He slung a loaded bag onto his pack horse and beckoned to the young squire he'd taken on as a body-servant after Marc's death.

"Maybe I just want to know how long I can be left in peace," Johanna countered.

"It shouldn't take me more than a few days to ride up to Ockham," he said, naming the northernmost of his manors.

Johanna looked relieved rather than disappointed at this hint that he'd be back soon. That suited Rochambeau well enough, but he decided not to pursue this slight advantage now. The middle of a cold courtyard, with squires and servants bustling abut their duties and people hurrying to hear a quick Mass before breaking their fast, was no place to start courting one's own wife. No, he'd let her have a few days to think over how well she liked her lord's absence; then, when she was in a mood to appreciate him, the little surprise he was planning would have all the more effect.

Johanna disappeared without a proper farewell, and that

disappointed him somewhat, but Aubrey didn't give him a chance to chase after her. "What are you going to Ockham for?" he demanded while Rochambeau was mounting.

Rochambeau looked down at his bastard half-brother with a twinkle in his eye. Sleepy and disheveled in the early morning light, with wisps of fair hair sticking up on his head and fists planted on his hips, Aubrey looked as if he suspected Rochambeau of plotting to steal one of his favorite toys. "My dear Aubrey, is it really so strange if I should choose to inspect one of my own manors?"

"Yes," said Aubrey uncompromisingly. "You've never bothered before. And you should take me if you're going on a tour of inspection. I'm your estate's seneschal, after all."

"Are you?" Rochambeau murmured. "I rather thought Johanna had usurped that role. And you'll notice that I'm not taking her."

Aubrey flushed painfully, and Rochambeau repented of teasing his brother. "Cheer up, Aubrey. If I were going to inspect my manors, of course I'd take you along."

"If? But you just said that's what you were doing."

"I said it shouldn't take more than a few days to ride to Ockham and back. Which is perfectly true. I did not, however, say that was where I was going."

After a long, puzzled moment of silence, Aubrey's brow cleared and he began to chuckle. "Oho! Tired of the lady already, Nicolas, and off to seek pleasanter companionship?"

Rochambeau shrugged, smiled, and rode off without confirming or denying Aubrey's guess.

Over the next few days, Johanna found that Malvern seemed oddly empty without Rochambeau. And her life seemed quite flat without his constant teasing, without the expectation that she'd encounter his tall form in mews or stable or that he'd appear in the bower with some mischievous comment to set her ladies aflutter. No matter how often she told herself that she ought to be glad of the few days' respite from their continual sniping, the truth was that she was bored. She began cutting out a new dress from some of the silks he had brought back from his travels, but she abandoned the project halfway through. What was the good of a tunic and surcoat in clinging red and gold silk if there was no one to be tantalized by the sight?

"Oh, you take the silk," she told Alais when she found herself heartily wishing she'd never begun the project. "Finish it up for yourself."

"Not my colors," said Alais wistfully, fingering the soft Eastern fabric that stretched and clung to her fingers like a silken spiderweb. "He bought all these silks with you in mind." And indeed, the gorgeous array of peacock colors, scarlet and gold and brilliant green and deep rose, could hardly have been worn by any woman except one with Johanna's striking black hair and white skin. The boxes of cloth from Persia and China and India had come to Malvern by sea while Rochambeau was making his leisurely way home overland—the closest thing to a direct message from him that Johanna had had in all those years, until the ramsom demand came.

"Then pack them up again," Johanna snapped, "and make yourself something out of that gray woolen stuff we wove last winter. Make me something, too. We might as well start dressing like nuns, since that's how we live."

She herself did not stay to supervise Alais's work but went of to order her horse saddled. Perhaps a day of riding on the windswept hills west of Malvern, flying her peregrine, would help to clear her brain of the disordered fancies which troubled her these nights—dreams of a tall, golden-haired knight who bent over her bed, whispering the words of love and commitment she'd never yet won from Rochambeau in the flesh. And never would. See, already he was bored! Johanna didn't believe for one minute that the man was inspecting his northern manors. He'd probably gone off to rejoin the court and she'd get a message to that effect in a few weeks. Meanwhile, she'd survived his absence for four years; there was no reason for a second desertion to trouble her so much.

Aubrey intercepted her on the way to the mews. "You're moping," he said bluntly. "Don't. He's not worth it. Besides, I'm sure—I'm almost sure he'll be back soon."

Johanna regarded him steadily while she drew on her leather hawking gauntlet. Aubrey's countenance, usually so open and guileless, was now clouded as though he was trying to conceal something from her. "Did he tell you where he was really going?"

Aubrey dropped his eyes. "He said he was going to Ockham," he mumbled.

"And you don't believe that any more than I do!" Johanna challenged.

"Maybe he's looking for someone to help him decipher your accounts. I think he's finding the task more difficult than he anticipated."

That hypothesis drew an unwilling chuckle from Johanna. "No, he'd have taken the rolls with him if he were looking for help, wouldn't he?"

"And he didn't?"

"He left everything strewn over that room in the old keep."

"It's not a very good place to leave valuable documents," said Aubrey severely. "The beams are rotten, and there's a lot of old wood shoring up the walls. Rats, too."

Johanna shrugged. "They're his documents. I'm afraid he's given up on deciphering them, though."

Aubrey glanced up with a mischievous smile that reminded her unbearably of Rochambeau. "Would that disappoint you?"

"By no means," said Johanna crisply. "But he will have to know what's in them someday. I'm just waiting for him to admit defeat so that I can translate the accounts for him. Or show him the secret and let him do his own translating. That way perhaps he'll believe . . ."

"Believe what?"

"I never told him," Johanna said slowly, "about the money I raised for his ransom. At first I was too angry, and now . . ." She shrugged. "There's never been a good moment. Besides, it's been too long. He'd think I was making up a story to excuse myself. But I—it's stupid, of course, for it makes no real difference—but I would like him to know, someday, that I didn't really intend that he should rot in France. And I certainly didn't intend that Marc should die in the escape attempt. If only your messenger had arrived in time, there wouldn't have been any need for an escape. And now, well, I'd rather he would only blame me for things I really did do." She sighed and bit at the fingertips of her leather gauntlet, pulling it half off her hand and then straightening it with little nervous jerks.

"You could call on me to back you up," Aubrey pointed out.

"And what could you prove? We never found out what happened to your man. Doubtless he was waylaid and robbed." It had been madness to send the man alone, without an armed escort to protect the silver he carried. She'd been furious with Aubrey when she found out how casually he'd handled the affair. But there was no use raking up old angers now. She had been equally furious with herself. In any case, didn't she know perfectly well that Aubrey was a bumbling incompetent in money matters? But one would have thought, even if he couldn't add a short column of figures twice and get the same result, that he'd know enough to send guards with the ransom money.

With an effort Johanna broke away from the old circle of thoughts. "Anyway," she said with an attempted smile, "call it a whim, but I'd like Rochambeau to know that I didn't betray him as badly as he thinks I did. And the best way would be if he discovered it for himself in the course of deciphering the accounts, don't you think?"

"It's clearly recorded in there?"

"One hundred and fifty marks from the abbot of Saintsbury for hunting rights to the forest at Ainscourt. One hundred and fifty marks to you for ransom to be sent to Avranches. Couldn't be more clear."

Aubrey still looked sick. He must feel terribly guilty about his messenger having lost all that money. "Don't feel bad," Johanna said, forcing a smile. "It's my own fault Rochambeau thinks I refused to ransom him. After all, if the plan had worked and the money had reached him in time, I never would have told him where it came from. It's just—well, I'd like him to know that Marc's death wasn't exactly my fault." But it had been. If it weren't for her own foolish pride, her desire to insult Rochambeau as publicly and deeply as he had once insulted her, he would not have believed it necessary to break out of Avranches, and Marc would be alive today.

"Don't you feel bad either," said Aubrey. He patted her shoulder and let his hand rest there for a moment. "It's a sad tangle, but somehow it'll all come right in the end. You and Nicolas, well, it was never a match made in heaven, was it? You need somebody who'll cherish you and care for you,

Johanna, not a rough, crude fighting man like Nicholas." He pulled her into an awkward hug and kissed her moistly on the forehead. "I would care for you always," he whispered.

Johanna freed herself as quickly as she could without using force. "Then it's a good thing it was Rochambeau I wed," she said with a shaky laugh, "for to tell you the truth, Aubrey, I don't much want to be cherished like a delicate piece of glassware! What I do want is a nice brisk ride over the hills. Coming?"

Aubrey shook his head and stepped back, accepting her laughing dismissal as he always did. Johanna never had been able to take his clumsy attempts at courtship seriously; she suspected Aubrey didn't mean them seriously, either. For all his courteous words, she never had the sense that he desired her as a woman or that he saw her as anything but Rochambeau's lady. He just wanted to cheer her up, Johanna thought, and, like his brother, he only knew one way to make a woman feel happy.

"Then I'll take a groom," she said, suppressing a secret relief. Aubrey was always as nervous as an old maid when he went riding with her, warning her to slow down, afraid her horse would stumble and he'd be blamed for a fatal accident to the lady of the manor. The grooms might have the same fears, but at least they knew better than to say anything.

For once, the promised tonic of a long afternoon outdoors failed to calm Johanna. A vague uneasiness possessed her which she found impossible to shake off. Rochambeau had been gone for a week and two days now, long enough for her to miss the constant stimulation of his company but not long enough for her to settle down into the placid routine that had occupied her while he was out of the country. It had been too long for the brief visit to Ockham that he'd hinted at, and she couldn't think of any attraction in that distant northern manor which could keep him there for so long.

Unless he had a woman up there . . .

"Good," said Johanna between her teeth. "It'll keep him from annoying me." Besides, hadn't she always known that would be the inevitable end of this mismatched marriage, that he'd tire of her and go off to find some other pretty doll to play with? Better to face it now than later, she told herself without conviction. The falcon responded to her unsettled mood, first refusing to rise to any of the game she started, then taking its first kill off to a high perch, where it sat and crunched up the hare in stark disobedience to her commands. The light was almost gone by the time she coaxed the peregrine down to her wrist again and set off homeward.

The villeins had returned from their daily work by the time she reached the village. Blue smoke rose from the huts clustered around the church, blending in with the pale blue evening sky, and the long lavender shadows crept across the stubble-filled fields. It should have been a peaceful scene. Why couldn't she look on it with the pleasure she'd felt before Rochambeau had returned to turn her life upside down? She was the one rebellious element in this ordered landscape, as out of place as the leaping tongue of orange that licked the sky above the walls of Malvern.

Fire. Johanna's heart skipped unevenly as she took in the meaning of that sight. Enemies? War? No, all was peaceful around the castle walls, and the great bell in the church tower was not ringing its warning note. She dug her heels into the gelding's side and tore up the narrow village lane at a gallop, shouting a warning at the men who lounged outside the alehouse. "Fire at the castle! Ring the bell! Bring buckets!" That was all she had time for, but she saw Alsi knuckle his forehead and set off for the church at a run. Alsi was bright; he'd organize the villeins and have help at the castle as quickly as possible. Meanwhile, her place was at Malvern.

In the outer bailey, all was smoke and confusion. A woman's shrill scream disturbed Johanna's gelding; exhausted though the horse was by the uphill gallop, it reared halfway up, and the falcon on her wrist bated and ruffled its feathers. Johanna leaped off the horse's back, handed the peregrine to a stable boy, and ran for the pillar of smoke that surrounded the old keep. Half a dozen servants were staggering around in disorganized fashion with buckets of water, while Aubrey shouted contradictory orders and yanked at his tousled blond hair with both hands.

"The records—save the parchments—throw water on the flames. No, not there, you dolt, you'll soak the rolls!"

As the bell in the church tower below them rang out its first warning notes, Johanna soaked her coif and tied it over her mouth and nose so that she could breathe while she looked over the damage. Before the tenth stroke of the bell had echoed over the village, she had organized the scurrying menservants into a bucket line to deal with what turned out to be a relatively minor fire. By the time Alsi and his fellow villeins had panted up the steep slope to the castle gate, the flames were out, and Johanna was investigating the smoldering pile of brushwood where the fire had evidently started. She thanked the villagers and sent them to the kitchens to get bread and ale in payment for their timely response while setting a couple of servants to clearing up the remains of the mess.

"How did it start?" she asked Aubrey. Her hair was a mess, she had smoke smudges and blisters on both hands, and she was aching with tiredness. But she was also too keyed up to go to the bower and let Alais fuss around her with gentle hands and meaningless babble. Striding back and forth outside the old keep, she listened while Aubrey, the hall chamberlain, and the marshal of the stables all offered contradictory stories. Some fool had been storing brushwood in the lower story of the old keep, some other fool had thrown kitchen trash that included live coals in the fosse outside the keep wall, but who had done what would probably never be known.

"No, don't bother." Johanna brushed aside the stable marshal's suggestion that the servants should be called for a general inquisition. "I can't see anybody coming forward to say they started the fire, can you? At least, I hope I don't employ anybody stupid enough to confess to something like this when they got away without being caught. And thank God there's not much damage done." The few old furnishings that had been left in the keep were gone, of course, but a handful of rotting tapestries and crude village-made tables were small loss. The important thing was that the structural beams had escaped damage. The new bailey wall that Rochambeau had thrown up around the castle incorporated the old keep tower into one corner of its structure, so damage there would have left the castle badly vulnerable to attack.

"Not much damage?" Aubrey gave her an odd look. "I must say, you're taking it well. I should have thought you'd be much more upset. I know Rochambeau will be, when he gets back."

"What, over some worm-eaten tables and a couple of writing stands?"

"Not that junk," said Aubrey. "But the estate records must have gone up with them. Didn't you say he left everything strewn around his workroom in there? The parchments would never have survived the fire."

"Oh, that!" In the excitement of the fire, Johanna had completely forgotten how Rochambeau left his workroom. Now she laughed with relief. "Yes, it would have been a disaster, wouldn't it? Fortunately, I'm not as bad a housekeeper as you seem to think me, Aubrey. As soon as I found out what a mess Rochambeau had left in his workroom, I tidied up the place and put all the parchments back in the locked chests in the strongroom for safekeeping. I was a little afraid he'd be angry with me for messing up his work, but as things turned out it was a most fortunate coincidence, wasn't it?"

"Fortunate indeed!" Aubrey looked as though he wanted to say something more, but whatever it was, his opening words were drowned out by shouts from the gate tower.

"Oh, for heaven's sake, what now?" Johanna exclaimed in exasperation. If Rochambeau had chosen this moment to come back, she thought, with her all tattered and smoke-smudged and the castle staff thrown into confusion, she would never forgive him. Ineffectively trying to pat her tousled curls back into place under her tight coif, she hastened toward the gate tower.

It wasn't Rochambeau, but what she found was nearly as bad. The crowd of curious onlookers, both castle staff and villagers, was too thick for her to see what was going on at first. One of the two men-at-arms on guard duty shouldered his way through the crowd to report to her.

"This young woman says she's a friend of the lord's," he announced, jerking a thumb back toward the center of the crowd. "Seeing he's not at home to prove the truth of her statement, shall I let her in or send her on her way, my lady?"

"Nonsense," said Johanna at once. "Malvern is not so poor that we need turn away guests, Umphrey! Whatever gave you such an idea?"

Umphrey dropped his voice to a confidential rumble and leaned so close to Johanna that she could count the grayish spikes of stubble on his roughly shaved chin. "Begging your pardon, my lady, but this ain't exactly one of your regular noble visitors. In fact, if you want my opinion, the young lady's no better than she—''

The disturbance at the center of the crowd moved violently forward. Two white-coiffed women and a turnspit boy were pushed out of the way with squawks of protest, and the object of the guard's worries stood revealed in all her glory.

''—should be,'' Umphrey finished with a gulp, rolling his eyes toward the girl whose appearance had caused such a stir.

Now that she got a good look at her, Johanna could fully understand why a crowd was standing around the gatehouse to gawk at the visitor. The girl was dark-haired like Johanna herself, but there all resemblance ceased. Instead of keeping her black hair decently covered under a linen coif, she wore it streaming down her back in a tangle of glossy curls mixed with strings of flashing jewels. Instead of being slender and straight like Johanna, she was possessed of a decidedly voluptuous figure which swayed slightly from side to side even when, as now, she was attempting to stand still. It was easy to assess her figure, because it was concealed by nothing more than a long tunic of thinnest gold-embroidered silk over a pair of loose silky braies—the most immodest mixture of men's and women's dress that Johanna had ever seen. The full braies were gathered at her ankles to reveal gilt shoes with long curling tips.

Before Johanna had a chance to reformulate the words of greeting that were strangling in her throat, the girl swayed forward gracefully, crossed her arms over her breasts, and went down on one knee at Johanna's feet. With the movement, the little silver bells that decorated the hem of her tunic tinkled merrily, and her dark jeweled curls tumbled forward to release a cloyingly strong perfume.

''I am Laila, Pearl of the Night,'' she announced in a low, melodious voice, ''and I had the honor to do my lord of Rochambeau some insignificant service when he was in the Holy Land. Now that I in my turn am a stranger in a strange land and in need, I have come to him for succor.'' She raised dark pleading eyes, made larger by the artful use of paint, to Johanna's face. ''Of your mercy, most gracious lady, may I be brought to my lord? I have traveled far to reach him, and I am most weary.'' In attempting to rise to her feet, she stumbled as though overcome by weakness. Two of the stable grooms and the hall usher's assistant rushed to catch her.

"I—ah—of course you may come in," Johanna said. She felt awkward and ill at ease before this gorgeously attired vision of Eastern splendor. And she would dearly like to know exactly what "insignificant service" this hussy had rendered her lord in the Holy Land. No, she wouldn't. She could guess precisely what it had been! But nothing would be helped by her making a scene in front of all these gawking servants and villeins. They had already been privy to more than enough of the discord between her and Rochambeau.

Increasingly conscious of her own disheveled, smoke-stained condition, she bent her knee the merest fraction of an inch and beckoned to the girl with one hand. "Pray follow me, ah . . ." What had the girl said her outlandish name was? "Laila. You shall have rest and refreshment in my own bower."

Leaving Laila to the attentions of her own waiting-women, Johanna slipped into her private chamber and tidied herself as best she might with Alais's help. Warm water and scent removed most of the smoke from her skin, but her hair, she realized with resignation, would go on smelling like fire and ashes until she had time to wash it properly and dry it in the sun for hours on end. Oh, well, at least she could be clean and neat when she faced this hussy and heard more about her "friendship" with Rochambeau.

She was debating between two severely cut dark tunics, either of them quite rich enough in embroidery and fabric to establish the dignity of her position as lady of the manor, when a fresh hubbub broke out in the courtyard. This time the babble was mostly of men's voices, overlaid by the snorting of horses and the chink of armor. A clear, ringing voice cut sharply through the noise with a tone of command that Johanna recognized instantly.

Rochambeau.

She stood quite still in the middle of the bedchamber, feeling the blood drain away from her face and hands until she was as cold as the tub of cooling water that stood to one side of the bed. At the same time, a flush of excitement darted along her veins, warming her from the inside out until she did not know what she felt.

"He's come back," she thought, first exultant. "Now everything will be different." Thought how it would be different, she could not say. Confused images and sensual memories crowded upon her, dizzying her with the flash of bright blue eyes, the melting sweetness of caresses from two strong hands roughened by swordplay. She'd railed at him, hated him, missed him, unwillingly and secretly loved him. Now he was back, and she didn't know what would happen next between them; but her knees were trembling and she felt her strength of resistance melting away.

Then a new and unwelcome thought struck her. What had brought him back so suddenly without warning? Could it have anything to do with the arrival of the heathen hussy who was even now being entertained in Johanna's own bower?

"Surely not," she whispered, almost unaware that she spoke aloud. "How could he have known?"

"Known what, my lady?" Alais's gentle eyes were cloudy with doubt, and her hands shook slightly as she combed out Johanna's long black hair.

"Nothing. It doesn't matter." Johanna shook her head briskly and stepped away from Alais. An inner voice cried out rebelliously that it wasn't fair. Was there never to be any peace between her and Rochambeau? Must each meeting be like going into battle? So be it. This time she was going to fight to keep what was hers, her position as the lady of Rochambeau and her power over the estates. Whatever else might or might not pass between them, Nicolas de Rochambeau wasn't going to insult her by keeping his heathen mistress in the same castle as his wife—of that she felt sure.

Suddenly the two dignified tunics that Alais had brought out of the chest, one of dark green wool and the other of dark blue, seemed entirely unsuitable for this particular kind of battle. Heavy bands of gold and silver embroidery, the weight of gold rings and chains, were not the weapons she needed against a foreign enchantress with scented hair and little bells on her transparent garments. And Alais, that silly girl, was fumbling with the clothes chest instead of helping her to decide which of these unsatisfactory garments to put on.

"I wish I'd finished that red silk dress," Johanna moaned.

"I did." With a quiet smile, Alais stood up from the chest

with a trailing, shimmering banner of red and gold in her arms. "I thought you'd want it someday."

"Alais, you're wonderful!" Johanna embraced the girl and would have kissed her, but Alais drew back with alarmed protestations that she would crush the fragile silks. "You shall have whatever else you choose out of Rochambeau's Eastern silks to make yourself a new dress for the Christmas feasts. And if none of the colors suits you, we'll just send him back to the Holy Land to pick out something better!" She raised her arms so that Alais could slip the clinging spiderweb material over her head, but her tongue kept rattling on with promises for Alais's future. It was one way to keep from thinking about her own immediate future.

"Yes, you should definitely have some better clothes. It's time we saw about a marriage for you, too. Your father hasn't said anything about it, has he? I thought not. Now that Rochambeau's back, we'll be entertaining more. There'll be a chance for you to meet some men of standing."

Alais pouted. "I don't like men of standing. They're all old and serious. I'd rather have a minstrel or a squire, somebody young enough to have fun."

"Do you think Aubrey's old and serious?" Johanna teased.

"Aubrey's different." Bright waves of pink stained Alais's perfect oval of a face.

Johanna regretted having brought up the subject. "And unavailable, at least as far as you're concerned! Do you think Sir Ilbod would let you marry beneath you? Forget Aubrey. Forget the nice boys who flirt with you. That's not what your father fostered you here for. His intent, and mine too, was that Rochambeau should use his influence to marry you well."

"Marry well!" Alais cried out rebelliously. "As *you* did, you mean?"

Johanna was shocked to realize how much she had sounded like her own mother, counseling Alais to accept the arrangements her elders would make for her. And yet—and yet—would she really change things, if she could go back? Would she rather have had Piers or Gautier? Her marriage to Rochambeau might not be a happy one, but Johanna found it impossible to imagine being married to anybody else. If only he would be *reasonable*—

She cut off that line of thought. He wouldn't, no use expecting it, and she had to show him he couldn't get away with planting his mistress in the house. And none of this had anything to do with Alais, who was a silly child without the sense to choose her own husband. "If my lord had been at home, we should have started looking about for someone two years ago, when you turned twelve. If we wait another two years, you'll be sixteen, as I was when I married, and that," Johanna concluded with a sigh, "is really to late for a girl to begin learning to accept a man's authority."

"Somehow I don't think your advanced age had much to do with it," Alais teased. "I think you and Rochambeau would have struck sparks off each other whenever you met."

"You may be right. There are certainly going to be some sparks flying now!" Johanna jammed a gold circlet down on her head in place of her limp and smoke-stained coif and exited the chamber with the long sleeves and train of red and gold silk floating behind her like the banners of an army marching to war.

Chapter Fifteen

ROCHAMBEAU REACHED THE head of the stairs just as Johanna pushed aside the heavy tapestry curtain that gave the bower a modicum of privacy even when, as now, the door was open.

"Ah! My very dear wife! How good of you to make a special effort to greet me!" His eyes flickered over the gaudy crimson and gold of her tunic and supertunic. A respectful kiss pressed on the back of her wrist, a sense of the powerful masculine force contained in his immaculate riding tunic and leather surcoat, and then he was past her and setting all the women in the bower aflutter, as usual. And Johanna had nothing better to do than trail behind him like a servant.

"Laila!" He certainly sounded surprised to see the exotic vision of silk and scent that bowed to greet him in the bower, but how could you tell what a man like Rochambeau was really thinking? Only one thing was certain: he also sounded pleased. Johanna's eyes narrowed to green slits as her husband lifted the Saracen girl from her knees, embracing her fondly and speaking to her in a foreign tongue that she could not understand. Arabic? She strained her ears, trying to guess what they were saying, but Rochambeau's words were entirely incomprehensible, and Laila's murmured replies were all but inaudible.

"Poor child!" At last Rochambeau released the girl and

turned to Johanna. "She has suffered many hardships on her way to me, as doubtless she has related to you already."

"As a matter of fact," said Johanna stiffly, "we have not yet had the opportunity for private converse. At the time when she appeared—"

She had meant to tell Rochambeau about the fire, but he interrupted her before she could do so. "No? What a pity. Well, you can talk later. Laila is a most entertaining conversationalist—in Arabic, that is—although, her English being limited, perhaps it would be better if I related her sad story to you myself."

He said it was a pity, but he sounded as pleased as a cat that's been accidentally locked in the dairy. Johanna's suspicions grew. Rochambeau had known damned well that this Eastern lightskirt was coming to Malvern; he'd stayed out of sight just long enough to make Johanna receive the girl herself so that she couldn't claim he'd forced her into it. More of his trickery! Well, this time it wasn't going to work. There were some insults no woman could be expected to swallow in silence.

"Perhaps it would be better if you did so," Johanna agreed. "In privacy. I am sure we both have much news for each other after your journey, my lord." She invited him into the inner chamber with a smile and a curtsy.

Once the door of the bedchamber had shut behind them, there was no more need to pretend calm for the benefit of her women. "Now," Johanna demanded, hands on hips, "suppose you tell me what's really going on between you and that hussy. No, on second thought, don't tell me. It's perfectly obvious. You and your Saracen dancing girls! She leaves this castle as soon as she's had a night's rest and a decent meal." Less than that she could not, in simple decency, offer, even to her husband's mistress.

Rochambeau raised his brows. "The poor girl seems to have offended you. Don't you even want to hear her affecting story first? It seems the pasha of Egypt cooled toward her after she had been lent to me for a few nights, suspecting that she could not feel true affection for him after enjoying the company of a Christian knight. She was sold into the most degrading service of a silk merchant who, inflamed by her beauty, took her with him wherever his business led him. He used her cruelly, but she had no thought of escape until one day they took ship for a cold northern land whose name was familiar to her. When they reached England she ran away from her master and, knowing no English but my name, begged her way through the countryside until by great good fortune she arrived at my gates.''

"Her English has improved remarkably since she set out on this journey of love,'' Johanna remarked. "And your Arabic may not be as good as you thought. It seems, whatever else passed between you overseas, you omitted to tell her that you were married.''

"Am I?'' Rochambeau asked simply.

"To the best of my knowledge,'' Johanna snapped. "The Holy Church has not yet dissolved our union. Unless that was the business you were about on this mysterious journey.''

"Even a man of my talents,'' said Rochambeau, "would have difficulty in obtaining a papal dispensation in eight days.''

"Eleven!''

"I can't tell you how gratified I am to learn that you have been counting them. Could it be that you missed me more than you are willing to admit?''

Johanna flushed. If she had missed him, why should she admit it? If he knew the power he had to stir her senses, he'd never bother learning to treat her as person or a wife. She'd always be his toy. And already he was bringing in new toys!

"I would have been foolish to miss you,'' she said at last. "Look what happens when you're here! We can't live in peace together for the time it takes to say one Paternoster.''

"Some folly is sweeter than wisdom.'' He moved toward her, and she backed away.

"Oh, no you don't. Don't come near me with that woman's scent clinging to you!''

"Jealous?'' He smiled as though she'd just offered him the highest compliment.

"Insulted!''

"Don't be. Perhaps she's not my mistress . . . anymore. Perhaps,'' he offered in softly insinuating tones, "I wouldn't need a mistress if my sweet wife were more forthcoming.''

"You take a strange way to sweeten my temper!''

"But if you don't care for me and don't want me in your

bed," Rochambeau inquired, "why should you object if I take care of my own needs in such a simple and obvious way? Charitable, too. The girl is in desperate straits, and we are commanded to be generous to the poor."

Johanna bit her lip and turned away to pick at the bed tapestries. How did Rochambeau always manage to put her at a disadvantage, even when he had committed so great a wrong as bringing his Saracen mistress into her household?

Before she could think of a way to answer that would stress only the wrong he'd done to her position and not the hurt to her feelings, the argument was over. The swish of tapestries and the gentle closing of the door were her first signals that Rochambeau had gone, evidently taking her silence for agreement. She heard his voice raised in greeting to Laila in the bower; a few more incomprehensible words passed between them, and then he clattered down the steps to the hall and she was alone, with her curious women in the outer chamber waiting to see how she took this latest insult.

There was, under the circumstances, only one way to take it. She would have to be so sweetly friendly to Laila that no one could know for sure how much she hated Rochambeau's gall in installing his mistress under her very nose. Gritting her teeth, she went out to pretend to make friends with the hussy. It was easier than she'd thought. Laila's halting English improved remarkably in the course of conversation, and some of the things she said made Johanna think that all was not as it seemed on the surface.

In fact, Johanna began to feel much better about Laila's presence the more she talked with the girl. She thought that she could even see a way to turn it to her own advantage—if her guesses about the mysterious Laila's true origin were correct. She went to the kitchens and ordered a generous supper to be served that night, placing particular stress on the dishes and drinks she wished to see served at the high table.

When people began gathering in the hall for supper, Rochambeau was surprised to see Johanna come down from the bower with a light step, holding Laila affectionately by the hand and chattering to her as if she and the Saracen girl were the best of friends. She smiled sweetly to him and with her own hands led Laila to a seat on the other side of Rochambeau's, brushing aside the girl's evident confusion at being placed at the high dais.

"No, no, my lord would never forgive me were we to fail to honor you!" she told Laila. "Besides, I wish for you to sit here at the high table where we can all talk together through dinner." The bright glance she darted at Rochambeau made him feel uneasy. Was she planning to stage a scene of some sort at the evening meal in hall? A public confrontation would only be embarrassing for all of them, not at all what he'd intended when he arranged for Laila to come to Malvern.

At the beginning of the meal Laila showed some unfamiliarity with the customs of dining in a baron's hall. Johanna instructed her in how to hold out her hands for the boy with the ewer to pour water over them, how to place meat and cooked dishes on her trencher of stale bread, and all the other small details of courteous dining.

"I am sure this must be so different from your Eastern customs," she cooed sweetly as Laila took up a chicken leg in both hands. "For instance, it was my understanding that you Saracens refrained from eating with the left hand, considering it unclean. You are very generous to adopt our ways so quickly."

Blushing scarlet, Laila dropped the chicken wing and surreptitiously rubbed her greasy left hand on her silken tunic. Johanna gestured for a page to bring fresh water and napkins with which Laila could cleanse herself. While this was going on, another serving boy poured wine into the large cup set between Rochambeau and Johanna, the smaller one set before Laila, and the second large cup shared by Aubrey and Alais. Johanna turned her attention to her lord and sweetly suggested that they should drink together in celebration of his homecoming. She sipped at the strong Gascony wine and passed it to Rochambeau, who took a hearty gulp to wash down the dust of the road that still coated his lungs. He was in the process of swallowing when a shriek from Johanna started him so that he choked, coughed, grasped the cup convulsively in both hands, and nearly strangled on the draught of strong wine.

"Oh, Laila!" Johanna exclaimed in sorrowful tones. "How remiss of me not to warn you!" She took the half-empty cup from Laila's nerveless fingers and twirled it between her own white hands. "This is wine, which is forbidden by your religion. Doubtless, as a good Saracen, you would not have tasted it before and could not possibly know what you were drinking. I am so sorry for the pollution which you have brought upon yourself because of my carelessness. Boy! Bring good clear water for the lady Laila. Her customs forbid drinking wine."

Laila looked distinctly sulky as Johanna took care to replace the wine cup with a wooden mazer containing only fresh, pure water from the castle well.

"You're very well informed about the customs of the East," Rochambeau commented with some surprise when Johanna was through fussing over Laila's cup. "How do you know so much?"

"We occasionally had the honor of entertaining returning crusaders while you remained away, my lord. I was always eager for news of you, of course."

"Of course."

"But they also told me much of the customs of the countries where they had traveled. Their tales served to while away many a weary hour in your absence, and I am grateful now for the chance that led me to hear them, since it permits me to serve your honored guest in the way that will make her feel most at home." Another small shriek from Johanna punctuated this statement, and she leaned forward just in time to snatch Laila's trencher away from her.

"A ragout of pork! Oh, Laila, indeed you must not eat that. I know it is forbidden by your religion, and I do truly apologize for allowing it to be set before you. We'll have something else. Page! Bring another dish to the lady Laila. No, not that one, you dolt, the rabbits were cooked in lard." A succession of dishes, each one looking and smelling more tempting than the last, was brought forward for Johanna's inspection. As she waved each one away, Laila looked more and more sullen. Finally, a plain dish of dried pease cooked almost without seasonings was pronounced acceptable, and Laila munched away at her Lenten dinner of pease and water while on either side of her the English couples dipped happily into the highly spiced dishes Johanna had ordered for this elaborate late meal. Rochambeau glowered suspiciously at his lady but could not accuse her of anything more than concern for the supposed preferences of her guest.

As the meal progressed, Johanna seemed to take it as her duty to draw out the silent, sullen Laila. Prattling away as Rochambeau had never heard her do before, she asked Laila innumerable questions about the manner of life she had enjoyed in the East. Where had she lived? Jaffa? What sort of city was it? How did the great barons and earls there dress? What was life like in their halls? Had she seen the trees of paradise from whose branches fell the spices they bought here in England at such great cost?

To all this rain of questions Laila gave halting and sometimes contradictory answers. Johanna politely did not question her guest's veracity, but she did permit herself sometimes to express surprise at the answers. So the houses in Jaffa were like those in London, of two or three stories with peaked roofs and a framework of cross-timbers? How strange that returning crusaders should have described Arab houses as white, flat-roofed cubes! And the great barons kept fires burning in their halls all year round? She had not thought they would wish for fires in the summer, when the heat was reportedly so intense that the crusaders in their shirts of mail broiled like crabs on a hot stone. And how strange that Laila had never heard the calls to prayer that were reputed to echo through the city five times a day. Surely, as a good infidel—

Laila's face worked oddly and she gulped back a sob. Rochambeau rose to his feet, intending to break off the questioning, but he was already too late.

"Ah, give over with your devil's questions, do!" Laila entreated Johanna in the unmistakable accents of a poor Londoner. "You can see well enough I've never been east of Southwark, can't you? *He* said 'twould be an easy part, like mumming in a Christmas play." She jabbed her thumb at Rochambeau with a venomous expression that made him glad she didn't have a knife. "Great lords' tricks! Said all I had to do was wear the clothes he bought me and say the lines he told me. He didn't say there'd be a witch here 'oo knew all about the East without ever having been there!"

Rising from her seat, she glared at Rochambeau. "Brought me here to make sport of me with your fine lords and ladies, didn't you? Well, I'm not havin' no more of it! And another thing! You said I'd get my belly full of good food. Look at this mess!'' With a clumsy gesture, she knocked the trencher with its load of pease porridge to the floor. "I've et better when I was begging along the loading docks! Poor sailors are more generous with their food than you and your fine friends! You can keep the gold you promised me, *my lord*. It ain't worth what I'm havin' to go through here—even if you meant to pay me honest, which I'll lay you didn't!'' Choking on another sob, she gathered up her trailing gauze skirts and ran from the hall.

Johanna rose to go after her, but Rochambeau laid an iron hand on her wrist. "Don't you think you've made enough mischief already?''

"You have a strange idea of what it is to make mischief,'' she retorted, but she made no attempt to free herself. "Alais, please go after that poor girl. She mustn't be allowed to run off in such a state. Apologize for us, tell her my lord and I are barbarians, say whatever is needful, but see that she stays here.''

"Why?'' Rochambeau queried as Alais hastened to do her mistress's bidding. "So you can stick a few more pins in her tomorrow?''

"By no means. But it seems to me that our household has some responsibility for her. If you brought her here from Southwark slums just to torment me, will you throw her back into those slums now that your game is over?''

"You are determined to think ill of me, no matter what I do. I promised to pay her well, and so I would have done.''

"If I hadn't sent Alais after her, she'd be gone by now, and then what good would all your promises of payment have done?''

Rochambeau threw up his hands in disgust. "Women! I don't understand any of you. Are you seriously quarreling with me because you think I've been unfair to the girl I hired to play the part of my mistress?''

"That, among other things,'' Johanna snapped. She drew her skirts about her with a swish of red and gold silk and marched toward the bower stairs.

Rochambeau caught up with her on the stairs. "Then let's continue the quarrel in private.''

"I have nothing more to say to you!''

"No? What about all those other things you wanted to quarrel with me about? Don't you even want the satisfaction of telling me what a beast I am?" He was holding her arm now, so that she could not get away from him without an unseemly struggle. They passed through the bower and into the great bedchamber, where Rochambeau made haste to shut the door before any of Johanna's waiting-women could come in to give her moral support.

At once she jerked free of him and stalked to the far side of the room, where she stood looking up at a slightly faded tapestry of St. Sebastian full of arrows. Rochambeau straddled a stool and sat admiring the view of her angry profile thus presented to him. Arms crossed below her sweet breasts, chest heaving with short, angry breaths, black hair tumbling loose under the gilt circlet, she was as lovely as he'd ever seen her—and as unattainable. He sighed. How had his clever plan gone so wrong?

"All right," he said at length. "Perhaps it wasn't such a good idea. But I only wanted to make you jealous. And you'll have to admit that part worked—until you figured out what I was up to!"

"I don't have to admit any such thing!" Johanna snapped, still pretending to study the tapestry. "Any woman would be offended at her husband's trying to install a mistress in her own household."

"Many women," said Rochambeau silkily, "have to put up with that particular insult. Especially those contumacious wives who deny their husbands the comfort of the marital bed."

Johanna whirled to face him. The gilt-embroidered ends of her long red sleeves and the curling locks of her loose black hair streamed behind her with the speed of her turn, and Rochambeau found himself forgetting their quarrel in his delight at the vision of angry beauty she presented. The soft silk clung over her breasts when she moved, showing each tantalizing rounded curve in a manner far more tempting than Laila's semitransparent dress.

"Don't ever make the mistake of thinking I'm a woman to suffer such insult," she warned him.

"Not unless I want to wind up like St. Sebastian in the

picture, stuck full of arrows like a cat that tried to fight a hedgehog?''

"You make a jest out of everything," said Johanna darkly. "But if you ever dream of doing such a thing to me in reality, I will kill you, and that's no jest. Do you think the only thing I know about herbs and simples is how to heal women's ailments?"

"Remind me to lock up the thorn apple leaves!" He couldn't help laughing, even though it only irritated her further. Didn't all this anger just prove she really cared for him? A woman who was truly indifferent to her husband would surely welcome his defection to another bed. If only he could get Johanna to admit her true feelings!

She crossed her arms under her breasts again, and Rochambeau wished he could just relax and enjoy the sight. Didn't she know how that motion emphasized the high, firm breasts whose perfect whiteness he remembered so well? And below, the spiderweb silk clung along her thighs, tormenting him with other and even more intoxicating memories. His eyes followed the tempting shadows and curves of her body, and he began thinking of ways to bring this particular quarrel to a speedy conclusion.

"Now, love, don't let's quarrel any longer," he said, rising from his stool and crossing the room so that he could put his arms around her. "I admit it was a silly idea, but don't you see that it only shows how much I love and need you, that I was prepared to go to such lengths just to arouse your jealousy? And how the devil was I to know you'd spent the years of my absence becoming an expert on Saracen life and customs?" He rolled his eyes on that last question, miming his discomfiture, and Johanna giggled reluctantly.

"It does seem an excessively roundabout way to go about getting your wife into bed," she told him, but she didn't push his hands away. He felt the softness of her under the clinging silks, and his desires increased until he could scarcely bear the time it would take to get her out of the surcoat and tunic.

"Mmm." He lifted the soft tresses of dark hair and kissed her white neck. "Straightforward ways never did me any good with you." Why did her hair smell like smoke? Better not ask. Ten to one it was some woman's magic to win his affections back from the Saracen girl, and by now she must know how little she needed charms and spells to get his attention.

"How would you know? You never tried them. From the day we met, you've lied and cheated rather than try to win my love by fair means."

Rochambeau sighed as Johanna freed herself from his embrace. Perhaps her hair smelled like smoke because she was always going up in flames.

"Does it matter now? We do love each other. That's all that counts. Not how we got there."

"What makes you so sure of that?"

Rochambeau chuckled. "If you can't see the evidence of my love for you rising before your very eyes, you must have forgotten some basic facts of male anatomy in the years since I've been away. And of course you love me, or you wouldn't have got so upset about the trick I played you with the Saracen girl." Desire was making him impatient. Hadn't they fenced with words long enough? It was time to join the more pleasurable battle between the bedsheets, the joust where he always won.

Johanna drew one deep, trembling breath and backed away from him. "There's a difference between lust and love. A difference you have yet to learn, my lord. You don't respect me, and you don't love me."

"Come to bed, and I'll teach you some other things about love!"

"*No.*"

Rochambeau's hands fell empty to his sides as Johanna sidestepped his reaching grasp. Chin tilted, green eyes flashing, she proclaimed, "You can force my body, my lord, but never my love!"

"Oh, God's body and bones! Are we back to that old song again? Johanna, I'm tired of seducing my own wife."

"And tired of your wager, too?"

"Wager? Oh, that business with the accounts." He had actually managed to forget Johanna's thrice-damned cipher in the two weeks he'd spent arranging for Laila's little act. "Are you really going to hold me to that?"

"Remember your promise? You said you'd leave me alone until you solved the cipher."

Rochambeau groaned. "And if I don't, it will only confirm you in your opinion that I'm a liar and a cheat."

"I hardly need confirmation," said Johanna pertly, "but, yes, that would be the general effect."

Groaning again, Rochambeau crossed the room and laid one hand on the door latch. "Sometimes, dear wife, you make me wish that I didn't have an objection to thrashing women. But since I do suffer from that handicap, I suppose I've no alternative but to go back to the old keep and flog my poor brains some more."

"You won't like—" Johanna started to warn him that he wouldn't find his workroom in the old keep tower just as he'd left it. But before she could finish the sentence, he was gone, leaving her with that curious feeling of emptiness and desolation that always followed one of their quarrels. Damn the man! Whenever he saw she was winning, he retreated so quickly that she could take no joy in her victory.

And what sort of victory was it that left her alone for yet another night in this great bed, while Rochambeau burned too many candles in some small room on the other side of Malvern? Johanna pondered the question through the sleepless night that followed, without finding an answer. All she felt certain of was that to go to Rochambeau's laughing embrace, forgiving all his tricks for the sensual passion he could inspire in her, would be a kind of defeat.

But a defeat that was beginning to seem almost preferable to this lonely victory.

Chapter Sixteen

Rochambeau was never quite sure how it happened, but by the next day his wife and the strolling mummer he'd hired to play the part of his mistress had become the best of friends. Laila, Pearl of the Night, the Saracen slave girl, was transformed into plain Margery from Southwark and given a position among Johanna's waiting-women. She and Alais vied with each other to see who could serve their mistress better. Margery had a slight edge in the matter because she wasn't distracted, as Alais always was, when Aubrey brought his handsome face within sight of the women's quarters.

"Such a fine man," Alais sighed. "Isn't it a pity his birth prevents his being knighted as he deserves."

Margery gave a disdainful sniff. "Some bastards can rise above it, and some can't. Look at me. Never knew me father, grew up begging for crusts from the sailors. At least I've the wit to be thankful for a good place like my lady gives me here. Don't see your Aubrey showing any gratitude to my lord for his generosity. He's got a nice manor on the other side of the county for doing flat nothing, and all he can do is whine about what more he'd like to have."

"It's not the same thing, Margery," said Alais gently. "Aubrey is the elder brother. He can't help but feel—well, cheated by fate, I suppose—when he sees Rochambeau holding so lightly the titles and honors that might have been his.

And as a dependent of Rochambeau's," she added with a telling blush, "he can marry only with my lord's consent."

Margery looked at Alais's flushed cheeks and downcast eyes and withheld her opinions about bastard half-brothers who affected to be galled by the charity they lived on. Alais was soft, anyone could see that, and maybe she'd not be so bad a match for Aubrey at that—two soft fools together. But Margery knew enough of the world to know that great lords arranged these things differently, considering manors and farms and money fiefs more important than the preferences of the people concerned. So it might be that Alais was destined for a more important person than Aubrey, and Margery had better keep her tongue between her teeth until she learned more of the castle ways.

She reserved her disdainful sniffs henceforward for Rochambeau. Say what you might, it wasn't a gentlemanly thing to do, trying to embarrass one's wife by bringing in a mistress, even a poor, painted fake of a mistress from the London slums. And especially when the wife was as noble and generous as the lady Johanna. Who else in the world would have troubled to think about poor Margery's fate when husband and wife were fighting like cat and dog? Most ladies would have had her whipped from the castle gate. Johanna had sent Alais after her with money and apologies and promises of a good position.

It didn't occur to Margery that Johanna might be using her in her turn, that Rochambeau must find her daily presence a galling reminder of the failure of his trick. But it occurred to Rochambeau every time he passed Margery on the steps or found her guarding the entrance to my lady's private chamber. Margery stuck her nose in the air and sniffed, Johanna gave her husband that three-cornered cat's smile, and Rochambeau retreated for another crack at the intractable cipher. His desperation seemed to be driving the solution farther and farther away from him. And all the while he was uneasily aware that Johanna had not yet forgiven him for the trick he'd tried to play with Margery.

"She's waiting to get revenge on me," he muttered to Aubrey after one particularly unproductive session with the enciphered accounts. "I can feel it in the air."

Aubrey lounged on a table and smiled sleepily down at his

brother. "This should be recorded by some monkish chronicler. In the third year of King Edward, Nicolas de Rochambeau was bested by a woman for the first time in history."

"I'm not bested yet." Rochambeau slammed his quill down on the writing stand and splintered the point. "I'll make sense of these accounts yet."

"If there's sense to be made."

"What do you mean?"

"Perhaps you're meant to be wasting your time. I've always wondered that a woman should presume to cipher and write like a clerk. Perhaps these rolls are nothing but a fake, meant to confuse you and keep your attention away from other problems."

Rochambeau shook his head. "She couldn't possibly run an honor comprising this many manors and keep all the accounts in her head. She had to be writing her records down somewhere, and this chest holds every piece of parchment in Malvern."

"Maybe she hasn't bothered to run the estate all that well. Why should she? She's not overfond of you. Maybe she'd rather ruin you for revenge."

"You don't understand the lady," said Rochambeau. "She might ruin me—and herself—for revenge, but she wouldn't cheat on a wager. And it would definitely be cheating to give me a set of meaningless accounts to decipher."

"You're being very defensive about somebody you can't know very well," Aubrey pointed out. "After all, I've been in the lady's company for the past four years, while you've been playing the knight in all the courts of Europe. Perhaps I know her better than you."

Rochambeau looked up without speaking. Something in his glance made Aubrey turn pale and slip from the table. "Do you, brother? Do you indeed?" He spoke softly, but at the same time one hand slipped to the handle of his belt knife. "It seems to me you have been more used to defend her against my wrath than to mutter vague accusations. What's changed, I wonder?"

"Nothing." Aubrey beat a hasty retreat. "I just thought you should be aware of all the possibilities."

"Oh, I am, Aubrey, I am. But Johanna's cheating does not happen to be one of those possibilities." The soft voice sent

Aubrey hastening from the room, beads of sweat standing on his brow.

Rochambeau unsheathed his knife and began to sharpen a new quill point. "I, on the other hand," he muttered to himself, "would cheat in a minute, if I could only figure out how. How did I ever work myself into a situation where I could only win by playing fair?"

It was that damned animal craftiness of women again. And he'd better find some way to circumvent it, before Johanna took a notion into her head to be revenged on him in some way that would make their relationship totally unsalvageable.

Unfortunately for Rochambeau, Johanna's inspiration for revenge came about long before he made any measurable progress on the cipher.

Dinners in the great hall were subdued affairs these days, with the lord and lady sitting at the high dais in an icy silence that cast its pall over the spirits of all the manor officials and well-born retainers condemned to sit near them. Only at the far ends of the long tables, where servants and dogs sprawled in happy amity among the greasy rushes nearest the door, was there a spark of gaiety to be found. It was for that reason that Aubrey took it upon himself to invite a traveling jongleur to dinner one day. He met the fellow on the road between Malvern and his own manor of Spelsham, where he'd been spending most of his time since the near-quarrel with Rochambeau.

"The boy's a de Bellay," Aubrey announced when he brought him into the hall just before dinner. "A younger son, but well born for all that he's chosen to stroll the roads with a lute under his arm."

"One of old Godfrey de Bellay's get? Aye, I can see it in your face." Rochambeau nodded at the slight dark-haired boy with casual interest. "Which one are you? Adam? Baldwin? Centor?"

"Somewhat farther down the line, my lord," responded the jongleur with a small ironic smile. "I'm Gilbert. The three sons you named, as well as Drogo, Eduin, and Fulbert, all preceded me in birth as in my father's estimation."

"A seventh son," murmured Johanna. She liked this slender youth with his black hair and quiet manner. "There's said to be some magic clings about such ones. Did no mysterious godmother attend your christening, to gift you with some trinket that would be worth more than all your older brothers inherited?"

"If she was responsible for my love of this," Gilbert laughed, holding up a finely carved lute worth more than all his clothes, "my father may have regarded it as a curse rather than a gift. He does not consider music an appropriate study for a knight's son. However, the other possibilities were limited. By the time I reached years of discretion, the patrimony had already been shared out. There wasn't even enough left to equip me with a horse and arms with which to practice the knightly profession. So I decided to take up another calling to which, in truth, I feel more attraction than to my brothers' more respectable pursuits in church and military camp. Perhaps during dinner I may persuade you that my choice of calling had some merit."

"After dinner," Johanna said with the quick smile that Rochambeau saw so seldom these days. "There's surely magic enough about your birth to entitle you to a seat at the high table with us."

Shaking his head slightly, Gilbert begged that he might first be allowed to prove himself by entertaining them during the meal. He preferred, he said, not to trade on his father's friendships. If his skill as a musician was not enough to earn his bread honestly, he would not earn the scorn of his fellow jongleurs, most of whom were of low birth, by using means of advancement denied to them.

Aubrey in his turn shook his head as Gilbert retreated to the modest place halfway down one of the long tables which he deemed more suited to his calling. "A foolish attitude. The boy will learn wisdom after a few years of struggling. Good birth is an advantage no one should lightly scorn."

Johanna did not miss the suppressed note of pain in his voice or the quick sympathy with which Alais pressed his hand. It was definitely time, she thought, to see about arranging a match for Alais. Sir Ilbod de Marti would not thank her if she allowed his daughter to form an attachment to Aubrey. With the dower he could provide, she might look higher than a bastard seneschal for a husband.

She did appreciate Aubrey's tact in pretending not to notice Alais's gesture of sympathy. He looked only at Johanna, and after a moment Alais took her accustomed place at the high table, eyes modestly downcast. A pity if she felt rebuffed, but it was good to know that Aubrey wasn't encouraging her childish attachment. He must know how little chance such a match had of coming to fruition. And was that one of the things that caused him pain when he reflected on his bastard birth? Johanna mentally added the finding of a suitable wife for Aubrey to her list of things to discuss with Rochambeau, should they ever get on civil speaking terms again.

At the moment, it didn't seem likely. Since their last quarrel, he had withdrawn himself from her society more completely than ever before. She saw him only at mealtimes and at Mass, when they were in company and there was no opportunity for private converse. Not, of course, that she had forgiven him for humiliating her with that playacting about his Saracen mistress, for tricking her into revealing how deeply he had the power to hurt her. But how was she ever going to forgive him if he didn't give her the chance?

If he'd gloated over his victory, she could have fanned up her hatred again into the white glowing fire that heated her blood during their quarrels. If he'd humbly apologized, without sandwiching his perfunctory apology between a laugh and an invitation to bed, she might have been persuaded to admit him back into her favor. Either alternative would have been preferable to this cold, lonely stasis. Johanna didn't like inaction; she twitched to be doing something, whether it was quarreling or reconciling. And she suspected that Rochambeau—damn him—knew that perfectly well!

Johanna was so deep in her own thoughts that she failed entirely to hear Gilbert's first song. Only the sound of Rochambeau's applause recalled her to her duty as hostess. "A beautiful tenson," she said vaguely toward Gilbert, smiling and nodding.

"It was a rondel," Alais hissed.

"My wife does not care for music." Rochambeau favored her with a bland smile and ordered a platter of special delicacies from the high table sent down for Gilbert to refresh himself with between songs.

Feeling guilty for her inattention, Johanna listened seriously to Gilbert's next two songs and found them unexpectedly pleasing. One was an old Provençal lyric whose meaning she could only guess at, but the sensual languor of the accompanying music and the glances he cast toward her made it tolerably clear that this was one of the standard troubadour effusions addressed to the lady of whatever hall the minstrel happened to be entertaining. The next selection was in much of the same vein, but in English, and Johanna enjoyed the sugary lyrics with their generalized compliments even though she knew it was only part of the game of minstrelsy. When she was young and foolish, she'd dreamed that Rochambeau would court her this way, with songs and sighs and languishing glances. Instead, he'd taken her in trade for two pieces of rich land and a remission of her father's scutage, expected her to be pleased with the sale, and left her as soon as his new toy displeased him.

Johanna gave a sharp sigh, and Gilbert broke off his last chorus in some confusion. Calling him to her side, she hastened to assure him that she intended no criticism of his music; it was only that she was somewhat distracted that day.

"Yes, my lady," Gilbert murmured, lowering his eyes. Johanna repressed another sigh, this time of irritation, and set herself to soothe away the boy's hurt feelings. At least concentrating on him might keep her mind off Rochambeau and her own bruised heart. This time, instead of inviting him to the high table, she commanded that he sit beside her and tell her the news of the road.

"Truth to tell, I am not in the mood for songs of love today," she confessed in a lowered tone, hoping Rochambeau would not hear her. "You know that women are fickle creatures, Gilbert, and a good troubadour must always pay attention to his lady's changing moods. Today I would rather be amused by any gossip you have picked up; later you shall give us all some more music."

It took a little more attention than that to charm Gilbert out of his sulks, but Johanna soon had him laughing with her as he related the story of how Leofric of Thonglands had recently persuaded his wide, Judith, to take a lighter hand with the household staff. Johanna remembered Judith well from the day of her disastrous wedding feast—a critical, house-proud woman who had been lavish in her predictions that Rochambeau would regret wedding an unschooled chit from a poor manor near the Welsh border. Well, perhaps he did regret it, but not for any deficiencies in her management of his manors. Johanna was not surprised to hear that Judith had terrorized her own servants for years, and she heartily enjoyed hearing the tale of the woman's discomfiture.

"He really made her do all the tasks herself?"

"Oh, no, my lady. Not *all* the tasks. Just those that weren't being performed to her satisfaction." Every time Judith threatened to have a servant whipped for incompetence, Leofric had intervened and dismissed the servant in question, then told Judith that she had better do the work herself so that the other castle servants could see how it should be done. Before Judith caught on to the game and learned a measure of tolerance, she had salted meat for the winter, burned her hands in the bake-ovens, and woven yard after dreary yard of coarse woolen for the ushers' Christmas robes.

"Then, of course, he called all the servants back and gave them presents for playing their part, and he gave Judith a gold chain to make peace with her. Now Leofric's household runs more smoothly than ever before!" Gilbert finished with a twinkle in his eye.

Johanna burst out laughing. "Perhaps I am lucky that my lord leaves me so much to my own devices here. I should not care to be lessoned so."

"My lady, it is inconceivable to me that any man could seek to change you in any way."

"You are not acquainted with Rochambeau." Johanna lowered her lashes, then raised them swiftly to give Gilbert a dazzling glimpse of bright, laughter-filled green eyes. She was thoroughly enjoying the game of double meanings and veiled flirtation they were playing, and Rochambeau's silent presence on her other side only added spice to the sweet dish of revenge. Hadn't he paid a girl to play the part of his mistress? He should see that, were she of a mind to retaliate in kind, she'd have no trouble finding a man to make love to her in earnest.

"It's not the lord of Rochambeau whom I most wish to know better," Gilbert murmured, leaning toward Johanna with a confidential smile. Her heart beat a little faster at the bold look in his dark, long-lashed eyes, but all she could think of was how wonderful it would be if Rochambeau ever looked at her like that, instead of taking her with his easy confidence.

"Hey, minstrel!"

Aubrey's voice, somewhat slurred and too loud, broke the fragile spell that was being woven between Johanna and Gilbert. Johanna looked around in annoyance, wondering if Aubrey was drunk. It was not like him to interrupt so rudely.

"The meal's over." Rising unsteadily from his seat, Aubrey pushed between Johanna and Gilbert and leaned both fists on the table. "Let's have some more music. None of those soft love songs this time, mind you. Something with a little jollity to it, know what I mean?"

"I think so." Gilbert laughed, and he retired to a bench between two side pillars to tune his lute for a new session. His face showed no resentment at Aubrey's interruption, nothing but courteous desire to please. Johanna supposed one of the first lessons a wandering musician learned was to control his reactions to rudeness or hostility from his patrons. Someone dependent on largesse for his bread dared not show the independence of a nobleman, no matter how gentle his birth.

She, however, was under no such restraint.

"God's teeth, Aubrey," she snapped. "Did you have to order the boy around like a paid servant? I was enjoying my chat with him!"

Aubrey looked down at her with pale blue eyes that showed no trace of any befuddlement from drink. "I thought it was time he did something the rest of us could enjoy equally."

Instead of returning to his own place at the table, he sat down between Rochambeau and Johanna. "Something lively, minstrel!" he called out again.

"Tired of love songs, Aubrey?" Rochambeau's smile held the subtly disquieting look that had been on his lips so often of late.

Aubrey leaned toward his brother and murmured, "They didn't seem to be having the desired effect."

"And that was?"

"I thought an hour of love songs might soften the lady's heart toward you."

"Did you indeed?"

The grooms and ushers at the far end of the hall had been

growing boisterous with the end of the meal and the promise of more entertainment. Now three of Rochambeau's hunting dogs burst into vicious war over a meaty bone one of the grooms had tossed into their midst. The master of the hounds slashed ineffectually at the dogs, all three locked together with their jaws fast about various parts of the bone; they rolled over in the rushes, tripped the master of hounds, and sent him staggering into an unwary servitor, who fell backward and spilled his greasy bowl of scraps over the ushers' table. Rochambeau swore under his breath and ran down the hall to restore order in person, too impatient to wait for his men to do so.

"Your pardon, minstrel," he apologized as he passed Gilbert. 'I'll be back in a minute. Why don't you go on and entertain the rest of the company?" Grabbing dogs and men impartially by any loose parts that presented themselves, he transferred the dogfight, the greasy ushers, and a few innocent bystanders to the courtyard. "Throw water over them all!" he snapped at the apologetic master of hounds.

By the time Rochambeau got back to the hall doors, Gilbert was already playing the first notes of a lively song as Aubrey had requested. Rochambeau, so quick to act in scenes of violence or games of love, stood frozen in horrified disbelief as the first gay notes rippled forth from Gilbert's lute.

"Oh, no," he murmured. "Not today. God, why are you doing this to me?"

The people seated at the high table were also immobile. As Gilbert innocently launched into the first verse of Rochambeau's mocking little song about his unsatisfactory wife, Johanna went quite white, and her eyes glittered like cold splinters of green ice. She was intensely aware that, just as had happened four years earlier, everybody in the hall was watching to see how she would react to a public rendering of That Song. To her, it appeared that Rochambeau, standing by the doors at the far end of the hall as if he wished to be as far away from her as possible, was also watching for her reaction.

He must have requested Gilbert to sing it. Hadn't he passed by the minstrel's bench on his way to stop the dogfight? The fight had been no more than a convenient excuse. But why would he do such a thing? Instant punishment for her momentary flirtation with Gilbert? Of course. The lord of the manor could install his mistress under her nose, and she was expected to fall into his arms in gratitude when he admitted it had been a hoax; but let her dare to smile at another man, and he instantly arranged for her public humiliation.

Johanna felt as though ice were slowly creeping into her heart, benumbing her until she could feel nothing at all except a cold intention to be revenged. How many times had she sworn never to forgive Rochambeau, for how many insults? It didn't matter. This was to be the last one. The trick with "Laila" had been bad enough. This time he had gone too far. This time she was going to humiliate Rochambeau as he delighted in humiliating and thwarting her, and she didn't care what it might cost her.

And the first step was not to show what she felt at this moment, with the eyes of everybody in the hall upon her.

Aubrey and Alais were stricken as still as she was. It remained for Rochambeau, the first to recover from his shock, to stop the minstrel with a curt command. Gilbert's voice died away in midnote, and his fingers plucked a crashing discord on the lute as he stared up into Rochambeau's stony face. Somehow, he realized, he had offended terribly. But how?

In the relieved babble that filled the subsequent silence, the people at the high table stirred again. Aubrey's large, warm hand clasped Johanna's icy fingers. "He didn't plan it, Johanna," he said in a rapid undertone. "I'm almost sure. He wouldn't have done that, no matter how angry he was with you. Didn't you see how he moved to stop it?"

Aubrey's instantaneous, clumsy defense of his brother only solidified the suspicions in Johanna's mind. "He did not seem to me to be in too much of a hurry to stop it. Everybody had time to enjoy the situation first."

Aubrey sighed. "Rochambeau has a demon of jealousy," he admitted. "But he wouldn't have affronted you so. It had to be a coincidence."

"Did it?" Withdrawing her hand, Johanna stood and looked down at Aubrey with measuring, cold eyes. "You're very loyal to this family, Aubrey. Sometimes I wonder what they've done to deserve your fidelity." She swept away from the high table as Rochambeau came back to it, passed him without acknowledgment, and walked straight to the bench where Gilbert de Bellay still sat gripping his lute. As she walked, one hand tugged convulsively at the triple gold chain set with rubies that adorned her neck, the prize item in the Rochambeau jewels, with which Rochambeau had gifted her before he went on crusade.

"A merry song, and well performed," she said in a clear, ringing voice that carried throughout the hushed hall. "I know not what reward my lord promised you, but on my own account I should like to thank you with this." The recalcitrant clasp of the chain at last came free, and the people near enough to see gasped in shock as she poured a glittering shower of golden chains and red fire over Gilbert de Bellay's knees.

"One of my women will come to you," she said in an undertone as Gilbert stared up at her. "Follow her instructions, and you will not regret your stay with us." She gave him a dazzling sweet smile that promised worlds of enchantment and swept gracefully back to the high table.

Chapter Seventeen

JOHANNA PACED UP and down in the tapestry-hung bed-chamber behind the bower, too impatient to sit still while she waited for her plot to come to fruition. Timing was crucial; if Gilbert didn't arrive before Rochambeau showed himself, her revenge would fail of its effect.

She had dismissed her women immediately after supper, saying that she felt no need of company or of help in undressing. They might think she was upset about Rochambeau's insult; with any luck, a few of them would speculate that there was something else behind the mistress's sudden desire for solitude, and those speculations might reach Rochambeau's ears in time. But Johanna had no mind to let her revenge depend on such chancy means as women's gossip. She'd kept Margery, the erstwhile Pearl of the Night, by her when the other women departed. It had been hard to ignore the hurt look in Alais's eyes as she saw the interloper preferred to her, but Alais was too innocent for the errand Johanna had in mind. It remained to be seen whether Margery was bright enough to carry it out faithfully.

"First you go to Gilbert and tell him to come to the bower after lights are doused in the hall," Johanna instructed Margery. "He'll be sleeping in one of the alcoves between the pillars on the west side."

"Aye, my lady. I know where he's to sleep," Margery interrupted with a twinkle in her eye.

Johanna sighed. "I suppose every woman in Malvern marked down his sleeping place. Well, try to get there before too many of the serving maids throw themselves into his arms, all right? I don't want the whole castle knowing of his visit to my room."

"Especially not Rochambeau?"

"Wrong," said Johanna crisply. "I especially *do* want Rochambeau to know of it. But not until Gilbert is already here. It would be best if you could accidentally encounter my lord after Gilbert has the message. Act confused and guilty, make sure he knows something's up, make him force it out of you. Cry a little, if you can manage it, seem to be delaying him, but finally confess that you've just sent Gilbert to my chamber." She looked at Margery's plump, beaming face with some doubt. "Do you think you can fool him?"

"You want me to make sure he knows Gilbert is coming to your chamber but make him think I don't want him to know it," Margery summarized. She crossed her arms over her bosom and bent to the ground in a swift, fluid motion that irresistibly recalled the Saracen slave girl. "Thy servant is but a tool in thy hands; may it be done as thou desirest!"

She looked up, black eyes brimming with laughter, and Johanna had to smile. "All right. I'd forgotten what a good actress you were."

Margery lingered at the chamber door, and Johanna had to urge her to go on. Any minute now, the torches would be doused in the hall, and the men who slept there would be settling to rest.

"You're sure this is what you want?" Margery asked.

Johanna nodded firmly.

"All right. Me, I wouldn't want to be caught crossing Rochambeau's will. I can think of pleasanter ways to die!"

"He won't kill me." Johanna pushed Margery through the door and drew the tapestry back across the opening. "I think . . . ," she mused, tracing the lines of gold thread that made the saints' halos in the tapestry glitter like jewels in the candlelight.

How long had she been waiting since then? Long enough for one wax candle to burn down almost half its length. Johanna eyed the tapestry that hung over the far wall of the chamber, trying to judge whether it moved slightly or whether it was just the flickering of the candlelight that gave it that illusion. Behind that hanging was the wall that this chamber shared with the upper gallery of the chapel; behind that hanging was the secret door that Rochambeau had cut between chapel and chamber; behind that hanging, if she judged Rochambeau aright, her husband would soon be standing. The man couldn't be direct to save his life, much less his honor. Any other baron, informed that his wife was about to betray him with a wandering minstrel, would come charging up the stairs to the bower with a drawn sword. Rochambeau would have to try and be clever. Thinking she'd forgotten the second entrance to the chamber, he would steal up through the chapel to catch her in the act before he made his move.

And for once, Johanna meant to use that compulsive cleverness against him. He should see nothing that gave him grounds to accuse her of adultery, but he was going to see and hear plenty that raked his soul over the coals. Under guise of complaining about her sad lot to Gilbert, she would be able to make it perfectly clear to Rochambeau what his failings as husband and lover had been. Her smile took on a dangerous sharp edge, and she waited, now still at the center of her enforced patience, for Gilbert de Bellay to come into the chamber and offer himself as the tool for her revenge.

"Go on, you great gowk!" hissed a sharp voice from the bower. The tapestry that hung between the rooms was jerked back, and a push from Margery's firm little hands catapulted Gilbert into the inner chamber. He had a bemused impression of tapestries in deep jewellike colors, illuminated by an extravagant use of wax candles in branched holders, but the room was dominated for him by the figure in the center of the ring of candlelight—a slender, green-eyed woman in a red tunic that molded to her body like the flames of hell, her long black hair falling down her back in glossy sheets that curled up at the very ends like a witch's hair.

"My lady." Gilbert's mouth was dry. This was the sort of happening other minstrels told stories about—the noble lady of the castle who was taken by their charm and showered them with rich presents. They smiled and whispered about secret meetings, hinting at names without ever saying them out loud, but making sure everybody knew. "This ring I had from a certain noble dame whose husband had been at court for two years, leaving her alone in their country manor. . . . Hush! 'Twould be all my life's worth to say her name, or why I had the jewel; let's just say she . . . admired my music.'' And the man would hold up the gold ring with its square emerald blinking in the light like a cat's green eye, making sure to drop enough mysterious hints so that everyone knew the identity of his "noble dame."

Gilbert had listened to such stories, envied the men who boasted of these conquests, dreamed that some day he too would know the joys of courteous love with a noble lady instead of the importunities of greasy serving maids. As a portionless minstrel, a seventh son, he could hardly expect to marry, and so he'd been free to pin his romantic fantasies on whatever unattainable ladies of high birth he happened to meet in his wanderings.

The sad fact was that such unattainably high damsels were few and far between, at least those who could inspire a young man's fancy to new songs of love. The chatelaines of great estates tended to be plump and busy with the duties of their position, more interested in seeing that the wool was properly carded and the liveries made up than in exchanging glances with a minstrel. And their daughters, almost without exception, had freckles and giggled.

So, at least, it seemed to Gilbert when he first set eyes on the lady Johanna, the embodiment of all his dreams. Every woman he'd known before had surely been fat or freckled or worse. He blithely forgot his current dream of meeting a fair-haired beauty with a rosebud mouth; far more exciting was this half-Welsh witch with her slanting emerald eyes and her edged smile that promised untold delights.

He'd been lying on his pallet in the hall, trying to ignore the grunts and snuffles of the men composing themselves to sleep on either side of him, when Margery interrupted his fantasies of Johanna with the message that had set his heart pounding with anticipation. When she gave him the jewels, when she prayed him to speak with her before he left, he'd imagined a tender scene in the bower, in the morning light— words of love hinted at but unspoken between them, perhaps the great liberty of kissing one of her white fingers, and a romantic memory to cherish in his heart as he set out on his travels again. And never would he have made a story of this "conquest," using her to improve his standing with others of his profession. He would have built her a secret shrine in his heart and worshiped her forever.

But that was before Margery jerked him rudely from half-sleep and led him to the bower. Gilbert barely had time to comprehend the difference between this reality and his dream. A public meeting in the bower, by morning light, with waiting-women all around to guard the lady's honor, would have been one thing; this midnight secrecy, this candlelit chamber dominated by the great tapestry-hung bed and the slender woman in her red tunic, had to mean something else entirely. Heart pounding, mouth dry with anticipation, Gilbert faced at once the fruition of his most secret dreams and the paralyzing fear that he might show himself not man enough to take what was, seemingly, being offered to him.

"Gilbert! How good of you to come." Johanna moved toward Gilbert, holding something that glittered in her hands. More jewels? No, a jeweled cup, from which rose the tantalizing aroma of hot wine beaten together with honey and spices. "I was . . . lonely," she confessed, her arch inflection giving a special meaning to the innocent-sounding words, "and I couldn't sleep. I would take it kindly if you'd share a cup of wine with me and perhaps entertain me with some more tales of your adventures in the world."

"Lonely," Gilbert repeated, bemused. His fingers brushed Johanna's as he mechanically took the offered cup, but her hand was withdrawn so quickly that he couldn't be quite sure the touch had been intentional. "Er . . . surely my lord Rochambeau is the proper person to assuage your loneliness, my lady?" Cowardly, craven words! Even as he spoke, Gilbert was rewriting the scene in his mind to fit his fantasies, telling himself that he would be in this noble lady's arms any minute now.

Johanna gave a deep sigh that made the tightly cut front of her red tunic strain over high, perfect breasts emphasized by the wide golden girdle. Her sooty lashes fluttered down, veiling those alarming green eyes. "Alas, my lord has very little interest in my doings, and I in his. That song you began tonight?"

"I feared I had offended in some way. Pray forgive me, my lady." Gilbert dropped to one knee, head bowed, and began a confused apology without being exactly sure what it was he was apologizing for.

"It was composed by Rochambeau," said Johanna. There was a steely bite to her voice that made Gilbert look up in surprise, but her appearance was soft, sweet, white, and feminine. Two sparkling tears trembled like diamonds at the tips of her lashes, and when she spoke again her voice quivered most affectingly. "You see, he has no desire for me, nor does he scruple to say so in public."

"That, my lady, is all but unbelievable," said Gilbert frankly. No man with blood in his veins could fail to react to this witch woman, this slender, green-eyed flame. Even now, as his fear and confusion began to wear away, he could hardly think for the throbbing of the blood that pounded in his ears. Yet something still seemed wrong to him about the whole scene.

"I assure you it is so," protested Johanna, "and how am I to know whether it is so unbelievable? I must be unattractive indeed, to have inspired such cold treatment. He has hurt me deeply, Gilbert, not even scrupling to install his mistress within these walls, making it very clear that he cares naught for my feelings. I am only a toy to him—and I will be no man's plaything!" On the last words, her voice rang out, unguarded, with a triumphant echo that again made Gilbert blink in surprise.

"I have a very sad and lonely life," Johanna sighed, again resuming her demure demeanor. She let her head droop like a wounded songbird. "I did not think you would be so cruel, Gilbert de Bellay. Perhaps it is as my husband says, and no man could desire me in truth." Two more large, glittering tears rolled down her cheeks.

"My lady, don't weep!" Gilbert reached out his arms to clasp Johanna, but she retreated swiftly, and he found himself grasping empty air. He rose to his feet and followed her, forgetting self-consciousness in the desire to assuage the hurts this lovely woman had suffered. "It's not so, indeed—only I could not believe my fortune at first—that you would deign to be so kind to a mere minstrel . . ." As he spoke in disjointed phrases, he reached for Johanna again. His fingertips brushed the trailing hem of an embroidered sleeve, tangled momentarily in a long black curl, yet never grasped her fully.

Johanna smiled and turned her back on him. "This girdle pinches me cruelly," she said in a coy voice, "and my women have all gone to bed. Pray, Gilbert, can you discover the secret of its fastenings?"

Gilbert's hands were trembling so that he could hardly untie the tight knots holding the girdle together in back, but that didn't seem to be the only problem. Somebody had tied and double-knotted all the laces in a tangle that was going to be the devil's own work to undo. And Johanna's smooth, scented skin under the red tunic, tantalizing him with flashes of white where the shoulder openings were closed with golden brooches, distracted him so that he could hardly have performed the task under the best of conditions.

"My lady, I fear this will be difficult to undo," he murmured in apology after working over the knotted laces for some time with sweaty hands.

"So are many things—like this unhappy marriage into which I was forced when scarcely more than a child. Have a cup of wine." Johanna blessed the tight knots with which Margery had fastened her girdle before leaving. It was difficult to flirt with this boy. He seemed to know no happy medium between awkward shyness and leaping on her like a stable boy with a serving girl. And where was Rochambeau? She didn't know how much longer she could preserve the appearance of flirtation without granting some favor to Gilbert. And she didn't even want to kiss the boy, much less . . .

Her thoughts shied away from the end which he doubtless expected. Strange, that something so wonderful with a bastard like Rochambeau could be completely unappealing with this slim, shy young minstrel! Gilbert was really a very nice boy, and it wouldn't hurt to grant him a kiss if necessary to keep him there until Rochambeau interrupted them, but the thought didn't appeal to her at all. And he had nearly finished the wine.

"Let me show you how much any normal man would desire you," Gilbert urged, setting down the empty cup and moving toward her again. His cheeks were flushed, and his eyes glittered with wine and excitement and danger. Johanna felt the danger thrilling her, too, but it wasn't Gilbert's touch she ached for.

"First undo this girdle," she insisted with a coy laugh that set her own teeth on edge. "Don't you know that every knight must do some service for his lady?" She turned her back again, prepared to endure another session of Gilbert's incompetent fumblings about the laces while she spoke barbed words to annoy the listener who must surely, by now, be lurking behind the tapestries! The gold threads in the border of the tapestry winked in the candlelight, and Johanna drew a deep breath of relief, unthinkingly tightening the girdle laces and setting poor Gilbert's efforts at naught.

"I think you must still be nervous about my husband," she said, raising her voice slightly to make sure that it carried well. "There's no need to be. Since the day we married, he has been at pains to make it clear to me that nothing I do can affect him in the slightest. Had I been a mindless doll to dance at his bidding, he might have been well pleased with me. Unfortunately, he married a person, not a toy, and this great puissant lord seems to be terrified of treating his own wife with the respect he would show to the least of his serfs. He doesn't respect me. Why should he care what I do?"

Gilbert's fingers, slippery with cold sweat, could not grasp the tightly knotted laces. "My lady, I know not. But such is the way of men."

"Yes," said Johanna with brooding bitterness. "Such indeed is their way with property. A wife, a cow, a field—all may be bought and sold with equal ease. All are only the lord's property to do with as he pleases!"

Gilbert had no answer for this last bitter statement. Such was the way of the world, and it had never occurred to him to question it. For himself, he would have been only too happy to have been the firstborn son, with an inheritance to step into and the chance of buying himself a beautiful wife like Johanna. "I don't think I can undo the laces without cutting them, my lady," he said miserably.

"A sharp blade is often the solution to such tangles."

The gilt tapestry parted in the center, and the tall figure of the lord of Rochambeau, his blond hair shining more brightly than the golden threads in the embroidery, stepped into the bedchamber from where Gilbert had thought there stood only a blank wall. Gilbert's hands jerked convulsively on the knotted strings, pulling Johanna backward so that she all but lost her balance. He put his arms out to catch her, and she pushed herself away, furiously aware that to Rochambeau it must look as though they were guiltily breaking out of an embrace. A show of guilt was not part of her plan.

"My lord!" She raised her chin, defying him to move against her. "I did not expect you."

"Clearly not," agreed Rochambeau. One hand dropped to his waist and came away with something that shone wickedly in the candlelight. Gilbert backed away from them, white and stammering. Rochambeau laughed and juggled with the knife. "I must thank you, de Bellay, for serving as my lady's tiring-woman. I had not realized Malvern was so poor that she had not a single woman to attend her at night. But I'm afraid you have much to learn of women's ways."

"I th-think so," stammered Gilbert. The man was laughing! He began to believe that he wasn't going to die on the spot, and the color began to return to his face.

"Some knots," Rochambeau said in a lecturing tone, "are so inextricably tangled that the only thing to be done is to cut them. There is nothing left worth saving of the original bond. Don't you agree, Johanna?" As he spoke, he put out one hand to spin her around and hold her in front of him. The belt knife slashed downward and the girdle fell at Johanna's feet in a mass of glittering golden threads.

"You're entirely right," said Johanna, kicking the expensive, ruined garment out of her way. "There is nothing worth saving."

Rochambeau's hand tightened around her arm, but he gazed over her head at Gilbert de Bellay with seemingly untroubled eyes. "You may go now, de Bellay. I'll attend my wife tonight."

Scarcely believing his good fortune, Gilbert stumbled from the room.

Left alone in their chamber, the lord and lady of Rochambeau gazed at each other for the space of a dozen breaths— she defiant, he thoughtful. Sheathing his knife at last, he pulled from his belt the braided leash with which he had struck at the fighting dogs earlier that night.

"I think," he said thoughtfully, "it is time to overcome my prejudices about beating women. You deserve a sharp lesson for this night's work, Johanna."

She stared as if entranced at the shining length of braided leather, dark with years of use. Could he mean it? Why not? He was a man, wasn't he? Of course he'd resort to force when trickery failed him. Having failed to charm her into compliance, he would now turn into a brute like her father, red-faced and ready to knock her down at any sign of opposition.

She could face the pain, she told herself. But the humiliation was another thing. If he struck her with his whip, there would in truth be nothing worth saving of the original bond between them. And, for some reason, Johanna found that she passionately did not want matters to come to that, even though she'd told herself a dozen times that the injuries he'd already done her were irreparable.

She raised her chin, wordlessly challenging him to carry out his threat. He took one step toward her, then another, and stopped when he was so close that she could see the even rise and fall of his chest beneath the close-fitting velvet tunic with its bands of silk embroidery.

"You may use me as you will, my lord," she told him, "but blows won't put you in the right! Nothing happened between de Bellay and me. Nothing would have happened, however long you waited to put in your appearance."

Unexpectedly, Rochambeau chuckled, though there was little mirth in the cold blue depths of his eyes. "Oh, I know that well enough, Johanna. You don't cheat, and you don't lie, and you wouldn't betray me—not like that, not sneaking behind my back with a boy scarcely out of his teens. If you took a lover, you'd probably announce the fact in broad daylight, with trumpets and heralds, and defy me to do anything about it."

Johanna's lips curved in an involuntary smile. "I hadn't quite thought that far ahead. But you're right. That would be the way to do it."

"Well, I suggest that you not even think about doing it," Rochambeau told her. "Because I would most assuredly know how to deal with such an action—just as I know how to deal with tonight's small contretemps! Take off your tunic."

The brusque command, coming after his almost friendly acknowledgment of the fact that of course she had not betrayed him with Gilbert, took Johanna by surprise. "Why? I told you, nothing happened!"

"I'm not punishing you for taking a lover, but for dragging that poor boy into your games. Whatever is between us, Johanna, you have no excuse for putting an innocent man at risk in that way. If I'd believed your little playacting attempt, I would have had no choice but to kill the boy."

"Maybe," Johanna suggested, *"He* would have killed *you!"*

Rochambeau's grim smile was cold and hard as the coiled braid of leather he carried in one hand. "Oh, I don't think we need worry about that possibility. We might as well not waste breath arguing over obvious facts, Johanna. You know as well as I do that Gilbert's no match for me. If you wanted me to believe that he was your lover, then you wanted his death; one follows from the other."

Johanna closed her eyes, unable to face Rochambeau's cold, remorseless logic. She had not thought that far ahead. Truth to tell, she acknowledged silently, she had not thought at all. She'd merely struck back at Rochambeau with the first weapon that presented itself. The fact that the weapon was a boy scarcely fit to take part in the bitter fight between them had not weighed with her at all.

"Would that have pleased you?" Rochambeau inquired. "To have men fighting with naked steel in your chamber? You've always resented the fact that I didn't waste months courting you like a popinjay with a crest of feathers in his helmet and time to waste tilting for his lady at tournaments, haven't you? But I didn't realize you were selfish enough to get your pleasure at the expense of a boy's life."

His hand fell on her shoulder. Mouth dry, Johanna tried to back away, but the long fingers hardened by years of swordplay held her as effortlessly as if she had been a doll. "You're wrong!" she cried out. "It wasn't like that. I didn't intend harm! You twist everything!"

In her frantic struggles to free herself, she actually managed to slip free of Rochambeau's grip, leaving the fold of her gown in his hand. There was a ripping sound, and the fine red cloth parted down to her waist. Rochambeau grabbed the tunic in both hands and thrust it down over her shoulders to her waist, leaving her creamy skin exposed above a low-cut chemise of finest silk.

"Go on!" Johanna shouted. "Strip me naked and beat me!

I always knew it would come to this between us! You'd rather kill me than respect me, wouldn't you?''

Rochambeau's hand trembled around the length of braided leather that he held clenched in his fist. Had he really intended to beat this woman into submission? He'd told himself that this time she had gone too far, that she had to be taught her place before her childish games got them into serious trouble. But now, staring at the perfect white skin bordered by folds of torn red cloth, he knew that he couldn't go through with it. Infuriating, sarcastic, maddening though she was, she was still his wife, his Johanna. To be cherished and loved, not to be hurt.

Why wouldn't she let him love her?

With a snarl of self-disgust, he threw his coiled whip down on the floor. The tight coils unwound like a snake writhing across the stone flags, rustling through the fresh-strewn rushes and sweet herbs that covered the floor. ''Oh, why should I wear my arm out on you? It's not worth the trouble.'' The thought of seeing pain in her eyes, of knowing he'd brought it there—he couldn't face that, but he dared not let her know how weak his love for her had made him. To keep her from seeing his weakness, he railed womanishly at her, hating himself more for every venomous word. ''You're nothing but a spoiled, selfish brat, left too long to run loose in the fields before you were wed and set to a woman's work. Your mother warned me I'd be buying a rare handful, but I thought you could learn. God help me, I even thought you had some fondness for me!''

''You did your best to destroy that fondness,'' Johanna defended herself. Arms crossed over her breasts, green eyes lowered, hair in disarray, she looked slight and pitiful where she stood in the middle of the chamber. Her voice quivered with unshed tears, but she was still fighting him.

Rochambeau loved and hated her for it at the same time. He wanted to sweep her into his arms and kiss away those tears, wanted to force her to her knees to apologize for her mischief making. Conflicting impulses froze him to the spot, unable to move toward her.

''And you've succeeded in destroying my hopes.''

She glanced up, so briefly that he caught just one flash of

emerald green before she veiled her eyes again. "What hopes?"

"I am not," Rochambeau told her, "entirely averse to enjoying a peaceful life as man and wife on my own estates. It would be a lot more comfortable than forever exiling myself to get away from a spitfire shrew who never forgives a man a single mistake. But there has to be a little give and take, Johanna."

"Seems to me that the giving is all on my side and the taking on yours!"

Rochambeau threw up his hands. "Enough! I'm tired. God's teeth, in the last months I've taken more barbed missiles from my own wife than I ever met with on crusade!"

Johanna bit her lip. "I haven't been very happy either," she said in a small voice. "If you understood how it's been for me—"

"No more, I beg of you!" Rochambeau cut her off. He was too tired, frustrated, and angry to listen to her petty grievances once again. "You've made it clear enough that you'll never forgive me for the heinous crime of marrying you, and I'm tired of trying to win you over. Forget about love. I will accept that you hate me. But you, madam, will accept that you must behave in a manner befitting the lady of Rochambeau. Is that clear?"

He was tired of her. That was all Johanna took in. What she'd feared would happen if she gave in to him had come about anyway, and she hadn't even had the few weeks of happiness that could have been hers if she had surrendered. He was tired of her; he would leave again in the morning. What else could he have meant by that remark about forever exiling himself from his own estates? Johanna stared at Rochambeau's tall, implacable figure through a mist of tears that blurred her vision. For once she was entirely incapable of telling herself that she wanted him to leave, that she'd be happier left alone to run the estates in peace as she'd done for the last four years.

That wasn't what she wanted at all. She wanted Rochambeau, wanted him with a passion that shook her to the roots of her being. But she hadn't wanted him as a casual visitor to her bed, slipping in and out of her life between one jest and another, using her for rest and relaxation between his jaunts around the country. She'd wanted him as part of her life, and she'd wanted to be part of his. Settling for anything less had seemed like self-betrayal.

Until now, when it became shatteringly clear to Johanna that she would settle for anything at all rather than give him up altogether. What did it matter if he knew the full extent of his power over her, if he used her as a plaything until he tired of her and then went back to his life of racketing around the country and making love to all the beautiful women he knew? At least she would have had those few short weeks, maybe months, of happiness with him. Now she would have nothing at all.

"Wait!" The plea was torn out of her as he moved toward the door to the chapel gallery. "Please. Don't go away. I—I love you!"

Even as she spoke them, Johanna sensed how inadequate her confession of love sounded, how false and strained the simple words could be in this context. But how could she convince Rochambeau of their truth? And even if she did so, what good would it do? She had already lost. He was tired of her. Whether she loved or hated him could only be a matter of indifference to him now.

She didn't need to see the slight shake of his head to know how utterly she'd failed. Suddenly she no longer had the strength to stand upright or the pride to hold her up when strength failed. Pride had become utterly unimportant in the face of her failure. She sank to her knees, holding out her arms in a last vain attempt to stop his departure.

"Please don't go. Not like this. We can try again. I'm sorry. Oh, God, I'm so sorry!" Johanna covered her face with her hands, trying to restrain the sobs that broke out despite her efforts at control.

Rochambeau stared down at his wife's white shoulders, half veiled by her long black hair, and his mouth twisted. Wasn't this what he'd wanted—to see her confess that she was in the wrong? But the victory was dust and ashes in his mouth, not the sweet wine he'd dreamed of.

"Don't kneel to me, Johanna!" Strain and confusion made his voice harsh. She looked up, startled, and he bent to raise her to her feet. "I don't want you like this, on your knees to me as a suppliant."

"I know." Elf locks of black hair stuck to the glimmering trail of tears on Johanna's white cheeks. Her eyes were flat and dull, the sea at low tide, the emerald fire extinguished. "You don't want me at all, do you? I knew you'd tire of me. Only I didn't think—so soon—but then, I've pushed you too far—" Her voice broke, and she turned away from him, fumbling to pull up the tattered red cloth of her dress. "You don't have to exile yourself this time, my lord. I'll go in the morning."

"And just where do you think you'll go?" He caught her by the bare shoulders, forced her to turn back and face him.

"To the convent of St. Sulpicia. It's on the road to Wales, near Pomeray. Do you remember? That was where you—rescued me from—the robber knight—" Johanna's voice was so choked by sobs that she could not go on.

"The hell you will," Rochambeau said, slowly and distinctly. He closed his arms around her, locking her against his chest. "You are my wife, and I am not giving you permission to go play at being a nun. You are going to stay right here and start acting like the lady of Rochambeau. Is that clear?"

Johanna raised her eyes to his face. The long black lashes were stuck together with tears; he wanted to kiss them. "But you said you didn't want me."

"I said I didn't want you on your knees to me," Rochambeau corrected. "That's not the Johanna I fell in love with. I want the woman I saw when I came into the chamber tonight, the one who had the courage to taunt me and defy me to my face. I want to win you, Johanna, not to destroy you."

"Fell in love?" Johanna repeated, as if she were stumbling over a phrase in some foreign language. "You fell in love with me?"

Rochambeau seriously doubted that she'd even heard the rest of his speech. It didn't matter. Her eyes were shining again, and she'd spontaneously reached up to put her arms around him, and she didn't even seem to have noticed that her dress was all but falling off her. The sweetness of her warm breasts, suddenly pressed against him, made him dizzy with longing.

"Oh, I didn't guess," she was saying now. "I didn't know!"

If only he'd guessed, himself, that a simple declaration of love would win him so much sweet complaisance, instead of her scornful laughter, he would have made it long ago. But one would think she'd have been able to figure it out. Rochambeau wanted to ask Johanna why she thought he'd gone to so much trouble to get and keep her, if she didn't understand that he loved her, but he refrained. He had other uses for his lips just now—kissing the soft mouth suddenly offered to him, tasting the salt traces of tears on her cheeks, and following the trail down to the scented, sweet curves of her bosom. His own wits seemed to be flying out the window; all his resolves about keeping Johanna under control were gone already. The only thing he could think about was how to get the last remnants of her wrecked dress off her before he went entirely crazy with wanting her.

And for the first time in a long career of discreetly removing ladies' dresses, his hands were shaking and he was fumbling like a lovesick boy. Fortunately, Johanna was cooperating. More than cooperating. She was attacking the laces of his own clothes even as she wriggled out of the dress. When she was standing white and slender in a pool of scarlet and gold, Rochambeau slipped one arm under her knees and the other under her shoulders and carried her to the bed.

Chapter Eighteen

THE CURTAINED BED was a small private room within a room, a secret place where Johanna nestled into her lord's embrace, for the first time without reservations. She had given those up in the shattering moment when she saw the abyss at her feet, the emptiness of a life without Rochambeau that her pride had almost forced her to. She was through now with her vain attempts to keep a part of herself separate from him. He wanted her; he said he loved her; she would have and give all she could now, freely, without worrying about the morrow.

The kiss that had begun while he was still fumbling with her dress and continued while he carried her to the bed now was prolonged almost beyond endurance. His lips moved over her neck and shoulders, sending waves of longing through her entire body until she was lost, dizzy, drowning beneath the overpowering current of love and desire. She moved involuntarily to escape a pleasure too strong, not of her seeking. "Ah, no, my sweet, don't go away from me," Rochambeau breathed against her naked skin. He kept her prisoner under his hands while he sought out and enjoyed every part of her, at last returning to drink of the sweetness of her mouth again.

Unbidden, her hands twined through the heavy silken curtain of his blunt-cut golden hair, then slid down along the muscles of his back, eliciting moans of rapture from him.

249

Limbs pressed to hers, molding her perfectly to the hard lines of his body, he parted her knees and lowered his weight onto her, filling her with a golden delight that radiated outward from her center. As he withdrew slightly, Johanna arched her body to keep him within her, to prolong the honeyed sweetness of that first moment. Rochambeau groaned.

"Don't move," he commanded. "I want to feel you around me. I want . . . you . . . Johanna!" With a cry of mingled pleasure and defeat, he plunged into her again, his whole body quivering above her with the tension of his desire, and Johanna rose to meet him. The rhythms of his need for her alternately shattered and rebuilt her being, finally flooding her with a sweet joy that felt like a million golden bells ringing in her veins.

For a long while they lay nestled close together after that almost unbearable crescendo, holding each other in a magic circle bounded by the softly swaying curtains of the bed all around them. Finally, Rochambeau stretched luxuriously, ran one hand over the black curling silk that flowed from Johanna's head down over her back and hips, and kissed her on one dark, satiny brow. "Is there some secret women's magic that you've been withholding from me?" he inquired quite seriously. "I don't remember it ever being quite like that before—even with you, sweetest and most delectable witch wife!"

The only magic, Johanna thought, was love—his confession of love for her, her discovery of a love for him that transcended the pride and reservations that had been keeping them apart. But she was afraid to say what she was thinking. In the grip of passion, he'd confessed that he loved her; now he might wish those words unspoken. Or—what would be worse—might not even remember what he'd said.

So, instead of speaking, she reached out her own hands to slide down the lean, scarred length of his hard body, ruffling the golden fuzz on his chest and stomach, darting lower to move over his thighs in lazy circles. She heard his breathing sharpen, felt the muscles of his thighs tighten under her hands, and reveled in her own power.

Rochambeau half closed his eyes, savoring the sweet agony of anticipation. "Where did you learn to torture a man so?"

"From you," Johanna whispered letting her fingertips trail a spiral course closer and closer to his loins, watching the play of emotion across his face and feeling the silky hardness that she just brushed with the tips of her fingers at the close of each spiral. "Do you want me to stop?"

"I plead for mercy." Rochambeau caught his breath and shifted so that she was forced to encircle him with her fingers. "It's not the same thing exactly."

"Then confess." If she could make a game of it, perhaps she could—within the game—get again the words of reassurance that she craved.

"What do you want me to confess to, witch wife?" He buried his face in the scented mass of her hair, feeling the crisp tendrils tickling his face and neck, lapping with his tongue at the soft whiteness of her skin beneath the glossy dark hair.

"That you . . . love me?" She hardly breathed the words, a hesitant thread of sound in the candlelit rosy stillness of the chamber.

"Haven't I proved that often enough?"

Johanna couldn't answer. She wanted to tell him that lust wasn't the same as love. That she wanted to be his wife, not his toy or his paramour. That a few hours of mutual pleasure weren't enough for her. She wanted a life with him, not a night.

But she couldn't speak. Hadn't she already decided that she would take whatever Rochambeau was willing to give, even if it was to be no more than this single night? In an agony of apprehension, she waited for him to tell her what it was she could have from him.

"Apparently not," he answered his own question. He groaned, and his fingers convulsively clenched her shoulders as her hands ceased their gentle stroking motion. "Johanna, this is not the best of times to wring words from me. I seem to be having some trouble concentrating."

"The remedy is in your power." Slipping down into the nest of crushed and dampened bedclothes, she put her arms about his waist and drew him down atop her. She'd been a fool to restart that old struggle; having already decided to capitulate, she might as well enjoy what there was to be had from her elusive husband. He was generous enough with his sensual expertise, if not with his words. She would take what she could get and be happy with that.

And what she could get from him was surely more than any woman had the right to ask for! This time, the first urgency of passion slaked, Rochambeau devoted himself to slowly and torturously unwinding her nerves, one by one, wrapping them around his fingers and playing on her as sweetly as ever he'd played on an instrument. Johanna alternately shivered and cried out with surprised pleasure as he discovered her own body for her, begged him to bring his long-drawn-out delights to completion, and pounded small fists against his chest with frustration when he only smiled and moved very, very slowly within her. His tongue explored the trails of passion first discovered by his hands; his nails drew feathery lines of desire spiraling against her skin; his strong body held her captive in the sensual, languorous rhythms of his mastery. She trembled, burned with exploding fires, cried out and clutched at him with shaking hands; even then he did not lose control, but forced her onward to experience new heights of passion before she had fallen back from those first peaks. Only when she was begging for mercy did he allow his own desires free rein, and then the tumultuous urgency of his need carried her away into a realm of pure sensation beyond anything she had known before. When at last they rested again, Johanna stroked the golden head that lay against her breast and told herself that she had no need now to hold back the words of love that rose to her lips. Rochambeau was hers at last, husband and lover.

Or was he? She'd given in completely, withholding nothing of herself from him, forgiving the way he'd forced her to become his initially. But what had he given her? As soon as his passion was slaked, wouldn't he be off again, remote, teasing, laughing at her, manipulating her, and effectively denying her a real place in his life? Tears squeezed between the black smudges of Johanna's thick eyelashes as she looked at Rochambeau where he'd tumbled to one side of the bed, his golden body stretched out as relaxed as a cat's. The even rise and fall of his chest was showing no sign of the tremors that had shaken them both only moments earlier. His eyes were closed, and he looked on the verge of falling asleep. No, not on the verge—those were definite snores she heard now.

Was that what it was like to be a man? To be gripped by passion one minute, and able to forget it all the next and walk way from the mystical joining as though you'd done no more than enjoy a good meal? Johanna could feel her nipples pulsing and the deep waves of desire within her contracting her flesh when she looked at Rochambeau and remembered what they'd just shared. She knew that now, having given herself to him without reservation, she could never be wholly free of him again. But what had it been for him? Pleasant, no doubt, not to have to seduce your own wife. Easier. A delightful experience. The belittling, trivializing phrases boiled up out of nowhere, scalding her like the hot tears that would burst forth despite her clenched fists and bitten lip. A moment earlier she had never felt closer to Rochambeau; now she thought she had never felt more alone. She turned her face away from him and wept silently into the crushed pink silks beneath her cheek.

"What—tears! What's this? Did I hurt you?" Gentle but firm, kind but inexorable, his hand on her chin forced her to turn her face back toward him and the light.

"Oh, go to sleep!" Johanna spat. "You got what you wanted, didn't you?"

"I was under the impression that we both got what we wanted." Rochambeau's deep voice sounded amused. "And I am sleepy. I've been up most of this night trying to make peace with my lady. I've just had a very pleasant time in her arms, and I was going to sleep happy. But I can't do that if you're still sad, Johanna. What's the matter?" he coaxed. "Are you angry that I tore your pretty new dress?"

Tender, humoring, subtly remote, his tone was all she needed to convince her of the truth of her own vision. Already he was slipping back into treating her like a child.

"Dress! Ten thousand devils fly away with the dress. It's you I'm crying over, you great fool." Johanna buried her face in his shoulder to conceal her tears, feeling the warm hardness of muscles gliding beneath the skin, tasting the salt of his sweat and her tears intertwined. "Oh, damn this crying! I know it bores you. You probably have scads of women weeping over you in bed and begging you not to leave them!"

"Not recently," said Rochambeau, a quiver of laughter under the concern in his voice. "And I've never had that experience with a woman I happened to be married to. What *is* the matter, Johanna? For years you've resented me for marrying you. But I should think one thing that would make fairly clear is that my intentions were permanent where you are concerned.''

"You c-couldn't get Sir Hugh's daughter any other way, though, could you?'' Johanna sniffled. ''You wouldn't seduce the daughter of one of your own vassals—and you did want me. I know that.''

"Not so much of the past tense there.'' Strong arms held her in place on his shoulder, offering a deceptively comforting circle of safety.

"All right. You still do. But that's only because you've been away for years and because I never completely gave in to you like all those other women. Now that you've won, you'll get bored with me and go away. You never thought about me, who I was and what I wanted; why should you start now? You saw, you wanted, you took—like a boy grabbing at a ripe apple—and now you're going to throw away the core!''

Rochambeau's deep, unrestrained laughter vibrated through his body. Johanna stiffened with insult and tried to break free of his embrace, but he twined one hand in the tick mass of curls at the back of her neck and forced her to look at him. "You don't look like an apple core to me, sweetheart. You look like a very tasty, tempting morsel indeed.''

"Wonderful. So maybe you'll nibble away for a little longer before you get bored!''

"You seem to have a very poor opinion of my attention span. I've got every intention of concentrating on this mysterious woman I took to wife long enough to understand her and her moods. Which just might take me the rest of my life.''

His hands caressed the stiff line of her backbone, molding her full hips against him and tantalizing her thighs with the memory of desire, until she relaxed against his body. "There, that's better. What makes you so insecure of your own attractions, dear heart? I can hardly believe this frightened girl is the woman I've been terrified of all these years.''

"You, afraid of me—'' Johanna laughed shakily. ''That's a good joke!''

"No jest. Why do you think I was in such a hurry to make you legally, irrevocably mine? From the moment you cursed me out in the middle of your father's fields, I knew no other woman could be my life's partner. I was terrified that I'd lose you if I gave you time to think about it, my love, especially considering the games you were playing with your father's squires, setting them all at one another's throats like ducks fighting for a crust of bread!''

"What a flattering comparison!"

"No more than you deserve. You were a little mischief maker, and you know it. But you were made for me, Johanna, and I for you. And I knew it then, and so did you—if you'll only admit it. Can you wonder if I betrayed myself by too much eagerness? It would have ruined both our lives if I'd let you get away."

Rochambeau paused, his lips setting in a firm line over some remembered sorrow, while he stroked Johanna's long black hair over her back and hips with one hand. "For a long time, I thought I might have ruined both our lives anyway. You seemed to hate me so much for hustling you into that marriage, and nothing I could do would win your forgiveness. I dared not show you how much I loved and needed you for fear you'd dominate me completely."

"Somehow I find that hard to believe."

"Try for an act of faith," Rochambeau advised. "It happens to be the plain truth. Something I'm not very good at telling, so you may not be used to the sound of it on my lips."

"I never thought to hear you admit so much!"

"Well, most women don't want truth from a man."

"All women want to hear that they're loved." She nestled luxuriously against his shoulder. "If that's true . . . ."

"Demand the truth, and you'll hear all of it," Rochambeau warned her. "Some parts may not please you as much as others. Yes, I love you, God help me! And I can't count the times I've asked God why He couldn't have let me wed a nice, quiet girl who would neither make trouble for me nor stir my blood to a frenzy. I can't get free of you, Johanna, you're part of my life, but I'll be damned if I'll let you rule me."

"I never wanted that."

"No?"

"I just want my own way."

Rochambeau burst out laughing. Johanna raised herself on

one elbow and glared at him suspiciously. "What's the matter with you? What's so funny about that?"

"You remind me," he gasped, "of the nice, peaceful baron who was always at war with his neighbors because all he wanted was the land that bordered on his own."

"Sounds perfectly reasonable to me. One has to protect one's borders."

"And after you've acquired the field next to yours, what about the field next to that?"

"Well, you have to—oh!" The paradox struck Johanna, and she began to giggle unwillingly. "Oh, I see what you mean. Oh, dear. Are you really afraid I'll try to take over everything, Nicolas?"

"You've certainly taken over the damned accounts," Rochambeau pointed out. "Mind you, I mean to decipher them, but for the moment . . . well, let's just say I don't want to see you in the armory, all right? Leave the lord of the manor a few trivial things he can call his own."

"With pleasure," said Johanna at once. "You can have the weaving and sewing and laundry. I'd be only too happy to leave those matters in your domain. And I'll take care of your horses and falcons."

"Women don't know anything about falconry!"

"Your mews are better kept now than when you left!"

For a moment they glared at each other like antagonists. Then Rochambeau's lips began to twitch, and he gathered Johanna back into his arms. "All right, I give in. I surrender. You are my liege lady, and I do you homage for this castle of Malvern . . . and for my life and soul, which you hold in your hands."

He gazed straight into her eyes with a tender, steady look that was everything she'd ever dreamed of winning from him. With a happy sigh, Johanna melted into his strong embrace, pressing her lips to the old white scar on his shoulder and letting the scented curtain of her hair fall over both of them. It seemed too good to be true. Her surrender had finally brought her what she'd fought for all along: Rochambeau's unstinted, unreserved love. Finally, after all their battles for dominance, she felt like his equal partner. His wife, not his plaything. And the mother of his heirs.

That was something she had yet to tell him. But . . . perhaps not tonight. She'd only had a few hours to enjoy being his wife. It was only in the last few days that Johanna had begun to feel sure that the changes she'd noticed in her body betokened pregnancy. And some men got very nervous when their wives were carrying. She certainly didn't want Rochambeau to begin treating her like a delicate thing that might shatter if he had his way with her. Not yet.

Thinking about how she did want Rochambeau to use her, Johanna drifted into sleep with a wicked little smile curving her lips. Rochambeau looked down at the ivory face cradled against his chest and marveled at how sweet and peaceful she could seem at such moments. With those dangerous green eyes veiled and her mouth relaxed in slumber, she might have been a lovely child instead of his delicious, tormenting, spirited witch wife.

No, not a child. She had been just blossoming out of her girlhood when he took her to wife; now she was a woman blooming in full beauty. The rich, sensual curve of her lower lip, her breasts like ripe fruit begging to be plucked, and the smooth white fullness of her hips belied the imagery of childhood. Rochambeau gently stroked her from shoulders to knees, and she sighed with pleasure in her sleep and sighed again as he gently eased himself out of the bed.

A few minutes ago, sated with the extremes of sensual pleasure that Johanna had brought to their bed, he had wanted nothing more than to sleep on her breast. Now, after the effort of explaining himself—something he'd never done for a woman before—he was twitchy, unable to relax. He kept going over what he'd said to her, wondering if the morning would see a resumption of their old battle or if she would let herself trust him at last.

"A plague on all this wondering!" Rochambeau muttered as he drew on his clothes. What he needed was some nice, challenging intellectual puzzle to take his mind off women and their wayward ways. Something like deciphering Johanna's encoded estate accounts—except that had been too challenging. If he started on that, he'd be up all the rest of the night with letters and numerals dancing before his eyes.

Something to read, then. He glanced around the room in search of inspiration, and his eye was caught by the hammered silver cover of an illuminated psalter. I had been one of the marriage gifts he'd ordered for her—gifts which, at the time, she'd taken as yet another deadly insult. He'd never understand why. But it seemed she hadn't scorned the pretty things in that chest, even though she had pretended to be angry with him at the time. Rochambeau smiled inwardly and wondered if he understood Johanna as well as he thought. He picked up the psalter and ran his hands over the raised figures on the silver cover, then flipped it open to glance at the illuminated initials and fine scribework he had bespoken but never looked at. As he recalled, the scribe had put in the lives of a few saints to fill the book out, after he copied the usual prayers. That would be unusual reading for Rochambeau, but it should be just the thing to put him to sleep.

It was strange, how certain sections of the psalter were so much thumbed over, while others were pristine and untouched. There seemed to be no sense to the selections, either; the much-used sections skipped from a prayer for women in childbed to the end of the Credo, then to the middle of the Litany. The intervening pages were crisp and clean, but these places where the book fell open were smudged with fingerprints from much reading. Rochambeau frowned in distaste as he saw that Johanna had even scribbled in the margins of the book in places, placing her own random series of letters and signs down the edge of the page. What had possessed her to treat this elegant gift as a toy, marking it up with a bunch of meaningless letters like a child's first attempts at writing, like . . .

Like a cipher.

Heart pounding with excitement, Rochambeau slipped the prayer book inside his tunic and glanced at his sleeping wife. Yes, her eyes were still closed. The dark lashes lay across her cheeks without a single tremor, and her breast rose and fell in an even rhythm. She was deeply asleep; she couldn't possibly have noticed him looking at the psalter.

With any luck, it might be two or three days before she realized it was missing.

Chapter Nineteen

IN THE MORNING, Johanna was surprised to be awakened by Alais and Margery. Their voices blended with the twittering of the women in the bower just outside, Alais's soft and concerned, Margery's sweet and strong with an occasional harsh note from years of shouting to be heard over unruly crowds at fairs and festivals.

"We were worried about you."

"You never sleep so late."

"It's after Mass, and nobody's been given their orders for the day."

This last roused Johanna to prop herself up on one elbow, blinking in the daylight that spattered through the narrow slits of windows on the far side of the chamber. The sudden movement made a wave of nausea go through her. Oh, no! She didn't want to be one of those women who was forever sickly when they were breeding. Sheer will forced down the queasiness in her stomach. She rubbed her eyes and tried to stare down Margery's straightforward, questioning gaze. Of course, Margery wanted to know what had happened last night. And Johanna didn't feel like telling her. She wanted to hold that joyful memory to herself for a little while longer.

The slight uncertainty she still felt in her midriff, the passionate desire that everybody would stand very still until she recovered herself, made it easy enough to produce an automatic burst of indignation while she tried to figure out exactly what she was willing to tell her women about last night.

"God's body and bones! Have I trained my staff so ill that they can't get on for one single morning without my eye upon them? Master Chamberlain can order matters in the hall. My women can get on with weaving cloth for the winter liveries. The cook can use his own judgment for dinner. He's always complaining that I don't give him enough freedom anyway."

Margery shrank back briefly, and Alais pushed forward, giving a soft cry of horror at the sight of the wrecked bed and torn clothes that littered the floor. "Oh, my lady! Your lovely tunic is all torn and wrinkled—and whatever happened to the girdle? Oh, I knew I shouldn't have left you to disrobe yourself. You're as careless as my little sisters, throwing your best clothes all over the floor . . ." She chattered on while her clever fingers repaired the mischief, smoothing the torn tunic across her arms and mourning over the rips.

While Alais fussed over the clothes, Margery looked Johanna up and down with a sniff. "Well, you're not bruised, that I see," she commented as Johanna shrugged off the bedclothes and stepped naked into the sunlight of a new day. "You must be a right clever woman to get away with your tricks."

"I didn't," said Johanna absently, scarcely heeding Margery's words. She stretched shamelessly in the light, feeling the golden tide of warmth and healing go right through to her bones. Alais clucked disapprovingly and pulled a linen chemise over Johanna's head. She looked about the chamber, feeling a little bit cheated that Rochambeau wasn't there. Of course, he'd have been up at first light and about the business of the manor. But Johanna had been looking forward to a leisurely morning in bed with him, persuading him to repeat the declaration of love he'd made last night, seeing his face light up when she told him that she might be carrying his heir already.

"Where's he gone to?"

"The minstrel? Oh, he's still here, the silly gowk, though God knows why he lingers," Margery answered.

Alais dropped her eyes and blushed, and Johanna found time in the midst of her more pressing worries to wonder if Alais had transferred her maidenly affections from Aubrey to

Gilbert. Really, from one ineligible to another—it was high time she took the girl in hand. But first Johanna wanted to set the seal on her own happiness.

"Not the minstrel! Rochambeau."

"Didn't know he was going anywhere. No, he's locked himself up in the strongroom, wouldn't even come out for a bite of bread and a sup of wine after Mass. You've upset him finely with your goings-on, my lady, for all he didn't beat you black and blue as you deserved last night." Margery's tone made it clear that her volatile sympathies had veered over to Rochambeau.

"No, no, I don't think he's upset." Johanna smiled to herself. Perhaps it was better this way. She could go to him in the privacy of the strongroom, and they could share her news without a gaggle of silly women listening and giggling at the door.

Her decision made, Johanna snapped out orders, sending her women scurrying. "Alais! Get my blue tunic down from the clothes perch. No, bring me my mirror first. Margery, send a couple of pages for hot water. Where's my blanchet box?" Last night had been wonderful but exhausting. Some women lost their beauty when they were breeding. God grant she wouldn't be one of those! Anxiously, she scrutinized her face in the ivory-framed mirror, searching for signs of redness or swollen eyes. Her skin was white and smooth as ever, but she still dusted it with the fine wheat powder in the blanchet box, just in case. The soft blue tunic, no jewels, her hair hastily pinned back under a veiling of fine linen—she was too impatient to make a better toilette.

"You're alive. Even the minstrel's alive. I don't see what you're in such a taking for," Margery said softly when Alais was out of the room for a minute.

"I'm not." The deep, secret smile lit Johanna's face again.

Margery looked, looked again, gasped, and took Johanna by the hands. "I've been thinking something of the sort. Your waistline ain't what it used to be—we had to lace that girdle too tight last night. Are you—?"

"Yes, I think so." Johanna faced Margery, eyes dancing. "Only, before last night I was too angry to tell him. And last night I was too busy." She smiled again, and Margery gave her a quick, impulsive hug.

261

"No wonder you look like a cat that's been locked in the dairy! Had a good old fight, did you, and made up afterwards? And now you want to tell him he's about to have an heir. Yes, you'll want to be lookin' your best for that. Turn toward the light." Margery inspected Johanna's face in the morning light and gave a little envious sigh. "You don't need the powder, that's the truth. Why d'you mess your face up with that stuff in the first place? Girl, if I had your skin like silk and your eyes like big green emeralds, I wouldn't bother with anything else."

"I'm getting old," Johanna said. "Almost twenty-one! I need all the help I can get."

Margery laughed again. "Ha! When you're thirty-five—well, say thirty, like me—then it'll be time to think of painting."

"Thirty!" Johanna stared in astonishment. "No. Your skin is so smooth and white."

"Paint," said Margery succinctly. "I learned a few tricks on the road. When you need 'em, I'll teach 'em to you, my lady. But this isn't the day for it." She pushed Johanna up from her stool and gave her an encouraging pat. "Go on, what are you worried about? If he didn't kill you last night, he's not likely to do so this morning. Especially when you tell him he's going to have an heir to the honor of Rochambeau!"

Alais, her arms full of silks from the bower chests, stopped in the doorway and almost collided with Johanna as she floated out. She looked at Margery, eyes wide. "What are you talking about? Aubrey is the heir to Rochambeau!"

"Not anymore, love," said Margery with a grin. "Not if that's a boy our lady is carrying under her girdle."

"Oh, dear," Alais said, setting her pile of cloth down. "Aubrey will be *so* upset."

If Aubrey resented the imminent arrival of an heir to Rochambeau, he didn't show it when he found Johanna in the garden and offered his congratulations. He was as considerate as any woman, proffering a wide hat to protect her from the sun, wondering if she ought not to go in and lie down at once, suggesting a strengthening posset of goat's milk and herbs.

"For pity's sake, Aubrey, I'm not an invalid!" Johanna snapped, and then she regretted her flash of ill temper as Aubrey's mouth whitened. "I'm sorry. You're very kind. But I don't want a lot of fuss made. It's too soon. I might not be with child at all, actually."

"No?" Aubrey looked surprised. "But Alais said—"

"Alais and Margery," said Johanna, "are all excited about having a baby to play with." She dropped her eyes for a minute, savoring the warm glow that rose inside her at the thought. She was excited too, but she didn't want to look like an idiot by acting the part of a breeding woman, letting everybody cosset her and keep her on cushions, when she wasn't the least bit sick. "It's too soon to be sure," she repeated.

"But you are sure."

Johanna felt a smile stretching all the way across her face and was aware that she must look like a grinning idiot after all. "I can't hide anything from you, can I, Aubrey? Yes. And what's more, it's going to be a boy. I can *feel* it. My mother was Welsh, you know. She had a little of the sight; she always knew when she was breeding and whether it would be a boy or a girl. I was even going to tell Nicolas this morning, but he was busy."

He was locked in his strongroom with the account rolls. That young squire Fulke, who disliked her, had said with a nasty grin that he had orders to see that no one at all disturbed his lord. Johanna wouldn't lower herself to squabble with Fulke, and she didn't want her joyous news for Rochambeau preceded by such an unpleasant scene. So she had taken herself and her glow of happiness out to the herb garden, where she walked the sweet-smelling rows of savory and medicinal plants and told her news to the bees that buzzed above the small flowers.

"But it's a little early for public announcements, don't you think? And I particularly don't want the news spread all over Malvern before Nicolas knows."

Aubrey nodded. He looked bleak suddenly, and years older than Rochambeau. Once again, Johanna realized tardily that she had been tactless. "Oh, I didn't mean you, Aubrey," she said at once, putting a hand on his arm. "You're different. I don't mind that Alais told *you.*"

"Yes, different." Aubrey's voice was heavy and dull. He

turned aside and suddenly lashed out with one hand at a flowering spray of lavender. Two bees rose into the air with affronted short buzzes, and the tiny flowers scattered over the garden path.

"Aubrey, what on earth is the matter?" Johanna took his hands and drew him back around to face her. His face was white and set, pinched in deeply at the corners of the mouth, and he wouldn't meet her eyes.

"Don't ask, Johanna. You don't really want to know."

"Dear Aubrey, of course I do. You've been like a dear, kind brother to me ever since I married Rochambeau. Why, I don't know what I would have done without your help and advice all these years, especially while Nicolas was away."

A sarcastic little voice in the back of Johanna's mind suggested that the estate would have done a great deal better without Aubrey's help and advice. She brushed it away. Aubrey meant well, even if he was somewhat bungling and totally unfit to handle financial matters, and she truly didn't want to see him unhappy. That much was true. Especially not on this glorious day of blue sky and opening flowers and true love fulfilled for her. She wanted everybody to be as happy as she was.

"Come, let us sit in the pleasance, and you can tell me what is troubling you." Perhaps the sun was too much for him; he did look dazed. Johanna gently led the unresisting Aubrey through the arch in the west side of the garden wall, into a green enclosure planted with grass and daisies and shaded by three ancient apple trees. Between two of the trees was a swinging seat just wide enough for two people. Johanna guided Aubrey to the seat and sat down beside him, still holding one of his hands.

"Do you feel better now?" she asked solicitously. "Perhaps I should call one of the grooms to bring you a drink of water."

Aubrey groaned and rested his forehead on his free hand. "Pay no attention. I suppose I shall get used to it in time."

"Used to what?"

"To seeing Nicolas taking so casually what I would treasure as my dearest possession."

Johanna thought this over. All she could think of that Aubrey might be referring to was Malvern and the rest of the manors that constituted the honor of Rochambeau. Could Aubrey possibly have hoped to inherit the honor from his half-brother? Surely not. He was older than Nicolas, and a bastard to boot, and he must have expected that Rochambeau's marriage would someday produce heirs. Still, she could see that the sudden reality of a son to be born to Rochambeau might be a shock to him.

"I don't believe Nicolas is casual about his estates, Aubrey. He may have been at one time, but now he is willing to settle down and take care of them properly. And I know he will value your help in teaching our children the management of the land." With the slight caveat that their children had better learn their arithmetic from her and not from poor, dear, muddled Aubrey.

Aubrey groaned again and turned away from her, resting his brow against the trunk of the apple tree beside him.

"We do value you, Aubrey," Johanna tried again. "We need you. You will always have a place here." Oh, dear, how patronizing she sounded! It could only make Aubrey feel worse, to be earnestly assured by a girl half his age that he would still be needed after the heir who dispossessed him was born. "I know how you love the land."

"Fiend fly away with the land and all that is on it!" Aubrey's fist crashed into the apple tree, leaving skin on the rough bark. "Ow!" He sucked his knuckles and looked almost sensible for a moment. "Sorry, Johanna. I didn't mean that. But how could you think it was the land I meant?"

"What else?"

"Haven't you guessed?"

Before she could rise, Aubrey's arm went around her waist, crushing her against him. With his left hand, the one he'd grazed on the apple tree, he caught her wrist and bestowed clumsy wet kisses on her fingers. "All these years . . . ," she heard between kisses. "Never speaking my love . . ." Smack. Smack. "My devotion . . ." Smack.

Johanna couldn't help it. She giggled.

"Aubrey, quit fooling around! Do you know, you sound exactly like Rochambeau's favorite hunting brachet when she licks his plate? Now, stop it, Aubrey, or I shall get angry."

"Yes, get angry!" Aubrey said rapturously. "Show me some feeling! Beat me if you want to! But love me afterward.

Please, Johanna. We can be quite private here; I've given orders that no one should disturb us. Just let me show you how I can make you happy, and you'll never care about Nicolas again. Beautiful Johanna, be mine once, and I'll worship you forever!''

His hands were pulling at her skirts. Johanna almost began to be afraid. And yet this was Aubrey, her dear old friend and companion. He didn't mean to hurt her. He didn't know how strong he was. He was just getting carried away. Maybe he'd been drinking.

"Aubrey, I really shall be angry if you don't stop this foolery!'' she warned, her voice rising to a high note that betrayed the fear she would not admit. "Aubrey, do you want me to scream for help? Think how embarrassed we'd both be! Now cut it out, right this—'' His mouth came down on hers, wet and hot. Johanna pushed with all her might, and Aubrey, off balance already, fell backward out of the swinging seat. His arms and legs flailed wildly in a desperate attempt to save himself. One hand scrabbled along the edge of the wooden seat, and he landed with a thump on his back in the middle of a patch of daisies.

Johanna tried not to laugh, but the picture he presented was too ridiculous for her to restrain herself. Her smothered giggles broke out in peals of half-hysterical laughter, while Aubrey raised himself on his elbows and glared at her.

"Think it's funny, do you?''

"Oh, Aubrey, I am sorry,'' Johanna gasped between bursts of laughter. "But you must see. If it's not funny, then what *is* it? You can't have been serious. You didn't really think I'd slip off into the pleasance with you for a quick roll on the daisies, did you?''

"No,'' said Aubrey slowly. "You wouldn't demean yourself so with the bastard son of the house, would you?''

His lips were set, and there was a hard glitter in his eyes that almost frightened her. Johanna told herself again that she was not afraid of Aubrey, but she couldn't help glancing at the arched gateway to the herb garden, measuring the distance to it. A gardener carrying buckets of water sauntered slowly past, and Johanna relaxed imperceptibly.

"You know it's not that, Aubrey. Now, please, be reasonable! You don't want me to take you seriously. It would spoil everything.''

Aubrey nodded slowly with resignation. As he got up and brushed himself off, he looked past Johanna to the arched gate, as if already regretting his outburst and longing to be away. ''Of course not. How could I want you to betray Nicolas? Please accept my apology. But Johanna . . .''

He knelt again and raised her fingers to his lips. She saw that his skinned knuckles were bleeding.

''Take this much seriously at least: you have my entire devotion and service, whatever may happen in the future. And not for Nicolas's sake, but for your own.''

Johanna felt horribly embarrassed. She'd always taken Aubrey's flirtatious compliments as another sign of his basic kindness, a wish to make up to her for the slights Rochambeau put upon her. She wanted to go on taking them that way, to continue thinking of him as a beloved elder brother. Besides, the gardener had shuffled to a stop and was gazing slack-jawed through the arched gate. They must present a pretty picture, like a knight vowing service to the lady he loved.

''You're too good to me, Aubrey, as always.'' Finally, she was able to free her hands without actually fighting. ''And I think you were right before, too. The sun is too hot for me. Shall we go in?''

It was actually shady under the trees, but Aubrey accepted her excuse with good grace.

Rochambeau remained closeted in his strongroom for the rest of the day, and Johanna worked off her growing impatience by going out hawking after dinner. ''I wish you wouldn't ride alone,'' Aubrey said worriedly when she told him of her intention and asked him to tell Rochambeau if he should emerge from the strongroom.

''I knew I shouldn't have let anybody know of my expectations,'' Johanna said. ''Look, Aubrey, I'm nervous. I need to be alone. It will calm me to go out. It is good for pregnant women to be calm and happy.''

''All right,'' Aubrey grumbled, ''but I don't like it.'' He went to the stables himself and fussed an inordinately long time over the saddling of Johanna's favorite mare, complaining that the mare was nervous from lack of exercise and might throw Johanna.

"She won't throw *me*," said Johanna, and immediately regretted her unkind emphasis. It wasn't Aubrey's fault that he wasn't good with horses.

An hour later, she regretted her words even more. The mare shied at a fallen tree, the girth of the saddle snapped, and Johanna hit a pile of soft brown leaves with a thump that knocked the breath out of her. Before she had regained her feet, the mare was cantering back toward Malvern.

It wasn't a bad fall, though it might have been fatal if she'd taken the rocky high path that she'd told Aubrey she was taking. Johanna blessed the chance that had made her choose this path through the woods instead; the leaves had made a nice soft cushion for her and the precious burden she carried within her.

Still, it wasn't what you would call a successful afternoon. She had to limp back through the woods in soft leather shoes that were never meant for walking. Her feet were sore, and as the sun sank Johanna felt just slightly nervous. That old woman whom the villagers called a witch had built herself a hut somewhere in the forest, with Rochambeau's permission. That would not be a very pleasant place to shelter for the night, but it would be better than staying out in the open.

Fortunately, she reached the edge of the forest before it grew quite dark and met some of Rochambeau's serfs who were honored to lend her their old white plough-horse to ride home on.

Somewhat less fortunately, Rochambeau had emerged from his isolation to take an evening meal and had noticed her prolonged absence. "I don't want you riding out by yourself," he commanded in his high-handed way when Johanna finally returned to Malvern. "It's too dangerous."

Once he knew she was pregnant, he probably wouldn't let her go up and down stairs by herself! And this was no time to tell him anyway, not when she was hot and tired and desperately wanted a bath.

Johanna waited up late after her bath, watching the candles burn down in their chamber, combing out her long black hair, and dreaming of the smile she'd see on Rochambeau's face when he came to her and she told him he was to be a father.

She fell asleep in one of those dreams, woke in darkness to feel his warm body beside her, and woke again at dawn to discover that the man had gone off to his strongroom again to pursue whatever secret project was taking him all that time.

"I've been forbidden to go out riding," she grumbled to Alais, "and this morning I actually feel too sick to garden. The estate accounts are locked up in the strongroom where Nicolas is, so I can't do any of our business work. I may be reduced to sewing."

She waved a pair of shears in the general direction of some green and blue Damascus brocades, and Alais tactfully removed the valuable fabric, substituting a bolt of home-woven woolen cloth for the servants' liveries. Johanna glared at the boring task and settled sulkily in a corner of the bower with her tapestry frame. The half-finished pattern of green leaves against a gold background had been gathering dust in a corner since Rochambeau's return. She'd had better things to think of.

She had better things to think of now, for that matter. Needle poised over the frame, Johanna sat with half-closed eyes and dreamed sleepily of the future until it was time to dismiss her women for the midday meal.

She meant to join them, but halfway down the stairs that led from bower to great hall, the smells of roast and boiled meat caught in her throat. She fled ignominiously back to the privacy of the chamber, green-faced and shaky. Perhaps it would be better to take a little nap while her ladies dined. Just a few moments on the bed, and she'd feel refreshed and ready for the afternoon . . .

It was midafternoon when she awoke, alerted by stealthy movements just outside the curtained bed.

"What's going on, Alais?" Johanna demanded, thrusting her head outside the drawn curtains. "Where are my women? Why did you let me sleep so late?" Scrambling out of the bed, blushing to have been caught sleeping in the middle of the day, she splashed cold water over her face and hastily straightened her crumpled tunic.

"I sent them away," Alais replied. "No, I didn't tell them anything. But they're going to guess soon enough, especially if you keep turning green and bolting out of the hall at mealtimes."

"A temporary weakness. I feel perfectly all right now." It was true; after her nap, Johanna felt ready to take on the world again. She certainly didn't intend to spend the next eight months dozing in her room!

"Good. You need to eat something. I saved you a bowl of numble pie." Alais whisked a linen napkin off a wooden dish filled with the rich stew of venison tripe and onions thickened with bread crumbs. The smell of the meat made Johanna feel sick.

"Take that away!"

"I thought so." Alais nodded, and Johanna began to feel that she'd been trapped. "Aubrey was concerned when you rushed out of hall like that. He went and asked Bruma for some remedies for your condition."

Johanna laughed weakly. "The only remedy is time. About eight months of it. And I don't want any of the witch's noxious messes, thank you. Just send down to the kitchens for a bowl of bread and milk."

Alais's lower lip stuck out. "The least you can do is listen to her, after Aubrey went to the risk of fetching her out of the forest for you."

Johanna sighed and agreed rather than anger Alais, although she didn't believe the woman could do any good. She herself knew more of herbal remedies than most of the so-called wise women she'd met. She had potions to bring a nursing mother's milk in or to ease the pangs of childbirth, herbs to strew under pillows to keep the fairies from creeping in and changing a child for one of their own, and even some well-guarded and dangerous recipes for driving out demons from a mad woman or calming a feverish one. But those were cures for real problems, not for a little dizziness and nausea that would surely pass in the course of nature. Her mother had always said that the first few weeks of pregnancy were just miserable, and there was nothing you could do about it but wait.

Her first sight of Bruma imbued her with a certain involuntary awe. Instead of the bent, shuffling, poor old woman she'd been expecting, a creature more like a walking tree entered the chamber. Gray of face and skin, tall and painfully thin, with limbs twisted by some creeping disease, the witch stalked in with no more covering for her skinny old arms and legs than a patched and faded cloak the color of autumn leaves after a rain. Her head was uncovered, and her long gray hair flowed loosely in obscene parody of a maiden's style; her deep-set black eyes glittered in a colorless face. Johanna crossed herself as that piercing, ironic glance fell on her.

"You need my help," Bruma stated, seating herself without leave on an embroidered cushion near the bed.

Johanna sat straight. "I have been thinking that I might help you," she countered. "It does not please my lord that any of his people should live in want. There are vacant cottages in the village where you could be sheltered from the winter winds."

"And who'd shelter me from the stones of the villagers?" the witch cackled. "Nay, nay, 'tis best for me and my boy to stay in the deeps of the woods, where your silly villeins fear to hunt us."

Johanna glanced at Aubrey.

"She has a son, grown to man's size but without a man's wit," Aubrey explained. "He cannot speak, but he's managed to put together a stout lodging for the two of them in the depths of the forest."

"He's a good boy, a very good boy. Strong, too. D'you want a strong, lusty man, m'lady? One who can't tell tales after? Ah, don't look so prim and proper! Many's the great lady would be glad of such a service as I can offer. Many's the one who has rewarded me richly for that and more!"

Johanna withdrew the edge of her tunic from the old woman's clutching fingers, trying to fight down the distaste that showed too clearly on her face.

"Enough of that!" Aubrey admonished Bruma. "You know what you were brought here for. Do it, and you'll have your reward. Else—"

"Else what? You'll have me flogged out of the parish, me and my fine boy? I've had *that* too often to fear it! Look!" With one gesture, the witch tore off her cloak, revealing shriveled breasts and a back deeply seamed with the scars of old floggings. "My master gives me a charm against feeling the whip," she crooned to herself, rocking back and forth and hugging herself with withered old arms. "My master gives me many secrets, my lady. Send the little girl away, and perhaps I'll share some of them with you, if you speak me fair.''

That was reasonable. Young unmarried girls like Alais shouldn't hear too many of women's mysteries. Alais gave Johanna a hurt glance, but she departed obediently at Johanna's nod. Aubrey stayed where he was, standing beside Johanna's chair with one hand resting lightly on her shoulder. She felt a little embarrassed at the idea of a man hearing this discussion, but on the other hand, she really did not want to be alone with the witch.

"I feel a little sick in the mornings," Johanna said. "It's really nothing, but since Aubrey has been so kind as to bring you here, I'd appreciate hearing of any remedies you may suggest.''

"Ah!'' Bruma's whisper penetrated through the fingers clasped over her ears. "Yes, my lady, old Bruma's got remedies for that kind of sickness. Do you want the child?''

Johanna straightened and clasped her hands in her lap. "Very much.''

Bruma looked disappointed at this answer. No doubt she did a good trade among village girls who'd been silly enough to get themselves into trouble. "And you want him—yon great lord—to be the father?''

"He *is* the father.''

"If you say so,'' Bruma cackled.

"Insolent! Shall I call Rochambeau's men-at-arms to flog you back to your hovel?''

Aubrey's fingers gripped her shoulder. "Don't offend her, Johanna,'' he muttered.

The witch didn't seem to have taken offense; no doubt she was well used to such threats. And no wonder, if she insulted everybody she met this way. Johanna was beginning to understand why the peasants drove the old woman away with blows and curses. She was a born troublemaker, and the sooner she left the castle the happier Johanna would be.

Still, Aubrey was right. It didn't do to offend a witch; her herbs and potions might be worthless, but who knew what evil powers would answer her command? The quickest and easiest way to be rid of her was to let her detail her nauseous remedies.

After some discussion of toad's eyes boiled in the urine of

a pregnant mare, and the wings of dung beetles pounded to powder, Bruma offered Johanna a small bag of herbs. "If you'll not take the stronger potions, then put a pinch of this in your morning posset. 'Twill give you strength and make the baby grow big and healthy."

"What's in it?"

Bruma cackled. "Ah, that'd be telling! D'you want to steal a poor old woman's secrets?"

"I know something of herbs myself," Johanna said calmly. "I'm not taking anything unless I know what it is."

Bruma shrugged defeat. "Creeping thyme, dandelion roots dried and pounded small, plantain, and . . ."

Johanna raised her brows and waited.

"Peach leaves."

So that was why she'd been so reluctant to disclose her ingredients! The only peach trees in this part of England grew against a sunny wall in the orchard of Malvern. And that also explained the slightly bitter smell that had made Johanna nervous about the witch's herbal concoction. Though it didn't seem quite like peach leaves . . . Well, no matter. Bruma doubtless had a few secret ingredients she didn't want to admit to. The ones she'd named were all standard remedies for breeding women, herbs Johanna might have chosen herself for another woman in her case.

Aubrey towered over her. "You'll take the herbs? Promise me, Johanna."

"I'm sure they'll do me a lot of good," Johanna replied evasively. She wasn't sure she wanted to take anything that came from the witch's hands. But the look of relief on Aubrey's face touched her. He really did care for he, Johanna thought sleepily. That scene in the pleasance—well, he'd been upset at the news of her pregnancy. But it was just like Aubrey to put aside his feelings of jealousy and try, in his clumsy way, to take care of her. "I'll make an infusion right away," she promised. "Would you pay Mistress Bruma and escort her to her home again?"

"Oh, I've already been paid—well paid!" the old woman giggled. "Thank you kindly anyway, Mistress Johanna."

She seemed very pleased with herself for something, either at Johanna's courtesy to her or because she thought Johanna was too stupid to figure out where the peach leaves came from. As Aubrey and Bruma were leaving, Johanna called out on impulse, "Oh, and Bruma—"

The witch stopped and looked back over her skinny shoulder. "Yes, my lady?"

"Next time you want peach leaves," Johanna said, "don't risk your old bones climbing over the orchard wall. My gardener will be pleased to supply you."

"Peach leaves."

Chapter Twenty

LATER THAT AFTERNOON, Rochambeau at last stumbled out of the strongroom, red-eyed, unshaven, and triumphant. Under one arm he carried the original account rolls in Johanna's cipher; under the other he held a stack of miscellaneous scraps of parchment covered with his jottings, deductions, and translations. As he made his way down the stairs to the level of the bower and chamber, he chuckled every now and then and patted the second stack with a satisfied grin.

When he peered into the bower, several of Johanna's ladies jumped up from their tasks, alarmed at the sight of his unshaven face and bleary eyes. Johanna herself was nowhere to be seen. "Where's my wife?"

Somewhat nervously, Margery directed him to the herb garden behind the orchard, and Rochambeau set off in that direction after telling his squire to stop tagging at his heels like a little lost puppy. Fulke shook his head as he watched his lord set off, still grinning and chuckling to himself. Not for the first time, he wondered if the lord of Rochambeau had finally lost his hold on sanity.

Unaware of his squire's worries, Rochambeau strode briskly down the narrow path that wound past the walled orchard to the herb garden. On this hot autumn afternoon, it was a delightful shady stroll, with the old apple trees just overhead and the stone walls covered with flowering creepers. But the herb garden wasn't shaded, and the sun beat down fiercely from noon till eventide. Even in the exultation occasioned by his new discoveries, he began to wonder what had possessed Johanna to come out and sit in the garden on a day like this.

She wasn't sitting, of course. He should have known better. Tunic hitched up into her girdle, feet shod in plain wooden clogs, she was digging away like a serf girl. Her back was to him, and he paused a moment to admire the fine strong lines of her body as she moved through the garden. He could just see the curve of her cheek under a coif that had slipped somewhat awry. Fine curling tendrils of black hair clung to her face in disarray, and there was a smudge of garden dirt under her eye where she'd wiped the sweat away with a careless hand. The whole sight put him strongly in mind of a day years ago when he'd surprised her at just such menial work in her father's gardens at Pomeray. She'd been angry then to be caught disheveled and looking like a peasant, but he'd kissed her anger away.

Rochambeau grinned and began to whistle softly, almost under his breath, while Johanna bent over the bush she was transplanting. He had to increase the volume of his whistling several times before she finally looked up. With a violent start, she dropped the spade she held.

"M-my lord! I didn't know—I thought it was a bird singing."

"Rather late in the day for that, don't you think?" Rochambeau stacked his account rolls neatly on the top of the low wall bordering the herb garden. "And I would have thought it was rather late for gardening, too." He grinned at Johanna and wiped a smudge off her cheek with his finger. She was so entrancing like that, with her beauty muddied and humanized and brought down to earth; and doubly entrancing for the evidence he'd found, proving that she really had wanted him back.

How should he tell her of his success? Rochambeau wandered to the edge of the garden, broke a sprig off an ugly-looking plant that shot up near the wall to a height of nearly three feet, crumbled the leaves in his fingers, and sniffed them. Johanna turned white and darted forward to knock the leaves from his hand.

"Don't touch that! It's not safe."

"I knew that," Rochambeau agreed. "I wondered if you

did. Nice little flowers you have growing here. Do you ever send the cook out to pick his own herbs? And what happens to us all if he mistakes wolfsbane for salad greens?''

"This," said Johanna stiffly, "is the medicinal side of the garden. The kitchen herbs are on the other side of the wall. And I assure you, all of my—our—people know better than to pick anything out of this side. I take care of it myself."

"So I see." His eyes slid over her bare legs and dusty tunic. Johanna flushed and put up one hand, aimlessly pushing some tendrils of hair back under her coif. What did Rochambeau want from her? He hinted at criticizing her for leaving her chamber and for doing common laborer's work in the garden, but he kept grinning as if nothing he said was to be taken seriously. The way his eyes feasted on her figure, tracing the curves that showed under her thin tunic, made her feel first cold and then hot all over. And he kept changing the subject, almost as if he didn't know how to tell her what he'd come for. Well, she had something to tell him, too.

"Nicolas, I—I wanted to tell you . . ."

Her voice trailing off, Johanna shook her head despondently. By Our Lady's mantle, she wasn't about to tell Rochambeau about her pregnancy when she was dusty and sweaty and working with her tunic unromantically hitched up!

"What?"

"Oh, couldn't we go inside? I'm tired," Johanna said with a sudden inspiration.

Rochambeau put his arm about her shoulders and guided her toward the garden wall. "I do believe you've been working too hard. It seems to have affected your wits. Of course, women's brains are more fragile by nature. You really shouldn't strain yourself by trying to do man's work."

"Turning over a few spadefuls of earth!" Johanna laughed in spite of her frustration. There was something extraordinarily comforting in the firm, warm, undeniable grasp of Rochambeau's arm around her. She'd been longing for this moment, when they could reconfirm the understanding they'd reached, when she could whisper her wonderful news into his ear. It should have been a beautiful, romantic meeting. Instead, fiend seize it, she was sweaty with work and besmudged with garden dirt.

"Not gardening," he corrected her as they reached the wall. "I was referring to your childish attempt at enciphering the estate accounts."

"Childish!" Johanna gasped in outrage.

"Well, it wasn't a bad cipher. Not bad at all," Rochambeau allowed generously. "Never had a chance, though, against a man's reasoning ability."

"Aubrey never could solve it."

"Well, Aubrey's not the greatest mind of our times, as you yourself have pointed out. I, on the other hand, found no great difficulty in cracking the cipher, once I was able to free myself from the care of a great estate and a quarrelsome wife long enough to concentrate properly. Sit here, my love, and I'll explain it all to you." Seating himself on the garden wall, he lifted Johanna bodily onto his knee. She sat upright within the circle of his arm, torn between indignation at his patronizing tone and sheer pleasure at being so close to him again.

"It was clear from the beginning that you'd employed a simple substitution alphabet," Rochambeau told her, smoothing out one of the account rolls before them. "I deciphered the marked words almost immediately. I must admit that your trick of changing the alphabet with every third word did take me some time to figure out, but once I realized that was what you had done, it was a simple process of reasoning to find and apply each new alphabet in sequence."

"I don't see how it was that simple," Johanna protested. "You never had more than three words to work with. You must have guessed a lot."

"I didn't have to make a single guess," Rochambeau told her. "You wouldn't understand the mathematical theory involved, of course, but I assure you that it's a simple matter of applying angles of refraction to an astrolabal correction of the numerological values involved. Dependent, of course, upon the qualitative addition of velocity and, uh, a geomantic divination of the Egyptian tables."

Johanna's head was swimming with all the strange words. "Oh," she said doubtfully. "Well, I didn't realize it was so easy to figure out. But then, I'm not educated."

Rochambeau chuckled and hugged her around the waist. "It was a very clever attempt for a beginner, Johanna. For a woman, you're really quite bright. And I must admit that you seem to have done a good job with the estate accounts."

"You translated everything?" The praise was balm to her bruised pride, but not if he was just saying that after glancing at a few pages. She wanted him to mean it. And she wanted him to have seen for himself that she'd raised the money for his ransom, that it had only been an unlucky chance that it hadn't arrived in time.

"Everything," Rochambeau said with an emphasis that made her heart leap. Did he understand now about the ransom? She wanted to hear him say it first. "And I must say that, barring a few careless errors which a more experienced accountant would have corrected, you have done quite well." He paused. "In fact, extremely well. In fact, you seem to be turning me into a rich man!"

"You were already disgustingly rich when you married me," Johanna protested.

"In land, yes. In men, yes. But somehow the estates never produced the income I would have expected. The country's many times richer than it was in my father's day, yet my manors were always in need of repairs, and the rents never brought in more than enough grain to feed my household. Oh, Aubrey always came up with money when I needed it for some specific purpose, but I never got the cash without having to listen to a long, groaning explanation about rents and expenses and labor services and how we mustn't squander our resources. Anybody would have thought it was his estate!"

"Aubrey," said Johanna demurely, "is a dear, sweet, kind man, but I don't think he was framed by nature to be a man of business."

"Neither were you," said Rochambeau. She looked up, shocked.

"Oh, I don't mean that you haven't done admirably," he corrected himself hastily. "In fact, I want you to keep doing it. I couldn't ask for a better estate manager—if you don't mind the chore. But God didn't make you for a *man* of business, my dear wife, and I'm very glad of the fact." Lifting her from his knees, he stood before her with his hands around her waist. Her heart beat faster as he looked down at her with a grave, sweet, serious smile—the look she'd dreamed of getting from him for so long. "And now, my clever, hot-tempered, difficult lady, we have a small matter of debts to settle."

"D-debts?" Her mouth was going dry, and she couldn't think for the pounding of the pulse in her throat. His hands had not strayed from her waist, yet she felt as though they were touching her everywhere at once. Her knees quivered, and her nipples sprang up, erect and throbbing under the tunic, aching for his palms to slide over them.

"A certain wager. I think you'll agree that I've won?" Rochambeau nodded at the pile of account rolls and miscellaneous parchments. "So. Are you going to pay up?"

Johanna grinned. "Wasn't I complaisant enough last time you favored me with your presence?"

"I don't know. I've been working on these damned accounts so long I can hardly remember."

"Perhaps I can refresh your memory."

"Good!" Rochambeau swung her high in the air, caught her, and started toward the castle with her perched on one shoulder. "You can start now."

"Wait," Johanna pleaded, and Rochambeau slowly set her down. "Let me pay my debts in my own way." If she was finally to have the time alone with her lord that she'd been dreaming of for two days, she wanted to make the most of it. She didn't want to come to him all muddy and probably smelling like a horse after her bout of gardening. "I promise you," she teased, "you'll not be disappointed. But give me an hour to cleanse myself and prepare our chambers, and you shall be received as befits the lord of the manor." In token of her promise, she stood on tiptoes and pressed her lips against his bristly cheek.

"Hmm. All right. Now that you mention it, I suppose I could stand to wash too. And very forbearing of you not to point out directly that I need it! One hour. And no tricks!"

Johanna stopped on the narrow path and curtsied demurely. "Oh, my lord, I never play tricks or cheat. I know better than to compete with your expertise in such matters."

Happier than she'd ever been in her life, she scampered up the path to the castle, while Rochambeau lingered behind to gather up his scattered parchments.

At the end of the appointed hour, Rochambeau approached

the bower with some trepidation, cursing himself for his own nervousness. How had it happened that these spacious and sunny rooms above the great hall, newly built by him for his own use, had turned into a women's preserve where he feared to tread? The outer chamber that he'd intended for a comfortable solarium where he could sit with his friends was now filled with giggling women and clattering looms. And the inner chamber, with the great bed that he'd commissioned from a master carpenter—the place where he'd expected to lie with his wife and where he'd planned to beget the next generation—that was now Johanna's private chamber, full of silks and perfumes and women's knickknacks, with a couple of her damned waiting-women hovering about and that girl Alais looking at him with big, scared eyes as though she thought he'd eat her up on the instant.

Even when he had brought his "mistress" to flaunt before Johanna's face, she had worked her own peculiar magic, transforming the exotic dancing girl into plain English Margery and making her into one of her own most devoted followers.

"A man's mad who brings a woman into his life," muttered Rochambeau, pausing with his foot on the bottom step of the stairs from hall to bower. "Take your eye off them for a minute, and they take over and change everything around so that you don't know whether you're the falcon or the hare!"

But honesty forced him to admit that the "minute" had been four long years; one could hardly blame Johanna for arranging things to suit herself in that time.

But he did wish that he didn't have to run the gauntlet of her waiting-women's glances and giggles on his way to her.

Summoning up his sternest look to forestall the expected giggles, Rochambeau marched up the stairs and pushed the door open. It had been closed but not barred, and the force of his push was enough to start its ponderous movement on the oiled iron hinges. Pushing the entangling folds of tapestry aside, Rochambeau entered.

The bower was deserted. Around him were the evidences of work in progress—the shuttle left in the warp at the master loom, the needles trailing bright silk threads over the tapestry frame. But the women whose clattering tongues and busy hands should have animated looms and frames and sewing shears were all mercifully absent. The afternoon sun sent gilded shafts of light through the tall, narrow window openings, catching the atoms of the air in a merry dance. There was no other movement, no sound at all.

Rochambeau remembered a legend he'd once heard of a castle where some enchantment caused all the people to vanish one day in the midst of their tasks, leaving the cradle still rocking, the pot boiling over, the shuttle dangling from the loom. There was something eerie in this absolute stillness, here at the heart of a manor that normally hummed with activity from matins to vespers.

There was a rustling sound from the inner chamber, and a slender white hand put back the tapestry that hung between the rooms. "Will you make haste, my lord?" Johanna called softly. "The water will grow cold."

"Water," Rochambeau repeated. What brains were left to him had fled at the sight of Johanna, wearing nothing but a length of one of the fine soft silks he'd sent back from Egypt. The shimmering white fabric hadn't even been sewn into a tunic; she wore it wrapped around her body, tucked under her arms to leave her shoulders bare. Their whiteness rivaled that of the silk, but under the single layer of clinging fabric he could clearly see the pink tips of her breasts and the dark triangle between her thighs. The silk clung to breasts and thighs, rustled with her every movement, revealing more than it concealed and accentuating all the soft femininity that lay hidden beneath her normal garb of tunic and surcoat and girdle and coif.

As he moved haltingly toward her, his brain registered the scent of rose petals about her body, mixed with the warm, feminine scent of her skin that was all the perfume she needed to drive a man mad with desire. Her unbound black hair fell in a glossy sheet to her hips, with the short ends curling about her face and framing her eyes, green, mysterious, and as promising as the sea.

"I had water heated for you," Johanna explained, beckoning him into the inner chamber with one white arm. "I thought you might wish to rest and bathe and talk a little while."

Rochambeau was on the verge of telling her that there was only one thing any man this side of the grave could possibly want when confronted with the sight of Johanna in an insecurely wrapped, clinging length of very thin silk. But he restrained himself, curious to see what other surprises she had planned for him.

The inner chamber had taken on a more welcoming appearance than he'd ever seen. Lengths of rose-colored silk were draped over the window slits, lending a soft glow to the light that filtered through. In each of the four corners of the room, candles added their own gentle radiance, and in one corner there was also a small brazier from which rose curls of scented blue smoke. The tapestries that hung around the bed had been looped back to show a wide surface covered with more of his Eastern silks, and before the bed stood a great wooden tub filled with steaming-hot water. Dried rose petals and sprigs of sweet herbs scented the water.

With a sigh of contentment, Rochambeau began unfastening his wrinkled surcoat. The hasty, cold wash he'd taken in his chamber could not compare to the luxury awaiting him—or to the delights promised afterward by Johanna's changed manner. Still, he looked at her suspiciously as she glided to his side, helping him to remove his clothes like any servant.

"Such meekness makes me uneasy," he murmured. "What are you planning, witch wife?"

"I thought you wanted a woman to be meek and obedient." The glitter of green light in Johanna's eyes, reflected in the candlelight, made her look sleek and smug as a black-haired cat.

"Not in bed!"

"We're not in bed—yet." Her deft fingers continued their task, gently kneading the taut muscles in his neck and shoulders and urging him toward the tub. Rochambeau sank down into the steaming water. The gentle, warm currents that swirled about him eased the ache of tension in his muscles but did nothing to soften the gathering ache in his loins. Johanna bent over him with a dish of soap, and he could think of nothing but the shadowy cleft between her breasts, accentuated by the tight-wrapped material. What if the twist of silk came undone? He could picture it all too clearly, the pure white fabric slowly gliding down over pink-tinged living skin, the taut, high breasts with their tempting rosy tips, the intoxicating curves down to her slender waist and firm hips.

As she bent over to scrub his back, the curve of her breast brushed against his face, and he felt his heart stop for a moment with the shock of that touch. More than anything in the world, he wanted to grab her around the waist, bury his face between her breasts, and rip off that clinging barrier of thin shimmering silk. But he'd promised to let her pay her debts in her own way. Rochambeau gritted his teeth and bore the sweet torture with good humor. He had to admit that so far she was far exceeding his expectations. It would be interesting to find out just how sweet and tempting and yielding she could be when she really tried.

If, that is, he survived the experience. His loins throbbed with renewed desire, and he couldn't suppress a groan as the soft fingers gliding down his back inflamed his fantasies.

"Did I hurt you? Am I scrubbing too hard?"

Johanna's voice and manner conveyed nothing but sweet solicitude, but he felt certain that she knew exactly what effect she was having on him.

"I think," Rochambeau said with restraint, "that if you want me to finish this bath, you'd best let me do so myself."

"As you please, my lord." Johanna withdrew to a large embroidered cushion on the floor a few feet away from the tub. She took up the lute that lay beside the cushion and began strumming it almost at random, creating a pleasant harmony of soft sounds that reminded him of the sleepy twittering of birds at night.

"I'm a little confused about the terms of our wager," Rochambeau told her.

"How so, my lord?"

"As I recall, we agreed that if I could solve the cipher, you'd be a good and loving wife to me."

"Something of that sort," Johanna agreed, still idly strumming the lute. There was a secret smile on her face as she bent over the instrument that made Rochambeau distinctly nervous.

"I don't recall anything in the wager about your ceasing to be Johanna."

She looked up. "Meaning?"

"All this sweetness and light and meek agreement. It's making me nervous. It's not like you. What are you really planning?"

The lute went crashing into the far wall with a sad cry of snapped strings that made Rochambeau wince in sympathy for the mangled instrument. "God's body and bones!" Johanna jumped off the cushion, her body tense and alive as fine-stretched wire under the clinging silk. "Is there no pleasing you? Did it ever occur to you that I might *want* to be your wife? That I'm tired of feuding? Even more tired of playing games? Damn you, Rochambeau, I've been bending over backward today to be everything you want in a woman! I've capitulated completely, and all you can say is it makes you nervous?"

"That's more like it," said Rochambeau with deep satisfaction. Now, at least, he felt sure she wasn't putting on an act. He got to his knees in the tub, ready to spring. "I didn't say I wanted you to act like a Saracen slave girl, Johanna. It's you I want in my arms—troublesome, quarrelsome witch wife!"

On the last word, as she made to stalk past him, he grabbed an end of the white silk in which she'd wrapped herself and gave a hearty yank. The fabric unwound, spinning her into his arms, and he pulled her down on his lap in the tub. It was barely large enough to hold the two of them. For a few breathless seconds, while Rochambeau laughed and Johanna spat like a drowning kitten, everything was a tangle of knees and elbows and the wet silk clinging over both of them. Then he got her straddling his lap, his hands firm about her waist, and slowly lowered her down onto him. The scented water foamed and eddied around them, her silken sweetness held him tight and warm, and his body plunged upward with uncontrollable force to complete his act of possession. Johanna sighed, and her green eyes closed, her hands tightening on his shoulders, and in that moment he knew she was truly, finally his.

There was no stopping now for either of them, no time for gentleness and finesse and all the tricks of love he'd learned over the years. They were ecstatically one, needing nothing more than their mutual desire, and it was over as quickly as a boy's first coupling with his girl in the long orchard grass. Johanna's long, shuddering sigh reassured him that he had not gone too quickly for her in his own urgency.

"Don't be angry, sweet love," he promised. "That was just by way of an introduction."

Johanna giggled. "My lord of Rochambeau, meet Johanna de Pomeray?" Her fingers slipped down from his shoulders to dabble in the cooling water, tracing impudent tickling lines down to his lean hips, where they were still joined.

"Something of that sort. Now we go on."

"To what?" Wide sea-green eyes, innocent now of any sarcasm. His love for her was a painful constriction in his chest. Why had be been afraid for so long to admit the power she had over him? He felt more free now, admitting the strength of his love, than ever before when he'd fought himself and tried to treat her as he would any other woman.

"To the rest of our lives together."

Rose petals and sweet herbs and wet silk clung to her shoulders. He kissed them away until she was bare to his lips and hands, then started over where new petals had clung.

"Are we going to spend the rest of our lives in this tub?" Johanna whispered.

"Mmm. Getting cold?" But he knew, and she knew, that wasn't why she had shivered.

Rising from the tub with her in his arms, he took three dripping steps to the waiting bed. Johanna squeaked in alarm as he dropped her in the middle of a priceless length of Baghdad silk. "The water—you'll ruin the silk!"

"What did you put it there for, then, hmm?" His tongue flickered along her earlobe and into the curve of her neck as he spoke, robbing her of the power of speech. "I always wanted to make love on silken cushions." One hand moved with tantalizing slowness over the curve of her breast, giving double meaning to his words. "And you're silk and fire and roses, Johanna. My wife. My lovely Johanna." The hand closed possessively, making her gasp with fearful delight while he gently parted her thighs.

With torturous slowness, almost as if in revenge for her earlier torment of him, he brought himself entirely within her, while every inch of her flesh welcomed him and cried out for him to possess her completely. Her breath changed from a caught sob to a gasp of pure pleasure as he settled himself against her, his hands curling over her taut, high breasts and giving them a life of their own, while his rhythmic, unrelenting, slow movements brought a rising tide of desire to draw her down fully into his power. There was still one rose petal caught in the hollow of her throat; he bent his head and licked it off, and she shivered uncontrollably at the satiny warmth of his tongue there, the unexpected small intimacy.

"Johanna, my love," he whispered shakily into her throat.

"My lord. My love. My life." She traced his lips with one finger as they moved up to drink the sweetness of her own. The passionate demand of his mouth pressed against hers, the insistent movement of his tongue against her own, wakened deep tremors of desire in her.

She gave herself to him unreservedly, clasping and opening to him, letting him prolong their mutual pleasure until it became a long-drawn-out, tormenting ecstasy that was almost too much to bear. As her own passion rose higher, he withdrew ever so slightly, making her wait while he gently, skillfully extorted the last drop of sweetness from the moments of anticipation.

"Now?" But his smile withheld something from her. She was completely his, and he was completely in control. She could have hated him if she had been capable of such sustained thought. As she gave a little moan of protest, his hands lingered gently along her back and sides, making a leisurely journey over her body that kept her intensely alive to his presence without ever completely satisfying the needs he awakened.

Johanna raised herself to lie closer against him, rubbing her aching, unsoothed breasts against the golden brush of hair on his chest. "Oh, please," she breathed, feeling the irregular movements of his own breathing as if they were her own. How long could they remain suspended like this, on the very edge of unspeakable pleasure? He held her so that she could not move, could only accept whatever he did to her; and if he didn't do it soon, she was going to dissolve into a small damp spot on the silks.

"Please, my lord!"

Rochambeau shook his head. "Don't call me that."

"Rochambeau!"

Still he kept her poised on that sharp knife-edge, moving just enough within her while he used his lips and hands to devastating effect. What did he want? Johanna closed her eyes and gave herself up to pure, aching, tantalizing sensation.

"Nicolas," she whispered into the rosy glow behind her closed eyelids. "Nicolas, Nicolas . . . my love . . ." He laughed then and entered her as deeply as he could, while she strained to receive him. The touch of his fingers on her breast was a wild, sweet, drunken joy that blended with the deeper sweetness of their two bodies joined as one, fitting together so perfectly it seemed they could never have been apart. Weakened by the sudden sharp release, she let her head fall back against the bed, feeling the silky tangle of her own hair covering them both like a dark, shadowy wood. Golden limbs rested against alabaster ones, while deep, slow shudders built up in the center of her being. When the shaking release broke forth at last, she thought it would break her too. Rochambeau's body still moved in its demanding, implacable rhythm on hers, forcing her to feel more than she dared, more than she had known was possible. The candle flames splintered into a shower of golden sparks, and the sun burned through the pink silken curtains as though she were at the edge of the world, being reborn in a new golden dawn. The blaze would have consumed her if Rochambeau's tautness had not relaxed in the same moment, bringing him down against her in a tangle of satisfied arms and legs.

"My lord?"

"Who?"

"Nicolas," Johanna amended. "I have something to break to you. You'd better sit up." She wanted to see his face when she told him that he was to expect an heir.

"Not now. I'm finding myself disinclined for conversation." His lips grazed the tip of her breast, making strange warm feelings happen between her legs. She looked down at the golden eyelashes and the trace of golden beard on his cheek and felt a deep, true, abiding happiness in this moment, something too precious to be spoiled by words. He was right. Talking could wait.

She pressed her lips to his forehead, impressing her love on him with the urgency of her newly freed passion. No longer was she sullen, resentful, waiting for him to force her into the inevitable response. Now she wanted to enjoy their loving as he did, taking her pleasure in the groans of delight she wrung from him. Her fingers traced lightly down his muscled ribs, passing over the taut curves of his hips until she found and grasped what she was searching for. "I think I hold something besides your soul in my hands," she whispered.

Rochambeau groaned and arched against her hands. "I'm not sure. That just might be everything there is of me. Sweet Christ, Johanna!" She had stooped to place her lips there, sending a tingling moist warmth through his body with the caress. "How much do you think a man can stand?"

"Let's find out." Johanna felt as free as a leaping flame, as if all the old unhappy remnants of pride and resentment and shame had been burned up when they came together. She could do anything, dare anything, feel anything. All she wanted now was to belong to Rochambeau in every possible way, to reclaim her own self by total surrender.

Intent on the sensations and the cries of passion she was wringing from him, she was startled to feel the heavy weight of his head between her thighs, the golden smoothness of his hair against the sensitive white skin. His tongue flicked out, tantalizing her most secret places with the hint of the same caress she had offered him, and she almost cried out at the intensity of the sharp pleasure he brought her.

"Two can play at this game, my sweet witch wife!" The vibration of his lips seemed to travel through her whole body from that melting center where he touched her so lightly. Johanna's hands shook, and she felt her own control melting away under the sweetness of that kiss.

"I can't bear it," she moaned, tossing her head back and forth against the crushed silks beneath them, while Rochambeau's hands held her open to his touch and his lips wrung tiny cries of passion from her. "No more—it's too much—how can I bear it?"

"Let's find out," he echoed her own words.

Too soon, yet not soon enough, Johanna's body trembled in a passionate release that seemed to have nothing to do with her own will. There was no question now of choosing to surrender herself to Rochambeau's loving. Neither of them had the power to stem the mighty current that swept them away. Somehow his mouth was on hers again, kissing her lips till they stung, while he thrust one leg between hers and she felt herself, incredibly, responding as though this were the first time he'd touched her. And she'd thought to explain to him the difference between love and lust! It was all clear to her now, but not in any way that could be put into words. This was love, this mutual delight and response, this sharing without words or signals. She felt the urgent intensity of his own desire as though it were her own and knew that the tremors of passion that shook her to the core of her being shook him too. Before, she'd been an instrument on which he played when he chose, powerless to resist the sweet music he drew from her, resenting her own lack of power. Now they were both the music and the instruments, the players and the song, and all that had gone before seemed like the games of children, like the hasty kisses she'd had from her father's squires, a childish mimicking of something beyond their comprehension.

How long they dallied there, loving and being loved, one soul in two bodies, Johanna could not have said. It seemed like only minutes; it seemed like eternity; it was all she wanted in life. But, inevitably, there came a time when their newly freed passions slowed, allowing her pulse to ease to a ragged drumbeat, giving her leisure to catch her breath and look about the tumbled room.

The sunlight had faded from the windows now, and the candles were burning down into their sockets. The tub of bathwater was now a chilly well in the middle of the floor, surrounded by soaked rushes. The silks she'd spread over the bed were crushed beyond recognition, as was the white length of finest silk that she'd wrapped around her own body. Johanna glanced around the room and laughed softly to herself, imagining what sharp-tongued Margery and shy Alais would make of the wreckage she and Rochambeau had left behind them.

With leisure came the recognition of other bodily needs. She was cold. And hungry.

"My lord, shall we send for—"

A gentle snore interrupted her. Johanna gazed down at her husband in loving exasperation. What a time to fall asleep! She didn't feel the least bit sleepy; she wanted to sit up in the warm circle of his arms and nibble on spicy ragouts. She wanted to talk over every incident of their stormy courtship and interrupted marriage, to revel in their new harmony and clear away all the old grudges. "Tell me again what you thought that first day, when you saw me in the cornfield? Didn't you think I was an ill-clad brat with appalling manners? No? You thought I was the most beautiful girl you'd ever seen, and you had to have me? Tell me how you felt, and I'll tell you how I dreamed of you . . ."

And most of all, she wanted to tell him of the precious gift she carried within her.

Johanna sighed and stroked Rochambeau's hair with one hand. He did not stir, so deep was his sudden slumber. Well, there'd be time for all that loving talk later. She wasn't sleepy, but then, she hadn't been up for two nights deciphering the encoded estate accounts! At last he'd worked honestly to win her, even when he no longer needed to do so, and—a smile quirked the corners of her lips—apparently it had been harder work than he'd been willing to admit when he found her in the garden.

Meanwhile, something could be done about her other needs. Johanna slipped on a plain blue tunic of soft wool, its warmth comforting her shivering bare skin, and went to the hall to order food. She was hungry now, and Rochambeau would want something when he woke up. She saw absolutely no reason why either of them should bother to dine in the hall that night. She would much rather sit on the bed and feed him sweet figs, one a time. And dried apricots, if there were any left in the castle stores. And some of those honey cakes with ginger that he liked so much. And just for him, she'd tell the cook to put in enough ginger and other spices to burn any normal person's mouth, since that seemed to be the way he liked them.

And maybe some cold meat, whatever the cook had on hand, and fresh hot bread and some bowls of soup, and . . . Humming under her breath, Johanna made her way to the kitchen and gave her order. The women who'd been expelled from the bower earlier, the castle servants setting up the long tables for supper in the hall, and the officials going about their business all looked at her curiously, most noting her satisfied smile, but none dared to say anything. And Johanna floated through the castle, almost, but not quite, oblivious of the presence of dozens of curious bystanders.

"Aubrey?" He'd touched her lightly on the arm to get her attention while she was giving her orders to the cook.

"You look . . . happy. And healthy. Did you take some of Bruma's herbs yet?"

One hand flew to Johanna's mouth. "Oh, dear, I forgot. I was feeling so good. I went out to work in the garden, and then Nicolas found me there, and I sort of forgot," she apologized. It had been nice of Aubrey to go to so much trouble for her.

"No matter. You're obviously healthy enough to do without them. Have you and Rochambeau been having a nice talk, then?" He smiled down at her, and Johanna was suddenly conscious of her tangled hair and the thinness of her single tunic. Oh well, what did it matter if for once she didn't look like the dignified lady of the manor? Everybody must know perfectly well what had been going on in the great chamber anyway.

Still, Johanna blushed and took her time about ordering a ragout of game birds and instructing the cook to spice the honey cakes liberally.

"He's deciphered the whole of the estate accounts," she told Aubrey, her head bent over the empty pastry shells offered for her inspection by the baker's assistant. "So I guess I lost that wager." Her shameless grin said more clearly than any words just how happy she was to have lost this time.

"And have you been going over all the accounts together?" Aubrey teased. "Is that why you've both been locked away all afternoon?"

Johanna smiled and felt the dimple coming out in her chin. "Actually, we hadn't quite gotten around to discussing the accounts yet. Somehow, other things seemed more important."

Aubrey put his arm around her shoulders in a brief, brotherly hug. "Well, Johanna, I'm glad for you."

He really did look happy. He must have gotten over his strange fit of jealousy, Johanna thought, and decided to accept the sisterly love that was all she could offer him. That thought removed the last faint shadow on her own happiness.

"And, do you know, I have the feeling today may be the start of a whole new era for these estates!" As if sensing that she'd be embarrassed to have him underline the new accord any further, he changed the subject at once. "There's no need for you to order your own food, though, like a servant. Why don't you go back, and I'll see that everything is brought up when it's ready—and by someone discreet," he promised with a sly smile, "who will know not to disturb you."

"Thank you, Aubrey. You're very kind." Still humming under her breath and floating several inches above the pavement, Johanna wandered back into the hall and started in the general direction of the bower. Once her feet were on the stairs, it occurred to her that Rochambeau might well be glad of some fresh clothes when he woke up. Of course, that too was a task with which she could charge a servant, but at the moment she was taking a positive pleasure in doing things for him with her own hands. Now, where had Rochambeau been sleeping since his quarters in the old keep were ruined by smoke? Probably in the strongroom, since it was there that he'd been deciphering the account rolls.

Johanna was relieved to find that Rochambeau's squire was no longer on guard before the room. She marched in and found just about the scene of chaos she'd expected—parchment and broken quills strewn over all flat surfaces, bowls crusted over with stale porridge in the corners, and clothes tossed at random over the high clothes perch that ran along one wall. She pulled down a few items, sniffed, and finally decided that a green velvet tunic with a silver border was not dirty, only wrinkled. Taking that and a few other reasonably clean garments over her arm, she was about to return to the bower when a bright page of jewellike colors caught her eye.

What a beautiful illuminated letter! It looked more suitable to a psalter than to a musty old account roll. In fact, it was from a psalter. Her psalter!

Johanna snatched the book up and leafed through the pages. What was it doing here? The truth struck her as she glanced down again at the writing stand from which she'd taken the book. On it were Rochambeau's first attempts at deciphering the accounts. And in her hands were the secret alphabets she'd used to encode the rolls in the first place, matching the letters of the alphabet to random phrases in the prayer book that told her when to switch alphabets and substitution codes.

Johanna snapped the book shut and stood quite still in the middle of the chamber, color flaming in her cheeks as she remembered all of Rochambeau's patronizing garbage about how he had so cleverly deciphered her code. She'd felt quite humble for a little while, to think that he'd cracked it so easily. Now—

The clean clothes fell in a heap on the floor. Clutching the psalter in both hands, Johanna whirled and marched back down to the bower with a determined tread. She and Rochambeau had some talking to do, all right, but not about their love life!

Chapter Twenty-one

THE TRAYS OF food were already waiting when Johanna returned to the inner chamber where Rochambeau slept, totally relaxed, with his long limbs sprawling across the bed and his mouth half open. She glowered at his recumbent form and repressed the urge to kick a steaming bowl of soup across the floor.

The cook had certainly done well at such short notice. Beside the soup was a tray of what smelled like fresh-baked bread, carefully wrapped in a clean linen cloth. Covered dishes of heavy chased silver would hold the meats, the ragout of spiced game birds, and the slices of beef in a sauce of dried figs and wine. And an entire round wooden tray held elaborate subtleties of flour and sugar, sweet and spicy round cakes and sticky confections of honey and dates, all the rich goodies for which Rochambeau had acquired such a taste in the East. Johanna planted her foot right in the middle of the cook's masterpiece, a pastry castle with towers of marzipan, and felt a vengeful satisfaction in grinding it to crumbs.

Still Rochambeau slept. Johanna wished he were on the floor where she could kick him instead of the food. She wished he might choke on his lying words, or on the sweets she'd ordered just to please his decadent tastes.

Thought and action were never very far separated for Johanna. Rochambeau awoke seconds later from a dream in which Welsh raiders were trying to shove their long pikes down his throat. Reality was no less confusing. His lovely green-eyed wife was kneeling on his chest, chanting Welsh curses, and grinding a dry crumbly mixture into his mouth and nose. Rochambeau coughed, choked, threw up both hands, and just managed to push her away before he smothered in the shower of crumbs. Sitting up, he spat the last crumbs out of his mouth and glared at Johanna.

"What in the name of God's holy saints are you up to now?"

"Here are your damned honey cakes," Johanna retorted, hitting him in the face with another pastry, "And I hope you choke on them!"

"I nearly did." He caught her wrist and twisted slightly until the battered cake fell from her fingers. "What's the matter now?"

"Astrolabal projections!" Johanna quoted bitterly. "Angles of refraction! Geomantic divination! Ha! You cheated again!" She bent to the floor and picked up something else which came flying at him, open pages fluttering like a butterfly's bright wings. Rochambeau caught the missile automatically; it thudded into his open palm, much heavier and harder than a butterfly, with a priceless page of illuminations crumpled in his fingers.

Johanna's psalter! He cursed his own stupidity in leaving it out in the strongroom, open to one of the very pages she'd used as a key for her secret alphabets. "You found it," he said lamely.

"You thought I was too stupid to check up on your story!" Johanna raged, conveniently forgetting that her trip to the strongroom had been the merest chance. "You couldn't even win our wager fairly, you—you cheat! How can I believe anything you say, when you'll say anything to get what you want?" Tears of anger stung her eyes. She'd been fooled by his glib talk of how he had deciphered her accounts. Had his honey-sweet words of love been just so much more talk, designed to keep her in his bed and in a receptive frame of mind from the beginning? How could she ever trust him? Jumping from the bed, she grabbed the tray of sweets and began hurling honey cakes at her bemused, naked husband.

Rochambeau caught the cakes with a juggler's dexterity and threw them back as fast as they arrived. They splattered on the wall above and behind Johanna's head with little sharp pattering sounds, like solid raindrops. He was playing with her. She hadn't got close to him, and he wasn't deigning to retaliate; he was just destroying the missiles so that she couldn't do anything more. And he was laughing! With a sob of pure frustration, Johanna swung both arms back to her side and spun the round wooden tray directly at Rochambeau's head.

He caught that too, but the subtleties and almond creams and other sweet things with which it was loaded showered about him in a sticky mess. A pastry figure of a knight on horseback broke itself on his nose. A dish of dates in honey flipped upside down over his head, streaking his yellow hair with long, dark, sticky streamers of sauce and decorating his naked shoulders with the dates. Rochambeau growled and grabbed the last remaining dish, a shallow bowl of almond cream, just before it spilled over his lap. Scrambling from the bed, he advanced slowly toward Johanna, the dish held threateningly overhead in one hand. She barked his shins with the lid that had covered the game birds, but he didn't even notice the blow. He did put down his dish, but only for the moment.

Backing her into the corner, he held her by one shoulder against the wall and slowly, with immense relish, tore off the blue tunic that was her only garment. The soft, old woolen fabric gave under his fingers as easily as if it had been the finest silk. Still holding her, he reached one hand into the dish on the floor and plastered the almond cream down the front of her body from nose to thighs. Johanna kicked and struggled and cursed him, and when the cream that slithered over her bare skin made her too slippery to hold, she got away to the other side of the food trays and started throwing lids. They clattered and clanged around his head, and she got in at least one or two good hits, but he didn't seem in the least incommoded. With a grin on his face, not even attempting to grab her directly again, he retaliated in kind. Every time she threw a lid, he reached into the uncovered pot and slathered her with a handful of the contents. The sticky sauce of figs and wine blended with the almond cream, and she got one of the little birds from the ragout tangled in her hair.

"What happened to your care for the accounts?" panted

Johanna, dancing up and down just out of his reach and watching for another chance to get under his guard. "Do you realize those figs cost two silver pence the pound?"

"Do they? Well, the beef's our own, so that costs nothing." Rochambeau popped a slice into his mouth as he spoke and chewed appreciatively. Johanna relaxed her own guard for a fatal moment and was taken by surprise by a tart of saffron and galingale that caught her in the midriff.

"Galingale is eighteen pence the pound," she pointed out, retaliating with the tray of bread rolls, "and you don't even want to think about how much saffron costs!"

"I don't want to think about—our!—accounts at all." The tray of bread had caught him in the midsection with a satisfying thump.

"Obviously not." Johanna looked about for something else to throw. All the spare parts of dishes had been used up, and she couldn't bear to waste the food. Perhaps she wasn't so very angry anymore. Actually, the first sight of Rochambeau's surprised countenance, with honey trickling over his hair and dates cascading down onto his bare shoulders, had made her feel a lot better. But she still wasn't ready to give up her indignation. "You couldn't even keep your mind on them long enough to win the wager honestly, could you?"

Rochambeau ripped out a couple of guttural noises which she assumed were Saracen oaths, since the words were like nothing she'd ever heard in any Christian language. "Johanna, I *couldn't* win the wager honestly. If I could, I'd have had you in my bed days ago. I've been beating my damned brains out over your thrice-cursed cipher ever since I came home. I was just about ready to give up when I saw the letters scribbled in your psalter and realized that they must be the key to the cipher. How did you think of changing alphabets every three words? Even if I'd realized that's what you were doing, I could never have figured out the sequence of alphabets without your psalter. Just consider, love. If I hadn't cheated, I'd have died of old age before we got together again. And that would have been a terrible waste."

"Oh!" A slow smile spread over Johanna's face. She reached up and pushed a sticky strand of black hair out of her eyes. The stickiness transferred itself to her fingers, and she reflexively licked them clean. Mmm, sweet lemon paste.

At some point, Rochambeau must have crowned her with a lemon tart, and she hadn't even noticed. "So it wasn't that easy, huh?"

"You know it wasn't." Rochambeau wiped his brow and came away with a handful of dates that tumbled out of his honey-smeared hair. "I never would have deciphered it if I hadn't stumbled on the key."

"So naturally, you had to cheat!" Johanna clung to her sense of grievance, now fast slipping away from her. "And you had to tell me how easy it was, make me feel stupid for trying to deceive you."

"Lending verisimilitude." Rochambeau shrugged. Then his blue eyes clouded over, and he looked almost embarrassed. "No, saving my pride. I couldn't bear to admit how nearly you'd outsmarted me."

"I did outsmart you! You admit you could never have figured it out on your own!"

"Results, my love, look at the results. I won, didn't I?"

"You certainly did not."

"I collected—and what else is winning all about?" Rochambeau shook the last of the dates off his broad shoulders and gave Johanna a heart-stoppingly sweet smile. "Come, now, love," he coaxed. "Are you going to tell me you're sorry we made up our differences? Would you really rather I'd gone off again, to leave you sleeping alone for another four years while our tempers cooled? I had the distinct impression this was one wager you were glad to lose."

"Well . . ." Johanna felt a blush rising under the stiffening paste of almond cream that encased her skin. It was true; Rochambeau's inspired cheating had given her what she most wished for in the world: a way to end a quarrel that she bitterly regretted. "It's just that I wish, just once, I would know whether to believe what you tell me!"

"You can believe this much." Rochambeau stepped carefully over the denuded food trays and put his hands on her arms, just above the elbows. "I love you, Johanna. I love you and need you so much that I'll do anything to get you—yes, even lie, cheat, steal. You're mine, and I'm not going to let you get away, and I don't particularly care what it takes to keep you with me. But understand this: *here* is where you belong!"

On the last words, his arms slid around her, meeting in the sticky, tangled mass of her hair, and he crushed her against him. Johanna's foot slipped in a puddle of wine sauce as she threw her own arms around Rochambeau's neck. The sudden thrust of her weight unbalanced him, he stepped backward into the ragout of game birds, and they went down onto the floor with a doomsday crash of silver dishes and wooden trays.

Rochambeau cursed. Johanna began to giggle helplessly.

"What's so funny?"

"I think we're stuck together." She pulled experimentally and found that the stiffening paste of almond cream had indeed glued their skin together, while her long hair, sticky with lemon tart filling, was doing its best to intertwine with the short honey-smeared strands of Rochambeau's head.

"I can think of worse fates." Bending his head, Rochambeau licked a morsel of almond cream from the tip of Johanna's shoulder. "Mmm, almost as sweet as you are. I could enjoy freeing us. It might take some time, though. And I don't like to start a meal with the sweets. Are we lying on anything more sustaining?"

Johanna wriggled and investigated the hard knobbly shape under her left thigh. Her hand came up with a small bird that had been cooked whole in its sauce of onions, cinnamon, and anise. "Partridge?"

"Thank you. Exercise always makes me hungry." Rochambeau crunched up the bird in two bites and offered Johanna a slice of beef that had skidded out of its pot and across the floor. She shook her head at the sight of the rushes and dust adhering to the meat.

"Thank you, I think I'll just have a little dessert." She plucked two dates out of Rochambeau's hair and nibbled daintily on them, while he applied himself to the task of gently freeing them from the glue of almond cream. His tongue ran over her neck and dipped down into the crevice between her breasts, glided over each breast in turn, and teased the nipples free. Johanna shivered in his arms and forgot to finish the second date as his lips closed over the tip of one breast.

"You're—paying a lot of attention—to just one spot," she murmured, trying to control her uneven breathing.

"I like to do a thorough job." The vibration of his lips sent new shivers through her body. "Don't worry. I'll take care of everything before I'm through." The other breast accordingly received his thorough attention, while Johanna tasted the long trails of honey that had trickled over his back and shoulders. Slowly, inch by torturous inch, he worked his way down her body, commenting from time to time on the delicious taste of almond cream mixed with essence of Johanna.

"The breasts impart a more delicate flavor, but I think it is best as a sauce for the inner thighs. What do you say?"

But Johanna was beyond saying. By the time he began to work over the remnants of cream that he had smeared over the dark triangle between her thighs, she was beyond coherent thought; nothing mattered except the raging need that he had awakened in her. She writhed on the rushes and begged him to finish, but he drew out the teasing game until she could no longer think or feel anything at all except the starbursts of ecstasy wherever he touched her. She could hardly have told the moment when their bodies were joined again; all blended into a sweet, sticky, uninhibited delight that began with her cries of ecstasy and ended with them rolling about on the floor, banging into furniture and silver dishes and making more noise than their fight had done.

"That," said Johanna with a pretense of severity, when they were lying quietly in each other's arms again, "was not a great success as a cleaning effort. Now we're decorated with rushes and honey instead of sweet cream."

Rochambeau's head was pillowed on her breast. He raised his eyes to her face with a lazy smile. "How was it as an effort in . . . other directions?"

Johanna grinned. "Maybe I'll wear almond cream to bed on a regular basis."

She stretched lazily, both arms above her head, and one hand knocked against the wooden tub that was still full of bathwater. It was cold now, but somehow she thought a little soap and water might be a good thing before she tried to face her waiting-women again. "Would you get off me? I want to wash."

"I do love the romantic love words you give me after our shared joy." Rochambeau obligingly rolled off Johanna's body and sat cross-legged against the foot of the bed while she knelt in the tub. The cold water made her shiver, but she scrubbed herself vigorously and was rewarded by a brisk glow that covered her skin and made her feel bright and awake once more. Stepping from the tub, she picked a warm robe from the clothes perch and wrapped herself in the soft green wool. The collar of the robe stuck to her hair and reminded her that there was one task she'd left undone.

"Oh, bother. I'll have to wash my hair." She gave Rochambeau a dirty look. "What did you rub into it, anyway? The lemon tarts?"

He nodded and dipped one finger into the remaining sauce of figs and wine that had once surrounded slices of beef.

"Aren't there any left? I like lemons. And they're expensive," she added, remembering the spice accounts that had been her first lesson in the complexities of estate finances. "At least—"

Rochambeau raised a protesting hand. "Don't tell me. I'm not a man to be niggardly with my wife. If you want to use imported lemons as a rinse for your lovely hair, I'd never criticize you on account of the cost. And no, there aren't any left. But that reminds me . . ." He stretched one long arm up to the surface of the bed and felt around, while Johanna knelt over the tub and dipped her long hair into the soapy water. "I never did get to eat those honey cakes you were trying to kill me with. You said the cook put in extra ginger?"

"Enough to burn your mouth," Johanna mumbled, scrubbing vigorously at her hair. "You won't be able to taste anything but spices."

"Excellent, just the way I like—ah! Here's one." Rochambeau popped it into his mouth, while Johanna dipped her whole head underwater, trying to rid herself of the remains of the lemon tarts.

When she came up again, water streaming down her damp hair and gurgling in her ears, Rochambeau was making a strange choking noise behind her. "What's the matter?" she called gaily. "Don't tell me our simple English cook put in too many spices for the great crusader himself?"

The coughing sound increased in intensity, and he gave a wheezing gasp that scared her. She swung around and saw that his face was changing color, while he bent almost double, clawing at his throat with spasmodic, ineffectual gestures.

"Nicolas!" Heedless of the water dripping over her, Johanna ran to his side and pounded his back. A few crumbs of honey cake flew out of his mouth, but not enough to account for the desperate wheezing that continued. A cold hand clenched around her own heart as she looked into his contorted face.

"Poison," he croaked between pitiful attempts to breathe.

"I know. Don't talk," Johanna commanded fiercely. "Breathe!" He couldn't be choking on crumbs; that wouldn't account for the way his limbs were twitching or the labored effort of his lungs. The cakes had to have been poisoned. But how—and why? No time to worry about that now. Running to the door, she shouted for her women, a servant, anybody! Then she knelt by Rochambeau again, supporting his head as he tried feebly to cough up the poisoned cakes.

There were people shuffling in the doorway, afraid to come in. They must be confused by the appearance of the chamber—food strewn over the floor, hangings ripped from the bed, and the lord of Rochambeau stark naked and in convulsions on the floor.

"Bring me vinegar!" Johanna snapped without turning her head. "Lots of it—at once!"

She was relieved to hear Margery's competent voice answering. She could trust Margery to waste no time questioning or explaining. Johanna called for a page, somebody, anybody, to help her hold Rochambeau's head and shoulders up while he writhed with the effects of the poison. What she got was Alais, looking pale and scared and weak.

"Hold him up like this," Johanna directed. "We have to get the poison out of his body before it contaminates the bodily humors."

Alais's face was dead white, and her hands shook under the weight of Rochambeau's body, and even in this time of crisis she had to modestly avert her eyes from his nakedness. Rochambeau's teeth grated together, and a few bubbles of foam flecked his mouth; his body convulsed in agony while they were trying to lift him to a sitting position. Alais's eyes rolled up until only the whites were showing. "Are you going to faint?" Johanna demanded. *"Don't you dare faint,* do you hear me, Alais?"

A pair of hard brown hands slipped under Alais's arms,

taking the weight from her. Johanna looked her thanks at Gilbert de Bellay and ignored the slump of Alais's unconscious body on the rushes. When Margery arrived with the vinegar, she and Gilbert worked together at the ugly business of getting as much of it as possible down Rochambeau's throat and as much as possible of the poison he'd ingested out of his body again. Johanna was vaguely aware that there were people around them in the chamber now, fresh torches brought in to light their work, Aubrey somewhere in the background muttering about the need to send for a physician. None of that mattered, any more than it mattered that her robe was gaping open in front or that it was spotted with sweat and vomit. All she cared about was that Rochambeau was still breathing, still fighting to live. As the night wore on, her legs cramped under her, and her back ached with coaxing him to sit up and drink more of the sharp vinegar draught. People came in and out, muttering worriedly; someone threw a cloak over Rochambeau to keep the chill of the night air from him; someone else tried to persuade her to leave his side for a moment, and Johanna resisted, snarling like a cornered animal, until they left her alone.

"Johanna, you should rest! Let me take over until a physician can be found."

That was Aubrey, kneeling beside her, his large hands with their sprinkling of blond hairs reaching out to hold his half-brother.

"Get out of my light," Johanna snapped. No doubt Aubrey meant well, he always did, but she wasn't about to entrust her lord's precious life to such a bumbler. Gilbert had shown himself quick-witted and steady-handed; his help was all she wanted.

"No—physician."

The croak startled them both. Johanna's green eyes flared wide with joy as Rochambeau's lips moved again. "Seen them—kill more than—they save," he whispered with great effort. "Leave—Johanna. She's got more sense than any of you."

His head dropped back, as if the effort of speaking had exhausted him, but his chest was rising and falling more regularly than before. Johanna bowed her head and let the tears

304

splash onto his broad chest. If only he could keep breathing now! She felt that if they could make it through the night, they would be able to defeat any lingering effects of the poison.

And if not? The tears fell faster. At last she had irrefutable proof of Rochambeau's trust in her. But at what cost?

Chapter Twenty-two

I N THE CHILLY blue shadows of dawn, Johanna rested at
last, kneeling by Rochambeau's bed with her arms on the
mattress. Her head nodded forward into her arms, and she
woke herself up with a startled jerk, momentarily bemused
by the strange surroundings. "Where—oh, Gilbert! Is there
any change?"

Across a narrow bed in the strongroom, across Rochambeau's sleeping figure, the strained white face of Gilbert de
Bellay recalled Johanna to her surroundings. His black hair
fell forward around his long, thin face, and his eyes were
dark smudges of exhaustion. "No change."

"But you watched with me. And you a stranger to us, and
one who almost got killed through my folly. Oh, Gilbert."
Johanna felt close to tears from exhaustion and strain. "How
can we ever thank you?"

Sometime in the small hours before matins, Rochambeau's
condition had stabilized to the point where she felt it was safe
to move him out of the reeking shambles that their bedchamber had become. He would rest better in a smaller, more
private room while the chamber was cleaned. And so she
moved him to the strongroom, where there was already a
narrow bed set up for his use. Parchments and account rolls
had been ruthlessly thrown into the great iron-bound chests
in no kind of order, freeing table space for the dishes and
utensils Johanna would need while she nursed her lord.

"This room is too small and entirely unsuitable. There's no place for you to sleep," Aubrey had protested.

Johanna flashed him a dangerously sharp look from under her tangled black hair. "I'm not going to sleep. Besides . . ." She paused. Rochambeau had been poisoned; until they knew why and by whom, he would be better off in this narrow room with just one entrance. Johanna had already learned how well Rochambeau's squire could guard that door. She and Fulke might never be friends, but if she should have to leave her lord for a few moments, she would feel safe with that hard-faced boy at the door. But this was no time to discuss the matter, not with servants and waiting-women and minor officials all crowding around with their big ears flapping. "This room will do very well," she said at last.

Aubrey grumbled and fussed about her comfort, but it was Gilbert who unobtrusively conferred with the waiting-women and sent for rugs and cushions from the hall. He made a soft place where Johanna could sit beside the bed and watch Rochambeau's face for a sign of any change, however slight. After those few sensible words in the chamber below, he had fallen into a delirious slumber that worried her somewhat. His long limbs twitched uncontrollably in his sleep, and his jaws clenched now and again with spasms that shook his whole body.

She sent everyone away except Gilbert and Margery, preferring to keep her vigil with those two who'd already proved their cool heads and ability to react quickly. Margery stayed by the door, ready to run and fetch anything Johanna might need, while Gilbert coiled his long limbs on the floor on the other side of the narrow bed and talked with Johanna in a low voice.

Gilbert, it turned out, had had some experience with the healing arts. He made a deprecatory mention of a season traveling with a wandering physician, half wizard, half quack, when the minstrelsy business was slower than usual. Earlier in the night, he'd told Johanna a little of those wandering days, hoping to distract her for a few minutes from her fears for Rochambeau. Now, as she crossed herself and prayed silently in the dawn light, Gilbert took up the tale of his master the quack again.

"My master would have said that anybody who survived a

night like this had a constitution too strong to kill with anything short of iron poisoning."

"Iron poisoning? What's that?" Had she overlooked something simple and obvious, something any man would know?

"Twelve inches of broadsword shoved down the throat," Gilbert explained succinctly. "It's been the death of many a good knight, and unicorn's horn won't do a thing to prevent or cure it."

"Oh, I see. Iron poisoning!" Johanna achieved the ghost of a chuckle. "Rochambeau *is* strong, isn't he? Do you think he'll be all right?"

"Master Bartholomew would have told you to be proud of him for lasting this long," Gilbert replied evasively. "And Master Bartholomew wasn't all quack. He talked a line of nonsense, but he never killed anybody that I knew about, and he taught me a little of the herbs and the influence of the planets over them."

"What did he teach you about poisons?" Johanna inquired anxiously. "Thorn apple, for instance?"

"You think that's it?"

Johanna sighed and rubbed one hand across her aching brow. "Well, it would be easy enough for anyone to get. I have some growing in the medicinal side of the herb garden. A very weak infusion of the leaves is good to calm feverish patients. The kitchen servants have all been strictly warned to stay out of the medicinal garden, and I keep the dried leaves under lock and key, but from my warnings, someone could know that it's dangerous. And he's been delirious off and on. That sounds like thorn apple, don't you think?"

Gilbert nodded. "Yes. My master told me vinegar was good against poisoning by thorn apple. But you've already tried that."

"And if that were all, he should be getting better by now. There must have been something else used." She looked up with wide panicky eyes in which rings of pale white surrounded the brilliant green of the pupils. "Oh, Gilbert, what if I've done exactly the wrong thing? I was so quick to think it was thorn apple, I never stopped to ask if anybody else knew better. What if I've killed him with my remedies?"

Gilbert reached across the narrow bed and patted her hand. "Don't worry, Johanna. Nobody ever yet died from drinking vinegar and water. And if you hadn't given him that draught right away, the thorn apple would have killed him before the other poison had a chance to work.''

Rochambeau's swollen eyes flicked open, slits of blue between lids red with the aftereffects of poison and vomiting. ''Making love—to my woman—again, de Bellay?'' he whispered.

''Oh, Nicolas! You're awake!'' Johanna flung her arms around his neck and nearly smothered him with joyful kisses.

''Trust a woman to state the obvious.'' Rochambeau's sarcastic voice was a mere thread of sound, but the intonations were wholly his. ''Awake, tired, and ready for something to eat. Why don't you go and rest yourself, love? Gilbert will feed me, and we can talk after.''

Johanna didn't like the idea of letting Rochambeau out of her sight for a single minute, but Gilbert and Margery persuaded her, pointing out that she'd be no use to anybody if she fainted on the floor from exhaustion. Better to take an hour's rest, surely, and return to Rochambeau's bedside later when he had broken his fast.

''All right,'' Johanna conceded, but only because she didn't trust anybody else to prepare Rochambeau's food. ''I'll fix a tray with some wine posset and bring it right up.'' A newly broached cask of wine, eggs broken into the posset before her own eyes, honey and breadcrumbs from the common kitchen stock—there'd be no opportunity for anybody to slip poison into the cup while she watched, and she meant to taste the food herself before giving any to Rochambeau.

Rochambeau sent Margery down to the kitchens with her. As soon as they were out of the room, he turned his eyes to Gilbert. ''Heard you talking,'' he whispered. ''Guessed . . . you know more than you want to tell her?''

Gilbert nodded, his young face grave with fatigue and responsibility. ''Do you feel numbness about the tongue and the roof of the mouth?''

Rochambeau nodded weakly.

''And a sort of tingling sensation all over your body? Your throat constricting? And something makes you want to clench your fists?''

Rochambeau tried to whisper his assent, but another convulsive movement of his jaw stopped him.

"It's all right," said Gilbert quickly. "Don't speak. Don't try to move."

"Tell me. Before Johanna gets back." The imperious whisper, through teeth clenched with the spasms of the poison, left no possibility of disobedience.

"I think it's wolfsbane. That grows in the medicinal side of the herb garden, too."

"I know, I know." Even in his weakness, Rochambeau's impatience came through. "Johanna grows a good many strange plants . . ."

"Don't talk! Do you want to kill yourself before your time?" For once, Gilbert's concern overrode the natural awe which the older man inspired in him. "I saw a case of wolfsbane poisoning once, when I was working with Master Bartholomew. The man had beaten his wife, and she—" He swallowed the end of his sentence. "Well, that doesn't matter. Master Bartholomew said his only hope was to lie completely still until the watery humors of his body had absorbed and vanquished the poison. There's no known remedy but time."

"And how long did it take the humors of his body to conquer the poison?"

"As a matter of fact," Gilbert admitted, "he died within three hours."

Rochambeau gave a ghostly chuckle. "Fine recommendation!"

"But, my lord," Gilbert pleaded, "you have already lived through the night. Master Bartholomew said, when that man died, that he never knew anyone to die of wolfsbane but the convulsions took them within one to eight hours. If you will just be still and patient—"

"I would be more interested in hearing what Master Bartholomew said of those who survived the poisoning."

Gilbert flushed and looked down. Rochambeau studied the taut cords of his thin neck and the dark blush along his cheekbones with a tolerant smile, detached as though their entire discussion was nothing more than an academic disputation. "Is it possible," he asked gently, "that Master Bartholomew never knew anybody to survive?"

Gilbert's unhappy gulp was all the assent he needed.

"Well, then." Rochambeau lay back on the bed, forcing his clenched hands to open by the sheer force of his will. "Perhaps you'd better take notes. This might be the start of a brilliant medical career for you, de Bellay. For I have no intention of succumbing to poison or anything else."

The brave words sounded well enough, but they were belied by the dark, sunken circles around Rochambeau's reddened eyes, the dank sweat that stained his golden hair, and the greenish pallor of his skin. Aubrey, bursting into the room with clumsy haste, seemed like the personification of strength and rude health beside his younger brother.

"My God, Nicolas." Going down on one knee beside the bed, Aubrey took one of Rochambeau's open hands in his own. "What have they been doing to you? You look worse every time I see you."

He had been appearing at the door at intervals all night, trying to get Johanna to lie down and let him take over the task of tending Rochambeau, but this was his first appearance since she had been persuaded to leave the room. Now he glanced from Rochambeau's pale countenance to Gilbert with an appearance of unease.

"Er, de Bellay, would you mind? I need to talk to Nicolas for a moment."

"Can't it wait? He should be resting."

"No," said Aubrey simply. "No, I fear this cannot wait, Nicolas. It touches on your very life."

"Then it's got some competition," Rochambeau whispered with a faint grin. "Young de Bellay has just been persuading me that it's as much as my life's worth to stir from this bed."

Aubrey glanced back up at Gilbert. "Is that true?"

Gilbert spread his hands unhappily. "I'm no leech. I think he's been given wolfsbane. My old master said that moving around would cause the poison to spread through the system faster than the bodily humors could absorb it."

"And that would kill him." Aubrey seemed pleased at his own quick comprehension.

"It might only paralyze him. He's very strong. Most men would have died already."

"If you two don't quit talking over my bed like this,"

311

Rochambeau warned them, "I shall begin to think I have died already. Aubrey, de Bellay stays. He's my medical advisor. What is so urgent that you had to see me at once?"

Aubrey frowned. "Nicolas, this concerns matters that you might not wish to discuss with strangers present."

"Then wait till Johanna gets back. She can take over from Gilbert."

"No!" Aubrey's recoil went through his body like a wave breaking against the seawall. "No, I have been waiting to see you without—that is, this concerns—it might concern Johanna."

"And in such a fashion that you don't want her to hear it." Rochambeau nodded at Gilbert, who tactfully withdrew to the doorway. He did not quite leave the room, but he was far enough away to accord the brothers a measure of privacy. Kneeling by Rochambeau's bed, Aubrey began in halting undertones to explain the urgent errand that had brought him there.

"I don't want to say anything against Johanna," he repeated over and over until Rochambeau snapped that he was growing weary of hearing what Aubrey did not wish to say; what *did* he want to say?

"I've been thinking." Aubrey paused and rubbed his head with one hand, sending his fair hair up into spikes like a cornfield after a high wind. "She didn't want you to read the estate books."

"Considering the ingenuity of her cipher," said Rochambeau dryly, "I'd say she didn't want anyone to read them."

"Yes, but whose business was it to do so, save yours? And as soon as you did decipher the books, this poisoning happened. She ordered the spiced cakes herself, Nicolas. I caught her in the kitchen, conferring with the cook."

"You're suggesting I should hang the cook?"

Aubrey shook his head. "Not until we know just what part Johanna took in the preparation. Nicolas, don't be angry, but listen to me! You know she keeps all the expensive spices, like ginger, under lock and key in the storeroom. She would have had to open a locked chest and give the ginger to the cook personally, such a quantity as she required for those cakes."

"Such is the habit of all good housewives."

The next words seemed almost to be dragged out of Aubrey. "She also keeps . . . medicinal herbs . . . in a locked chest in the storeroom. Including leaves of thorn apple, and God only knows what else. Young de Bellay mentioned wolfsbane."

Rochambeau could have mentioned that he'd seen the plant growing in Johanna's medicinal garden, but he lay back against the bed as though the effort of speaking was too much for him. His eyelids flickered shut, then opened halfway. He watched Aubrey's face intently as the indictment went on.

"She ordered the honey cakes, but she ate none of them. Did she press them on you in any way?"

Rochambeau's lips twitched as he recalled the way he'd been awakened from his nap with Johanna kneeling on his chest, grinding the sweet spicy cakes into his mouth and nose. "You might say that."

His words were barely audible; the strength and determination to survive that he'd shown while talking with Gilbert seemed to be ebbing away now. Still, he roused himself to make a feeble protest. "Everyone knows that she does not care for sweets . . . and that I do. It would be the safest way to poison me without harming her."

"Who," asked Aubrey unanswerably, "other than Johanna herself, would be concerned to keep her alive while killing you?"

"She nursed me devotedly all night long. And Gilbert will confirm that her remedies are the best he knows of."

"Do you know," asked Aubrey, "exactly what was in the draughts she gave you? She *said* it was only vinegar and water, and none of us had the wit to test it for poison." He picked up an empty vessel and sniffed at it. "Not enough left to discolor a bit of unicorn's horn now."

"I hope not," Rochambeau half whispered with a faint grin. "She's a better housewife than to leave that particular vessel standing full. That's not one of the ones I drank out of, Aubrey. I used it for other purposes."

Aubrey almost dropped the empty dish, a look of disgust on his face. "Never mind. The principle is the same. How do you know she was really trying to keep you alive? She drove all of us away, Nicolas. Perhaps she feared lest you might accuse her when you regained consciousness."

Before Rochambeau could summon up his waning strength to reply, Aubrey followed that suggestion with a series of damning questions that seemed to fall on the dying man like the blows of a smith's hammer on the anvil.

"Who tried to keep the estate accounts from you? Who was the first to know that you'd deciphered them after all? Who keeps poisonous herbs growing in her garden and makes concoctions of them in her stillroom? Who ordered the cakes made so spicy that no one could have tasted the poison? Who would have had an opportunity to mix spices with other noxious ingredients before she handed the makings to the cook?"

Rochambeau's eyes were closed again, his pallor was even more pronounced than before, and he breathed shallowly and quickly. Aubrey stood and looked down at him with a face in which nothing could be read but sorrow and concern. "I don't make this accusation lightly, Nicolas. I have watched her devious ways for years without speaking out. But now, when it is a question of your very life, I cannot reconcile it with my conscience to remain silent. You are weak, unable to protect yourself, vulnerable to her witch's tricks. Please, for my sake if not for your own, take some precautions. Let me oversee the preparation of all your food until you are fully recovered."

Rochambeau barely moved his head from side to side on the linen bolster. His sweat-dampened hair clung to the linen, dark matted locks streaked with gold.

"Please, Nicolas!" Aubrey knelt again, taking Rochambeau's limp hands in his. The pulse beat strong and fast, too strong for a man who seemed so weak. "It's your life I'm thinking of. If I'm wrong, then let the lady prove her innocence—but later, when you are well and can oversee the trial. This is no time to let infatuation blind you to the danger you are in. All I ask is the chance to stay by you and prepare your food, to see that she doesn't get to attack you again."

Again Rochambeau shook his head. "Not—good enough," he whispered.

"God's finger joints! How much of a case do you want me to prepare?" Anger blazed in Aubrey's eyes and died out as quickly, to be replaced by the look of loving concern he had worn since coming into the room.

"You . . . have to sleep . . . too," Rochambeau pointed out, drawing each breath with obvious pain. "If I take what you say seriously, Aubrey, the danger is too great for half-measures. Call my squire."

Fulke had been standing just outside the door of the strong-room, silently keeping watch. Now, impassive before his lord's obvious weakness, the boy listened to Rochambeau's orders with no sign of emotion.

Johanna, Rochambeau decreed, was to be arrested immediately. Young Fulke was to take six men of the castle guard with him, showing them his ring as security that the orders did indeed come from the lord. He pulled off the archaic gold ring with its carved stone, the seal of the lords of Rochambeau, and handed it over to Fulke as he spoke. His hands were damp with sweat, and he had lost flesh in the night; the ring slid off easily, too easily. Aubrey stirred and muttered that it was a bad omen.

"Where is the lady to be kept, my lord?"

"In the barred cells under the old keep. She may have what comforts she wishes, cushions and food and drink, but she is to be kept absolutely alone, and you are to guard her at all times. Keep the door to her cell as faithfully as you have kept mine, Fulke, and I shall sleep the sounder for knowing you are there."

Fulke bowed and had turned to leave when Rochambeau called him back with one last order. He was to have all Johanna's food tasted before it was passed into the cell with her, and he was to see that she knew it.

"Is that necessary?" asked Aubrey. "It's your food we should be protecting, not hers."

"If she is really a witch," Rochambeau pointed out, "there may be potions she would wish to take to increase her powers. Or she might wish to poison herself so as to escape trial. I mean to have her kept absolutely safe until I am able to deal with the matter myself. I—"

Rochambeau fell back against the pillow in another convulsion before he could finish the sentence. His jaws clenched until the cords in his neck stood out and his hands clawed feebly at the coverlet. Apparently at the last of his strength, he beckoned for Gilbert. Aubrey left them together and accompanied Fulke to search for Johanna. It might well be, he thought as he left, that the lord of Rochambeau would never recover sufficiently to deal with Johanna in this life. And in that case, what would become of her? Would she stay walled up in the old keep cells forever?

Chapter Twenty-three

It seemed to Johanna that the mixing of the wine posset for Rochambeau took forever. She was so tired that she could hardly keep her eyes open, yet it was necessary to oversee each step herself, to ensure that only those ingredients she doled out to the cook and tasted personally were used. The need for sleep grained the corners of her eyes and tormented her with the illusion that the hard stone floor beneath her feet was actually a soft mattress into which she could float, if she would just shut her eyes and let herself fall. She deliberately concentrated on the small sensations that anchored her to reality: the cold grittiness of the stone flags under her bare feet, the bell ringing outside to call the castle folk to Mass, the pungent smell of the healing herbs she had ground up to mix into the posset.

At last the task was done, and Johanna gripped the heavy cup in both hands. She would let no one else carry it to Rochambeau; that had been her mistake yesterday. Oh, if only she hadn't let Aubrey take charge of having the food sent up! He was such a great, blundering, kindly fool of a man, without a suspicious bone in his body; anyone could have poisoned the tray under his very eyes. But who would want to kill Rochambeau? Johanna swayed slightly and recovered her balance with an effort. No use trying to think now; she was too tired and distraught. First she must exert all of her willpower to see that Rochambeau lived. She would

317

not let him die—she could not—not now, when they'd just discovered each other after all those wasted years! Later, when he was out of danger, there would be time to sleep, and think, and talk.

Head bent over the steaming cup, she hurried along the maze of wooden passages that connected the cooking shed with the great hall. She turned a corner too sharply and almost ran into the man who stood there, blocking her way. Hard hands on her arms steadied her, but too late to prevent the wine posset from splashing down the front of his surcoat and staining the straw beneath their feet with a pale red puddle. Johanna's eyes filled with tears.

"Look what you've done, you fool!" she snapped at Fulke. "And who told you to go loitering about the kitchen where you don't belong, getting in people's way? I thought I could trust you to keep guard over my lord as I told you to do. You'd better get back there at once. I'm going to have to go back to the kitchen and make another posset, thanks to your clumsiness."

"No," said Fulke. His hands were still closed over her arms. Johanna felt a moment's irrational fear. No one had ever held her so, except Gautier once when he stole a kiss she wasn't ready to give. And Fulke's stern young face didn't look as if he were interested in giving or receiving kisses. She hadn't realized how he had grown since he had left with Rochambeau; she still thought of him as the pesky little page who was always underfoot in the guardroom. But it was a grown man who held her now, taller and stronger than she—and why should that matter? Wasn't she the lady of the manor?

"What nonsense are you talking, Fulke?" she demanded. Fear and anger, both uncalled for, made her tongue sharper than she meant. "You waste precious time with this foolery. Will you get back to your post, or shall I call the castle guard to teach you your duty?" With a glimmer of relief, she saw, over Fulke's shoulder, the glint of mail. She couldn't think why men armed for castle-guard duty should be wandering about the kitchens at dawn, but it was reassuring to know that, if Fulke had indeed gone mad, help was at hand.

"They've come with me," said Fulke, as if he could read her thoughts. "And I am doing my duty. My lord's orders supersede yours." He didn't deign to do anything so human

318

as smiling, but there was a pleased glint in his eyes as he let go of her with one hand to fish in the purse at his belt. He drew out a heavy gold ring with a carved stone set in the middle.

"Rochambeau's seal." Johanna recognized the ring but could not connect it with Fulke's presence there or his unexpected insolence.

"My lady Johanna" said Fulke formally, "I am commanded to conduct you under guard to a place of safekeeping, where you shall remain until the time is right for you to answer certain questions concerning this poisoning of Nicolas de Rochambeau."

Johanna passed her freed hand over her forehead, brushing away the little black curls that had escaped her hastily bound coif. "Questions? I don't understand. It was thorn apple, I think, and something else, but I don't know what. Gilbert de Bellay might have some ideas." She glanced up at Fulke's face with sudden horror, thinking that his delay and his strange speech might make all too much sense. "He's alive still? Oh, tell me he is no worse!"

"My lord's condition is none of *your* concern anymore, witch wife," Fulke snapped. "Don't you understand plain Norman French? You're under arrest. For poisoning him. My lord's own orders."

"Then he's still alive." That was the first thought that entered her mind; only slowly did Fulke's words sink in. "But I—you're mad! I wouldn't poison Rochambeau! I love him!"

"So you have made abundantly clear since his return to Malvern," said Fulke with heavy sarcasm.

Johanna scarcely heard him; she was fighting the hard hand that clamped about her left arm, calling out to the guards she saw behind Fulke in the passage. "Guards! Help! This squire's lost his wits!"

The mailed men did not stir. She recognized the two in front and appealed to them personally. "Edric, Osmund, won't you tell this boy to let me go? There's been some terrible mistake!"

Edric looked down at his feet; Osmund shuffled uneasily and stared up at the ceiling.

"They follow *my* orders," said Fulke, and there was a

trace of creamy satisfaction in his voice. "I bear my lord's seal. Now, my lady, will you walk with me or be carried?"

Still clutching the empty wine cup in her nerveless fingers, Johanna mechanically accompanied Fulke down the rest of the wooden passageway. Edric and Osmund stood aside to let them pass, then fell into step behind them, while four other guards marched ahead. All were in full armor, having just been taken from the castle watch, and so she was surrounded front and back by the glint of steel and the heavy clang of mailed footsteps.

When they came to the short open space between the passage and the great hall, Johanna automatically started for the hall and was almost pulled off balance by Fulke's tug on her arm. "Not there. You're to stay in the old keep cells."

The daze of unbelief which had brought Johanna unprotesting this far cleared now. "No. I must see my lord!" She yanked unavailingly at the hand like iron that held her arm so tightly, protesting, "You don't understand. It's a mistake. I must see Nicolas. He'll explain to you that you're making a terrible mistake. And I have to take care of him. I can't be locked away from him, not now!"

"You've taken care enough already!" Fulke dragged Johanna forcibly away from the shallow steps leading up to the doors of the hall. She hit him with the wine cup, and he twisted it out of her hand with a sharp motion that sent a shooting pain up her wrist. Edric and Osmund moved closer, coughing apologetically and holding out their own hands to restrain Fulke.

"Er—she is the lord's wife," Osmund pointed out.

"Been a good lady to us while he was away. Run the manor 'bout as well as a man could, I reckon," put in Edric.

On the far side of the bailey, Rochambeau's falconer hobbled out and called in his cracked old voice, "Trouble, my lady?" He stroked the great fierce gerfalcon that perched on his arm and grinned as if to indicate that he'd be happy to unhood it at her request. Beyond him, the groom who cared for Johanna's horse ambled to the stable door and stood there, smiling vacantly and swinging a horseshoe in one hand.

Fulke's hand fell away from her wrist, and Johanna straightened up, trying to control her panicky breathing. A little sense was returning to her now. There were those in

Malvern who loved her, perhaps felt more loyalty to her than to the lord they'd hardly seen in the past few years. She could call on their assistance and precipitate a brawl that might momentarily disconcert Fulke, she could play on Osmund's and Edric's conflicting loyalties, but to what end? She would only succeed in delaying the inevitable for a few minutes longer. Between Rochambeau's armed men, used to fighting in Saracen wars and French tourneys, and the lackeys of the castle, there could be no real contest.

And yet, how could she let herself be locked up away from Rochambeau like this, without even a chance to protest her innocence? There must be some way in which she could turn this unexpected support to advantage. She looked up at Fulke, who seemed irresolute for once.

"You see," she said quietly, "the people of Malvern will not like to see me dragged to a prison cell like a common thief. Nor do I think my lord would be pleased to hear of a brawl in the courtyard. Perhaps you'd best mend your manners. We can sit in the hall and discuss this like civilized beings."

As if taking his agreement for granted, she lifted her skirts and stepped up into the high-vaulted, shadowy hall. Fulke, taken by surprise, followed just half a pace behind her. He didn't attempt to lay hands on her again, but his malicious whisper was hot on the back of her neck. "Perhaps the folk of Malvern will be better pleased to see you burned as a witch and poisoner!"

Johanna meant to ignore him and go right on up to the strongroom to see Rochambeau, if he would let her go that far; but before she'd taken more than three steps into the hall, Aubrey came hurrying to meet her with hands outstretched.

"Johanna." He took her hands in his and gazed down at her with tears in his blue eyes. "I am so sorry. It is a terrible mistake. Thank God I came in time to save you from being incarcerated in the cells!"

Johanna felt weak-kneed with the relief that flooded through her at Aubrey's words. "I knew there was a mistake. How did it happen? How is Nicolas?"

"Sleeping when I left him."

"Oh!" Johanna sat down on one of the long benches that lined the alcoves in the hall. She wanted more desperately than anything in the world to see Rochambeau again, to have him tell her in his own voice that Fulke had run mad or had laughably misinterpreted his order. She wanted to know—no, to be reassured of what she knew already in her blood and bones—that Rochambeau could never, even for a moment, have thought that she wished to take his life. But how could she let her need for reassurance outweigh his need for healing sleep? Aubrey's kindly assurance would have to be enough.

"It's all right," she said, wiping one hand across her eyes as if the gesture would clear away the cobwebs that seemed to fill her tired head. "I'll speak with him when he wakes. Meanwhile, can you do something about this?" She nodded her head at Fulke, who hovered inches away like a hunting dog balked of his prey, and at the embarrassed men of the castle guard who shuffled behind him.

"Certainly. That's what I came for." Lifting his head, Aubrey addressed Fulke directly. "Rochambeau has changed his mind. The keep cells are not fitting for a lady of gentle birth. He wishes you to escort her to her own chamber, there to be kept under strict guard until he is ready to interrogate her."

Fulke grumbled and demanded to see some confirmation of this change in orders. Johanna heard his words as some kind of annoying background noise, barely audible over the roaring in her ears. Aubrey had said it was all a mistake, yet now he spoke as though Rochambeau had indeed given the order for her arrest!

"I must speak with Nicolas," she said, rising unsteadily on legs that seemed too weak to support her. "He cannot have meant it. Please, Aubrey!" How strange and mad it seemed, to be pleading with ineffectual, kindly Aubrey for the chance to see her own husband. "I'll wait very quietly until he wakes up. I won't disturb him—"

Aubrey was shaking his head. "Better not, Johanna. Not now. If he sees you now, or if anyone speaks of you, he may order you cast into the keep cells again. It was all I could do to obtain this slight favor. Give me some time first to soften his anger against you. In a few days, perhaps he will consent to see you."

Johanna clutched at Aubrey's arm, feeling the floor dip and sway under her feet. Blackness crowded in on her vision, a darkness full of menacing shapes and shadows. "He thinks I sought his life?"

"Johanna, he is a desperately ill man. The poison may have disordered his reason. Please do not take it like this. You have only to stay in your own chambers for a few days, then I'm sure everything will be straightened out. That is—" Aubrey coughed as if to cover up his deep embarrassment. "I'm almost sure he will consent to speak with you privately before the trial. Only, it would not be wise to insist on seeing him now. He keeps saying something about treachery, that the child of a traitor could only be a traitor. I'm afraid you may be paying for your father's sins."

"My father is no traitor. Nor am I." Anger stiffened Johanna's backbone, giving her the strength to let go of the comforting support of Aubrey's arm. "As will be proved in due course." And how she was to carry out that promise, she had no idea. But that didn't matter now. All that mattered was the pride and anger that enabled her to walk unsupported down the length of the great hall, up the short flight of steps that led to the bower, into the empty bedchamber that her women had cleaned out that morning. The stone flags of the floor were scoured clean, the stained and dirty hangings had been removed; there'd been no time to bring in fresh rushes and clean linen for the bed, and Dilys fluttered before her, apologizing as if Johanna were still the lady of the manor and not a prisoner under suspicion.

"Never mind, Dilys. This is good enough for a prisoner." Johanna sat down on a clothes chest and gazed unseeing at the barren room, the floor and walls still damp from their hasty scrubbing. A puddle in one of the depressions on the floor had soaked the hem of her cloak; she regarded the dark semicircle of the water stain with as much interest as anything else. She was barely conscious of Aubrey's apologetic explanations that Rochambeau had insisted she be kept alone, without even one waiting-woman to keep her company. Solitude was all she desired at the moment—solitude and a chance to think out what to do next.

That Rochambeau had mitigated the severity of his first orders, allowing her to be confined in her own chambers instead of in the cells below the old keep, was the only positive thing about the situation. And that wasn't much, compared to the crushing weight of the discovery that he believed her guilty of poisoning him. What did it matter whether she lay in the comfort of her own bed or on the straw of the cells? All that mattered was that for all his words of love, Rochambeau had condemned her without even giving her a chance to speak in her own defense. What had happened in the short time while she'd been in the kitchen to make him believe her guilty of so monstrous a crime? Or perhaps he'd thought it all along. Hadn't he added his weak voice to Aubrey's, trying to persuade her to leave him for a while and get some rest? Perhaps all night while she worked to save his life, he had been secretly fearing that she would try to finish the job she'd started, afraid to voice his suspicions until he could get her out of the room on some excuse.

The pain of that thought was almost intolerable. Johanna felt as though a mailed hand were closing around her heart, crushing it inside her chest. There was an actual physical pain shooting up through her chest, wracking her throat with unshed sobs. She'd tried to make peace with Rochambeau, to make up for all their bitter wrangling in the past, but she had been too late. The one day of peaceful love that they'd shared was not enough to wipe out years of hatred and suspicion and old grudges. And here was the proof of it: when someone made an attempt on his life, he immediately suspected her.

"I can't bear it!" she exclaimed aloud. The pain in her chest was choking her. She wanted to die of it. That would be a relief. But people didn't die of unhappiness. Not quickly, anyway. It might take years.

She might have years. How long did Rochambeau mean to keep her locked up? Fulke had hinted something about a trial. Presumably that would have to wait until Rochambeau had recovered his strength—or until . . .

No. She would not contemplate the other possibility. If he died believing her faithless, her own life might as well end too. As long as he lived, there was hope; it was that shred of hope that hurt so. If only she could reach him, speak to him herself, find out exactly what he thought of her. There had to be some way to refute this monstrous charge.

"Think," Johanna commanded herself. But her exhausted mind would not obey her orders. Everything seemed mixed up together, as if it were all happening at once: Rochambeau's sickness, their lovemaking, the first meeting in her father's fields, all their quarrels and passionate nights and angry days. When she tried to remember the exact sequence of events that had led up to Rochambeau's eating the poisoned cakes, her mind drifted back to the sweet lovemaking that had preceded that, and she found herself weeping like a child. When she tried to recall exactly what Aubrey had said in the kitchen, the memory of that conversation blended with the one four years earlier, when he'd broken the news to her that Rochambeau meant to have her father arraigned as a traitor if she didn't marry him. How she'd hated Rochambeau for that blackmail, and how unimportant it seemed now!

Tears of sheer weakness streamed down Johanna's face. Rising unsteadily, she made her way to the bed and fell face-down on the straw tick, all that remained after her women had taken away the stained coverlets and feather mattress for cleaning. Before her cheek touched the rough sacking surface, she was asleep, without even time to feel the sharp points of straw that pricked through the coarse cloth.

The heavy, fitful sleep lasted several hours. She was tormented by strange dreams, and she moaned and moved restlessly about on the bed, but she could not break the spell of exhaustion that held her captive in deep sleep. At one time she thought the old witch from the forest was laughing at her; then it seemed that Rochambeau himself walked through the wall and stood looking down at her with a grave sweet smile that held the promise of everything she'd ever wanted from him.

"You don't believe it, do you?" she cried out in her dream. "Oh, tell me you don't believe it!"

The sound of her own voice broke the dream, and she woke to the crushing disappointment of finding herself still alone in the chamber. She sat up, looking bemusedly at the bars of sunlight that slanted across the room and proclaimed the hour to be late in the afternoon. Her limbs were stiff from lying so long in the awkward position in which she'd collapsed on the bed, and one side of her face was all red and sore from the prickly straw tick. But her mind was blessedly clear again.

"Oh, how could I have been such a fool?" she laughed at herself. "I'm not a prisoner at all!" The dream about Rochambeau walking through the walls had been sent her for a purpose. The outer door might be locked and guarded, but what of the secret entrance through the chapel gallery?

Tossing her cloak back over her shoulder, Johanna padded barefoot over the cold stone floor and slipped her hand behind the tapestry. Yes, the door was there as she remembered, and if she could but discover the secret of making it move, she could leave at any time she wanted. There must be a stone to push, a lever to pull; she would have plenty of time to explore the wall. Once she got the door open, she'd be free in the chapel gallery, and then . . .

Then what? Johanna sat back down on the clothes chest and pulled the cloak closely about her shoulders as she considered the possibilities. Everyone in Malvern must know by now of her arrest. If she simply walked through the chapel and tried to make her way back up to Rochambeau's room, she would be seen and taken prisoner again before she'd gone a dozen paces. She would have to wait until late that night, when the castle would be dark and everyone asleep. Even then, it would be tricky to make the circuit from the outer chapel door, back through the hall, and up the stairs to the strongroom on the floor above this without arousing a sleeper or being challenged by a guard. And if Rochambeau's door was guarded?

Johanna shook her head impatiently. "I can't afford to think about that," she told the tapestry-hung walls. Nor did she dare to think about what might happen if she reached Rochambeau and he still refused to believe her. Now that she was rested, she could see that from a purely logical point of view there was much to condemn her. Everybody knew that she worked with herbs and that there were poisonous plants in the medicinal garden; she'd warned the castle servants of that herself, to make sure that they didn't accidentally pick wolfsbane in mistake for horseradish, or thorn apple for salad greens. Rochambeau himself had seen her administer a weak dose of thorn apple to that peasant woman to calm her fears. And in their bitterest quarrels, hadn't she threatened Rochambeau that if he raised his hand to her, he might do well to have his food tasted thereafter?

"But we love each other," she protested to the walls. "He knows I didn't mean it."

If he knew that, what was she doing here? Come to think

of it, if he wanted her locked up, what was she doing in the only chamber in the castle that had a back way out?

The clink of dishes at the door interrupted her train of thought. Johanna jumped up as Aubrey came into the room, carrying a tray awkwardly in both hands, while a little page held the door and the tapestry for him.

"Aubrey! What's happening? How is he?"

Aubrey shook his head. "Weak. No better."

"But still alive?"

"Just."

The single word sapped her hopes and strength. Johanna sank back down on the chest, supporting her aching head in one hand. "Aubrey, please. Help me to see him. If—" She hadn't wanted even to consider the possibility, but now it had to be faced. She forced the words past a constriction in her throat that threatened to strangle her. "I cannot bear it if he dies, and me not there. Please, Aubrey! *You* know I would never have done anything to hurt him! And—and he can't really think it, or why would he have ordered me kept in this room? I don't have to be a prisoner here any longer than I choose."

Aubrey looked startled. "You don't?"

"Send the page away," Johanna commanded with belated caution. When the boy was gone, she pushed aside the tapestry that hung over the wall between this chamber and the chapel gallery. "There's a door through here. Rochambeau had it put in secretly when he had this new tower built."

"Yes, I know," said Aubrey.

"You do?"

He smiled. "There was a time when Nicolas kept no secrets from me. I'd meant to use it to come and comfort you, if Fulke tried to keep me away; but even he wouldn't deny the lord's brother entrance." A shadow of resentment crossed his face. "The little brat insisted on personally tasting your food before I brought it in, though, and in his clumsiness the first tray got spilled and I had to send to the kitchen for more. That's why it took me so long."

"Well, then." Johanna couldn't really work up much interest in the food; the thought of Rochambeau's distrust had robbed her of all appetite. It had been a kind thought of Aubrey's, but it was just like him to get distracted by irrelevancies. "I don't know the secret of opening the door from this side, but it can't be too difficult to find out. And he knows I know of it, for he used it to come to me the other night when we weren't on good terms." Her throat ached with unshed tears as she recalled that night. What a fool she'd been, not to enjoy Nicolas's love when she had the chance! Now it might be too late.

No, she wouldn't think that. He wouldn't die, not her brave, strong, golden knight who laughed at all obstacles. But if Aubrey believed he was dying, it might incline him to help her. That was, she told herself firmly, the only reason she would even pretend to think he was dying. Inside herself, she had to have faith that he would live, that they'd both be given a second chance. She looked up at Aubrey with tears swimming in her green eyes, making them seem larger and more luminous than ever.

"You see, Aubrey, if he'd really suspected me of poisoning him, he'd never have sent me to this chamber, of all places. Doesn't that prove it will be all right for me to see him? Please, take me to him now!"

Aubrey shook his head, a look of pity clouding his face. "Johanna, Johanna, there's something I must tell you." He took both her hands in his; the dry, feverish warmth of his palms startled her until she realized that her own hands were like ice. "Rochambeau didn't give that order. I lied to Fulke."

"It was your idea to keep me in here? But why?"

"I couldn't bear to think of your being locked up like a common prisoner."

Johanna's laugh was harsh and brittle. "No, I'm a very uncommon prisoner. Witch and poisoner—that's what Fulke named me! Isn't he afraid I'll turn myself into a bird and fly out that window?" She laughed again and, frighteningly, found it hard to stop.

"Johanna!" Aubrey's hands squeezed down on hers until the brief pain brought her to her senses. "Don't lose heart. I'll do what I can. Surely, if you speak with Nicolas, he'll see the injustice of his suspicions. But I dare not take you to him now. There's a strong feeling against you in the castle. Someone would make an outcry. Rest and eat the food I've brought you, and after dark I'll come with a hooded cloak to conceal you. Then we can slip upstairs to see him."

Johanna cast an anguished glance at the golden late-afternoon light that slipped through the tall narrow windows. How could she wait until dark, with Nicolas upstairs, fighting for his life?

"You must have patience." Aubrey's voice was steady and reassuring now. "Think, Johanna! Will you risk all, only to see him a scant hour or so earlier? Let me arrange all, so you shall come to him in safety and privacy."

He went on, murmuring reassuring words, but Johanna hardly heard him. She was hurting from the double disappointment: that Rochambeau hadn't sent her to this chamber as an oblique indication of her innocence, and that Aubrey wouldn't take her to see him immediately. Either discovery would have been hard to bear; together, they were almost insupportable.

She reminded herself that she had been prepared to wait until nightfall to make her own move. If she'd hoped for a few moments that Aubrey would help her reach Rochambeau earlier and then had lost that hope, she'd really lost nothing. Besides, he was right. It would be foolish to risk being sent back to even straiter confinement, when an hour or two would vastly improve her chances of slipping into Rochambeau's chamber unnoticed. But she had thought that with Aubrey by her side she might have gone openly and unchallenged.

"Do they hate me so much, the castle folk?" She spoke almost at random, senses and wits dulled by sorrow, but unwilling to give up so soon. "I thought that some of them, at least, knew me and loved me by now."

"All of us who know you must love you," said Aubrey simply. The unforced tribute brought new tears to Johanna's eyes. She dashed them away almost angrily, telling herself that this was no time to give in to self-pity. "But the men who went with Rochambeau to the East, and who fought their way out of French captivity with him, don't know you as we do."

"And," Johanna added dryly, "they have little reason to love me, as no doubt they blame me that the ransom did not reach them in time."

Aubrey's big shoulders moved uneasily. "They think it was never sent."

"Oh, yes, I was forgetting that." Rochambeau would know differently by now, if he had indeed deciphered the entire account rolls as he claimed. But what did it matter? There were worse things between them now than the matter of a missing hundred and fifty marks.

"Their loyalty is to Rochambeau," Aubrey went on. "To them, you're an interloper, a stranger, half Welsh, and they've seen the bitter quarrels between you and Nicolas. Now he lies dying—"

"No," Johanna interrupted swiftly. "Not dying. I'll not believe that."

"As you wish. They believe it, and they're scared and angry and looking for someone to blame. It may have been as much for your own safety as for any other reason that Nicolas had you locked up."

"Oh, do you really think so?"

Aubrey coughed and looked away, and Johanna felt a sharp stab of disappointment under her breast. Of course he didn't think so. He was just trying to make her feel better.

"All right," she said dully. "I understand. I'll wait. But, Aubrey . . ." She caught at his sleeve and felt his arm tremble under her hand, as a lover trembles at his lady's touch. "You will be back?"

Aubrey stooped to brush her forehead with his lips. The caress lingered a little longer than Johanna had expected. Against her will, Johanna found herself remembering that strange scene in the pleasance, Aubrey's declaration of love and jealousy and the way he'd grabbed at her with clumsy, greedy hands.

If she shrank back from him now, he would know she was remembering that scene, he would feel she didn't trust him anymore, and he would be hurt.

And she had to trust Aubrey. He was her only friend now. Johanna stood quite still, only a slight relaxation in her tense muscles betraying her relief when at last Aubrey drew away from her.

"I shall not fail you, Johanna," he promised. "But you must promise me something in return."

"Anything."

Aubrey gestured at the tray of cooling food. "Eat your soup!" He drew off the linen cloth that had covered the tray and fussed over the soup for a moment with his back to her, stirring it up so that a rich meaty smell drifted through the chamber. "Come now, just a few spoonfuls," he coaxed. "It won't do any of us any good if you faint from hunger before I can take you to see Nicolas."

Johanna forced herself to smile. "All right. I think I can manage that much." She took a few sips of the cooling soup and tried to keep from wrinkling her nose at the bitter aftertaste. The cook must have thought she'd acquired Rochambeau's peculiar tastes, to have seasoned the dish so highly. She forced down a few mouthfuls under Aubrey's approving gaze, but as soon as he was gone she pushed the bowl aside. She couldn't eat while she was so worried about Nicolas. And she felt funny, too, dizzy and confused. Well, a lot of women felt ill at the beginning of a pregnancy and did their work in the hall and bower regardless. She wouldn't be weaker than they were. But perhaps she would just try to take a little nap before Aubrey returned.

Chapter Twenty-four

THE SOUND OF the tapestry being brushed aside, followed by the creak of a door slowly moving on ponderous hinges, startled Johanna out of the half-slumber into which she had fallen. She had been leaning back against the wall. When she moved, stiff limbs and cramped muscles protested the shock after hours of cold stillness.

The sound came from the wrong side of the room—from the chapel side, not from the door to the bower. Johanna was on her feet in an instant. The blood rushed from her head, and she swayed, clutched at the wall to regain her balance, and tried to remember what she was doing in this dark empty chamber.

"Johanna?"

The whispered voice was Aubrey's. Johanna relaxed slightly. "Here."

He came toward her, a darker shadow among shadows. "You're awake."

"Of course I am! God's teeth, Aubrey, is this a time for sleeping?"

"I didn't mean to suggest that you lacked the finer feelings," Aubrey said mildly. "Only that you've been a long time without sleep, and I wish you had rested while I was away. We've a long way to go tonight."

"Only upstairs, surely?"

He didn't reply directly. "Are you still wearing that cloak?

Take it off. It's too light. Here, this will do better." Fussy as an old maid, he draped a heavy, dark hooded cloak about her shoulders, pulling the hood down low over her forehead to obscure her features. The coarse stuff of the cloak was rough with many patches, and a sharp, acrid smell rose from the folds, something vaguely familiar that Johanna could not quite recognize. "I have a bundle of supplies, too. You'd best take that under your cloak; it might rouse suspicion if anyone saw me carrying it."

"Supplies! What for? We're only going up to the strong-room."

"No. Johanna, you must leave here at once. It's not safe for you here. I don't know how much longer I can protect you. Rochambeau's guards are in an ugly mood. There's talk of a burning. They're afraid, you see."

"I don't understand." Unexpected chills shook her body; Johanna was grateful for the warmth of the coarse cloak. "I have to see Nicolas. He can protect me, surely." And if he didn't want to, then she had no more wish to live.

Aubrey's heavy sigh told her before the actual words struck her ear. She shrank inside the cloak, feeling the chill of death already about her. "Johanna, you cannot see Nicolas. He—"

"No!" There was a roaring in her ears. Aubrey's lips kept moving. She didn't want to hear him, but the words forced themselves on her.

"He died at sunset, Johanna."

"No." The room dipped about her. Aubrey's hands bit into her waist.

"Johanna, don't faint now! We can escape, I promise you that."

She shook her head, too numb to speak. What was the use now in escaping? All her hopes had been concentrated on reaching Rochambeau. If he had died believing her his murderer, what did she have to live for? "You let him die. And I wasn't even there." For the moment it was all she could think of, that this crazy tangle of suspicions had cheated her of the right to sit with him in his last minutes. It should have been different; she should have been in his chamber with the last glow of the setting sun, not waiting patiently here below. If she'd been there, perhaps she could have saved him some-how, if only by the sheer force of her will. She clung to the thought of sunset, Rochambeau still alive, herself with him; she couldn't think beyond that to the dark reality of his death.

Aubrey's arm was tight about her shoulders. "Forgive me that I brought the news to you, Johanna. But it was better you should know. Now there is no reason for you to remain here."

Johanna shook her head slowly, wondering at Aubrey's senseless words. "Where should I go? What would I do? I'll stay here, with Nicolas."

"Johanna, you cannot stay!" The sharp urgency in Aubrey's voice, the tightening arm around her, were like very slender threads binding her to a reality she hated and wanted to flee from. She shook her head again, trying to drive away the annoying buzzing of his voice. All she wanted was to be alone in the darkness, where she could sit quietly and remember Nicolas and pretend that it hadn't happened yet, that he wasn't dead.

"I told you. The men of his personal guard talk of witchcraft, of burning you. They're not minded to wait for trial. For the moment you are safe enough—it will take them some time to gather up their courage—but before the night is out they will come for you. I won't let that happen, Johanna; I cannot see them hurt you. I would rather die protecting you, keeping the chamber door; but after they cut me down, they will still take you. You must leave at once. Thank God you told me of the chapel door! It gives us a chance."

"But where should I go?" Johanna's head felt numb, battered with Aubrey's explanations. It didn't seem real. Yesterday she and Nicolas had been laughing and loving each other in this very chamber; today the rich silk hangings and the Eastern cloths had been stripped from the chamber, Rochambeau lay dead upstairs, and Aubrey spoke of her death as though it were something she should fear. If Nicolas had died believing her his murderer, Johanna could think of little else for herself to do save to follow him.

Aubrey brushed her question aside with an impatient shake of his head. "Does it matter? Perhaps your father will hide you for a while. Or you may leave the country—that would be the best way, no doubt. For tonight, I've shelter for you. The old witch in the forest is dead, and I know where her hut is. I can take you there tonight. You'll be safe enough. The villagers don't know she is dead yet, and they'd be afraid to meddle around there. Later we will contrive something.''

"The villagers don't hate me," said Johanna slowly. It was all too much to make sense of. Aubrey was tugging at her now, urging her once again to make haste.

"All the better, but come on, now. Once you're safely away, I will put it about that you've been seen on the way to Wales, to your mother's kindred. That should keep them from searching the forest. Then we can contrive what to do next. For now, even if anyone should see us, they'll think you are Bruma. I told folk that I meant to seek her out, to see if she had any cure for Nicolas.''

Johanna's fingers brushed the patched surface of the cloak. "This was hers?''

"An admirable disguise, don't you think?''

Her flesh shrank from contact with that foul old woman's clothing, but she had no strength to resist. It was easier to go along with what Aubrey wanted her to do, even if it did seem strange to her that Rochambeau's men should talk of burning her. Her head had felt fuzzy ever since she woke in the darkness—no, earlier—since she had tried to drink the soup Aubrey had brought. She was too tired to think or plan or argue, and Aubrey's compelling certainty swept her along.

Aubrey led her out through the chapel gallery, leaving the door ajar behind them. When Johanna reached to swing it shut, he grasped her hand to stop her. "Leave it," he whispered. "Later I'll come openly to visit you and 'discover' the open door. We have to provide some explanation for how you got away, else they really will think you turned yourself into a bird and flew out the window!'' His whispered chuckle irritated Johanna's overstrained nerves. Now that she'd consented to his plan, Aubrey seemed actually to be enjoying himself. A shaft of moonlight cutting across the chapel floor showed his grin, and he drew her along with exaggerated tiptoe gestures, finger to his lips, as though this were all some sort of game to him.

She started automatically to protest that Rochambeau would be angry to have his secret exit discovered, and then the crushing weight of remembrance bowed her down: Rochambeau would never be angry again, never smile at her again, never take her in his arms—and he'd died thinking she had killed him.

Johanna bit down hard on her lip, until the pain and the trickle of blood distracted her. There would be time to weep later. Now she had to follow Aubrey and let him save her life, though she couldn't quite remember why it mattered.

Outside the chapel, they slipped from shadow to shadow toward the unguarded postern gate. There was one risky moment when one of the guards patrolling the outer walls looked down into the courtyard just as Johanna prepared to slither across an open space. Aubrey flung out his hand against her breast to hold her back, and for a long breathless moment they stood frozen there.

Even when the guard was out of sight, he would not let her move. "His partner may follow," he whispered, pressing her further back into the safety of the shadows. She stood passively between the wall and Aubrey, unable to get away from him and hating the physical contact. He was tall, broad-shouldered, and blond, a little soft in the belly from years of good living, with soft features reflecting his vague kindly nature. Aubrey was like a blurred copy of Rochambeau, as if a sharp pen-and-ink drawing had been dipped under water for a moment, softening and blurring all the fine edges and harsh lines that made Rochambeau what he was. To have Aubrey so close to her, one hand gripping hers, his other arm thrust across her breast, was like a mockery of the embraces she'd had from Rochambeau. How could she stop thinking of him, while every word and gesture of Aubrey's reminded her?

Finally, Aubrey was satisfied that no more guards would come for a while, and they made it to the postern gate without incident. He had the key that would unlock the little door, and the bundle he'd given her contained a feather and a bottle of oil. With these he oiled the wards and the hinges so that no grating sound should alert the people within the castle. To keep her mind from her grief, Johanna forced herself to think how impressively efficient Aubrey had been for once. How had he managed to procure a disguise for her, the key to the postern, a quill and a pot of oil to treat the rusty lock, all in the short time since Rochambeau's—

She caught her breath on a sharp indrawn sigh. Since sunset; that was a better way to put it. Blessed Virgin, would she ever be able to look at another sunset? Perhaps she wouldn't have to. Aubrey was taking an inordinately long time with the lock. Perhaps the next, and the last, light that she saw would be the glow of the flames about the stake.

Finally, the door swung open, and they were free of Malvern. Johanna choked back a sob. She might never see it again, this place that had become home to her, the one of all his castles and manors that Rochambeau loved best.

She kept turning back to look at the pile of golden stone, while Aubrey hurried her through the sleeping village. When the forest rose up, enshrouding them in the tall trees that grew right up to the edge of the village, she felt as though her last link with Rochambeau had been broken. A merciful numbness sustained her through the next tiring stage of the journey, through a forest choked with underbrush where wild things snorted sleepily at their passage and moonlight turned a tangle of branches into a menacing skeletal figure. Here she had to be grateful for Aubrey's help and guidance; without him, she would surely never have found the old witch's hut. It must have been built in the deepest part of the forest, because thorny vines and small trees grew up unchecked, making an impenetrable tangle.

When they finally reached the hut, standing silent and blank in a small clearing with trees crowding close around two sides and arching over the roof, Johanna felt a moment's revulsion. The thing seemed solid enough, with good logs and earth-plastered walls, but it was a crazy leaning shape with a low roof that slanted nearly to the ground on one side, one nearly triangular window, and a door covered with the hides of small creatures, stretched out and nailed onto the wood like a grisly verderer's display. Except that a verderer would take foxes and other predators that spoiled the game, not the small harmless hares and mice and forest birds that decorated this door.

As they came closer, a smell of rotten meat came to Johanna's nostrils, and she realized with horror that it wasn't just skins that Bruma had used to decorate her door. There were entire small corpses there, split and gibbeted with their paws nailed to the wood, and some of them had not been dead very long at all.

"I can't go in there," she gasped, backing away.

"Don't be foolish, Johanna." Aubrey's tone had changed subtly, as though he had gained strength and certainty from the hour they'd spent in the forest. He was no longer the kindly, bumbling half-brother who pleaded with her to do what was necessary; he spoke as a master. Now he wrenched the door open and pushed her inside the dark, malodorous hut before she could object again. "You're tired," he told her. "Rest. There's clean straw in the corner. I'll be back, when I can, with food and wine."

He blocked the door. She could not get out without fighting him, and to what purpose? This must be the only refuge he knew of, else he'd not have brought her here. He would think her a hysterical woman, not worth listening to, if she protested again. But there was one thing Johanna felt she must know before she could sleep in this place.

"What did Bruma die of?"

Aubrey chuckled. "Nothing contagious. She stumbled and broke her neck while she was out gathering herbs. Don't worry, Johanna, this place is cleaner than many a villein's hut, and sturdier built."

That was another thing. Who had built this strong though crazily designed hut? Not the old woman Johanna had met. Oh, yes. She had said something about her son. "There was a boy—a half-wit?"

"He won't trouble you. I've offered him a place in our stables. It's warmer and drier than he's used to, and the table scraps are better than his mother's cooking. He won't be back."

Johanna wished she could feel as certain as Aubrey sounded. But before she could question him further, he had swung the door shut again, leaving her in blackness. She groped her way to the pile of straw in the corner, fearing every moment to touch some other unspeakable remnants of the witch's activities.

The straw was warm and soft and smelled fresh compared to the musty interior of the hut. There were not even too many fleas. Johanna knew she was too worried and unhappy to sleep, but she was grateful for this comfortable place to rest while she waited for Aubrey to come back. She burrowed into the straw, using it to cover herself so that she need not keep Bruma's cloak wrapped around her.

The next thing she knew, it was morning, and her limbs were stiff and cramped from sleeping curled on the hard floor all night. There was a bad taste in her mouth, and her head ached, but at least she felt like herself again, wide awake and able to think. She must have really needed the sleep.

Sitting up and brushing the straw out of her hair, Johanna took stock of her surroundings. The light that came in through the one triangular window showed her a cleaner, emptier place than she'd believed the cottage to be last night. Indeed, it looked as if somebody had gone through it, throwing out most of the witch's personal possessions and leaving only a three-legged stool and a ragged blanket. Aubrey must have cleaned it up for her. How thoughtful of him! But when had he had the time to make all these arrangements? Surely not in the brief interval since sunset and the darkness when he'd come for her—

Sunset. Johanna's teeth clamped down hard on her lower lip. For a few moments she'd actually managed to forget why she was there: Rochambeau dead, herself in danger of being burned as a witch and a poisoner and the cause of his death. She could hardly believe it now. Aubrey's brief whispered communications last night, their stumbling journey through the woods—surely all this was the stuff of nightmare!

But the barren hut where she sat was real, the hard-packed earth beneath her and the rustling straw as real as the scratches from thorns and whipping branches marking her face and arms. So all the rest must be real too, and she would never see Rochambeau again. Their happiness had ended before it had fairly begun, and it was all her fault for driving him away. If she hadn't been so hateful to him after their marriage, he would never have left her. Why hadn't she forgiven him at once for his threats against her father? Why hadn't she seen that he had only threatened her because he wanted her so much? Why hadn't she had the good sense to take what happiness she could in their marriage? Now it was too late, irrevocably too late, and she wanted to throw herself facedown in the straw and weep her heart out.

But if she once gave way to her grief, she would have no strength left to face the demands of the new day. Soon Aubrey would be back with news and food. Johanna found, to her surprise, that her body was making its usual demands, just as though this were a day like any other. They would have to plan for her escape then; she could hardly stay in this hut forever. And it would be a poor return for Aubrey's kindness to saddle him with a soft, weeping, hysterical widow who was as incapable of planning as a child.

She owed Rochambeau something, too: to discover who his murderer really was. Who would have wanted to kill him, and why? Some old enemy, some grudge she knew nothing of? Perhaps Aubrey, when he came, could tell her to which servant he'd entrusted the tray of food; that might give her a clue. Had there been anybody in the chamber when she had come back from Rochambeau's strongroom, or—

It was no use; the memories were too vivid. She couldn't go on without breaking down. Later, perhaps, when the pain of losing Rochambeau wasn't so intense, she would be able to think it all out and figure out just what had happened. For now, Johanna found that she could only stay calm if she concentrated on very simple, mundane things, like how to comb the snarls out of her hair with her fingers and whether there was any water in the hut for her to wash with.

Her explorations revealed no water, but there was an earthenware jug with a cracked lip in one corner. There must be a stream or a well nearby, and it was early enough yet that there'd be no one about—not that there ever would be anyone in this deep, isolated center of the forest. Aubrey had warned her to stay inside until he returned, but presumably he hadn't thought of the problems this entailed. Men really were not very good at envisioning the practical details of a situation. Johanna picked up the jug and pushed with the tips of her fingers at the door of the hut, reluctant to touch it any harder while she remembered the tiny corpses festooning the outside.

It was stuck. She would have to give it a good push, after all.

The full strength of her arm didn't budge the door. Johanna braced her feet on the floor and set her shoulder to the boards. This time the door shifted a bare quarter of an inch, and there was a dull clanking sound when it stopped.

She had to repeat the experiment several times before she

was convinced of what had happened. "God's bones," Johanna swore, resting and wiping her forehead with the back of one grimy hand. "He's put a bar across the door!"

If that wasn't just like stupid Aubrey! So convinced that she was a foolish creature who had to be locked in for her own safety that he forgot entirely about certain small matters like providing water! Johanna could almost have laughed if it hadn't been so irritating. Well, she would just have to get out some other way. The half-wit son of the witch could hardly have built a hut much stronger than the villeins' cottages, and some of those were so shoddily put together that you could tear the daub-and-wattle walls down with your bare hands.

This one wasn't. It was sturdily constructed of good, stout logs pegged together from the outside. It occurred to Johanna, somewhat tardily, that while Rochambeau's villeins obeyed the laws about gathering only dead wood from the forest, the witch and her son had felt no compunction about chopping down whole trees to make themselves a nice solid dwelling. The one window was quite effectively barred by a three-pronged branch too thick for Johanna to break. She considered breaking a shard from the earthenware jug with which to saw through the branch, but that did seem excessive. After all, she might have to hide there for several days, and that jug was the only utensil in the hut fit to carry water. She would just have to speak to Aubrey about this nonsense when he returned. Fuming, angrily conscious of her sweaty, grimy condition, Johanna pushed all the straw together in one corner and sat down to await Aubrey's arrival.

Waiting gave her too much time to think, and none of her thoughts led anywhere pleasant. By midday she was growing seriously worried. What could be delaying Aubrey? She jumped up in relief when at last she heard the crackle of leaves and twigs under someone's feet outside. But the heavy, shuffling step did not sound like Aubrey's. Johanna peered cautiously through the window and shrank back against the wall at the sight of a shambling heavyset boy with one eye closed in a permanent grimace. He was carrying a jug in one hand, and he was headed straight for the window. Before she could move out of sight, he gave her a cheerful, wide-mouthed grin that slightly reassured her. This was no enemy, apparently.

He set the jug down on the outer windowsill and greeted Johanna with a series of unintelligible gurgles. This must be the witch's son, the one Aubrey had so kindly taken in when his mother had died. Was he half-witted or only mute?

"Let me out of here," Johanna tried. She stuck one hand through the narrow space left by the forked stick and pointed toward the door. "The bar—can you lift the bar?"

The boy grinned and gurgled some more but made no move toward the door. He tried to shove the jug through the same narrow space in the window. His face puckered up in frustration when it refused to fit through the opening.

"Break the stick," Johanna suggested, but the boy didn't seem to hear her. Deaf as well as mute, she concluded. She tried by signs to get her message across, but he was signing vigorously at the same time, and nothing resulted but confusion. Finally, Johanna understood what he wanted of her. She picked up the earthenware vessel that had been left in the hut and held it up to the window opening. The boy grinned and stuck the narrow neck of the jug through, so that he could pour water into Johanna's vessel.

"Well, you're not half-witted, anyway," Johanna muttered. But apparently he had been ordered not to let her out. What was this mummery of Aubrey's? Had he even considered what must be her fate if he were unable to get back to the cottage for several days? Rage consumed her, flaring white-hot when the boy poured out the last of the water and shambled away as if he had no more concern for her.

"Hey, come back! Let me out!" Johanna gripped the forked stick that barred the window and shouted in vain at the boy's retreating back. He disappeared into the forest without another look.

The brief interval of human contact left Johanna feeling more lonely than before. She was hungry, too. She drank down half the water and wondered hopefully if the boy would return with food. Even scraps from the kitchens would be better than nothing. Her stomach growled as she recalled the slabs of trencher bread soaked with gravy from the meal and the baskets of meat scraps and other leftovers that were distributed to any beggars who came to Malvern after a meal. Once she'd felt embarrassed to hand out table leavings; now the same food would have been a feast to her.

Thinking about food had one advantage at least: it kept her mind off worse things. Composing herself again on the straw, Johanna used the last of the water to wash her face and hands and then set about making up a feast-day menu, from roast peacock stuffed with grapes and breadcrumbs to a spice plate loaded with sugar plums and honey-glazed cinnamon tarts. Rochambeau would want too much ginger in the cinnamon tarts, of course . . .

She was not quite crying when she heard Aubrey's light step outside. There was a clanking sound as he lifted the bar that had held the door shut. She was on her feet and facing him when he entered the hut.

"What happened? What took you so long? God's bones, Aubrey, what possessed you to lock me in like this?"

"I wanted to keep you safe," Aubrey answered unapologetically. He set a bundle down on the floor and took Johanna in his arms, running his hands up and down her long, slender arms and holding her closer to him than she liked. "Don't scold, Johanna, it mars your beauty. I'm always going to keep you safe from now on. Safe and close to me."

His smile of pure satisfaction frightened her; it seemed so out of place. She withdrew from his embrace as quickly as she might without seeming rude. "I'm sure you meant well, Aubrey, but it really wasn't a good idea. What if you had been unable to come back and let me out?" She tried to speak softly, not to annoy him; the very effort irritated her nerves almost beyond bearing. How things had changed in the last few days! Suddenly she was pleading with Aubrey for the most basic rights. First she'd had to beg him to let her see Rochambeau; now she was dependent on him for food and drink and, more, for her very freedom.

And he had never let her see Rochambeau. A premonitory chill made Johanna shiver. Aubrey seemed too happy, too much at peace, for a man whose beloved half-brother had just died and who was risking his own life by rescuing his sister-in-law. He was kneeling on the ground now, unpacking his bundle and whistling a gay tune between his teeth.

"I've brought you half a roast capon," he announced, "fresh bread, and some of the good Gascony wine. No cups, unfortunately, or dishes. We'll have to eat with our fingers and share the bottle. I shan't mind if you don't. I've shared with less beautiful ladies in my time."

"I'm not hungry," Johanna lied. How could Aubrey expect her to calmly sit down and start eating as if nothing were wrong, without a word of explanation? "And Aubrey, we've got to get some things settled. I know you're only trying to protect me, but I really can't stay locked in this hut any longer. If you won't guide me out tonight, I'll set off on my own." Could she walk all the way to Pomeray without being recognized? Johanna didn't know, but anything would be better than the torturous inaction of this day. But her chances of reaching Pomeray would be better if Aubrey could be persuaded to get her a horse.

"You're not going anywhere," said Aubrey calmly. He spread out a linen napkin with a flourish and set the food out on it with as much delicacy as if he were serving in the king's hall.

"I'll wait till tomorrow," Johanna bargained, "but only if you promise to bring me a horse."

Aubrey shook his head and concentrated on carving up the roast capon. "No, it's too dangerous. I prefer to have you here where I can watch over you."

"God's body and bones!" Had he gone mad? Johanna stared with disbelief at the golden back of his head, bent over the napkin where he was somewhat messily dismembering the fowl. "Aubrey, I do appreciate what you've done for me, but it's my life, and it's for me to say what risks I will take."

"Not anymore." Aubrey looked up with a peaceful smile. "Won't you sit down and have a bite to eat, Johanna? You must be famished by now. I waited until now," he explained with simple pride, "to make sure you'd be hungry enough to take food from my hand." He waved a chicken wing in the air and beckoned to her.

"From your—Aubrey, are you feeling quite well?" Perhaps he was feverish. Perhaps he too had been poisoned, and this was the first sign.

"It works with falcons," Aubrey pointed out. "First you catch them, then you tame them. I've caught you now, Johanna, and within the week you'll be coming quite tamely to my hand. So forget all this talk about going anywhere."

He bit into an enormous piece of crusty new bread and

washed it down with a gulp of wine. "You are simple, Johanna. Did you really think I meant to help you flee the country? Right here is where I want you. It's convenient to the castle, it's private enough for our pleasures, and nobody ever comes this deep into the forest. The villagers think the witch is still living here, and huntsmen won't fight their way through the thickets. It's the perfect place to keep you!"

His casual mention of pleasures made Johanna feel sick at her stomach. Still, she couldn't believe that Aubrey meant what he seemed to be saying. "Aubrey, you're not keeping me anywhere! What made you think I would consent to stay with you?"

"I don't recall asking for your consent." Aubrey's strong white teeth bit cleanly through a slice of roast capon, and Johanna felt the familiar nausea and dizziness attacking her again. Perhaps she should sit down and eat something—no, that would be seeming to accept Aubrey's mad plans, whatever they were. She sidled toward the door, hoping to get past him while he was greedily occupied with the food, but one of his hands shot out and grabbed her ankle when she was closest to him. A quick yank brought her down with a thump on the dirt floor. "Sit quietly," he advised her. "You can't get past me, and I don't want to have to hurt you." Then, as though nothing at all had happened, he went on munching at the chicken and bread.

"You've always thought I was simple, Johanna. Maybe you're the stupid one. You and Rochambeau and all the others."

"What others?"

Aubrey glowered over his mouthful of chicken leg.

"All of you who thought I didn't mind growing up in little brother Nicolas's shadow. Starting with our father, who so generously recognized me as his bastard son and had me brought up with Nicolas and taught to aspire to a life he never meant to give me. The rules were set from the beginning. He was the heir; I had no place save what he gave me out of charity. We were both sent to the monastery for schooling. The monks praised his brains and flattered him; they never gave me aught but the rough side of their tongues. They knew which of us would grow up to inherit the honor of Rochambeau, which of us would be able to endow the monastery with rich lands. When we came home, girls couldn't resist him, but they never saw me. He was younger, handsomer, stronger, better at everything. He was knighted when he reached twenty-one. I was twenty-three, and the old man thought I should be pleased to be his squire.

"I was the older; I should have been the heir. He should have married my mother, but a Rochambeau was too proud to marry a merchant's daughter. He thought he'd done enough when he recognized me and had me brought up with Nicolas. All my life I've watched Nicolas taking what should have been mine—and taking it casually, as though he didn't really care one way or another. I had to practice for hours in the tiltyard, and even then I couldn't equal what he did without trying. When I courted girls, they laughed at me, but he didn't have to court them. If it weren't for dear brother Nicolas, my life would have been entirely different. The old man would have had me legitimized. I'd have been the heir. I'd have been knighted. I'd have led men into battle. I'd have been the one the girls flocked around. And all these years, knowing that, I've smiled and scraped and been ever so grateful to dear brother Nicolas for giving me a place at his table—and you all believed it! I'm not simple, Johanna dear. You are."

"He gave you more than a place at his table. He gave you a manor of your own; he trusted all the accounts of the estates in your hands."

Aubrey laughed. "Yes. Very generous—one small manor out of his twenty!"

He wiped his mouth with the back of his hand, took a long drink of wine, and went on talking. His pale eyes glittered at Johanna, but she felt as if he didn't quite see her, and that was more frightening than anything else. Where was Aubrey? The bumbling, kindly elder brother she'd believed in for so long had disappeared. Now she looked into this man's eyes, and there seemed to be no person at all behind their pale gleam.

"Managing the estates served me well enough while Nicolas was off fighting Prince Edward's petty wars."

"Yes," Johanna said slowly. "I begin to see why your manor was so rich and well kept, while Rochambeau's own

346

estates hardly brought in enough rents to keep them going. You stole from him to enrich your own lands, didn't you?''

''And you thought the accounts were muddled because I was too stupid to add and subtract,'' Aubrey acknowledged. ''It wasn't a bad life for a while. I was in charge of the estates, people turned to me for everything, and I kept Nicolas supplied with just enough money to keep him happy away from the land. But it was never really mine—never mine, as it should have been! And then he came home, and I thought it was all over.''

He beamed and patted Johanna's leg. Her flesh cringed from his touch, and she felt grateful that his mind wasn't really on her.

''I've you to thank that he didn't find me out immediately, Johanna dear. He came home with his head stuffed full of good resolutions about settling down and learning estate management and taking care of his lands. But the first thing he did was go on a tour of the outlying manors, and the first thing he saw on that tour was you!'' Aubrey gave a reminiscent chuckle. ''That was the first time in my life I'd ever seen Nicolas vulnerable, doubting, unsure of himself. He wanted you so badly, you see, and with girls always having fallen into his lap like ripe fruit before, he'd no idea how to court you.''

Johanna sighed for what was now lost irrevocably. Aubrey's words cast a whole new light on what she'd thought of as Rochambeau's high-handed behavior. If only he'd told her this four years ago! Now it was too late. She was Aubrey's prisoner, and Rochambeau—

But that didn't bear thinking of. She was still alive, and she had to find some way of getting away from Aubrey. Johanna swallowed the lump in her throat and encouraged Aubrey to go on with his story.

''Well, I have to confess that I didn't, at first, see the possibilities of the match. I just wanted to see Rochambeau, for once, lose something he wanted as badly as I'd always wanted his place in the sun. And after managing the estates all these years, I knew a lot of dirty little secrets, including your daddy's dealings with the Welsh. So when Rochambeau sent me to Hugh to arrange the marriage, I threw in the blackmail threat on my own account—saying it came from Rochambeau, naturally. I thought that if Hugh had any balls at all, he'd tell us to take it to court, or maybe he'd even kill Nicolas. Instead, the poor, crawling, cowardly bastard meekly handed you over. I could have kicked myself! Mind you," Aubrey said reflectively, taking some more wine, "I can understand him better now. He probably would have paid good money to be rid of you, you nosy, contumacious bitch. Well, you'll learn better manners now. I'll have plenty of time to teach you."

Johanna hardly heard his threats, so occupied was she with the revelations he had just made. "You were the one who threatened my father with a traitor's death! All these years I've blamed Rochambeau. All these years you let me blame him. And he never even knew why I hated him so!"

Aubrey grinned mirthlessly. "Yes, it was an amusing situation, wasn't it?"

"I could kill you for it."

"I'll take good care you don't get the chance." Aubrey slid his hand up and down Johanna's leg. She gritted her teeth and tried to think of something else. "Not tame yet," he commented, feeling the tension of her muscles. "Never mind, I've plenty of time to school you. No one will ever come to let you out, Johanna. You'd best make up your mind to like my face a little better—it's the only one you'll ever see. I wonder how long it will take to make you love me?"

"Don't hold your breath."

"No? Well, first we'll teach obedience. Love can come after, as it does in most marriages." Aubrey settled himself comfortably against the wall and went on with his reminiscences.

"After the wedding, it dawned on me that I'd still gotten what I wanted. Rochambeau might have married you, but he didn't have you, not in any way that mattered. And it was driving him mad!"

"And you did what you could to keep us at odds with each other." Johanna remembered how many sympathetic little talks Aubrey had had with her in those difficult weeks, how often he'd seemed to excuse Rochambeau while only inflaming her hatred of him. At the time, she'd thought him well-meaning but clumsy; now she saw the cunning, vicious mind behind those casual comments, and she felt coldly afraid.

How could she outwit Aubrey and escape from him? He'd been outwitting her and everybody else for years!

Aubrey's reminiscent grin chilled her blood. "It wasn't hard, though, was it? Not with a spitfire like you! You were easy, the two of you, and as long as Rochambeau's mind was on you, he wasn't examining his accounts. I knew it couldn't last, though. He *would* keep taking you to his bed. And once he got you pregnant, there'd be an heir to supplant me. I was at my wit's end what to do, when he went charging off on the crusade. I never dared hope you'd annoy him that much." He eyed Johanna with mild curiosity. "Just how did you do it, anyway?"

Johanna pressed her lips tight and looked away. What on earth could make Aubrey think she'd give him the satisfaction of recounting the details of her quarrels with Rochambeau?

"Don't want to be friendly, eh? Never mind. We'll have plenty of time to talk over the years."

The vista of long years as Aubrey's prisoner made Johanna feel utterly desolate. But it couldn't come to that. Surely it couldn't! Isolated as this hut was, sooner or later somebody would pass by, or she'd find a way to free herself.

But how much later? And what would she be like by then? Even one night in Aubrey's power was too much to contemplate. By the time she freed herself, she might be mad in truth, a fitting replacement for the witch who'd lived here.

"Bruma didn't stumble, did she?" she interrupted Aubrey's self-satisfied discourse. "You killed her because you wanted the use of this hut for yourself. How long were you planning this?"

"Only since you let me find out you were breeding. I couldn't risk you giving Rochambeau an heir, Johanna. If he died without children, I could have taken over the estates, bastard or no. Mind you, Johanna, I didn't want to do it. It would have been such a damned waste to let you die without ever making love to you. I was almost relieved when you came back from your ride unharmed."

"You cut through the saddle girth!"

Aubrey nodded. "Not cut. Tore. It would have looked like an accident, Johanna. And if you'd taken the witch's herbs, she would have been blamed for your death. But I realized I would have to twist her scrawny neck to make sure she didn't tell who had paid her to mix that poison. And once she was dead, it occurred to me that this cottage would be a much better solution to the problem. I'm glad you didn't take the poison, Johanna. I mean that sincerely."

"I can't tell you how flattered I am."

Aubrey chuckled and waggled one big finger at her. "Sarcasm, Johanna? You'll have to curb that wicked tongue of yours. I like my women quiet and obedient. Don't worry, though, you'll have plenty of time to learn my little ways."

His soft, plump hand caressed her hair and ran down her spine. Johanna felt a shiver of revulsion at the confident touch, but she was afraid to slap him away. Perhaps she could keep him talking for a while, until—until what? No matter. Talking was better than having him fondle her like this. She moved sideways against the wall, away from Aubrey's hands, and asked another question at the same time.

"I see why you had to get me away. But why did you have to kill—" Her throat closed over Rochambeau's name, and she swallowed a sob.

"Nicolas? He signed his own death warrant when he deciphered your accounts. He would have seen the record of the money you raised for his ransom. And he's not as stupid as you. He would have asked me all sorts of embarrassing questions, like exactly which of my men did I send with the ransom money and how could they have been so careless as to be waylaid and robbed. Then he might have started looking at the rest of the estate records, from before you took over, and he would have figured out how much money I'd been channeling into my own manor from his. I had to get rid of both of you before he understood the implications. Fortunately, you made it easy for me, letting me bring up the food for you both. I knew he'd eat the honey cakes; I knew you didn't like sweets. Wasn't it elegant? He dies; you're suspected of having poisoned him. I offer to save you and spirit you away to the forest. You and your brat are out of the way as heirs to Malvern, and I get the pleasure of you for as long as I want to keep you. That's what I call a truly elegant solution." He smiled as if expecting Johanna to share his satisfaction. "And now, Johanna, I've wasted more than enough time in explanations. It's time for you to start earning your keep—on your back, where a woman belongs."

"You can rot in hell first! Do you really think I'd couple with the man who killed my husband?"

Aubrey sighed. "I don't like fighting for it, so you'd best learn to receive me sweetly whenever I come to this hut. If you don't, you'll have no food until you cooperate. I don't think it will take long to tame you to my hand, my little falcon."

"Some things make starvation seem a pleasant fate." Johanna tried to speak firmly, to keep the fear that chilled her brain from freezing her entirely. "You'll never have me, Aubrey, and you can't keep me prisoner for long. It won't work. Somebody will see you coming here, or somebody will pass by the hut. You'll be better off if you let me go now, and we'll forget this conversation ever took place. I promise to leave, not to accuse you."

She was beginning to plead with him; she couldn't help it. The worst thing was that he didn't even seem to hear her. That blank, glazed look was back in his eyes, and she sensed that she could not reach behind the empty blue stare.

"It's too late to bargain, Johanna," he said softly. "You don't have any choices left. And I've a mind to see what it was that kept Rochambeau in such a tizzy over you all these years. What do you have that's so much better than what any other woman keeps under her skirts?"

He rose to his knees and reached toward her. Johanna tried to scramble away from him, but her legs were numb from crouching so long against the wall. Prickling with pins and needles, the muscles wouldn't obey her commands, and she went down on her knees in the straw as he grabbed at her. She felt a moment of sick disgust at the touch of his hot, dry hands on her legs. He crouched over her, and she pushed him away with weak, ineffectual hands.

"Aubrey, no!" she panted, fighting the nausea that threatened to overcome her. "Think! I'm your brother's wife. 'Tis incest, against the ban of the church!"

Aubrey casually consigned the church and its bans to the lower depths of perdition.

"That's where *you* will go, if you do this thing!"

"You talk too much." One broad hand covered Johanna's mouth. She thrashed in panic as Aubrey lowered his weight onto her; she kicked out wildly and was rewarded by a grunt of pain from him. He raised himself, clutching at his groin. Johanna brought up her knee and drove it with all her strength into the tender area his hands cupped protectively. Aubrey screamed, and one hand lashed out, catching her across the face and knocking her back into the straw as she struggled to stand up.

Her whole head throbbed from the blow, and for a moment her vision blurred. She waited in sick anticipation, knowing herself to be at the end of her resources. But Aubrey painfully raised himself, bent almost double with both hands cupping his groin, and limped toward the door.

"You have a way—of diminishing—a man's ardor," he told Johanna with a sickly smile. "But I'll be back. And if need be, I'll have the witch's idiot son hold you down while I finish the job."

Johanna managed to get to her hands and knees in the straw. Her head was swimming, her cheek felt swollen to twice its natural size, and her jaw ached from the blow. She prayed that Aubrey would indeed leave, knowing she was powerless to keep on fighting him.

He had one hand on the door when the sound of a hunting horn sliced through the air, floating through the tangled thickets and filling the hut with its golden echoes. Johanna started up, feeling new strength with the sound she'd thought never to hear again. No one but Rochambeau had ever used that horn with its pure tone and its compelling echo. It was one of the treasures of the house; no one would dare; no one else could have brought that clean, strong note to it.

"He's alive!" she cried out exultantly. "You lied about that too!" She was at the window, face pressed to the forked stick and her lungs filling with the fresh clean air, before she remembered that she was exhausted and sick and barely able to stand up. At the end of her resources? Nonsense! Not while Rochambeau still lived and was so very close to her.

In the next moment, she thought of a dozen reasons why somebody else could have taken the horn on the day after Rochambeau's death. But they didn't matter. The look on Aubrey's face told her that her inspired guess had been correct.

"If he's not dead now, he soon will be!"

"I doubt that." Holding on to the forked stick that barred

the window, Johanna grinned through her bruised lip at Aubrey. "You couldn't kill him by stealth. You'll hardly be able to do it face to face. He's alive, Aubrey, and we'll cut through this web of lies you've woven about us. You've lost!"

Pressing her face to the window again, she took a deep breath to call to Rochambeau. Aubrey grabbed her by the neck and dragged her away from the window, and her cry for help turned into a strangled scream, cut off almost as soon as it had begun.

"I've not—lost—yet," Aubrey panted, wrestling her down onto the straw. He tore off her coif with one hand and stuffed it into her mouth, tying it in place with his girdle. Strips torn from her own gown bound her wrists and ankles while she thrashed helplessly under his weight. A lucky kick had freed her before, but this time Aubrey wasn't distracted by lust. He coolly and competently used the weight of his body to pin her down while he tied her quite thoroughly.

"There," Aubrey said with satisfaction, surveying her bound and helpless body. "That should hold you until I get back. It's true that Rochambeau has chanced to come nearer this cottage than I thought he would. I think I'd better go out and tell him that I've searched all this end of the wood to no avail. Oh, don't look such daggers at me, Johanna. He'll believe me, you know. Why wouldn't he believe dear, old, loyal, bumbling Aubrey? Especially when I show him the evidence that you've escaped to Wales."

Johanna felt sick again. Evidence? Of course, while Aubrey was laying his plans to entrap her in the witch's hut, he must also have been making up the story that she had run for the Welsh border. She wondered dully, without really caring, what evidence Aubrey would have planted to persuade Rochambeau to call off the hunt.

And what good would it do him, since Rochambeau lived? She asked the question with her eyes, and Aubrey read her mind.

"He won't live long," he told her. "Maybe I lied about his death, but I heard what Gilbert said about the effects of wolfsbane—you didn't. The physician Gilbert worked for said that a patient's only chance of life was to lie absolutely still until the effects of the poison had dissipated. Instead, the fool has dragged himself from a sickbed to search for you. How long do you think sheer will can keep him going? Especially since I haven't used up my stock of wolfsbane yet. By the end of the day, he'll be dead, mad, or paralyzed. And nobody will look for a second poisoning, since Gilbert so obligingly predicted those effects from the first attack. Indeed, I may not even have to use my reserve supply. We'll see how it goes. The effort of searching for you may be enough to kill him without my help. You still have a chance to cause your husband's death, Johanna. Isn't that interesting? You lie there and think about it, and I'll be back to let you know how it all came out. I'll wager you will be in a more cooperative mood by then.''

Johanna closed her eyes and slumped back against the straw. Her body proclaimed her defeat and exhaustion. She must seem utterly negligible to Aubrey now, hardly worth the trouble of tormenting, a defeated woman who could well be left alone until he had leisure to deal with her.

Chapter Twenty-five

A DOZEN MEN were gathered in a glade not far from the witch's hut, resting their horses and casting worried glances at Rochambeau. The marks of the previous day and night were plain on his face; for the first time in any man's memory, the lord of Rochambeau looked like a mortal man. Sheer force of will had roused him from his sickbed with the news that morning of Johanna's disappearance. His old imperious temper had forced servants to bring him his customary rich clothes and his men to mount and follow him on the hunt. But the effort it had cost him showed in his white face, in the taut lines of neck and shoulders. He was fighting sickness and exhaustion and the aftereffects of poison with nothing but his will. His men were beginning to wonder how long that would hold him erect.

Most of the men were from his personal guard, the ones who'd followed him to the East and back again by way of a French prison. They would have followed him through hell if he had suggested the detour. But Aubrey also spied Gilbert de Bellay, insecurely mounted on a borrowed horse that pranced with too much energy for the slight minstrel to control. He smiled to himself. Gilbert looked too worried about his horse to be paying much heed to Rochambeau's symptoms. If it were necessary to slip the lord of Rochambeau another dose of wolfsbane, Gilbert would think that the renewed symptoms were caused, as he'd predicted, by violent exercise.

And it might not be necessary. The harsh, unfiltered light of day showed Aubrey that his golden younger brother had aged overnight. The hands that gripped his reins were too tight, as though they would shake if he let himself relax. His lips were tense with the effort of controlling excruciating pain. He looked desperately tired and desperately worried. Aubrey breathed a sigh of relief. He might have failed in his first object, that of keeping Rochambeau on a sickbed until repeated doses of poison overcame even his strong frame, but it wouldn't be hard to persuade this sick man to return to the castle and let big brother Aubrey manage the search.

"Nicolas, what are you doing out of bed?" It was not hard to assume an appearance of concern as he strode forward to greet his brother. Rochambeau's insistence on hunting Johanna down himself might fit in very well with Aubrey's plans for his untimely death, but his presence in this glade so near the hut could spell disaster. "Did Gilbert not warn you not to move, lest the poison bring on paralysis or worse?"

Rochambeau looked down at Aubrey, lips compressed over his pain. "Johanna's gone."

"She's not worth chasing after. If the witch has fled into Wales, to her mother's people, good riddance to her. In any case, you'll hardly find her here, so close to the castle, after so many hours have passed."

"You knew she'd gone, then? And did not tell me?"

"I feared this very thing." Aubrey covered his slip quickly. "That your desire to see justice done would rouse you from your sickbed to chase after the slut."

"You are speaking," Rochambeau reminded him, "of my lady wife." The black horse on which he sat raised its head and nickered softly, great hooves shuffling near Aubrey's feet as if the animal sensed its master's unease and anger.

"Lady murderer, you mean!" Aubrey stepped back from the great horse but refused to retract his accusation. "Lady poisoner, lady witch. You're well rid of her, Nicolas. Let her escape into Wales. We can go on very well together as we've always done. And now, won't you return to Malvern? I will see to all that's needful."

"I'm sure you will." Rochambeau bared his teeth in a grin

that reminded Aubrey of a wolf he'd once seen caught in a poacher's trap, his lips drawn taut with teeth gleaming menace and defiance. The beast had disappeared that night, gnawing its own leg off to get free. The thought of that ferocity and determination had troubled Aubrey at night for many a month. Now he found himself unable to meet his younger brother's piercing blue eyes, just as long ago he'd dropped his eyes before the trapped wolf's burning yellow gaze.

"But perhaps," Rochambeau went on, speaking so softly that the men waiting a few yards away could not have heard him, "your idea of what's needful might not square with mine, dear brother. I think it was not chance that brought you to this part of the forest."

"What do you mean?" Aubrey heard himself stammering slightly and hated himself for once again being intimidated by his golden younger brother, the legitimate son, the favorite one. Rochambeau was a dying man, he told himself; condemned, if not by the poison he'd already taken, then by the further dose which Aubrey still held in reserve. He put one hand to his tunic to feel the reassuring small bulge of the witch's leather bag of herbs against his chest. Then he forgot bag, herbs, and all to stare in open-mouthed astonishment as Rochambeau vaulted from his horse as lightly as he'd ever done in the tiltyard, tossing his reins to one of the men-at-arms behind them.

"The reports of my illness were—somewhat exaggerated," Rochambeau told Aubrey, moving toward him with his old catlike grace. "It's true that Gilbert feared lest movement bring on a recurrence of the poison's effect, but even when he was warning me of it, I was not as weak as you believed. Though I was still too weak to protect what is my own as I should have liked. That, Aubrey, is why I ordered Johanna locked up. Not because I believed your foul stories for a moment, but because I wanted her where she would be safe from you until I was strong enough to see to you."

"Brother, if I accused Johanna, 'twas only because I felt it my duty to communicate my suspicions," Aubrey stammered. He backed away from his advancing brother, feeling more intimidated now than when the black gelding had almost trampled him.

"Indeed." Rochambeau's momentary baring of teeth could hardly have been called a smile. "Since my return home, I've suspected you of making mischief against me, Aubrey, but I was reluctant to move against you until the case was proven. What I found in the accounts might have pointed directly to you, had I had the chance to ask Johanna about it, but the poisoning came too quickly. I was even more reluctant to think you guilty then. There used to be some fondness between us, Aubrey, or so I thought. You're my only brother."

"Half-brother," Aubrey corrected. "The bastard who should be grateful to be recognized as one of the family." He felt breathless and light-headed, half convinced the game was up. It was hardly worthwhile to maintain the pose of smiling, brotherly amity that he'd kept up all those years until it corroded his vitals. After all, he still had one move to make on the board. His knowledge of Johanna's whereabouts might not save his position at Malvern, but it should serve to buy him a horse and gold and a chance to make a fresh start elsewhere—that is, if he could get away before Rochambeau found out how he'd use her. And with Johanna still a pawn in his possession, why bother anymore with the old pretense? "If you think that watching you enjoy what should have been mine was calculated to increase my brotherly love, Nicolas, you erred sadly."

"So it seems." Rochambeau's tone was mild enough to give Aubrey new confidence. He raised his eyes to Rochambeau's face and as quickly dropped his gaze. The blue fire in those eyes burned through him, exposing all his paltry shifts and contrivances for the maneuverings of a weak, inferior man. He knew what a poor cheat he must seem to Rochambeau, and he hated his brother worse for making him know it.

"You don't bother to deny anymore?"

"What would be the use?"

"Not much," Rochambeau agreed. "You overplayed your hand when you stole Johanna out of her chamber. I've had a few words with Fulke. He should never have believed you when you told him the change of orders came from me. In the old keep cells she'd have been safe from you."

For the first time, Aubrey noticed that Rochambeau's squire was not among the searchers gathered in the glade.

"It was clever of you to have her put in the bedchamber, Aubrey, with the secret door known of only by us two. But didn't you think it was also risky? I never believed Johanna would run away; that, like cheating, is not in her nature. And there was only one other person who could have taken her that route. I had no more doubts when I found that secret door open, Aubrey. And, as you see, the rest of your plan didn't work. I followed your trail, Aubrey, not the false one you laid to make it seem as though Johanna had gone into Wales."

He gestured to the men who had dismounted and clustered behind him. "Take him."

Aubrey drew his belt knife before the words were finished and pointed it at his own throat. "I can die before they touch me." As he spoke, he backed slowly toward the shelter of the trees. Once among those entangled branches, swords would be useless against him. "And then you'll never find your precious Johanna!"

Rochambeau raised his hand, and the men-at-arms stopped their slow advance toward Aubrey. "Where is she?"

"Where you'll never find her!" Three more steps, two, and he'd be in among the trees where he could bargain without pretending that he meant to kill himself. He dared not turn around to see what was behind him; he had to watch Rochambeau's eyes now, as a man stares down a savage wolf. As long as Rochambeau believed that his hope of finding Johanna lay in Aubrey's hands, Aubrey's life was safe, and he could bargain for the rest. A branch brushed the back of his head, lifting the bright strands of hair; he felt leaves crunching under his feet. Another step—

His instep came down on the stub of a branch. He stumbled sideways away from the unexpected pain, and before he could recover his balance, Rochambeau was on him. The blue eyes burned like the eyes of the trapped wolf. Aubrey put up a hand to cover his throat, stupidly, as though he had been attacked by a wild animal that would use teeth and claws against him. The moment's confusion cost him whatever slight chance of escape he might have had. Rochambeau's knee jabbed into his groin, and one hand was at Aubrey's throat while the other was chopping down like an ax on Aubrey's right arm. His wrist snapped back under the hard edge of Rochambeau's hand, and the knife dropped from fingers gone suddenly numb. There was a rustling in the leaves as somebody picked it up.

Burning in arm and groin from Rochambeau's sudden attack, Aubrey let the men-at-arms twist his arms behind him and haul him into the clearing again. Once he yelped with the surprise of pain when they grabbed him by the wrist. "Do they have to be so rough? I think my wrist is broken."

"Quite possibly," nodded Rochambeau. His fighting fury had been overlaid with icy coolness that gave Aubrey hope. The man was sensible again; they could bargain.

"If you want to know where Johanna is, you'll treat me better."

"Will I?" Rochambeau nodded to the men who weren't holding Aubrey. "Build a fire, you three."

"What for?" The day was warm enough for autumn. Beads of sweat were clustering on Aubrey's temples from the brief exertion of the fight.

"Think," said Rochambeau. He borrowed a sword from one of the men-at-arms and tested its edge. "This one will do. I'd hate to ruin good steel, but this feels as though you've been chopping wood with it, Osmund."

Pale yellow flames licked at the pile of twigs and branches that had been gathered at Rochambeau's orders. He sat down cross-legged in front of the fire and laid the sword blade in the midst of the flames. "It shouldn't take long to heat up," he said, smiling at Aubrey as though they were discussing some mundane matter of estate management. "Perhaps you'd like to tell me where you've hidden Johanna, while we're waiting?"

The beads of sweat on Aubrey's forehead turned icy cold. He tried to wipe his face on his sleeve, but the men behind him were holding him too tightly. "Nicolas, you can't mean it. You wouldn't torture me for the sake of that—"

Rochambeau blew gently on the fire to encourage the flames, and Aubrey thought better of the epithets he had been about to apply to Johanna.

"All right," he said. Drops of cold sweat were running down his face now, falling salty into his mouth. "I'll tell you. But you'll need my help to guide you there. There's a cave in the hills between here and the Welsh border. I found it years ago, when I was out hunting, and last week I stocked it with provisions for Johanna. I took her there last night and left her with two men to see she didn't run away. I've just returned from there now. It's a long way from here. I couldn't describe it, but free me and I'll guide you there." Free me, he amended silently, put me on a good horse, and I'll damned well find some way to lose you all in the mountains when you least expect it, preferably into the path of some Welsh raiders.

Rochambeau heard the undercurrent of malice in Aubrey's voice. It sickened him to think of how much he'd missed or deliberately not heard all these years. In his unwillingness to face the fact that Aubrey hated him, he'd put Johanna in deadly danger. For that he would never forgive himself. "How far would you say it is? Who are the men? If you've been almost to Wales and back, where's your horse? Why did you come back through the forest?"

He deliberately fired the questions at Aubrey too fast to give him a chance to think. Aubrey's stumbling, vague answers confirmed his suspicion. His half-brother's pale, sweaty face made him feel sick. The sword blade was growing dull red in the fire now. Could he really torture a man he'd grown up with? Rochambeau set his teeth and thought of Johanna, who might be needing him now. God knew what was happening to her while he played word games with Aubrey. Would he once again sacrifice her for his reluctance to hurt Aubrey? But he had to be sure. Aubrey was just incompetent enough to have lost his way coming back from the cave, as he claimed under the interrogation. He might well have been thrown and lost his horse too; the man sat a horse like a sack of flour. Rochambeau knew he couldn't torture any man, let alone his half-brother, for sheer incompetence. But if he believed Aubrey's story, if he let him lead them on some wild-goose chase through the mountains while his friends spirited Johanna away and held her for ransom or worse . . .

"You didn't say who are the men you left with her," he reminded Aubrey. "I find it hard to believe any of my men would stoop so low."

"They're from the village." Aubrey's throat moved convulsively; his eyes were fixed on the glowing sword blade.

"Their names!" Rochambeau laid one hand on the hilt of the sword.

Aubrey's eyes darted from side to side of the clearing as he tried to think of some story. "Ah . . . Coluin. He's always hated you for having had an affair with Elfleda before their marriage; she never stops comparing him with you. And some friend of his, I don't know the fellow's name."

Rochambeau drew a deep breath of relief and stood up, drawing the heated sword from the fire. At least now he knew he would not be acting unjustly. "You're lying, Aubrey," he said. "I saw Coluin working at his smithy as we left the castle. Now you'd better get ready to tell me the truth."

He raised the sword till the red-hot point was aimed at Aubrey's eyes and prayed the threat would work. If Aubrey didn't crack now, he didn't know if he would have the will to go through with it. And if he didn't go through with it, what would happen to Johanna?

A high-pitched, uncanny shriek wavered through the wood. Startled, Rochambeau lowered the sword point slightly. One of the men holding Aubrey let go to cross himself. "The old witch. I thought her was dead."

"Her is," said his mate. "Seen the body, I did." His grip loosened, and Aubrey tore himself free. With one desperate thrust, he threw himself onto the point of the sword Rochambeau held. The heated blade sizzled as it sank into his chest. Rochambeau dropped the sword too late; already the blood was spurting out. Aubrey went down on his knees, clutching his chest with a puzzled expression as though he didn't know what had happened.

Rochambeau dropped to one knee beside him. There was blood spilling out of the corner of Aubrey's mouth, blood mixed with bubbles. It was a sure sign of death; he'd seen too many wounded that way, in battles and in tourneys, to hope that Aubrey could recover.

"Tell me!" His hands fastened on the dying man's shoulders.

Aubrey grimaced. "Never—find her now." He spat out blood and raised himself slightly. "Rather die this way—than you torture me to death. You'd rather too—eh? No stomach for it, Nicolas. But you'd have done it—you'd have done it for the witch! If it hadn't been for her—coming between us—poking into everything—"

His head fell back, and the blood gushed out of his mouth and nose. Rochambeau's hands cradled the massive shoulders for a moment; then he laid Aubrey gently down on the ground and rose, eyes blank with sadness.

"I wouldn't have killed him," he said, staring out into the darkness of the tangled woods. "He was my brother. I don't think I would have killed him . . ."

Chapter Twenty-six

THE HIGH-PITCHED SCREAM echoed again through the woods. This time it sounded uncannily like someone calling Rochambeau's name. Two of the men-at-arms crossed themselves, and the rest began arguing over whether Bruma was dead, and, if so, why did her voice seem to be coming from the thickest part of the forest instead of from hell, where she was presumably roasting by now?

" 'Tis an unquiet spirit, and no wonder," muttered Osmund. "Somebody ought to send for the priest to exorcise her."

"The priest won't go without a guard. Not in there."

"You're all a lot of blithering idiots," snapped Gilbert. "Souls in torment have no power to trouble us on earth. Something living made that cry—an animal caught in a trap—"

"Doesn't nobody dare trap in there where t'old witch lived," pointed out Edric.

"All right, a wounded bird—"

"Birds dunna fly over t'witch's copse."

"Then it's the poor old woman herself," Gilbert suggested, "and maybe she needs our help."

Instead of cutting off the argument as he'd hoped, this sparked a new round of debate. Had Edric been drunk when he thought he saw Bruma's body? Had she used her magic arts to raise herself from the dead?

"Whatever," Osmund concluded, looking somewhat pale, "her gave the poison to Aubrey, and if master's not dead, 'tis not her fault, and if she's not dead, I say she ought to be! Let's go and kill her properly this time!" He drew his sword and pointed it toward the thicket.

This suggestion raised a general round of acclaim but no definite forward motion. However, the shuffling of the men as each tried to indicate his desire to go in the second or third rank did arouse Rochambeau from his grief and guilt.

"What's that you want to do?" He stood up. "Kill the old woman? No, there's been enough killing today. Let her go free. She doesn't make very good poisons, anyway. In case you haven't noticed, I'm still alive."

But his appearance was hardly reassuring, Gilbert thought. Aubrey's death had only added new lines of pain to his face. And now they might never find Johanna. Did Rochambeau have the will to live without her? He'd never thought anything could drain Rochambeau's magnificent vitality. His strength had brought him through the attacks of poison and delirium; however, that had been before the news of Johanna's disappearance had turned Rochambeau's face gray and bleak like a cloud-swept winter sky.

"Perhaps," he suggested, more to stave off the moment when they had to return to the castle in defeat than with any positive hope, "we ought to go and interrogate her. She was Aubrey's ally; she might know something about Johanna."

Rochambeau's face lit up as though Gilbert had just returned his wife to him, safe and healthy. "I'll be bound she does. Well, men, who'll follow me?"

"Like to interrogate t'old witch with that sword he used on Aubrey," muttered Osmund, falling in behind Rochambeau. He was still ashamed of the way he'd been manipulated into helping arrest Johanna, who'd been a good lady to him in all the years when Rochambeau was off gallivanting on crusade. If they found the lady alive, perhaps he'd be able to make it up to her. Failing that, the next most satisfying thing would be to sheathe his blade in somebody. Bruma seemed the best target, now that Aubrey was gone.

Rochambeau was too impatient to creep along the winding path where low-growing branches swatted at his face and tangles of briers wound about his ankles. Sword out, he did his best to destroy a good blade of Nuremberg steel by using it like a woodcutter's ax on the small branches and saplings that grew in his way. The men behind him did the same, expanding the path to three times its original width as they marched along and several times narrowly missing one another's arms and legs. Gilbert followed at a prudent distance to the rear, ready to bind up the wounds of the first man who got a finger amputated by his neighbor's eager sword.

As they neared the hut, the cries became intelligible words. Somebody was definitely calling Rochambeau's name. A woman. And not an old woman, either. Rochambeau redoubled his efforts and burst through into the last ring of trees that surrounded the hut, panting with the exertion. The white hands that clutched the barred window were heart-stoppingly familiar.

Rochambeau sprang forward, relief and joy battling in his face, while Edric vainly warned him that the old witch might have taken on the form of a young and beautiful woman just to trap him.

"Not *this* woman," Rochambeau flung back over his shoulder. "There's only one of her." Then he was at the window, tearing the forked stick out with one wrench of his shoulders, and he'd no more time to spare for his superstitious men. Johanna was pale, her hair disordered, one side of her face swollen and bruised—but she was alive, and he could reach through the window and take her hands.

"I knew you'd come for me."

"Are you all right? Johanna—" Rochambeau became belatedly aware that half his personal guard was overseeing this reunion. "I see your lungs are in good shape, anyway," he said, affecting a calm he was far from feeling. "How's the rest of you?"

Johanna ground her white teeth together. "Rochambeau, God rot you, stop making polite conversation and let me out of here!"

"Ask nicely," Rochambeau advised.

An inarticulate low growling sound came from the interior of the hut, and a piece of an earthenware jug flew out of the window, narrowly grazing Rochambeau's right ear. Behind him, Edric shrugged and retreated a pace, putting up the sword with which he'd meant to kill the witch if she tried any funny business on his master. It wasn't inconceivable that she could have taken on Johanna's form for purposes of deception. But now his doubts were settled. "That's the lady Johanna, all right. Know that temper anywhere, I would."

Osmund and the rest nodded solemn agreement.

Meanwhile, Rochambeau had unbarred the door of the hut and was drinking in the sight of Johanna, enticingly disheveled and definitely all right. Her tunic was torn open at the top, and the bottom was missing strips, giving him glimpses of white skin and slender ankles; one sleeve was missing altogether, and her bare arm showed a line of reddish welts about the wrist that made him momentarily want to go back and kill Aubrey all over again.

"What happened to your arm?"

"Oh, that." Johanna glanced down, bemused, as though she'd already forgotten. "Aubrey tied me up. I had to break the jug with my foot and saw through the cloth with one of the broken shards. It took a little while. I was afraid you'd give up and go away before I got free . . . I was afraid he'd come back . . ." She shivered, her green eyes growing wide as she recalled unspeakable fears.

No explanations mattered as much as driving that fear out of her eyes. "He's not coming back." Rochambeau took two paces into the hut and clasped her to his chest, squeezing her tightly against him until he could feel the warm, soft outlines of her breasts and stomach and thighs against his body.

Belatedly, between kissing her tangled hair and trying to get her face turned up to his so he could kiss that, it occurred to him that she might have some reason to be shy of him.

"Oh, by the way," he said between kisses, "I never believed you had tried to poison me. I hope you didn't get too angry with me when I had you locked up. It was for your own safety."

"I thought you hated me." Johanna nestled closer against him. "I couldn't believe it at first, but Aubrey kept saying how angry you were and how it wouldn't be a good idea for me to go to you yet. He said he would try to calm you down first."

Rochambeau ripped out several Arabic curses. "Aubrey," he said between his teeth when he'd relieved his feelings in this manner, "came to me with evidence that you'd poisoned me. I knew he was plotting something, I didn't know what, but I was still so damned weak—that was yesterday morning—that I thought you'd be safest locked in a cell where he couldn't get at you." He took Johanna by the shoulders and held her a few inches away from him so that he could look at her face. "You do understand, don't you?"

Johanna nodded, but big tears filled her eyes. "Then that's all right." Rochambeau proceeded to kiss away the tears. He got carried away with this project and started to move down to kiss the long slender line of her throat, the curve of white shoulder that showed enticingly through her torn clothes, the—

"Here now," he said as a sob shook her slender body, "what are you crying for now?"

"Aubrey told me you were dead."

"As you can see," Rochambeau pointed out, doing his best to crush her ribs with his embrace, "Aubrey exaggerated slightly."

"But you shouldn't be moving around. Aubrey told me that Gilbert's physician friend said—"

"Did Gilbert happen to mention that Master Bartholomew never had a patient who survived poisoning with wolfsbane? There just might be some flaws in his method of treatment. I'm very much alive and intend to stay that way. Or is that what you're crying about?"

A muffled sound, somewhere between a sob and a laugh, was his only answer. "I could *kill* Aubrey," Johanna vowed.

"Too late." Rochambeau's jaw set, remembering the anguish of those moments when Aubrey had died by his hand. "I already did."

"Oh, Nicolas!" At last Johanna looked up at him, green eyes wide and soft with sympathy. "I am so sorry."

And she was perhaps the only person in his life who could understand how he could grieve for Aubrey and feel guilty over having killed him, instead of gloating over his victory like a proper hard-drinking, hard-fighting baron—she, the person Aubrey had wronged most sorely. Rochambeau folded his arms tightly around his green-eyed witch wife. "Come, Johanna. Let's go home." It was all he could find to say past the unmanly lump in his throat, and all inadequate, but she seemed to find the words enough. They went hand in hand along the widened path to the glade, she refused to let him carry her, and she rode before him on his black horse the rest of the way back to Malvern, where he could keep his arms around her waist and reassure himself that she really was there.

Once back at the castle, some of Johanna's other basic instincts reasserted themselves. She took one look in her mirror, gave a faint shriek of fright, called for buckets of hot water and a tub, and ordered Rochambeau from their chambers until she had had a chance to repair the damage.

"I've got a better idea," he told her. "I'll give you a bath."

Johanna shrieked again as he stripped off her torn and dirty clothes and tumbled her into the tub in full sight of a half-dozen waiting-women. Alais cried out in alarm and Margery frankly laughed, arms clutching her well-padded ribs. "Shoo, scat, we don't need your help!" Rochambeau dismissed them with flapping gestures of one hand, while with the other hand he rubbed six months' supply of lavender-scented soap into Johanna's hair.

"Nicolas!" Johanna protested, wriggling under his soapy hands. "That's all the scented soap I made for the winter. And I won't be able to distill any more essence of lavender until spring. Do you want to be scrubbing off with ashes and mutton fat for the rest of the season?"

"I'll take you to the cold-weather fair," Rochambeau promised. "We'll buy up all their soap and all their scent. I can afford it, can't I? I happen to have the best estate manager in Christendom . . . and the dirtiest!" Kneeling over her, he pretended to sniff in disgust at the white skin he'd just been lathering. Johanna grabbed a handful of his hair and yanked his face down to the surface of the bathwater. Rochambeau came up spluttering and spitting dried rose petals.

"Oh no you don't," he told Johanna, lifting her bodily out of the tub. "I recall your propensity for starting fights, but you're not getting out of your wifely duties so easily this time."

"*I* start fights?" Johanna placed one hand on her bosom in an assumption of outraged innocence, a difficult pose to maintain while Rochambeau was carrying her, wet and naked, to the bed.

"Who else?" Rochambeau dumped her onto the mattress

and stood over her, grinning and unlacing his tunic ties. "I'm a most peaceable, quiet man—if not provoked. Just ask anybody in Malvern. And, as I was saying, wife, you're not getting out of it so easily. I won a wager some time ago. You promised to welcome me to your bed whenever I wanted, and I'm ready to collect the second installment." His clothes went flying over the bare stone floor, and he knelt beside her on the bed, running broad hands over the slippery surface of her breasts.

Johanna shivered with pleasure and half closed her green eyes. "Are you sure you should be doing this? Gilbert said—"

"Gilbert," said Rochambeau, stretching out beside Johanna, "is an excellent musician and a terrible leech. I feel better now than I have since I woke this morning to find you gone." He grazed her lips with his and savored the sweetness they held in reserve, the tremor of her awakening body beside his. "A little healthful exercise is just the thing to drive the poisonous humors from the body."

Gazing down at his wife's slender form, he caught his breath as a fierce stab of desire took him by surprise. For so long he'd been used to thinking of Johanna as a child to be seduced into loving him, teased into good humor. But it was a woman who'd fought so gallantly for his life, then for her own, against Aubrey's machinations. The green eyes raised to his face were darkened with the sorrows of the last few days; her mouth seemed softer, fuller—even under the bruises left by Aubrey's blows—more exquisitely formed than ever for loving. Even her white body, half veiled by the tangle of crisply curling dark hair that fell about her shoulders, seemed somehow softer and more womanly than when he'd first seen and loved her. The girl-child he'd met in her father's fields had been a white leaping flame, slender enough to break between his two hands. In the years that intervened, she'd turned into a softly rounded woman, with full breasts and hips and long white legs, a woman made for love. He stroked his palms down her shoulders and arms, slid his hands under the gentle weight of her breasts, lifted the glossy cloak of her hair, and very slowly kissed each rising nipple in turn. He felt her shiver beneath him and saw her eyes darken with desire.

Johanna's initial impulse to protest was silenced by the rapid pulsing in her blood as Rochambeau slowly, gently brought each of her senses to full arousal. Her skin tingled where he touched her, she tasted his lips and tongue, smelled his skin, and heard only the words of love she'd so long desired to wring from him. Now, at last, without any plotting or show of cleverness on her part, he was giving her in full measure all that she had ever desired.

"My love . . . my life . . . my only love . . ." he murmured. Johanna twined her arms about his neck and pressed her lips to his cheek. He was alive, he loved her, and suddenly she didn't want to hear the words she'd waited for so long. She wanted him to take her by storm as he'd done so often in the past. Who wanted a gentle courtship when you could be swept up in the whirlwind of Rochambeau's loving? She ran soft fingers over his body, lingering for a moment over the muscled swell of his buttocks and drawing him down to her, trying to excite him into forgetting mere words. The feeling of his hardness against her thighs increased her urgency.

"I couldn't live without you." Rochambeau resisted her pull, propping himself over her and running one finger over the bruised curve of her lip. "Have I mentioned that lately?"

"I don't think I can last much longer without you." Her hands glided up to his shoulders to grip the thick golden locks that fell about his face, holding him close to her in a kiss that gave additional meaning to her words. She arched against him, wanting to feel his strength and life inside her, the final proof that he was alive and that the last few days had been only a nightmare. When he drew away and raised his head, she moaned in protest.

"Darling Johanna. Still impatient?" One finger traced the gently swelling curve from waistline to hips, and she moaned again under his touch. "We have time, you know. Every night for the rest of our lives."

Not quite every night, Johanna thought, as she recalled the news she hadn't broken to Rochambeau yet. But they should have a few good months before she got too big for these games.

"And today," he continued while his fingertips just grazed the triangle of dark curls between her thighs, "today I'm going to take my time and enjoy fully what I've earned—now that

371

I no longer have to hurry you along for fear you'll break something over my head if I give you a moment to think.''

"I never did!" Johanna gasped indignantly.

"Not for want of trying. It's just my good luck that you throw like a girl, with your elbow out. If you're quite through trying to murder me, love, perhaps I'll teach you to throw straight. How could you suspect me of believing you had poisoned me? I knew that if you did kill me, you'd want to have the satisfaction of doing it with your own hands, and slowly."

"I think that's what you're trying to do to me," Johanna gasped. She had given up all attempts to hurry Rochambeau's lovemaking, but the tension building in her body under his firm, knowing hands was driving her wild with anticipation. He kissed her breast and then moved lower, following the line his fingers had traced out with slow gentle kisses whose warmth made her tremble deep inside. The taut longing grew within her until she thought she could bear no more waiting.

"Do you need me?" His fingers brushed over the dark curls again, then dipped within her, sending a brief shock of pleasure through her, then retreating before she could fully enjoy the moment.

"You know I do."

"You fought it long enough."

"I'm not fighting now."

"No. Paying your debts?" Another light, tantalizing touch.

Beyond speech, Johanna could only move her head from side to side.

"Johanna." His face above her was still and grave. "I want you to be with me because that's what you want more than anything on earth. Because that's the way I want you. Because nothing less will do for me."

"Oh, God, Nicolas," Johanna moaned, "you've had me that way from the first day."

"You could have fooled me."

"Evidently I did!"

"Impudent wife!" He bent his golden head over her, and she gasped aloud with mingled shock and pleasure when the warm, moist tug of his lips replaced the teasing movements of his fingertips. His tongue flickered out, sending new jolts of almost unbearable pleasure through her with every movement. Her body felt warm and heavy, as if slow, warm currents were washing through her limbs. She let her hands fall to her sides, fingers uncurling, as the tormenting sweetness of his kisses carried her away on that slow tide.

She floated there, hardly conscious of what was happening to her, until the throbbing of desire peaked and her fingers clutched convulsively at his golden hair. "Nicolas!" It was too much; she couldn't bear it. She tried to find some way to tell him he must stop before she broke into pieces from the intensity of the shivering that possessed her.

"What do you need?"

The vibration of his lips against her skin set her off again, trembling and shaking with pleasure too sweet to be prolonged; yet prolong it he did, drawing out the golden moment like a single chord of music in air, like a taut string ready to be plucked.

"You. Only you." It was true; it had always been true. Only in confessing it, at long last, had she won him. Sated and lazy now, Johanna caressed the smooth golden hair under her hand until he drew himself up on the bed beside her.

"Don't you want to be my seneschal of the estates?" he teased. "Don't you want me to promise—"

Johanna covered his mouth with her hand. "No. No promises."

"But you have them anyway," he murmured through her hand. He took her hand, separated the long white fingers, and kissed each one lingeringly. "My love. My life. My honor. All in your hands, Johanna."

Johanna discovered that her fingers were more sensitive than she'd ever thought possible. A moment ago she'd been sated; now she felt her need for him growing again. She sighed and put her free arm around him, holding him close to feel the strength of his body against her.

"Tell me again what you want from me." His hands moved over her body with deft, knowing touches, reawakening passion wherever they glided, setting her white skin aglow from within. She moved almost mindlessly under him, open and aching to be filled, wanting nothing but the release that only he could bring to her.

"You," she whispered, clutching feverishly at him. "Only you. Always you, Nicolas. It was always you, damn you, and you know it!'' And if he did not accept her surrender soon, there just might be nothing left of her to give to him. She was melting away under his touch, dissolving into the heavy, warm, liquid current that flowed through her body; a little more, and she would wash away altogether.

"I like to hear it, though. You gave my pride quite a battering in the last few years. Tell me again what you need?''

"Are you going to make me apologize individually for every single day of the last four years?'' She ran her hands down his sides, feeling the muscles tense under her fingertips, knowing from his sharp intake of breath that he felt as much need and desire as she did.

"It's a tempting thought. But I think I'll have to defer collecting the rest of the debt until another time.'' With a groan of surrender, he entered her at last, and she felt the fullness of him deep within her, calling forth an answering response from the innermost core of her being. The long-drawn-out desire that had made her slow and heavy now quickened to a pulsing beat that demanded release. They found the rhythm that built up and up again until they were together at last in fulfillment. Johanna heard him cry out with wonder and delight and heard her own voice answering him. It seemed to her that waves crashed around them, or winds carried them into the sky, and yet all the time she knew exactly where they were. Together. And nothing else mattered.

When she could breathe evenly again, Johanna found herself lying peacefully beside Rochambeau, her head cradled on his shoulder, feeling the rise and fall of his chest as if it were an extension of her own breathing. His golden hair fell over her cheek, and one of his hands was spread possessively over the curve of her breast.

"We have to talk,'' he told her when he saw her lashes flicker.

"Now?''

He laughed. "Well, I'm not going to be doing anything else for a few minutes at least!''

"I didn't mean that.'' Johanna raised herself on one elbow and looked down the long form of her lord with frank admiration. "But I'm hungry. Aubrey said I couldn't have anything to eat until I . . . cooperated with him.''

"Bastard!''

"Yes. I think that was the problem."

"I didn't mean that literally."

"But it always bothered him." She shivered, remembering the envenomed speech he'd made about his envy of Nicolas. "I never knew how much. Did you?"

"I should have guessed. He was always one to blame circumstances for his misfortunes. It wasn't his illegitimacy that kept him from getting a good place in the world, you know. Exceptions can be made. If he'd shown any aptitude for fighting, my father would have found somebody to overlook his birth and take him on as a knight. If he'd shown any taste for study, we could have gotten a dispensation to have him ordained. But he never would work at anything. And he was always complaining how unfair it was that skills came easily to me. Yes," Rochambeau concluded, blue eyes darkening, "I should have guessed."

Johanna slipped a thin silk cloak over her shoulders and tied it in place with a braided cord. How could she distract Rochambeau from his grief and guilt? "I'll tell you something else you should guess, my lord," she said with forced cheerfulness. "If I don't get something to eat soon, I will faint from hunger."

Margery was waiting in the bower. The other waiting-women were nowhere to be seen, and Johanna guessed that the Pearl of the Night had driven them away to give Rochambeau and his lady some privacy or perhaps to make sure that she got the first gossip to come out of the inner chamber. The only thing that surprised Johanna was that Margery had even succeeded in banishing Alais.

"Where's Alais?"

"Crying over Aubrey."

"Oh, of course." Johanna bit her lip. Someday she would have to explain to Alais about Aubrey's death—after Rochambeau told her how it had happened. It was a task Johanna was not looking forward to.

"With Gilbert comforting her." Margery gave Johanna a bright-eyed, knowing glance. "Give him a few days, and I don't think you'll have to explain too much to Alais. She won't want to think about the past."

"A few days," Johanna repeated, uncertain. Should she let Gilbert spend this time with Alais?

"Surely you can think of something else to do with yourself? Why don't you ask Rochambeau for some suggestions?" Margery was almost, not quite, laughing.

Johanna hastily ordered some food to be sent up from the kitchens and retired before her blushes overcame her.

"Good girl!" Rochambeau was sitting cross-legged on the bed; he applauded her soundlessly as she backed into the chamber and shut the door. "Don't worry about other people's love affairs for a while, Johanna. I want all your attention. And I know how to get it."

"Yes, but Sir Ilbod will not be pleased if Alais runs off with a penniless musician." Johanna bit her lip, pausing uncertainly in the middle of the chamber.

"Gilbert isn't going to run away with her. And if it's serious, I'll find a place for him here. The boy's too bright to waste his life as a strolling jongleur, and Sir Ilbod, with four daughters to marry off, won't complain too much about Alais's choice of husband."

"Six," Johanna corrected absently. "He's been busy since you left."

"Whatever. If I pay her dowry, he'll be happy enough to see her settled with a boy of good family. All I have to do is ask my seneschal of the estates to sell off a few more hunting rights."

"Hunting rights!" Johanna had forgotten all about the account books Rochambeau had deciphered and the story those accounts told to anybody clever enough to read them. Now, as she remembered what she'd hoped he would find out, her cheeks flushed crimson, and she caught both hands together under her breasts.

"I never saw anybody look so guilty." Rochambeau grinned and extended one hand to her. "Be careful, my love. You've been found out in the act . . ."

"Of . . ."

"Of loving your husband, I think. You sold those hunting rights to the abbey to raise the money for my ransom, didn't you? The time is right—just about a week after my messenger arrived—and the money was given to Aubrey. You meant him to send it to France."

Johanna nodded slowly.

"You had second thoughts, then, after you refused to pay the ransom?"

"I always meant to pay it," she admitted. "I just wanted to make you angry."

"And you succeeded!"

"Better than I intended. I thought the ransom would get there almost as soon as your messenger returned. But Aubrey's man never got to Avranches, and we never heard what happened to him. He must have been robbed and slain on the road, or—oh!" Johanna raised one hand to her throat, battling with the shock of a new betrayal. "Of course, how stupid of me. He never sent the money."

"Doubtless he never intended to," agreed Rochambeau. "Unlike you, my love, Aubrey really was very well pleased to have me languishing in the dungeons of Avranches. And I was poisoned as soon as he discovered that I'd deciphered your accounts, before I could start asking inconvenient questions about the money."

A tap on the door interrupted them. Johanna went to the door and took a laden tray from Margery. "Watched everything being cooked myself," she said with a wink. "And there's absolutely no spices or honey in the dishes, so you'll be able to taste if anybody did slip something in as shouldn't be there."

"If it tastes like anything at all," grumbled Rochambeau when Johanna repeated this to him.

"It'll do you good to get used to good plain English cooking again." Setting the tray on the bed between them, she took a thick slice of roast mutton and clamped it between two pieces of bread. It was possibly that best thing she'd ever eaten, or was it? No, Johanna decided, there was also a lot to be said for the thick porridge, rich with currants and cream, which Margery had included on the tray. She spooned it up greedily while Rochambeau watched in amusement.

"Are you going to eat all day to make up for the meal you missed this morning?" he inquired when she had polished off the bowl of porridge and was looking wistfully at a dish of pears stewed in wine and honey.

Johanna dipped one finger into the sweet sauce and licked it while regretfully deciding that she was, after all, too full for the pears. Perhaps later. Yes, definitely later. While she waited, she could break her news to Rochambeau.

"I expect I'll be eating extra for more than a day or two," she responded at last, nibbling on a thin flat cracker that she'd just discovered under the basket of leavened bread. "Seven and a half months is my best estimate."

"What?"

"You heard me." Johanna finished the cracker and decided that she did, after all, have room for at least one of the sweet stewed pears. "I'm eating for two. I'm surprised you didn't figure it out already. Aubrey knew. That was why he had to get me out of the way. He didn't want you to have an heir. Give that back!" With an indignant cry, she reached for the bowl of stewed pears, which Rochambeau had taken off the tray.

"In a moment. I suddenly feel that I'm going to need to keep up my own strength. God's body and bones," Rochambeau marveled, raising his eyes heavenward. "I'm going to have a green-eyed witch of a daughter. How will I ever keep the two of you in line? One Johanna is more than I can deal with."

"A son," Johanna corrected. "An heir. We can have a daughter later."

"Yes, well, we won't quarrel over details. But don't you think these pears would be better with a little ginger to spice them up?"

"I know better ways than that to season a bland dish," Johanna whispered. She crawled around the big tray, took the bowl from Rochambeau's hand, and set it carefully on the floor. "And if you'd just move that tray, I could start demonstrating . . ."

"Insatiable woman!"

"You've had three stewed pears. That ought to keep your strength up quite sufficiently for the next hour or so."

And so it did.